# The Wurst Is Yet to Come

# THE WURST IS YET TO COME

### A Bed-and-Breakfast Mystery

# Mary Daheim

**WILLIAM MORROW**
*An Imprint of* HarperCollins*Publishers*

THE WURST IS YET TO COME. Copyright © 2012 by Mary Daheim. All rights reserved. Printed in the United States of America. No part of this book may be used or reproduced in any manner whatsoever without written permission except in the case of brief quotations embodied in critical articles and reviews. For information address HarperCollins Publishers, 10 East 53rd Street, New York, NY 10022.

HarperCollins books may be purchased for educational, business, or sales promotional use. For information please write: Special Markets Department, HarperCollins Publishers, 10 East 53rd Street, New York, NY 10022.

FIRST EDITION

Library of Congress Cataloging-in-Publication Data has been applied for.

ISBN 978-0-06-208983-0

12  13  14  15  16   OV/RRD   10 9 8 7 6 5 4 3 2 1

*To my granddaughters, Maisy and Clara, who give me hope
that the future is in good hands. You are much loved.*

# Author's Note

The story takes place in October 2005.

# The Wurst Is Yet to Come

# Chapter One

**J**udith McMonigle Flynn heard the knock at Hillside Manor's back door, wondered which friend or family member had forgotten the key, and hurried to see who was on the porch.

"Joe!" she cried, looking through the small window and turning the doorknob. "Why can't you . . ." The knob fell off in her hand. "Come to the front," she said to her husband, whose round face looked miffed—and wet—from the October rain.

Joe Flynn narrowed his green eyes at Judith as he held up the other half of the doorknob. "Warzdadamtolbag?" he shouted.

"I can't hear you," Judith replied, gesturing at the leaky downspout where rainwater dripped with a noisy *plop-plop-plop* into a steel bowl by the steps.

Joe tossed the doorknob aside and stomped off the porch. Sighing, Judith trudged back down the hallway, through the kitchen, the dining room, and the entry hall. She opened the front door just as Joe appeared on the walkway.

"What did you say?" she asked, irritated by her husband's scowl.

"I said," Joe responded, dripping rainwater off of his navy-blue raincoat, "where's that damned Tolvang? Your handyman was supposed to be here today."

"He couldn't come," Judith replied. "His truck broke down."

"No kidding," Joe muttered, heading straight for the kitchen. "Did the crank fall off, so he couldn't start that old heap?"

Judith traipsed after him. "The crank is leaving mud on my clean floor. Bad day or did you stop off to see Mother first?"

Joe was in the back hallway, hanging up his raincoat. "Why would I want to see your ghastly mother? Wasn't it bad enough I had to go through about a million background checks for the police department all day? Why did I take on this job? It's not worth the money."

"Because we *need* the money? Because you like your former partner, Woody Price? Because you're still a cop at heart?"

"Hmm." A faint smile tugged at Joe's mouth. "All of the above?" He entered the kitchen and put his arms around Judith. Brushing her lips with a kiss, he sniffed. "You smell like a lemon."

"I've been squeezing lemons for a meringue pie," Judith said, leaning against Joe. "Renie gave me a whole bag of them."

Joe tipped Judith's chin to make eye contact. "Why would your goofy cousin do that? No," he said quickly, putting his finger on her parted lips. "I don't want to know. Let me guess. She's growing lemons in the basement instead of sweeping out the dirt she tracks in?"

Judith shook her head.

Joe frowned in concentration. "Somebody sent her a bag of lemons after trying her god-awful Shrimp Dump recipe in the parish cookbook?"

Judith shook her head again.

Joe sighed and released his wife. "I give up. And by the way, I hate lemon meringue pie."

"So does Bill," Judith said, referring to Renie's husband. "I'm making it for Arlene and Carl Rankers when they arrive tomorrow to take over the B&B while I'm in Little Bavaria."

"Damn, I forgot you were leaving so soon," he said, moving to the family liquor cupboard. "I keep thinking this is Tuesday."

"You could've gone with me," she said accusingly.

Joe shook his head. "Not with this unique assignment. I've got until Monday to wind it up. I feel as if I've still got another three, four million records to go through. No wonder I thought it was only Tuesday. Drink?" he asked, holding a fifth of Scotch.

"Yes, please," Judith said. "Renie thought they were onions."

Joe paused, bottle in hand. "What did she think were onions?"

"Lemons," Judith said, checking the oven to see if the pie was done. "Renie was in a rush at Falstaff's and grabbed a bag of lemons she thought were onions, but didn't notice until she got home. She wondered why her bill was fifteen bucks more than she expected. Lemons cost a lot more than onions, so she gave some to me."

"Why didn't she return them?" Joe asked, pouring their drinks.

"Because . . ." Judith frowned. "Renie doesn't like making exchanges. She gets all mixed up with numbers."

"She gets all mixed up with lemons and onions," Joe said, handing Judith her Scotch-rocks.

"She has a deadline today for designing a corporate Web site," Judith explained, opening the oven and removing the pie. "I baked individual meringues for the guests' social hour." Glancing at the old schoolhouse clock, she saw it was ten to six. "I'd better set everything out on the buffet. We're full tonight, thank heavens. The economic downturn is hurting the hospitality industry. Ingrid Heffelman was chewing off my ear today, saying how everybody at the state B&B association is complaining about vacancies." She shot Joe a sharp glance. "As usual, she told me to give you her best."

"Wish I knew what it was," Joe said breezily. "Maybe I'll find out while you're gone."

Judith glared at Joe. "Don't even think about it. Have you ever seen Ingrid Heffelman up close? Renie calls her Inbred Heffa-lump."

"Renie's got a bad mouth," Joe said in his usual mellow tone. "I've seen Ingrid a couple of times. I'd describe her as . . ." He took a sip of Scotch and gazed up at the high kitchen ceiling. "Rubenesque."

"You mean she looks like the painter? Maybe it's her beard."

"Hey, when have I ever given you cause to be jealous?"

"How about the twenty years you were married to Herself instead of to your fiancée, who happened to be me?"

"Good God," Joe muttered, "that was another twenty years ago. Now *we've* been married that long."

Judith removed a tray of crab and mushroom hors d'oeuvres from the oven. "Are you crazy? It's only been sixteen. You can't count any better than Renie. And don't you dare say it *seems* longer."

The gold flecks danced in Joe's green eyes. "It seems like only yesterday."

"Right." She transferred the hors d'oeuvres onto a serving platter. And berated herself for being waspish. Judith and Joe had managed to make unfortunate first marriages that had kept them apart for two decades. Fate had not been kind—until a homicide case at Hillside Manor brought them together again. "I'm sorry," she said, platter in hand. "I just wish you were going with me to Little Bavaria instead of Renie. In fact, I wish I'd never taken on the task of helping out at the state's B&B booth during the Oktoberfest. I'll be working and Renie will be bitching. She gets bored easily. And neither of us likes beer."

"Nothing wrong with good beer," Joe remarked, swiping an hors d'oeuvre off the platter.

"Nothing right about this whole gig," Judith said. "Ingrid made it her own little project to get the B&B booth. I got the impression that the organizers weren't all that crazy about the idea because they wanted to focus on tourism in their own part of the state. But Ingrid persevered, probably by being her usual obnoxious self."

"Gosh," Joe said in mock surprise, "you don't like her much."

"That," Judith responded, heading for the living room, "is true—and the feeling is mutual."

Five minutes later, as she was setting out the meringues, the Wilsons and the Morgans from Omaha showed up for the social hour. They gushed appropriately and Judith chatted with them for a few minutes before the businessman from St. Paul arrived along with the newlyweds from Salem, Oregon. Judith returned to the kitchen just in time for yet another confrontation between Joe and her mother.

"See here, buster," the old lady said, wagging a finger at her son-in-law, "just because you *claim* you had to work late doesn't mean my supper should be late. I had to ram the back door to get inside. It's busted. Where's my useless daughter?" Gertrude Grover leaned from her motorized wheelchair to see beyond Joe. "There you are. Well? Did you ruin whatever slop you're going to feed me?"

"Mother . . ." Judith began, dismayed that Gertrude hadn't bothered to put on any rain gear except for throwing a sweater over her head. You'll catch cold. Your hair's wet."

"*You're* all wet. What's for supper?"

"Beef Stroganoff." Judith noted that Joe had left the kitchen and Sweetums had entered it. The cat rubbed his wet fur against her leg.

Gertrude glowered. "Like my niece Serena makes?"

"Renie uses about a gallon of sour cream," Judith said. "It's not good for your cholesterol."

"You know my cholesterol's perfect," the old lady declared.

Judith did know, and couldn't understand how her mother, who considered grease a food group and smoked like a chimney, could have such a low—and healthy—reading. "I use a different recipe, and that's—ow!" Judith jumped as Sweetums clawed her leg. "Damnit, you've trained that wretched beast to attack upon silent command!"

Gertrude looked smug. "Okay, we're even. Dish it up and bring it out." She turned the wheelchair around and headed back to her converted toolshed apartment. With a last malevolent look at Judith, Sweetums followed, his big plume of a tail waving in triumph.

Judith rubbed at her leg, thankful that the cat hadn't torn her slacks or drawn blood. After Judith delivered her mother's dinner, Joe strolled in with the dregs of his drink and sat down.

"Your mother's off base," he said after Judith had dished up their servings. "As usual. I like your version better than Renie's."

Judith avoided looking at Joe's slight paunch. "It's much less fattening and the wine adds some zing. In fact," she confessed, sitting down opposite her husband, "it's not beef Stroganoff. It's beef bourguignon. Mother doesn't trust food with French names."

"I figured as much," Joe said. "I know my way around a kitchen."

Judith smiled. "Yes, you do. You're a good cook."

Joe shrugged. "I'm not a chef like Dan was. When Dan worked at being a chef—or at anything else. Why him? I always wondered."

"He was the only one who asked me. What else could I do when you left me knocked up with Mike?"

Joe lowered his eyes. "Don't remind me. I haven't gotten drunk since the night Vivian hauled me off to the JP in Vegas."

Judith jumped as she heard someone come through the back door. "Arlene! Are you here to get prepped for your B&B stint?"

"No," their neighbor replied. "I stopped to see your mother. She's excited about the fun Carl and I'll have with her while you're gone." Arlene's pretty face beamed. "What a sweetie! You must exaggerate how she upsets you, Judith. I've never heard her utter a harsh word."

"That," Joe said, "is because she saves them up for us."

Arlene shook her head. "Joe's such a card. May I borrow a can of cream of chicken soup? I don't want Carl to have to go up to the store. He's worn out from painting the kitchen and he still has to fix the upstairs plumbing and check out the roof. That windstorm last week loosened some of the shingles. Oh—he should come over and fix your back door. It's broken, you know."

Judith was used to Arlene's contradictory reasoning. "Sure, you know where to find the soup. Pantry, third shelf. Joe can repair the door." She shot him a meaningful look.

Arlene started back down the hall, but stopped. "By the way," she said, "where will you be staying in Little Bavaria?"

"A B&B called Hanover Haus," Judith replied. "I'll write it all down for you. Several of us who are manning the innkeeping booth will be staying there, too. I've never done anything like this before, but Ingrid Heffelman talked me into it." *Cajoled, badgered, browbeat* were the words that rushed through her mind. And *compensation* for Ingrid not pulling her B&B license after so many dead bodies had shown up at or near Hillside Manor since Judith had been an innkeeper.

"You'll have a wonderful time meeting new people." Arlene said. "I hope none of them are murderers." She kept on going down the hall.

"I'll work through the weekend, either here or at city hall, to wind up this job for Woody. The last few months have been a big headache since he was appointed a precinct captain just as the mayor ordered a departmental investigation. I assume you haven't forgotten what happened last January?"

Judith sighed. "Hardly. Having you supposedly under arrest drove me to the brink. In fact, that episode almost got me killed."

"I figured you'd recall our nerve-racking start to the new year." Joe polished off the last of his dinner and stood up. "What time does the train leave tomorrow?"

"Nine-thirty," Judith replied before taking a last bite of broccoli.

"I'll drop you off on my way to headquarters."

Judith shook her head. "Bill volunteered."

"Bill can un-volunteer," Joe said. "The last time he took you and Renie to the train, she had him so confused that you almost missed the damned Empire Builder. I'll call him. He'll thank me."

Judith didn't argue. Renie's weird rationale for changing clocks to and from daylight and standard time the previous October had been so confusing that Judith had tried to forget it ever happened.

"One thing, though," Joe said, putting his plate and cutlery in the dishwasher. "Promise me you won't get into trouble."

Judith smiled ingenuously. "Don't worry. I won't have time to do that. I'll be busy with the booth and making nice with potential guests."

Joe frowned. "What's Renie going to do?"

"Who knows? I'll probably spend the rest of the time keeping her from antagonizing people that I'm making nice with."

Joe didn't look convinced. "You didn't promise."

"That's dumb," Judith said. "I already told you what I'd be doing. Isn't that good enough? We'll be coming back Monday morning."

Joe shrugged. Judith sensed what he was thinking. They both knew she never made promises she couldn't keep.

**R**enie wasn't a morning person. Judith wasn't surprised to see Bill Jones's grim expression as he carried his wife's suitcase to the Subaru. "She's coming," he said, opening the rear door and shoving the luggage across the seat. "Any chance you can leave her in Little Bavaria?"

"You'd miss her," Judith said, trying to sound convincing.

Bill scowled. "She just missed me with a cereal bowl. I'm going back inside to calm down Oscar. He gets agitated when Renie gets up before he does. It interrupts our discussion of the morning newspaper."

"Ah . . . right," Judith said as Bill saluted both Flynns before heading back into the house. "Damn," she murmured, "just when I was feeling sorry for Bill, he had to bring up that stupid stuffed ape!"

Joe seemed unfazed. "Oscar can't be that stupid if he can talk about current events."

"Joe!" Judith glared at her husband. "Don't you dare buy into—"

"Hey, here comes Renie. Look, she's kissing Bill good-bye. She can't be all that grumpy. Or maybe she's biting him. Is he bleeding?"

"That's lipstick," Judith said in disgust. "Don't make any smart-ass remarks when she gets in the car, okay?"

Renie, attired in a forest-green cable-knit sweater and matching slacks, marched out to the car and got into the backseat.

Joe spoke first. "Good morn—"

"What's good about it?" Renie snarled. "It's mother-jumping eight o'clock and no human being should be up in the middle of the mother-jumping night!" She slumped down and fumbled with the seat belt. "Hey, this sucker's broken! You want to get me killed?"

"Yes," Joe murmured.

"It's not broken," Judith said, craning her neck to look at her cousin. "It's just . . . tricky."

"Bill's waving bye-bye," Joe said.

"The hell he is," Renie snapped. "He just gave me the finger!"

"Well . . ." Joe said, "it looked kind of like a wave."

"Ha! He . . . there! I got it fastened. Let's rock."

The ride downtown was in morning rush-hour traffic, but mercifully, Renie kept quiet. The sun had come up and it promised to be a crisp, beautiful autumn day. Judith kept her eyes straight ahead while Joe muttered an occasional rude remark about less competent drivers. They reached the train station at ten to nine.

"Grab a cart," Joe said. "I'm in an impound area and I'm already late. I don't want to have to arrest myself."

Judith leaned over to kiss Joe. "I love you," she said.

"Right. Go. Somebody's pulling up behind me."

"Men!" Judith said under her breath after she'd dragged the travel case out of the car.

Renie had snatched a cart from an elderly couple who seemed confused. "Dump your case here," she called to Judith. "Don't run. You'll dislocate your phony hip. I don't want any more crap this morning."

Wincing at the Subaru's squealing tires as Joe rocketed away from the station, Judith joined Renie by the door. "Those poor old people," she whispered after the cousins had gone inside. "Why couldn't you get a cart on this side of the door?"

"What door?" Renie retorted. "You think I can see this early?"

"You can sure bitch," Judith said. "Watch where you're going with that cart. It's not a NASCAR entry. You almost ran into that baby carrier on the floor."

"The baby should have wheels on that thing," Renie muttered. "Have we got tickets?"

"Yes. We have to check in at that desk when the conductor arrives. The line's already forming."

Renie stopped so abruptly that Judith almost fell on top of her. "Then I'm going to sit down right here."

"But there's a man——"

"Oops!" Renie yipped as the bearded man who was already sitting in the chair let out a cry of surprise. "Sorry," she mumbled, and moved over to an empty seat. She glared at her cousin. "I told you I couldn't see. You should've warned me."

"I tried to," Judith said in an irritated tone. "Why don't you just shut up and sit there?"

"Okay."

Judith wasn't surprised by her cousin's sudden docile change. After sixty years of being closer than sisters, they knew each other better than anyone else did. Sometimes they didn't like each other very much, but their bond was so strong that nothing short of global destruction could sever it. Thus, Judith barely noticed that Renie had gone to sleep.

The bearded man leaned across the empty chair between them. "Is your friend all right?" he inquired in a deep, faintly accented voice.

"What? Oh—yes, she's fine. My cousin isn't an early riser."

"You're cousins?" the man said, still speaking softly. "You don't look alike."

"No," Judith said. "My cousin's sort of small. I'm not."

"Your coloring is not the same . . . excuse me, I apologize." He chuckled, apparently embarrassed. "I should not be so bold."

"It's okay," Judith said, smiling. "Are you from around here?"

"No," he replied, stroking his short gray beard. "I'm from Los Angeles. But I grew up partly in Germany. Tuttlingen, to be exact."

"Ah," Judith said. "My maternal ancestors came from that area."

He held out his hand. "I am Franz Wessler. And you?"

"Judith Flynn," she said, shaking hands. "My husband's Irish. That is, Irish-American."

"Very nice to meet you. You are going far?"

"No, only to Little Bavaria."

He beamed, sporting a gold eyetooth. "So am I! I have family there. You are going to Oktoberfest?"

"Yes." Judith smiled again. "It's nice not to have to drive over the pass. The train didn't used to stop at Little Bavaria, you know."

Franz nodded. "True. I have not been there for some time."

"Oh?" Judith's dark eyes showed her genuine interest in other people. "Do your parents live in Little Bavaria?"

Franz nodded again, though he had turned grave. "My father does. At ninety-six, he is elderly, but in robust health. Still, you never know how much longer anyone has. I have not seen him since 1999. I felt I should waste no more time."

"I understand," Judith said. "My mother is elderly, too. Nobody lives forever." *Except my mother,* she thought. *Maybe God doesn't want her.* And immediately she felt guilty. Gertrude's parting words that morning had been to not drink any beer or act like a strumpet.

"Does he live alone?" Judith inquired.

"Ah . . . no." Franz avoided Judith's gaze. "*Mutter* died years ago."

An announcement asked passengers to line up for the conductor. "That's us," Judith said, noting that Franz carried only a briefcase.

He stood up. "I hope to see you in Little Bavaria."

"You may," Judith said. "Enjoy the view. It should be lovely with all the trees in fall colors. We're lucky the weather's clear today."

Franz picked up his briefcase. "After you."

"No, go ahead. It may take me a while to wake up my cousin."

"Well . . . if you insist." Franz sketched a bow and got into line.

Renie, however, was awake. "I heard that," she said, vaulting out of the chair. "You're already picking up strange guys?"

"Keep it down," Judith warned, rolling her travel case behind a couple with two small children. "If you were eavesdropping, then you know that Franz Wessler has an aged father in Little Bavaria. I have to be polite to everybody. They might be potential B&B guests."

Renie plopped her suitcase on the floor. "Are you going to mention Hillside Manor's mortality rate? Or tell them that if a problem arises, emergency vehicles are always parked by the cul-de-sac?"

"Pipe down," Judith whispered. "Why didn't you stay asleep? I could've put you in a luggage cart and shoved you to the train platform."

Renie shrugged. "That's what my son-in-law Odo does when I have a temper tantrum in one of those horrible big-box stores. Then, as I sail out the door, I throw him my credit card. Those places make me crabby."

"Odo is a smart man," Judith murmured. "Anne was lucky to get someone who could put up with all her peculiar proclivities."

"Huh?" Renie stared at her cousin. "Like what? Our daughter is perfectly normal."

"Oh," Judith said, gazing at the high ceiling, where the original century-old plaster flower motif was being restored, "her obsession with casino gambling, her fascination with old cemeteries and ghost towns, her so-called work meetings that are only an excuse to dine and guzzle wine. Not every husband would humor her."

"Ha! Mike married a bossy Valkyrie with a big mouth," Renie

countered, glaring at the three-year-old boy who was tugging at her slacks. "Why doesn't he tell her to back off?" She held up a hand. "Don't say it. Because she could throw him through the front window?"

Judith leaned closer to Renie. "Listen up, coz, since you chewed out Kristin last Christmas, she insists she'll never come to any family gathering where you're present. How do you like that?"

"I like that a lot," Renie retorted, ignoring the older little boy, who was trying to show her a couple of Matchbox cars. "I did it for your sake. She had no right to call you a doormat."

"You would," Judith shot back—and suddenly began to cry.

"What the hell . . . ?" Renie muttered as the younger child yanked so hard on her slacks that she almost fell over her travel case. "Damn! Beat it, twerp!" She turned back to Judith. "Why are you crying?"

"Oh . . . I . . ." Judith sniffed a couple of times. "Mike called last night to say the Forest Service is transferring him to a new ranger post."

"When? Where?"

Judith took a tissue out of her purse and wiped her eyes. "He doesn't know. He's been in his current job for ten years. It's time."

Renie frowned. "Oh, coz, I'm sorry. They were just an hour away, and the little boys are growing so fast . . ." She seemed at a loss for words.

Judith had gotten herself under control. "They could go anywhere in the United States. Even Hawaii or Alaska."

Renie glared at the older boy, who was racing his Matchbox cars between the cousins. "Is Mike upset?"

"Well . . . yes. They have to take Mac and Joe-Joe out of school. And both he and Kristin liked being close to a city, and this area is home to Mike. Joe isn't happy about it either."

The cousins had moved up almost to the conductor's desk. Only the little boys' parents were waiting ahead of them. Judith glimpsed Franz Wessler heading through the door to the train.

The big clock on the far wall informed her that it was 9:25. She noticed that the line behind them reached almost to the length of the waiting room. Their departure was going to be delayed, but that was the least of her concerns. The trip to Little Bavaria would take less than four hours.

"How soon?" Renie asked.

The question startled Judith. "How soon? Oh—you mean before they find out where they're going? I'm not sure. They'd probably move after the first of the year."

"Then they'll be here for the holidays," Renie pointed out.

"Maybe." Judith's lips barely moved.

"What do you mean?"

"I told you. Kristin won't come to family occasions if you're there."

Renie's face puckered with disgust. "What a brat! Don't worry. I'll have a little talk with her. She'll come and behave herself or I'll fix it so that Mike can mail her to your house in a padded envelope."

"You want to end up in the ER?" Judith shot back. "She's twice your size."

Renie shrugged. "True, but I'm sneakier. She'll never know what hit her."

"Don't. Please. You'll only make things worse."

"How could I?" Renie said. And jumped—and swore.

Judith looked down at the toddler, who was wide-eyed and slack-jawed. Renie snatched his hand out from under the cuff of her slacks.

"Get your stupid car off my leg, you little twit! What do I look like? The Brick Yard?"

It was his turn to burst into tears. The boy's mother turned around just as her husband got to the desk. "What's wrong with Ormond?" she asked in a vague voice. "Did he hurt himself?"

"Not yet," Renie said, "but if you don't move this pest and the one hanging on to my backside, I'll stuff them both in the baggage car."

"I beg your pardon?" the young woman huffed. "Ormond and Thurmond are amusing themselves. Don't you like children?"

"Only as an appetizer," Renie snapped.

"Excuse me?" The woman took a step toward Renie. Ormond's crying had dwindled to a whimper. Thurmond, who looked about five, scrambled to his mother's side. Their father had finished at the desk.

"Come on," he said. "Let's get on that iron horsey, guys!"

Both boys scampered off with him, but their mother lingered. "Stay away from our sweeties, you . . . *monster*." Getting a frozen stare in return, she turned to Judith. "Are you responsible for her?"

Judith blinked. "Ah . . ."

"Skip it," the young woman said. "If you two bother us on the train, I'll call the conductor." She rushed off, flipping a long woolen scarf over one shoulder as if it were a penalty flag.

Judith approached the conductor, who, she realized, looked distressingly familiar. "Good morning, Mr. Peterson," she said in her friendliest tone. "We're only going as far as Little Bavaria this time."

Mr. Peterson didn't conceal his relief. "That's . . . good. I mean," he went on with a quick glance at Renie, "it's a delightful town, especially this time of year. Have a pleasant trip." He handed the tickets back to Judith. "You, too, Mrs. Bones."

"It's *Jones*," Renie growled.

Judith practically shoved Renie toward the door. "A natural mistake," she murmured. "Mr. Peterson probably was thinking about the bodies that littered our route on the Boston trip."

"Big deal," Renie grumbled. "Which car are we in?"

"Second one down," Judith replied, checking the seat numbers.

Renie went first. They reasoned that if Judith fell forward, she'd land on something soft. Unless, of course, she fell backward.

Judith noticed Franz Wessler toward the rear of the car. Renie saw the family of four behind their own seats.

"Damn!" she said under her breath. "Do we have to put up with those little hoodlums the whole trip?"

"We could go to the café for coffee," Judith suggested, placing her suitcase on a shelf at the coach's near end. "I wonder if most of these people are going to Little Bavaria, too."

"Some of them are," Renie said. "They're dressed German-style."

Most of the costumes were worn by a dozen or more older people, but there were two younger couples and four teenagers in lederhosen and dirndl outfits. Letting Renie take the window seat, Judith avoided eye contact with the couple behind them. The little boys were whining. The older child demanded ice cream. Their parents were asking if the train had a play area.

"They're going to Little Bavaria," Judith whispered. "Try not to turn any of them into victims."

Renie merely shook her head and continued staring out the window as they began a snail-like pace north through the tunnel under the downtown area. The coach lights flickered; the little boys wailed in fear. Renie lay back and groaned.

"It's ni-ni time, darlings," the mother said. "How about a nice nap?"

"It's dark!" the older boy shrieked. "No nap!"

"Oh," the father said, chuckling, "you know they like to sleep with the lights on. We can't change their routine."

"Of course not, but . . ." Mom shut up as the car's lights went on and the train began to pick up speed. The boys quieted.

"Where's Mr. Peterson?" Renie muttered. "We can't go to the café until he takes our tickets."

"It could be a few minutes," Judith said, wincing slightly as one of the boys kicked the back of her seat. "It's a fairly long train."

"Right." Renie sat back and continued staring into the darkness.

They were out of the tunnel and headed north along the Sound by the time Mr. Peterson showed up. Renie kept looking out the window while Judith handed over their tickets.

"Excuse me," the conductor said, leaning closer. "I saw you speaking to the bearded man in the station. Do you know where he went? He's supposed to be in this coach."

Judith shrugged. "No. Maybe he's in the men's room."

"Maybe." Mr. Peterson moved on.

"Let's go," Renie said, standing up. "I'm hungry."

Judith led the way, moving cautiously down the aisle. They had to walk through another coach car before reaching the café. Fortunately, there were still adjacent stools at the counter. Judith ordered coffee and a bran muffin. Renie asked for hot chocolate and a doughnut.

"The kids went to sleep," Judith said. "That helps."

Renie nodded. "Why don't I check out the observation car? We could avoid the hooligans and get a better view. After the next stop, we'll be heading toward the pass."

"Sure," Judith agreed. "You've cheered up."

"Yeah, it's after ten," Renie said, before licking hot chocolate off her upper lip. "I'm almost human."

"True." Judith surveyed the other café patrons. "Franz isn't here."

"What?"

"Franz Wessler, the man who sat by us in the station."

Renie's shoulders slumped. "Please. No mysteries this time, okay? Let's take a trip without homicides, disappearances, or near-death experiences. I'm not as young as I used to be. I've come off the bench for Joe instead of working on La Belle Époque's spring catalog."

"Stop griping," Judith said. "We're only going to be in Little Bavaria for three full days. What could possibly happen?"

Renie turned to stare at her cousin, slowly shaking her head. Along with her artist's talent, she was a history buff. Thus, she knew history had a way of repeating itself—especially for the cousins.

The journey up the western face of the mountains had been beautiful. Gold, orange, red, and brown foliage shone in the late-morning sun. As they climbed to the summit, only traces of old snow lay in the shade of the tall cedar, fir, and pine trees. They'd passed the green-tinged river, trickling waterfalls, and small towns clinging to the cliff sides. By the time they began the brief descent into Little Bavaria, they had returned to their seats.

The station wasn't more than a sleek blue canopy with a bench on the edge of town, but a bus was waiting to drive passengers to their destinations. Judith couldn't help but scan what looked like about forty people who had disembarked. To her relief, the family of four was walking in the opposite direction. She saw no sign of Franz Wessler, but decided not to mention the fact to Renie. Maybe a relative was meeting him.

"Gorgeous day over here," Renie said as they walked to the bus. "It's always either warmer or colder on this side of the summit."

Judith nodded. The mountains divided the state not only geographically, but in almost every other way. The western half was damp, cool, hilly, and much more heavily populated. To the east, the larger part of the state had a Midwestern air. Agriculture dominated, with wheat fields, orchards, and farms scattered over great stretches of almost flat land. Summers were hot; winters were cold. The western side was damp and rainy; the eastern part got far more snow. The very earth changed from dark brown to brick red where the Ice Age had carved out the arid land that had been spurned until great dams were built under President Roosevelt's New Deal.

But at the 1,100-foot level, Little Bavaria clung to the mountainside in alpine splendor, a fitting tribute to its namesake.

"Good," Renie murmured when they'd pulled onto the main street, "they haven't spoiled it. I was afraid they might get *too* kitschy. This kind of Bavarian architecture is sufficiently elaborate in and of itself."

"*Danke,* Frau Jones," Judith said with a wry smile. "Your artistic talent is showing. I must confess, every time I've been here, I actually feel as if we were back in Germany almost forty years ago."

"That's the point," her cousin said with a nod at the balconied buildings with their bright flags fluttering in the autumn breeze. "Very smart of the locals to keep it simple. Where is Hanover Haus?"

"It's in the middle of town on the right-hand side," Judith replied. "When I told the driver where we were staying, he said it's the third stop."

Several of the older visitors in costume got off at the first hostelry. The two younger couples with their quartet of teenagers made their exit next. By the time the bus reached Hanover Haus, a half-dozen other people disembarked with the cousins. Judith recognized two of the women as fellow innkeepers. She was about to greet them, but both suddenly seemed preoccupied with looking elsewhere. Judith shot Renie a quick glance. "What's wrong with them? Did they snub me?"

"Who are they?" Renie asked in her normal tone.

Judith made a face at her cousin. "Keep it down, will you?" She slowed her pace midway through the small lobby. "Let's wait until everybody else checks in. In fact, let's go back outside."

"With our luggage?" Renie retorted. "We'll look like pathetic waifs."

"We'll shove them into that alcove," Judith said, indicating a recess by the entrance. "I don't want to get off to a bad start running into people who believe what Ingrid Heffelman says about me being a ghoul."

Renie cooperated. A moment later, they were outside. "I spy a café," she said, pointing to the Gray Goose Beer House. "Let's eat."

Judith didn't argue. They walked two doors down and entered the pub. It was almost full, but several patrons were obviously leaving. After a brief wait, the cousins were seated at a table by the fireplace. Their server was a careworn blonde whose nametag identified her as HERTHA.

Judith barely had a chance to glance at the menu, which was attached to a wooden plank. "Which brat do you recommend?"

"The special's duck," the server said in a jaded voice.

"Okay," Judith said. "A kaiser roll and a small green salad, please."

Hertha turned to Renie, who was scowling. "And you, ma'am?"

"Ma'am would rather eat this menu plank than bratwurst," Renie declared. "I've cooked so many of those things for my husband that—"

"Hey, brat," Judith interrupted, "order something else."

Renie's expression grew puckish. "Why not? I'll have the pastrami on light rye. And I'll bet your name isn't really Hertha."

"Right," the server said wearily. "It's Ruby. Does it matter?"

Renie grinned. "No."

Ruby leaned closer. "We use German names for the tourists."

"Dumb," Renie remarked—but smiled.

Ruby trudged away. "I don't think she likes her job," Judith said. "I'm not sure I like mine if the other innkeepers give me the evil eye."

"You'll win them over," Renie said. "Just don't find a corpse."

# Chapter Two

After getting their bags, the cousins noticed the lobby was empty except for a buzz-cut young man at the desk. His nametag read HANS. When he turned to get their keys, Renie murmured, "Jake or Rick?"

Judith mouthed, "Brad? Alex?"

Renie shrugged.

Their room was on the second—and top—floor, overlooking the main street. "Not the best vantage point," Renie noted. "The brochure says the rear balcony has a river and mountain view."

Judith also moved to the window. "We have a balcony, too."

"So? You want to gaze at the other tourists or the alpine scenery?"

Judith glanced at the gas fireplace. "It'd be too cool during the evening to sit outside. It's pleasant now, though." She studied the brochure. "There's a dozen rooms, plus a bridal suite. No vacancies, so with two to a room, that's twenty-six guests. How many are innkeepers?"

"Is this a game? How many innkeepers does it take to fill a B&B? I give up. In fact, I don't care. You said there were only eight of you manning the booth," Renie said, flopping down on the queen-size bed.

"That's today's schedule," Judith replied, still gazing out the window, "but it changes daily to give as many innkeepers as possible a chance to recruit guests. We got to choose our own lodging because we get only a small stipend. It *is* a self-promotional opportunity."

"How come your group has never asked me to design anything for them? That brochure sucks scissors."

Judith turned around and leaned against the armoire between the windows. "Do you really want to work with Ingrid Heffelman?"

Renie kicked off her shoes. "Sure. I've faced off with worse clients than Inbred Heffalump. Think mayor, think governor, think—"

"Stop." Judith sat down in one of the room's two armchairs. "We have to be at Wolfgang's Gast Haus at six, but first I have to attend a rally-round-the-booth meeting that I assume you'd hate."

"I wouldn't do that if you promised me a date with Hugh Laurie."

Judith assumed a put-upon expression. "I thought you might've changed your mind."

"About Hugh Laurie?" Renie sat up. "He's here?"

"No, you idiot. I mean you'd be curious how innkeepers do business at the administrative level."

Renie yawned. "Sounds dumb."

"Okay, then I'll meet you at Wolfgang's," Judith said. "It's two-thirty now, so I'm going to get ready. The meeting's at four."

"Two hours? Are you nuts?"

Judith avoided Renie's gaze. "There are some presentations. And speakers. Maybe discussions. Statistics demonstrating the need to—"

Renie had snatched up a pillow and put it over her head. "Please! Be quiet! You think I don't get stuck with enough of that bilge in my own job? I'll see you at the bar."

By three-fifteen, Judith was walking the two blocks to Wolfgang's Gast Haus, where the meeting would be held. The cocktail party indicated informal attire, so she'd changed into black tailored slacks and a black sweater with two rows of tiny silver bars around the boatneck. Spotting the B&B association's booth, she saw one of the innkeepers she'd recognized at Hanover Haus. Judith hesitated. Eventually, she'd have to meet the woman. *Now or later,* she thought, and put on her friendliest smile. "Hi," she said to the fortyish strawberry blonde. "We've met. I'm—"

"Flynn," the woman interrupted, shaking Judith's hand without enthusiasm. "You own the B&B on Heraldsgate Hill." She made the last word sound like some kind of hell.

"You," Judith said, keeping her smile in place, "have two B&Bs, one in the Langford district and the other near the north city limits."

"Three," the woman replied. "I recently bought out Hermione Wingate's Teal Lake B&B. She and Elrod retired to Taos, New Mexico."

Judith wished the annoying woman was wearing a nametag. She tried to visualize who was in charge of the booth. Dinkle or Dunkle or Dumble . . . something like that. It suddenly came to her. *Denkel, Eleanor Denkel.* "Is there anything I can do here now, Eleanor?"

Eleanor looked at the clock tower across the street. "It's three-twenty-six. You have enough time before the meeting to sweep the area around the booth. The broom is in the corner by the state maps."

Judith tried to keep her expression pleasant, feeling a bit like Cinderella in her festive sweater. "Okay. Ah . . . you *are* in charge of our booth, right?"

"Indeed I am," Eleanor said. "The Oktoberfest chairman is Herman Stromeyer. He'll speak to us at one of our meetings. As you probably know, the honorary chairman is one of Little Bavaria's longtime leading citizens." The merest hint of a smile tugged at Eleanor's thin lips. "He's my dear grandfather, Dietrich Wessler."

Judith didn't know. Before she could ask if Franz Wessler was related to Eleanor, the other woman pointed to the booth. "Do you see your broom?" she asked.

"My . . . ? Yes, thanks."

Judith walked away, thinking that Eleanor should be wielding the broom. Or riding on it.

The meeting was as soporific as Renie had predicted. It was one of those occasions when Judith was grateful that she rarely had to leave Hillside Manor to conduct any part of her business. Midway through a tedious statistical recap of who, why, and when guests visited state B&Bs during an average year, Judith felt sorry for Renie, who often had to suffer through such sessions as a graphic designer.

By the time the drone fest concluded at 5:50, she was fighting the urge to nod off. Eleanor had the last word, which was *"Getränk!"* Judging from the applause, it had something to do with getting drunk. For once, that sounded like a good idea to Judith.

The travel packet stated that the cocktail party was for all the Oktoberfest exhibitors. A sign in the lobby pointed to the ballroom just down the hall from the registration desk. Not that Judith needed the information—she merely followed the crowd.

The high-ceilinged room with its display of hunting horns, antlers, archery equipment, and paintings of the real Bavaria was filling up. Except for Eleanor Denkel, who was almost enveloped by a half-dozen people who seemed eager for her company, Judith didn't recognize anyone. She headed for the bar, hoping Renie would show up soon.

The bartender was a good-looking young man whose nametag ID'd him as Fritz. He poured Judith a hefty Scotch-rocks. "Are you really Fritz?" she asked.

He grinned. "All the bartenders are Fritz." He gestured at his vis-à-vis, an older man with a shaved head. "Him, too, but he's a genuine Fritz. The waitresses are Heidi or Hertha. Saves on printing—and remembering names."

Judith glanced at Fritz II, who was serving what looked like rum and Coke to the other B&B owner she'd recognized at

Hanover Haus. "Thanks, Fritz." She turned away just as a wave of excitement erupted by the main door. "What's going on?" she asked over her shoulder.

Fritz had started to serve a goateed man in lederhosen. "The Great White *Vater*," he said. "Dietrich Wessler."

Judith moved closer, but could see only a thatch of silver hair. Most of his admirers were speaking German. A hearty guffaw and a rumbling bass quieted the crowd. She assumed the speaker was the Oktoberfest honorary chairman—and Eleanor Denkel's grandfather.

"My, my!" a female voice cried softly. "Can you believe his age?"

Judith realized that the fair-haired speaker was the other innkeeper she'd recognized earlier. "I can't believe it until I see him."

"He's ninety-six," the woman said, straining to stand on tiptoes for a better vantage point. "You're tall, Judith. Can you see his face?"

"Only his hair," Judith said, unable to recall the woman's name.

"It's all his own," she said, turning so Judith saw her nametag: CONSTANCE BEAULIEU, as in BEW-ly, who owned a B&B across the Sound.

"How are you, Connie?" Judith inquired.

Connie, a pretty, bouncy woman, smiled brightly. "Just ducky doodle. Isn't this a wonderful place for a cozy get-together?"

"Yes," Judith agreed, surprised at the other woman's friendly about-face. "Lovely time of year, too."

The audience erupted into laughter. "What did he say?" Connie inquired. "I don't speak German."

"Nor do I," Judith admitted. "You're staying at Hanover Haus?"

Connie nodded. "Charming, isn't it? Very European. Very old world. Very *authentic*."

"You mean," a third voice said, "because it's actually a *room* as opposed to a meat locker?"

Judith gave a start. "Oh! Connie, this is my cousin Serena Jones. Connie's an innkeeper, too."

"No kidding," Renie said, holding on to her cocktail glass with both hands. "Hi, Connie. Call me Renie. Who's the old fart doing the stand-up routine? Looks like he's too old to stand up, let alone do a routine."

Judith turned just enough so that Connie couldn't see her face and shot Renie a warning glance. "That's the festival's honorary chairman, Dietrich Wessler."

Renie shrugged. "No kidding. How come he's not funny?"

"How would you know? You don't speak German."

"So what?" Renie's face turned droll. "How many German comedians can you tick off on your fingers?"

"Coz . . . Hey, how could you see him? You're short."

"My mascara fell out of my purse and rolled into the audience," Renie explained. "I had to crawl between all those Germans. It was like the Redwood Forest. Those legs! Those thighs! That lederhosen! *Mein Gott!*" She grinned. "How's that for German?"

Fortunately, Connie Beaulieu had moved on, perhaps to get a better look at Herr Wessler. "Please," Judith begged, "try not to embarrass me while we're here. This is my job, my living, my career."

"I thought that Connie person was someone you wanted to avoid," Renie said, looking puzzled. "I was rescuing you."

"She was fine," Judith declared. "Kind of silly, but pleasant. Maybe it was because she was with Eleanor Denkel, who was not."

"Not what? Not Eleanor Denkel? Who was she instead? Is this another game?"

Judith heaved a heavy sigh. "Coz . . . I think I need a refill."

"Why not? Herr Gasbag is still going at it. The crowd's eating it up. Speaking of eating, where are the hors d'oeuvres?"

"I don't know," Judith said, moving back toward the bar. "Probably on the other side of the room. I can't see beyond Wessler's admirers."

What she could see was Franz Wessler, moving away from the bar with a cocktail glass in hand. He espied the cousins and smiled.

Judith felt an odd sense of relief. "Mr. Wessler," she said, smiling. "I thought we lost you along the way."

"Please—call me Franz." He smiled at both cousins. "I don't believe I've formally met your . . . cousin, correct?"

"Yes." Judith introduced Renie, who behaved with proper aplomb.

"Charmed," Franz declared, flashing the gold eyetooth. "Have you met my father? As usual, he has drawn all eyes—and ears—to himself."

"Oh, of course," Judith said. "Then you are . . . Eleanor Denkel's . . . ?" Uncertain of the relationship, she let the question dangle.

"Uncle," Franz replied. "Her father and I were brothers. Alas, he passed away some years ago. I have not seen Eleanor since . . . I am not certain how long. You are also an innkeeper?"

"Uh—that's right," Judith said, momentarily diverted by the entrance of an oompah band. "I know her only slightly."

"Ah." Franz looked beyond the cousins. "I must pay homage to *Vater*. We have only had the briefest of conversations since I arrived."

"I thought we'd lost you on the train," Judith said. "The conductor couldn't find you when he collected our tickets."

"Oh?" Franz frowned. "He did not look very hard. Excuse me. I mustn't let *Vater* tire himself before we dine."

Renie jabbed Judith's arm. "Don't," she said, raising her voice to be heard as the band began to play.

"Don't what?" Judith said, moving briskly to the bar.

Renie scooted along to keep up. "Wonder if Franz was lying or being evasive. Worse yet, don't speculate that he strangled Mr. Peterson and threw him off the train from a trestle in the mountains."

"I won't," Judith said testily, though similar thoughts had flashed through her mind. "He was probably in the restroom."

They reached the bar. Judith didn't have to ask for her refill. Fritz I remembered she was Scotch-rocks. "You're a good bartender," she said. "When my first husband owned a restaurant, I often worked the bar and it isn't easy remembering what strangers drink." *Especially with the Meat & Mingle's tawdry clientele, who couldn't remember either, and would have been satisfied if I'd served them Liquid-Plumr.*

"It's a knack," Fritz I said. "How's CC and 7UP doing?"

"Fine," Renie said, holding up her half-full glass. "Where's the food? I'm starving."

Fritz's words were drowned out by some very loud oompah. He grinned helplessly, then waved a hand toward his right and pointed straight ahead. Judith nodded and accepted her refill. Luckily, the band was playing on the opposite side of the room.

"Holy cats," Judith said as they hurried away, "that's really loud."

"It's sure a lot of oompah," Renie agreed.

A couple was dishing various appetizers onto sturdy paper plates. Judith did a double take, recognizing the blond woman in the tight pink sweater as Hertha—or Ruby—from the beer house. "You're serving yourself," she said, moving alongside their lunch waitress. "Are you Ruby for the rest of the evening?"

"Oh—it's you," the faux blonde said with mild interest. "Yeah, I worked the early shift." She used her free hand to grab her companion's arm. "Hey, Burt, this is . . . I don't know your names," she admitted.

"I'm Judith, this is my cousin Renie." She shook Burt's hand. "Do you live here, too?"

"No," he replied, ducking his balding head with its fringe of curly brown hair. "I'm a blogger."

Judith cupped her ear. "Do you log in this area?"

Burt looked puzzled. "Huh?"

Renie set down her drink and pantomimed chopping a tree—or striking out at home plate. "You know—axes," she clarified.

Ruby smirked. "Burt's a *blogger*."

"That's . . . nice," Judith said. "Any particular kind of blog?"

"Political," Burt replied, all but shouting to be heard over the band. "You realize human beings are regressing, don't you?"

Judith stared at him just long enough to feel embarrassed. "Well—isn't that social commentary? I mean, it's—"

But Burt was shaking his head. "No, no, no. It's why the world is in such a mess. Politically. Especially this country. We know too much, but we don't think. Our brains are atrophying."

The tuba player blasted out a couple of notes that made Judith wince. Some of the guests were dancing as they melted away from where Dietrich Wessler had held court. "Yes," Judith practically yelled, "glad you won a trophy. Downhill or cross-country?"

Burt cupped his ear. "What? This country makes you cross? Downhill is right. A slippery slope of sloppy stupidity."

The hissing sibilant sounds sprayed Judith, forcing her to back away and bump Renie's arm. "Hey," her cousin yelled, "watch it!"

"Let's get out of here," Judith said through gritted teeth.

Renie speared a chunk of pickled herring. "Sure."

At least Judith thought that was what her cousin had said. But when she turned around to gaze at the dancers hopping, bopping, and practically jumping out of their dirndls and lederhosen, she had no idea how they could brave such a mass of frenzied Teutonic flesh.

"This is worse than trying to get through Nordquist's annual sale," Renie shouted. "Where did Ruby and Burt go?"

"Who knows?" Judith yelled back. "Who cares?"

Judith's ears were ringing. Many of the dancers were her own age, some much older. She was amazed at their vigor, but appalled at her own reaction. The frenetic participants became a blur, but a long minute passed before the music came to a cacophonous halt. Judith's body sagged. The dancers broke ranks amid much panting and laughter.

"Where will we go?" Renie asked Judith in a normal voice. "Won't your B&B colleagues report you to Inbred Heffalump as a deserter?"

"At this point," Judith declared, her face set, "my ears are ringing so much that all I need to make me really nuts is—"

A piercing scream came from the middle of the room, where Eleanor Denkel was swaying and clutching at her breast. The sudden silence was almost as deafening as the oompah band. Then, like viewing a slow-motion pantomime, the cousins watched the dancers moving lead-footedly toward Eleanor. The circle around her began to close—but not before Judith glimpsed Dietrich Wessler lying on the floor with a pool of blood creeping across the hardwood.

# Chapter Three

Judith grabbed Renie's arm. "Drop everything," she whispered. "We're *really* out of here!"

"But . . ." Renie's mouth was agape. "How?"

The crowd was focused on Eleanor—and what Judith could only guess was the corpse of Dietrich Wessler.

"There's a door behind the bar," she said, moving as fast as she could manage. "I'm not sticking around for this one."

The bar was deserted. Apparently the Fritzes had joined the rest of the stunned onlookers. Judith barely heard the muffled screams, curses, and agitated buzz from the big room as she set her glass on a stool. "Lose the appetizers," she murmured to Renie, moving behind the bar. To her relief, the door was unlocked. It opened onto an area filled with cartons of liquor, mixers, produce, and other edibles. A large shelf holding dinnerware was on their left, a stack of chairs was on their right. Slowing at the next door, Judith opened it cautiously. A short hall led to double doors she thought might be the kitchen.

"Damn," she swore under her breath. "We're trapped."

Renie was still holding her plate of hors d'oeuvres. "Why don't we stay here until they move the stiff? We've got food."

Judith gave Renie an exasperated look. "That's the dopiest . . . wait. Can you fake illness?"

"Sure. What kind? I need symptoms."

"Food poisoning—allergies. Your peanut reaction. Look puny."

"I'll have to hold my breath."

"Whatever." Judith was at the double doors. "I go first. We'll make this quick. Don't fake your own death."

"Looks like Herr Wessler didn't have to fake his," Renie said, trudging after her cousin. "Seemed real to me."

Apparently the disastrous news hadn't yet reached the kitchen. The hired help was busy with dinner preparations. Judith looked around for anyone who might be in charge. At last she spotted a man in a chef's toque berating a line cook over some slices of veal.

"Excuse me," she called. "Are you Chef . . . Brfle?" She had no idea what the burly man's name was. "Help us, please."

"What?" he barked, wiping his hands on a towel.

"My cousin has a severe peanut allergy. She thinks there may be peanuts in the food. Is that possible?"

The chef scowled. "How can I tell? She looted the place!"

Judith tried not to waver as she heard distant sirens. "Either you have peanuts or peanut oil in the appetizers or you don't. Which is it?"

The chef glanced at Renie, who was leaning against a shelf, panting slightly and blinking rapidly. "No," he said emphatically. "No such ingredients used for the cocktail party. Please leave. We're busy."

"How do we get out?" Judith asked. "My cousin needs fresh air."

The chef jerked his thumb over his shoulder. "That way. It leads to the garbage. Fresh air is down toward the river." He turned back to the line cook, who was cowering over his veal.

Judith had to lean against the heavy outer door to open it. Garbage stench or not, she took a deep breath as the door closed behind them. "Nice job, coz," she said as Renie reluctantly put her appetizer plate's leavings in a Dumpster. "How do we get back to Hanover Haus? Except for the light by the door, it's pitch-dark— and cold."

"We could walk around the building," Renie suggested. "It sounds as if the EMTs have arrived. Maybe they could give us a ride."

"Not funny," Judith murmured. "Do you have a flashlight?"

"Yes, on my key chain. Bill bought it for me," Renie went on, searching in her suede shoulder bag, "so I could see to start the car and not put the key in the glove compartment instead of the ignition. I'll go first so if you fall, you can—"

"Fine," Judith said impatiently. "Move before the cops show up."

"There's a path," Renie said uncertainly, heading down the slope that led to the river, "but I don't think it takes us back to the main street. Damn! This light's so small I can't see more than three feet ahead."

Judith paused for a moment. "The hotel lights are above us now. Can you imagine what's going on inside?"

"I sure can. Everybody's probably wondering where FASTO is."

"Oh, God!" Judith cried. "Don't mention that Web site. Why couldn't my so-called admirers have come up with an acronym besides Female Amateur Sleuth Tracking Offenders? I'm sick of people who can't read calling me FATSO."

"You're too self-conscious about your weight. You're tall, you can weigh . . . hold on. The trail veers off by a bench up ahead."

"Good." Judith looked up. "The clouds are moving. Maybe we can see by the moon. That'd help," she added, carefully picking her way along the dirt path. "They may look for us. We're witnesses."

"Stop thinking like a cop's wife," Renie said as they passed the wrought-iron bench and began climbing back up the hill. "Hey— I'll bet I know where this goes. I noticed a nice restaurant on my way to the hotel. We could have dinner."

Judith started to protest but thought better of it. "Yes, we could claim that we left before the disaster."

"Now you sound more like a perp." Renie stopped and let out a little yip. "I see a ghost! Look, up there by the big rock."

Judith edged closer. She saw the white spectral figure—and a jack-o'-lantern. "It's a Halloween decoration," she said in disgust.

"Did you miss the witches and black cats and pumpkins around town?"

"Guess I was focused on all the Bavarian stuff," Renie replied. She moved on, looking up the riverbank. "Wow—lots of flashing lights over by the hotel. Looks just like the cul-de-sac in front of your B&B. You can't feel homesick here."

"Coz . . ." Judith began, exasperated.

Renie gestured at her cousin. "Let's book. The moon's out. I see steps leading to wherever we're going."

Feeling unusually weary, Judith kept a firm grasp on the handrail as they climbed a dozen stairs to level ground. They were in between two buildings divided by a paved walk. "If we're where I think we are," she said, "whatever's on our left isn't far from Hanover Haus. Is that where you saw the restaurant?"

"Right, Mad Ludvig's. There's a picture of his ersatz medieval castle outside. Stay put. I'll make sure there's a rear entrance."

Renie moved quickly away from where the path ended and onto a grassy patch close to the riverbank. Only a faint light from a coach-style lantern shone down as the moon was suddenly obscured by drifting clouds. Suddenly Judith heard her cousin let out a strangled cry before turning around and racing back to the top of the stairs.

"What now?" she demanded in alarm.

"A bear is there!" she gasped. "Look!"

Judith could see only a dark form moving in back of the two-story building. Then the creature moved into the lantern's glow. "It's somebody in a bear suit," Judith said in disgust. "Have you ever seen a real bear walk upright like that?"

Renie let out a big breath. "Damn! Scared by a bear that's not a bear. If I see any lions and tigers, don't let me panic. Whoa! That bear's got bigger teeth than I do."

Judith caught only a glimpse of the bear-suited person, who had turned the corner and was ambling toward the front of the building. "Those are tusks. It must be a boar, not a bear. I think the boar is one of the symbols of Bavaria."

"Bear, boar, body," Renie noted. "Makes Halloween seem tame."

Judith didn't argue. "There must be a door by that lantern. Shall we go in the back way and pretend we're coming out of the restrooms? Unless the restrooms aren't in back."

Renie had regained her aplomb. "We'll say we got lost trying to find them," she said, leading the way. "Let's hope this door is unlocked."

Luck was with the cousins. The entry led into a short hallway with two doors, one marked FRAUS, the other, HERRS.

"Should be 'Hiss' and 'Herrs,' " Renie murmured, moving toward what she hoped would be the dining room. Instead, it was the bar, which was crowded. The cousins exchanged perplexed glances. "What should we fake now?" Renie whispered.

"Indignation at waiting so long?" Judith suggested after a pause. "You do that sort of thing better than I do."

Renie shrugged. "Okay." She gestured discreetly at an arched doorway. "Restaurant?"

"Has to be," Judith murmured.

At a few minutes after seven, the dining area was jammed. Renie approached a petite waitress with blond braids wound around her head. "How much longer?" she asked in a cranky voice. "We've been waiting for twenty minutes. Our reservation was for six-forty-five."

The waitress, whose nametag predictably identified her as HEIDI, blinked twice at Renie. "We don't take reservations."

"What?" Renie shrieked. "I called this afternoon. I asked for a reservation at six-forty-five and . . . Hertha said that would be fine."

"Hertha's new," Heidi said. "She must have made a mistake. You'll have to wait in line. There are four parties ahead of you, but you're the only pair. I can probably seat you in fifteen minutes."

Renie sighed. "Are you sure? We're starving."

Heidi looked at an inglenook where two young people were

holding hands and gazing into each other's eyes. "I hope so. Romeo and Juliet finished eating ten minutes ago. They should get a room. Meanwhile, I'll remind Hertha that we don't take reservations. Sorry for the confusion."

Judith held up a hand. "Don't bother Hertha. It's a natural mistake. Which one is she?"

"Depends on which Hertha," Heidi said. "We have four new hires for Oktoberfest." She moved away, responding to an older man's wave.

"Well?" Renie said. "Did I do all right with the lying?"

"Too much," Judith said. "You should've stopped after the part about calling this afternoon. Lying is an art. You never overdo it."

"You ought to know," Renie murmured. "You're a champ."

"I don't really lie," Judith protested. "I fib for worthy causes."

"Ha!" Renie nudged her cousin. "The lovers are going off to do what lovers always do. We're in luck."

Heidi, however, was engaged in a serious conversation with a tall man in a forest-green Bavarian jacket. It was another five minutes before the vacant table was bussed and the waitress motioned to the cousins.

"Sorry about that," Heidi said, looking distressed. "The manager just told me there was a terrible incident at Wolfgang's Gast Haus just a few minutes ago." She shook herself. "Sorry. I shouldn't have mentioned that. But it kind of upset me."

Judith frowned. "An incident? What was it? Food poisoning?"

Heidi gulped. "No. Someone was stabbed." She looked around to make sure no one could overhear. "The poor man's been the town's patron forever. A saint, some call him. Who'd do that to such a beloved old guy?" Tears glistened in her eyes. "Excuse me. I'm so upset." She jammed her hand into her dirndl's apron pockets and stumbled away.

"Not beloved by everybody," Renie murmured.

"Damn," Judith said. "We should've stayed. Maybe I could help. Think how horrible Franz must feel—and even that dink, Ellie Denkel."

"Too late now," Renie said airily. "You made the right choice to get out of there. Think about Ingrid Heffelman. Think about Joe. Whatever you do, don't think about whodunit."

But of course Judith couldn't think of anything else.

**A**fter both cousins had ordered the venison steak entrée, Renie tried to steer Judith away from dwelling on the tragedy. She was, of course, doomed to failure.

"Stop, coz," Judith finally said after her cousin had tried to talk about Wagnerian opera. "I'm not an opera fan, and even if I were, doesn't everybody always end up dead?"

"Not in *Meistersinger*," Renie assured her. "It's a comedy."

"You already told me there were no German comedians."

"Well . . ." Renie hedged. "*Meistersinger*'s not exactly falling-down funny, it's more . . . um . . . sort of . . . well . . . nobody dies."

"Unlike at the hotel," Judith pointed out grimly.

"You don't even know if the *Grossvater* is dead," Renie pointed out. "Maybe he was only wounded."

"I know a corpse when I see one."

Renie shrugged. "You see what you want to see."

Frowning, Judith realized that her cousin might be right. "There was blood," she finally said. "He's very old. Still, Franz told me his father was in good shape."

Heidi, looking as if she'd regained her aplomb, came to ask if the cousins wanted dessert. Judith was uncertain; Renie wasn't.

"I'll have the Black Forest cherry torte," she said.

"Ohhh . . ." Judith refocused on the menu. "Apple strudel, please. Have you heard anything more about the incident at Wolfgang's?"

"Not really," the waitress replied, looking worried. "All we know is that our usual clientele isn't showing up. My manager thinks they might be people who were at the hotel when Herr Wessler was stabbed. The police may be questioning them."

Judith ignored Renie's glare. "Will Herr Wessler survive?"
Heidi shook her head. "I don't know."

"You'd better bring our desserts," Judith said, trying to smile. "Coz's disposition won't improve until she's gobbling your torte."

Somehow the cousins finished their dessert, paid the bill, and left without alluding to what had happened at the hotel. Mainly that was because—or at least Judith reasoned—they didn't speak to each other until they were on their way to Hanover Haus.

"Go ahead," Renie said. "Look back to check on the crime scene. You'll burst if you don't satisfy your curiosity."

Judith's stubborn streak prevailed. "No."

With a resigned sigh, Renie stopped and turned around. "Hmm. I wouldn't have expected that."

Judith didn't rise to the bait, but kept moving.

Renie had to hurry to catch up with her cousin's longer strides. "Wow! You don't see a guy hitting a cop with a trombone very often."

Judith's strong profile was set in stone and her dark eyes were fixed on the inn's door. She didn't say a word. Once inside the lobby, she ignored the stout, older woman at the desk and headed straight for the stairs. Walking too much on pavement had depleted her physical resources. Neither cousin spoke until they were in their room,

"Okay," Judith finally said, "I won't mention Wessler again. I have to be at the B&B booth by nine, so I'll set the alarm for seven-fifteen."

"Seven-fifteen?" Renie shrieked. "I haven't been up that early since I had to get drunk to make an early plane to London!"

"Don't tell me about your fear of flying or your guzzling of Wild Turkey before a flight. You embarrassed Bill, Joe, me—and yourself!"

Renie looked puzzled. "I don't remember. Did we get to London?"

"Oh, shut up!" Judith threw her handbag on the bed. "It's eight-thirty. Leave me in peace. It's been a long day."

"It sure has," Renie groused, heading for the bathroom. "Hey," she yelled, "there's no tub, only a shower. I hate showers. They scare me."

"Buy a fifth of Wild Turkey," Judith shot back. "Just stop griping."

Renie glowered at her cousin. "I think I will. I saw a liquor store across the street." Whirling around, she opened the door— and saw a tall, dark-skinned man in a police uniform.

Judith saw him, too, and couldn't suppress a little gasp.

The officer removed his hat. "Are you Judith Flynn?"

"Never heard of her," Renie said. "Excuse me, I'm going—"

"Answer the question."

"Never heard of her," she repeated.

He nodded at Judith. "Is that Ms. Jones?"

"Your guess is as good as mine," Renie muttered, forced to step aside as the officer entered the room.

"I'm Lieutenant Alex Hernandez," he said. "Ms. Jones, Ms. Flynn, you're wanted for questioning in the death of Dietrich Wessler. Would you both please come with me?"

# Chapter Four

The cousins exchanged beleaguered glances. "Okay," Judith said, picking up her purse and jacket. "But we can't tell you anything. We left before anything happened."

"Too much oompah," Renie remarked.

"Oh?" Hernandez said, arching his dark brows.

Judith realized her slip of the tongue. "We had dinner at Mad Ludvig's. Our waitress told us there'd been some kind of accident."

The officer made a gesture for the cousins to go out the door. "Please. You can tell me all about it downtown."

Judith reluctantly followed Hernandez, but Renie stopped on the threshold. "Downtown? What downtown? Aren't we already there?"

"Sorry," he said over his shoulder. "I transferred here only a few months ago. I was a city cop for ten years. Come along, Ms. Flynn."

"I *am* coming," Judith retorted, already halfway down the stairs. "I prefer 'Mrs.,' not 'Ms.' I like being married."

Hernandez ignored Judith's remark. "Where's Ms. Flynn?" He turned to see Renie still in doorway. "Hey, move it. Do I need backup?"

"*I'll* back up if you don't stop calling me Ms. Flynn," she snarled.

"Fine, *Mrs.* Flynn," he said, making a sharp motion with his hand. "I guess you like being married, too."

"Sometimes," Renie said. "But I like it better when you call me by the right—"

"Hey!" Hernandez shouted. "Do you want to get arrested for impeding justice, Mrs. Flynn?"

Renie crossed her arms and leaned against the doorway.

The officer took two steps toward Renie. "I'm not kidding." He reached for his cell.

Pointing to Judith, who was at the bottom of the stairs, Renie gazed innocently at Hernandez. "Why don't you ask her? For all I know, she might enjoy getting arrested instead of having her husband in jail. That episode made her fractious," she went on, alluding to the nerve-racking events of the past January.

"Coz," Judith yelled, "cooperate! We can sort it out downtown. I mean, at headquarters."

Looking mulish, Renie slammed the door behind her and stomped downstairs so fast that Hernandez had to lean against the balustrade to keep her from bumping into him.

The woman behind the desk stared at the trio marching out the door. "Their credit cards better be good!" she called after them.

"Up here," Renie muttered as Hernandez opened the cruiser's rear door.

The cousins heard the locks click while the officer went around to the driver's side. "Stick with Mrs. Flynn," Judith murmured.

"What?" Renie said, aghast.

"Try it. He's already baffled. It might work for us."

Renie had no chance to respond. Hernandez was behind the wheel, driving westward three blocks down the main street and turning right. The police station was on the next corner, discreetly tucked out of sight. The sturdy gray one-story building took up half the block and bore no resemblance to the rest of the local architecture.

"Gee," Renie said loudly, "that looks like a jail. How do you say that in German?"

"The Clink?" Judith suggested.

"No," Renie said, "that was a real English prison, and a very notorious one. I suppose in German it's *der Klinker*—with a *K*, right, Lieutenant Fernandez?"

"It's *Hernandez*," the officer snapped. "I don't speak German."

"Oh." Renie sounded uncommonly meek. "Sorry. I have trouble with names. I get them mixed up sometimes."

Judith elbowed Renie. "Knock it off," she said under her breath.

Hernandez got out of the car, opened the rear door on Judith's side, and ushered the cousins into the police station. To Judith's surprise, the small reception area was vacant except for a fair-haired young woman behind the service counter. Various maps and flyers covered the walls, but the only local decor was the mounted head of an elk with enormous antlers and a wanted poster hanging around its neck.

"Call me a taxidermist," Renie whispered to Judith. "I'll bet that thing with the horns on its head is the former police chief."

"Shut up," Judith said, barely moving her lips.

"Interrogation room," Hernandez said to the young woman, before speaking to the cousins. "Follow me."

The room was small and spare with a window that Judith assumed had one-way glass since she couldn't see anything except dim reflections. There was a table with two chairs on each side, a small file cabinet, and another, much smaller table with a coffeepot on a hot plate.

"Would you like something to drink?" Hernandez inquired, indicating that the cousins should sit down.

Judith and Renie both declined. The officer sat down across from them, opened a laptop, and cleared his throat. "We understand that you attended the cocktail party this evening at Wolfgang's Gast Haus. What time did you arrive?"

"About six," the cousins answered in unison.

"Please," Hernandez said. "One at a time. Mrs. Flynn?"

Renie made a face. "Maybe it was six-oh-five. Or maybe six-oh-three. It might even have been——"

"Close enough," the officer interrupted before nodding at Judith. "And you?"

"Six."

Hernandez nodded in apparent approval. Perhaps deciding that Judith was prone to more succinct answers, he kept his dark eyes fixed on her. "What did you do once you got to the party?"

"I went to the bar and ordered a drink."

"And then?"

Judith gestured at Renie. "She joined me. Then I recognized someone I knew—vaguely—so we chatted a bit."

Hernandez had an unsettlingly steady gaze and rarely blinked. "You remained together?"

"The three of us, yes."

"And?"

Judith thought back to the sequence of events. It had been only three hours since the cocktail party had begun. Yet it seemed much longer. "About the same time Dietrich Wessler entered the ballroom, we met some recent acquaintances. Many of the guests rushed to greet Mr. Wessler, but we merely watched."

"Did you know Wessler?"

"Ah . . . no," Judith said, reluctant to mention the older man's son, Franz, by name. "Someone told us who he was and how large a role he plays in this community."

"Did you meet him?"

Judith shook her head. "A large crowd had gathered around him and we were outsiders. Besides, I think he was speaking in German."

Hernandez finally made some notations on the laptop. "What did you do next?"

Judith hesitated. "The band started up. A couple of people tried to talk to us, but I couldn't hear over the music. My cousin and I went back to the bar."

The officer frowned. "How long had you been at the cocktail party at that point?"

Judith glanced at Renie. "Less than half an hour?"

Hernandez frowned slightly. "You already needed refills?"

Renie finally spoke up. "She did, but I didn't. I already had mine. The drinks were free—and stingy. I like lots of ice. There wasn't enough booze to make a newborn goofy. Not that I'd want to do that—nobody likes a drunken baby rolling around in the crib and crying off-key."

"Certainly not." Hernandez looked even sterner as he turned back to Judith. "Go on."

"We went to the appetizer table," Judith replied. "The band had started to play and it was really loud. We couldn't hear ourselves think. A bunch of people were dancing. It was raucous and so noisy. Then," she went on, pointing to Renie, "she got concerned about her allergies, so we went to the kitchen to ask the chef about nuts."

"Nuts?" Hernandez seemed bemused.

"Yes," Judith said. "Peanuts mainly, which aren't actually nuts, but legumes. She has a life-threatening allergy to them. We spoke to the chef and he assured us they hadn't used peanuts or peanut oil. But not wanting to take chances, she threw her plate away outside of the kitchen and we left to have dinner at Mad Ludvig's. We'd just returned when you arrived at Hanover Haus."

"I see." Hernandez drummed his fingers on the table. "So you weren't at the party when the tragedy occurred."

Judith leaned forward. "Can you tell us what happened? We only heard that it was something terrible and involved Mr. Wessler. Of course we heard sirens when we were going to the restaurant."

The officer's expression didn't change. "Dietrich Wessler apparently died from a stab wound."

"That's awful!" Judith cried. "How could such a thing happen?"

"That," Hernandez said, "is what we'd like to know."

Judith didn't dare look at Renie, nor did she utter another word. Her nerves were so taut that she had to fold her hands in her lap to stay calm. She wondered if the interrogation had concluded. If so, it seemed incomplete. Had the local police interviewed every person at the cocktail party? Of course they might have called in the county sheriff or even the state patrol. Judith estimated that there had been a hundred—maybe more—people in the ballroom, excluding the band and servers. The kitchen help, the front desk, the people in charge would all have to be questioned. Yet no one else seemed to be in the station except the young woman at the desk. Maybe there were prisoners in the cells. If so, who was guarding them? Most of all, why had she and Renie been brought to police headquarters? Couldn't Hernandez have asked his routine queries at Hanover Haus?

"Very well," he finally said, closing his laptop. "That's it." Although he'd leaned back the chair, his eyes were still unwavering. "Thank you. Do you need a ride back to your inn?"

"Yes," Judith said, starting to get up, "if you don't mind."

"By the way," the officer said quietly, "which one of you is FASTO?"

Judith's jaw dropped. She had to lean on the table for support. "I beg your pardon?"

He pointed to Renie. "It's not you, Mrs. *Jones*. Mrs. *Flynn* is tall. It says so on the Web site." He gazed at Judith. "Well?"

Judith sat back down again. "I'm FASTO. How did you know?"

A faint smile touched Hernandez's wide mouth. "We do our homework, even here in Little Bavaria. Someone mentioned that one of the innkeepers had a knack for solving mysteries." He tapped the laptop. "You weren't hard to find. Trying to dupe me was a waste of time."

"That Web site does not have my approval," Judith asserted. "Some silly people got the notion that I'm an amateur detective. It's ridiculous. I've just been in the wrong place at the wrong time too often. Not to mention that my husband is a retired homicide detective. In fact, he's now a private investigator."

Hernandez leaned back in the chair. "The wrong time? How many wrong times can there be in sixteen years? Shall I start with the fortune teller or just allude to your recent encounter with some big Paines?"

Judith held her head. "Ohhh . . ."

"Relax, coz," Renie said. "I'll bet Inbred Heffalump ratted you out to those other B&B people. Doesn't she always?"

"She thinks I'm a disgrace to the innkeeping profession," Judith blurted. "You know what she's like."

Hernandez sat up straight. "It's too bad you left early. It might've helped us if you'd seen something. You're obviously a keen observer."

Judith's conscience got the better of her. "Okay, so we didn't leave before it happened. But I truly didn't see anything that would help. In fact, that's why we left. I didn't want to get mixed up in another murder case. I'm beginning to feel hexed."

"Beginning to?" Hernandez said mildly. "I'd think you might've felt that way after you found a body in your British Columbia hotel elevator."

"Don't rub it in," Judith warned.

"So what did you see?" Hernandez asked.

Judith took a big breath. "Probably what everybody else did from the same angle. The music and the dancers stopped. The crowd sort of melted away from the middle of the ballroom. And there was poor Mr. Wessler lying on the floor. I didn't see a knife. At least I don't remember it. But I did see some blood. That's when my cousin and I took off."

Hernandez inclined his head. "How about before it happened?"

"Nothing, just what I told you earlier. No strange behavior on anybody's part, nothing suspicious. Just a typical cocktail get-together except for the enthusiastic dancing and the loud oompah band." She turned to Renie. "Am I missing something?"

"No. I never got a really good look at Wessler until I saw him lying on the floor. That was after *I* got off the floor."

Hernandez raised an eyebrow. "You were on the floor? You were dancing?"

Renie shook her head. "I can't dance worth a hoot. Very disappointing for my husband. My experience on the floor involved my eyelashes. Don't get me wrong, my lashes are real, but I dropped—"

"Never mind," Hernandez interrupted. "So far no one else has given us much help either."

"How long was the knife?" Judith asked.

Hernandez held his hands apart. "The blade was no more than three and a half inches."

Judith nodded. "Yes, that makes sense." She paused. "I suppose that was how it was planned."

Hernandez frowned. "Beg your pardon?"

Judith grimaced. "Is this an official homicide?"

He shook his head. "We won't make it official until after the autopsy. But I don't see how it could've been an accident."

Judith shrugged. "If it was murder, it was premeditated. In that crowd, with all those bodies so close together in constant motion and the noise such a distraction, who'd notice a small weapon like a steak knife? Was Mr. Wessler dancing? I didn't actually see him in the blur."

"Yes. He's a very vigorous old man. *Was*, I mean." Hernandez looked chagrined. "That's the strange part. He seemed to have been loved by everybody around here."

Sadly, Judith shook her head. "No, not quite everybody. Unless," she added, "someone loved him to death."

# Chapter Five

To her dismay—but not to her surprise—Lieutenant Hernandez insisted that Judith keep in touch.

"I realize you couldn't see much under the circumstances," he allowed, after stopping the squad car in front of Hanover Haus, "but judging from your history, you have an uncanny way of getting people to open up. You're also very impressionable—in the literal meaning of the word. It's possible that something you saw or heard this evening may come back to you. Chief Duomo would like to have you drop by tomorrow morning. He's very impressed with your credentials."

"Then he's easily impressed, especially about me being so impressionable," Judith said glumly. "Or something like that. Okay, but it'll have to be after eleven. I'm working the B&B booth until then."

"That's fine," Hernandez said. "I'll let him know. Thanks again. And," he added as Judith started to get out of the car, "be careful."

"Hey," Renie said, "coz is always careful. Nobody's tried to kill her for almost ten months."

"Yes," the officer murmured. "So I understand." He saluted before pulling out onto the street.

"Damn!" Judith cried. "What happened after I fingered the killer last January was never on the FASTO Web site because

Joe and Woody wouldn't allow the full story to reach the media. How do these cops know about it?"

"Because they're cops?" Renie said, opening the door to the inn. "It's the Blue Network. Word gets out."

Judith sighed. "You're right. Let's just hope none of this current disaster gets back over the mountains to Joe."

The woman behind the desk looked up. "You're back," she said, sounding disappointed.

"They let us out on bail," Renie said. "If any of our customers show up, send them to the right room. You might want to pat them down first to make sure they brought cash."

Ignoring the woman's startled face, the cousins went upstairs.

"Why," Judith asked as they entered their room, "do you have to make things worse?"

Renie looked innocent. "Like how? Hey," she went on, shifting gears, "maybe we should stick with the charade that I'm you?"

Judith removed her jacket. "What for? The cops know who's who."

"But what about everybody else?" Renie countered. "I don't mean we'd switch places, but we could pretend I'm taking over the sleuthing and let you off the hook with your B&B detractors. You investigate and I take credit. Then Inbred Heffalump can stick it in her mail slot."

Judith started to scoff, but paused. "Could we carry it off?"

"What's to carry? The burden is light, the reward is heavy. For you, I mean."

"What if I don't want to sleuth?"

Renie's expression was reproachful. "Coz . . ."

Judith sighed. "Let me sleep on it."

"Sure."

Half an hour later, the cousins were in bed. Each had brought a book for late-night reading. Not long after ten-thirty, Judith felt drowsy. "I'm turning out the lamp on my side. Okay?"

"I want to finish this chapter," Renie said. "I've only got three pages to go. Do you know who Bill James rates as the greatest second baseman of all time?"

"No," Judith admitted, switching off her light. "Who?"

"Joe Morgan," Renie replied. "He gets my vote, too."

"Lucky Joe. G'night."

A couple of minutes later, Renie shut her book, turned off the other lamp, and settled down. Judith had closed her eyes, trying to erase the image of Dietrich Wessler on the ballroom floor. She'd almost succeeded when a chomping noise disturbed her.

"Damnit," Judith said, lifting her head, "are you chewing gum?"

"You know I chew Big Red before I go to sleep," Renie replied.

"I'd forgotten," Judith said. "Can you stop?"

"Not until I've had at least four sticks."

"How does Bill stand it?"

"He wears earplugs," Renie said, smacking and snapping away.

"Why did you ever start that?"

"I like Big Red," her cousin replied. "It's soothing, and only a problem if it gets on me when I go to sleep while I'm still chewing."

"It's disgusting," Judith declared. "Please try to chew *quietly*."

"Can't," Renie said. "I've got big teeth. All the better to chew with. Done with Stick Number One."

"Oh, God!" Judith wailed into the pillow.

"Hey—if God hadn't wanted me to chew gum in bed, he wouldn't have—"

"Stop! At least shut up."

"Okay."

But the chomping continued, sounding like Clydesdale horses slogging down a muddy road. Judith pulled the covers over her ears in an effort to lessen the irritating noise. After almost five minutes, Renie apparently finished the final stick and rolled over onto her side. Judith expelled a big sigh, but was wide-awake. Trying to get into a drowsy state, she chose to think of something pleasant—like Renie lying in the parking lot under an enormous wad of Big Red gum.

**W**hen the alarm went off the next morning, it was Renie's turn to gripe. By the time Judith emerged from the bathroom twenty minutes later, her cousin had gone back to sleep. Breakfast was served beginning at seven-forty-five. Judith stopped at the front desk to ask the young man called Hans how to get to the dining room. He informed her it was through the hall at the other end of the desk. The cuckoo clock on the far wall sounded the quarter hour as Judith moved on.

A half-dozen guests had already gathered around the table that was set for twelve. Judith nodded pleasantly, if vaguely, before going to the trestle table by the wall, where she selected a bran muffin, fresh fruit, and a sausage patty. After pouring a cup of coffee, she wondered how Renie would react to the meager offerings, compared to the more lavish breakfasts Judith provided at Hillside Manor. Thankful she wouldn't be around to find out, Judith sought a place at the main table. The only person she recognized was Constance Beaulieu, who was sitting next to a thin-faced man with a handlebar mustache. A swift glance revealed that they were wearing matching wedding rings.

"Good morning, Connie," Judith said pleasantly, sitting down next to the man she assumed was Mr. Beaulieu.

"Oh, Judith!" Connie gasped, a hand at her breast. "Isn't it just awful about Mr. Wessler? Did you see all that blood? I almost fainted!"

Judith nodded. "Just enough so that we—my cousin and I—left. Does anybody know what happened?"

The supposed Mr. Beaulieu laughed hoarsely. "If anybody does, they aren't telling us."

"Oh," Connie said, her hand moving to the man's arm. "This is my better half, George." She beamed at him. "I told you about Judith Flynn, darling. Now you can see for yourself."

*See what?* Judith thought and couldn't help but frown when George leaned slightly closer. "Yes," he murmured, his mustache twitching a bit. "It's those dark eyes. Gypsy eyes. They reflect. Both outwardly and inwardly."

"Excuse me?" Judith said, trying to smile. "I'm not a Gypsy. That is, I've nothing against Gypsies, I just—"

"No, no," George said, lifting a hand in protest. "The quality of looking deeply to see things others don't. FASTO is clearly a corruption of Fausto. Feast of Fools, eh?" He chuckled richly.

Before Judith could say anything, Eleanor Denkel entered the dining room with a small, balding man trailing behind her like a pull toy. In fact, his long ears and drooping eyelids made him look like a bloodhound.

"Judith!" Eleanor exclaimed. "Who killed *Grossvater?*"

"I've no idea," Judith said, surprised.

"But if you don't know," Eleanor said crossly, "who does?"

Judith tried not to show her exasperation. "I'm not a wizard. Besides, my cousin and I left right after it happened."

"But," Eleanor protested, "you're FATSO!"

A sharp riposte almost shot out of Judith's mouth, but she squelched it in time. "Actually," she said calmly, "I'm not. That Web site is all a mistake. It's a cover-up for my cousin Serena. She doesn't like to be pestered by her admirers."

Eleanor gaped at Judith. "No! But Ingrid told us . . ."

Judith waved her hand. "Of course Ingrid would say I'm *FASTO*. I insist she does that. But if you study the Web site, you'll see that in every homicide case, my cousin is there in the background. And that's where she'll stay. Even now, she's on the case." *The* pillow*case,* Judith thought to herself. *Not exactly a bald-faced lie. . .*

"But," Connie said, "why are you telling us this now?"

Judith shrugged. "Everyone at this table is an innkeeper or associated with an innkeeper, right?" She paused to take in the nods and murmurs of agreement. "We have a bond," Judith went on, "so I can be candid. Besides, you know how Ingrid often chides me for being a sleuth. It's merely a ruse to cover for my cousin. We're all in the same business, so you should know I'd never be able to do such a thing." She forced a laugh. "How could an innkeeper have spare time to play detective?"

More nods and hushed agreement ensued. Judith turned back to Eleanor. "I'm afraid I haven't been introduced," she said, motioning at the little man half hidden by Eleanor's solid figure.

"Oh," Eleanor said, grabbing the man's hand and yanking him forward. "This is Delmar, my husband. Delmar, this is——"

"So I gathered," Delmar said, limply shaking Judith's hand. "Nice to meet you, Mrs. Fatso. I mean, Mrs. *Flynn*. I've heard about you from Ellie."

"Yes," Judith said, her smile frozen in place. "And some of it—alas—is untrue. But now we all have a little secret."

"That *is* exciting," Connie burbled. "I just *love* secrets."

The Denkels had moved over to the trestle table to select their breakfast. Judith buttered her muffin and couldn't help but wonder if she'd dug herself a very deep hole. She suddenly shivered—and wondered if the hole might be her own grave.

The conversation turned to Wessler's murder. Apparently the other innkeepers had already offered condolences to Ellie on her loss, perhaps the previous evening. Judith thought Ellie seemed remarkably composed. After a few desultory remarks about the horror of it all, Judith leaned toward the Denkels, who had sat down across from her.

"I met your uncle Franz at the train station back home," she said.

"Oh?" Ellie's expression was taut. "Until last night, I hadn't seen him in years."

Judith nodded. "He mentioned that he hadn't been here for some time. Was he terribly upset about his father's death?"

Ellie glanced at Delmar. "Could you tell how *Onkel* Franz reacted?"

Delmar, who was gnawing on a hard roll, shook his head.

"My uncle doesn't show his feelings," Ellie said. "He's a stoic."

"Maybe," Judith said, exercising one of her tactics for getting people to open up, "that serves him well in his work."

Ellie frowned. "I've never considered that. But he does have to distance himself from it. Emotionally, I mean."

Judith nodded. "Perspective—that's so important in his field of expertise. Keeping his distance."

"Oh, yes," Delmar put in. "And his eye—a genuine camera."

"Not to mention his nose," Ellie added.

Judith nodded again. *What does Franz do?* she wondered. A photographer? An architect? A garbage collector? Maybe his job wasn't important in terms of what had had happened to his father. But once Judith's curiosity was aroused, it had to be satisfied. Thus, she soldiered on. "Is Los Angeles really the best place for him these days?"

Ellie grew thoughtful. "Yes," she said after a long pause, "I suppose it is. Naturally, he travels a great deal." She grimaced. "Not to our part of the world, though."

Connie giggled. "Oh, Ellie, don't be so hard on your uncle. He was ever so charming last night—or was before your grandfather got stabbed. He was telling me about his latest documentary."

*Thank you, Connie,* Judith thought. "What," she inquired, "is this one about?"

Ellie looked sour. "Some African children's disease. Dreadful thing. I'll never watch it. In color, too. Disgusting symptoms, I'm sure."

"But," George Beaulieu said, leaning past his wife, "hasn't your uncle's humanitarianism won him several awards?"

Ellie shrugged. "Probably. He seldom writes or calls. I suppose he's too busy saving lives and doing good."

Judith glanced in the direction of the rest of the people who were eating their breakfast at the other end of the table. They were involved in their own conversation. She wondered if, being innkeepers or spouses or somehow connected, they were discussing Dietrich Wessler's murder. While Franz's documentary films sounded worthwhile, they didn't seem to have much to do with why his father had been killed.

Indeed, Delmar Denkel was now talking about a recent movie he'd seen on TV that he'd found offensive. It seemed he'd been so offended that he could hardly wait for it to end over two hours later. Judith wondered if he'd lost the remote. She finished eating and took a last sip of coffee. With a smile and a nod, she excused herself. It was eight-thirty—time for her to start heading to the B&B booth.

To her surprise, a voice called out to her just as she reached the main street. "Mrs. Flynn! Wait up!"

An auburn-haired young man Judith had noticed at the end of the table hurried to catch up with her. "I'm Gabe Hunter," he said. "I own a B&B across the Sound on the Kingfish Peninsula. My folks ran it until they retired. You may know them—John and Mary Lou Hunter."

"Yes, I met them once at a state meeting. They were fun people."

"They still are," Gabe said as they headed for the booth. "I'm on duty with you this morning. What did you think about the corpse crashing the party last night? I mean, so to speak."

"It was horrible," Judith replied, wondering if Gabe was pumping her or just making conversation. "My cousin and I took off. What happened after that?"

Gabe grimaced. "I was by the main entrance. I got there late because I stopped in the city to do some shopping. Traffic was horrendous—it took three hours to drive from downtown."

Gabe paused while he and Judith made way for a couple with a toddler in a stroller who was waving a blue-and-white-checkered flag with a crest bearing the words FREESTAAT BAYERN.

"Anyway," Gabe continued, "I checked into Hanover Haus and headed to Wolfgang's. I was getting into the mood of the place. Between the strolling musicians, the two-footed animals, the jugglers, the horse-drawn wagons, and the Bavarian architecture, I was in kind of a daze."

"Yes," Judith agreed. "The town has great charm."

Gabe nodded. "Anyway, when I got to Wolfgang's, the dancers were blocking my way into the ballroom, so I waited for the band to finish. When it did, I headed to the bar, but it suddenly got so quiet—eerie, really. Then I saw that old guy on the floor." He shook his head. "I thought it was a Halloween prank—or the start of a mystery game. People began screaming, but I still didn't get it. I found the bar, but nobody was serving. When I heard sirens, I knew the panic was genuine. End of bad joke, start of grim reality."

They'd arrived at the booth. Judith studied Gabe. He was average height with pale blue eyes and a fading suntan. His engaging manner compensated for unremarkable features. "Did someone take charge?" she asked as they entered the booth.

Gabe looked puzzled. "You mean one of the guests?"

"The victim's son and granddaughter were there. I wondered if they took over. Someone obviously called the police and the EMTs."

"Oh. I see what you mean," Gabe said. "It was pandemonium. Anyone could've called 911. Everybody's got a cell."

"True." Judith paused to get her bearings. The morning was overcast, but would probably clear later in the day. Even now she could see the mist slowly rising up the mountains that all but encircled the town. Her gaze shifted to the neighboring booths. A sporting-goods store was on her left, a Bavarian meat vendor on her right. So far, most of the dozen or so pedestrians seemed disinclined to check out the exhibitors' offerings. Maybe, Judith thought, it was the crime-scene tape across the front of Wolfgang's Gast Haus that put them off.

Apparently, Gabe was wondering the same thing. "How do the guests leave Wolfgang's?" he asked, jabbing a thumb over his shoulder. "Are they trapped inside until the police finish investigating?"

"How did you leave last night?" Judith inquired.

"Oh." Gabe grinned sheepishly. "They had a cop at the front

door. It looked like he had a checklist. Either I was okay to take off or not on the list of people they still had to question."

"I assume you were asked to give some sort of statement."

Gabe nodded. "They wanted to know what I saw, where I was staying, why I was at the cocktail party. Oh—my name, address, all that stuff. Routine, I suppose."

"Yes." Judith was about to add that it sounded that way to her, too, but stopped short. She didn't want Gabe to know she'd had any experience with similar situations. He was new to the business and perhaps didn't know of her reputation as FASTO. "Here come our first visitors," she said as a young couple approached hand in hand. Judith put on her innkeeper's face and went to work.

The next two hours were busy, answering questions, handing out brochures, quoting prices, and, on at least three occasions, trying to figure out which language the foreign tourists were speaking. Hindi, Urdu, Tamil, and Arabic were among the guesses made by Judith and Gabe. They were having better luck with a middle-aged Chinese couple whose English was understandable, when Renie showed up at the booth just before eleven. Mercifully, she hung back until the Chinese visitors had gone on their way.

"Hi, coz," Judith said cheerfully. "We're almost done here. Meet Gabe Hunter," she added, turning to her fellow innkeeper. "This is my cousin. You may have heard me mention her at breakfast this morning."

Gabe frowned. "I did?"

Judith realized Gabe had been engaged in conversation at the table's opposite end. "Oh. Well . . . this is Serena Jones. She's . . . here."

Renie shot Judith a curious look, but smiled and shook hands with Gabe. "Your backups are on their way. Connie and some guy named Phil are taking over. Phil forgot his glasses." She turned around. "Here they come. Oops! Phil just walked into a lamppost. Guess he didn't get his glasses after all."

"I don't remember Phil," Judith said. "Is he staying at Hanover Haus? He wasn't at breakfast."

Renie glared at Judith. "Breakfast wasn't at breakfast. By the time I got downstairs, the dining room was empty. Even the coffee urn was dry. You owe me, coz. It's an early lunch or I turn Little Bavaria into Dresden circa February 1945."

Judith winced. "Don't say that with so many Germans around. That wasn't one of the Allies' better ideas."

Gabe, who had been handing out brochures to a wholesome-looking couple who could've stepped out of a Norman Rockwell painting, turned around. "I read about that not too long ago. Half a million casualties in a city that wasn't a strategic target? That literally sounded like overkill. So close to the end of the war, too."

Renie shrugged. "Guess the Americans and the Brits hadn't had breakfast either. Come on, coz, Phil seems to be walking again. And no, he's staying at some other place on the river."

"Go ahead," Gabe said. "I'll wait for the newcomers to get settled."

Glad to avoid Connie, Judith grabbed her purse and exited the booth. "Where to?" she asked Renie.

"There's a pancake haus almost on the other side of Wolfgang's," Renie replied, leading the way. "You're lucky I'm still civil."

"Don't forget," Judith said, wishing Renie wasn't practically running, "I'm supposed to meet the police chief this morning."

"He can wait," Renie retorted.

Judith spotted the Pancake Schloss some fifty yards away. "Slow down! Hey—there's a police car parked outside the restaurant."

"Of course," Renie said. "According to the Little Bavaria guidebook, this place also has good doughnuts. I figured maybe you could kill two birds with one scone. They have those, too. And *Schloss* translates as 'palace,' in case you've forgotten our visit to Germany."

"I sure haven't," Judith snarled. "You were horrible that morning when we took the ship up the Rhine. Our breakfast was late, and after it finally came, you got mad at me for some stupid reason and poured a pitcher of cream all over *my* food."

"You'd filled the room with your stinking hair spray," Renie countered. "I was damned near asphyxiated."

"Too bad you weren't," Judith said, still irked at the long-ago memory of Renie's rotten morning mood. "Remember, the cops know who's who. Let's hope they don't rat me out to any of the innkeepers who think you're the sleuth," she added as they went inside the Pancake Schloss. "You were right—Ingrid can't get snarky with me this time."

The cousins were lucky. Their timing was such that most of the breakfast patrons were gone and the lunch crowd hadn't started to arrive. The restaurant was only half filled, but the current customers included two men in police uniforms in a booth near the back.

"Hey," Renie said, "I bet one of those cops is Chief Duomo. He's got a big round bald head. Isn't *duomo* the Italian word for 'dome'?"

"Maybe," Judith agreed, not waiting to be seated. "Let's join them."

The bald man didn't seem surprised by the cousins' arrival. "Mrs. Flynn," he said, looking droll. "Park yourselves. You, too, Mrs. Jones."

Renie nodded, sliding into the booth next to a lean-faced, hawk-nosed officer who regarded her with curious, heavy-lidded eyes. "Don't stare," she said, reaching around him to snatch a menu. "You're kind of skinny, but I'm part cannibal when I'm really hungry."

The officer had backed away when the menu almost hit his chin. "You've got the teeth for it," he remarked.

Judith, who didn't have much room next to the rotund police chief, tried to smile. "Could you hand me a menu? I assume you're . . ."

"Fat Matt Duomo," the chief interjected. "Go ahead, call me

that. I don't care, I don't have to. I'm the chief. Can I call you FATSO?"

Judith hesitated as Fat Matt handed her a menu. "Why not? Everybody else does. Except," she went on, "the B&B contingent. I've already told them my cousin is the real sleuth."

Duomo shot Renie a sharp glance. "Why'd you do that?"

"Because," Judith admitted, "I'm tired of the woman who runs the state association dumping on me when I find a dead body every so often."

Duomo chuckled. "Cramps your style, eh? Your rep's damned amazing. It makes us cops look dumb, but you're the goods, Mrs. F."

"A lot of luck—much of it bad—has been involved," Judith said, looking up at the hovering waitress whose nametag identified her as GRETEL. "I'll have the waffle sandwich with spicy link sausages. Coffee and apple juice, too. Thanks." She handed the menu back to Duomo.

Renie twirled a strand of chestnut hair, which, as usual, looked as if she'd combed it with a garden tool. "Buttermilk pancakes, one egg over easy, hamburger steak medium, large apple juice, and decaf."

The tall and rangy Gretel glared at Renie before hurrying away.

"Hey," Duomo said, "didn't introduce Major Schwartz, my second in command, title courtesy of fighting in 'Nam. Silver Star, Purple Heart, Jewish grandparents died in Buchenwald. Got quite a few folks around here whose families had some real bad experiences with the frigging Nazis. Fact is, Ernie here should be chief, but refused the promotion." Duomo grinned. "He didn't want the headache. Can't say I blame him."

"Hi, Ernie," Renie said. "I mean, *Major*."

"Ernie's fine," Schwartz said, "since we'll be working together."

Judith felt it was time to get down to business. "Can you update us about your investigation?"

"Sure," Duomo said, "if we can get more coffee. Where's Suzie?"

"Suzie?" Judith echoed.

"The waitress," the chief explained. "She didn't want to be a Heidi or a Hertha. She likes Gretel better. What the hell—she owns the place."

Judith was curious. "Why does she wait on tables?"

"Shorthanded during Oktoberfest," Duomo replied. "One waitress had a baby, another one sprained her ankle. Suzie and her husband started this place ten years ago. Done real good, best breakfast in town, open twenty-four hours during Oktoberfest and Christmas."

The cousins' food arrived. "It looks wonderful," Judith said, smiling at Suzie aka Gretel. "Thank you."

"You're welcome," Suzie said without enthusiasm. "You two guys want more coffee or are you just taking up space being baffled?"

"Come on, Suze," the chief said indulgently. "We do our best. Yeah, more coffee. Thanks."

Suzie stalked away.

Judith frowned at Duomo. "Isn't it a bit soon for her to give you a bad time about Wessler's murder?"

"That's not what she meant," the chief said, looking pained. "She's talking about her husband."

"What about him?" Judith inquired, buttering her waffle.

Duomo's expression grew even grimmer. "He was murdered last August. Maybe you could help us with that one, too."

# Chapter Six

Judith was taken aback by the new request, but felt obligated to at least show interest. "What happened to Suzie's husband?"

Chief Duomo sighed heavily. "Bob Stafford was a lawyer, but he got tired of working for Legal Aid after the first ten, fifteen years. They decided to move away from the big city, maybe set up practice in a small town. That wasn't too long after Little Bavaria started building a big rep as a tourist stop. Not just October and December, but ski season and camping—all the outdoor stuff. Once they got here, they couldn't find any place that made decent pancakes. So instead of going back to the law, they built this restaurant—Bavarian-chalet style with their living quarters upstairs. It was a big hit."

The chief paused as Suzie wordlessly refilled their coffee mugs. "Everything went along real smooth," Duomo continued after Suzie was out of hearing range. "That is, until early August, when Bob brought in some threatening letters, unsigned, about how whoever wrote the damned things had gotten a raw deal from Bob at Legal Aid. There were five of them, but we couldn't trace the sender. The next thing we know, Suzie reported Bob as missing. We found him not far from the Pancake Schloss by the river, apparently drowned. But we did an autopsy. The coroner's report showed that death was caused by a blow to the head before he ever hit the water." Duomo sighed again. "We haven't solved the case. Hell, we don't even have a suspect. Everybody liked Bob, so we figure it had to be the letter writer."

Judith swallowed some sausage before speaking. "Postmark?"

It was Ernie who answered. "The city—where else do all the nut jobs hang out?"

Judith couldn't suppress a small smile. "Believe me, they're everywhere. I've found killers all over the world—cities, small towns, island retreats, villages."

"Yeah," Duomo agreed grudgingly, "I've read your Web site, but the bigger the place, the more of the nuts. Besides, whoever wrote the letters was bitching about Bob's legal work and that was all in the city."

"I assume," Judith said, "you still have the letters?"

"Hell, yes," the chief retorted. "Handwritten, too. Even called in an expert who told us the sender was probably paranoid, a schizo, a psychopath, a real head case. I could've told him that, even without all those initials after my last name."

Renie nodded. "My husband's a psychologist," she said. "In professional terms, Bill would describe the writer as 'crazy as a bedbug.'"

Ernie eyed her with sleepy-eyed amusement. "He sounds like my kind of shrink."

Renie shrugged. "Bill doesn't mince words."

Duomo gestured at Judith's plate. "Your grub's on me," he said. "Can you come back to the station after you're done here?"

"Yes," Judith said, "but I didn't sign up for two homicides. Unless," she went on, narrowing her eyes at Fat Matt, "you feel they're linked."

The chief looked indignant. "Linked? Hell, how would I know? You're the sleuth. How 'bout this? Do a two-fer and I won't tell your B&B gang you aren't FATSO."

Judith sighed. "I'll give it a shot, but it's virtually a cold case. Don't expect much from me. Are you two leaving now?"

"Yeah," the chief replied. "You'll both have to move so we can get out. Time to arrest somebody . . . for something. Let's hit it, Ernie."

After the policemen made their exit, Renie fixed Judith with a knowing expression. "We're almost finished. When do we grill Suzie?"

"Now," Judith said, checking her watch. "It's after eleven-thirty, so the lunch crowd will start showing up. We need coffee refills."

"I see Suzie coming." Renie made a windmill motion. "Quick, make tears, put on your widow act. You know how, even if you didn't cry much over Dan's moundlike body."

Judith took a tissue out of her purse just before Suzie arrived at their booth. "Want me to take away the cops' stuff?" she asked.

"Oh—no," Renie said in a worried voice. "We need more coffee. Decaf for me, that is. My poor cousin's having a bad day."

Suzie slipped an order pad in her apron pocket, jabbed a pencil into her dark hair, and frowned. "What's wrong? You two flunk plea bargaining with the local lawmen?"

Judith sniffled; Renie scowled. "Hardly. My cousin's husband was a retired cop. He passed away recently under tragic circumstances. Can you cut her some slack, please?"

"Oh." Suzie looked faintly chagrined. "Sorry. I had no idea."

"Of course you wouldn't," Renie snapped. "It isn't every day that a husband gets whacked. Sometimes they just blow up. I mean, blow away. You know—like withered autumn leaves."

Suzie glanced over her shoulder, apparently to see if she was needed elsewhere. "Let me get your coffee—and decaf."

"Not bad, coz," Judith murmured. "Though you tend to overdo it. I didn't realize you could lie—I mean, fib—almost as well as I can."

"It's part of my job," Renie said. "I have to lie all the time, like when I tell CEOs and public officials and academics they're actually smart." She turned solemn. "Start sniffling again."

Armed with two coffee carafes, the Widow Stafford refilled

the cousins' mugs. "Sorry I was abrupt. I recently lost my own husband."

Judith dabbed at her eyes. "So many widows, so much crime."

"Foul play, huh?" Suzie remarked, still holding on to the carafes, but leaning against the back of the booth on Judith's side. "Same here. What's this world coming to?"

"Does it matter?" Judith said in a woebegone voice.

"No." Suzie looked even grimmer. "You're not a local. So why were you talking to the cops?"

Judith crumpled the tissue and cleared her throat. "My husband passed through Little Bavaria shortly before he passed on. That is, he was killed on the highway about ten miles from here near the summit. Hit-and-run, but it may've been deliberate. He was changing a tire when he was struck. I know it was in another jurisdiction, but I thought maybe your local police would have some . . . clue. The county sheriff on the other side of the mountains is baffled."

"Big surprise," Suzie muttered. "Same here with my husband. He was found by the river. Fat Matt and his crew don't have a clue either. And now they've got this mess with Herr Wessler. Wouldn't you think someone would've seen the old coot get stabbed?"

"Oh," Judith said in distracted voice, "that's so awful! It must've been an accident. Did you know him?"

"Sure. He was an institution in this town. He came to Little Bavaria before it was Little Bavaria." Suzie again glanced around the restaurant. "Hey—have to help the other customers. I put on a good dinner, if you're interested." She wheeled around and dashed off.

"I liked the tire part," Renie commented. "Ambiguous."

"That happened to some guy a while ago. I saw it in the paper."

Renie nodded. "That's why I'm glad we took the train. I don't mind when Bill's driving, but otherwise, this pass makes me nervous."

Judith dug in her purse. "I'm leaving a tip. I assume the chief picked up our tab, but just in case we want to come back here for dinner, it might be a good idea to butter up Suzie."

"She loosened up," Renie noted.

"But we didn't learn anything," Judith pointed out, putting a five-dollar bill by her plate. "She didn't even mention the letters."

"Won't the chief have them?"

"Probably." Judith didn't speak again until they were outside and going back down Main Street. "I prefer not getting side-tracked with Bob Stafford's murder. Assuming that's what it was."

"What else could it be?" Renie asked.

Judith looked up at patches of old snow as the morning mist rose up the mountainside. "He could've fallen and hit his head on a rock. Still . . ." She shrugged. "When it's not full of tourists, only a couple thousand people live here. If the letter writer who killed Bob wasn't local, he—or she—would have had to arrange a meeting. It sounds odd."

"I won't argue," Renie said. "I'm just a dupe. Or a dope. Do you have anything on your official schedule today?"

"Not until four," Judith replied. "We have an event at town hall with the Oktoberfest organizers. Beer tasting and a concert to follow."

"I wish I liked beer better," Renie said. "They can't serve the stronger German version here . . . whoa! What's going on by our B&B?"

"Oh, I forgot! At one o'clock they have a big procession and the official opening ceremonies. They're assembling everybody. Look, here comes a guy in an old horse-drawn wagon."

"How do you know the horse is old? He looks kind of frisky to me."

"I meant the wagon," Judith said, with a reproving eye for her cousin. "We haven't gone that far down the street, but it starts from just beyond the *Kinderplatz*. That is, the play area for kids."

"I get it, I get it," Renie muttered. "So where are we going? I don't feel like marching in a parade."

"Neither do I," Judith said, and turned around. "Why don't we check out the scene of the crime?"

"You mean Wolfgang's? That's in the other direction."

Judith shook her head. "Where Bob Stafford was killed. It happened behind the Pancake Schloss. There must be a trail."

"You realize the river will be higher now," Renie said as they approached the high bank in back of the restaurant.

"Of course. We were raised on a river at the family cabins, in case it slipped your mind. Here's the path." Judith studied the trail that zigzagged down the steep embankment. "It looks doable. You first?"

"Of course," Renie said.

The trail was a fairly easy walk. The cousins were more than halfway down when Renie stopped. "Hey—this is weird. Take a look."

Judith saw a wide spot dug out alongside the dirt track. It was overgrown with grass, weeds, and wild strawberry vines. "It's some kind of marker. What does it say? I don't want to bend that far."

" 'HRH,' " Renie said, pushing some of the vines aside. "Just dates: 1919 to 1979. His Royal Highness? A family pet buried here?"

Judith looked incredulous. "A sixty-year-old dog? Get real."

"A parrot, maybe. They live to be really old, just like our mothers."

"It has to be a person. The cleared area is big enough for a body."

"Of course," Renie said. "You've found another corpse. Too bad he or she died so long ago or you could figure out whodunit. Buried HRH here, I mean. Some people do die of natural causes."

"Why here? Why not in the cemetery?"

"Hey—forget it. Let's go down to the river and finish the ghoul expedition, okay?"

Judith gave in. A few moments later they were standing by the river. As ever, the riffles of water over rocks had a soothing effect. "No oompah bands. No emergency vehicles. No sniping rival innkeepers."

"No fish," Renie added. "Not like there used to be. But we've still got the mountains." She looked up above the tree line to the peaks with their crevasses of snow. "Civilization will get us yet."

"I hope not," Judith murmured. "If only people would stop moving here. Then they complain about the rain and the gray skies. I hate to do it, but when guests exult in a sunny day in the city, I tell them it's so rare that I might go blind. It's fine for them to visit, but why must they *move* here? All the new construction on Heraldsgate Hill is insane."

"Tell me about it." Renie stopped staring at the mountains. "So is this your crime scene?"

"It must be." Judith was quiet for a few moments. "The river would've been lower in August when Bob was killed. The initial reaction was that he'd fallen and hit his head on a rock, but all I see now are a few pebbles. What do you figure? Another ten feet of bank, maybe?"

"Probably, given the channel here. It's very wide and most of the snow would've melted much earlier."

Judith nodded before turning to look up at the bank. "How much could anyone have seen from there in August?"

"Quite a bit. Very little now, of course, only the river and the other side. Anyone walking by might've spotted Bob. Or, of course, walking along down here."

"But unless it was a fisherman, why do that in the first place? I suspect Bob got a call at the Pancake Schloss from somebody who wanted to meet him by the river. But why not mention that to Suzie?"

"Busy time of day?" Renie suggested. "She seems to go on auto-pilot when she's working."

"True. He might've told her and she didn't even hear him. Or he wouldn't have wanted to distract her." Judith paused, chin on fist. "That'd indicate he wasn't worried about whoever he was meeting."

Renie kicked at a broken branch by the river's edge until it landed in the water and was carried off downstream. "Not the letter writer?"

"Probably not. Bob was sufficiently upset or maybe just annoyed by the letters to take them to the police. Yes, the timing is right, but if Bob had common sense, he'd have insisted that the letter writer meet him at the restaurant or somewhere more public." Judith made a sweeping gesture. "This place suggests that he knew his killer."

Renie's gaze again took in the mountain view. "I assume you're trying to connect the dots between Bob and Wessler."

"Not quite." Judith sighed. "At least not yet. Come on, let's go."

"Go where?"

"To see the cops," Judith said.

The uphill climb took a little longer. Finally, the cousins reached the main street, but had to stop three blocks away from the Pancake Schloss. The town was abustle, forcing Judith and Renie to wait for the passage of a half-dozen vehicles and an antique fire engine. They were about to cross when a woman leading two Saint Bernards caught their attention. It struck Judith that the dogs seemed to be leading *her*, given that they were in the street and not on the sidewalk. "Excuse me," she called to the cousins. "Can you help?"

Judith stepped off of the curb. "I don't know much about dogs," she admitted. "What do you want me to do?"

"Could each of you grab one of the dogs' collars and lead them out of the street? These animals don't seem to want to obey me."

"Apparently not," Renie grumbled, but approached the nearest dog. "Okay, Bernie, let's go . . ." She almost fell over as the Saint Bernard jumped up and began licking her brown sweater. "Hey! Stop! It's cashmere!"

The other animal went for Renie, too. "They smell hamburger steak," Judith muttered, trying in vain to grab the second dog's collar.

"Damnit!" Renie yelled, backpedaling away from the dogs. "I paid a hundred and sixty bucks for this sweater!"

A sharp whistle cut through the air. The dogs instantly retreated. A stern voice called out, "Siegfried! Dolph! Here, here!"

The Saint Bernards stood as if at attention. Judith gaped at Franz Wessler. "Thank goodness! Are those your dogs?"

"No," Franz said, patting both animals. "They belonged to *Vater*." He looked at the breathless woman, whose heart-shaped, piquant face had turned pale as she reached the sidewalk. "Are you all right, Klara?"

"Yes, yes," she replied, letting go of the leashes and running a hand through her blond hair. "I should never walk them." She lowered her glacial-blue eyes. "I'm sorry, Franz."

"*You're* sorry?" Renie snapped. "What about my sweater?"

Judith nudged Renie. "Can it, coz."

Franz chuckled. "*Meine Liebe* Klara, did I not always say you were more in love with him than with me? Let us walk the dogs together."

Holding the leashes in one hand, he offered Klara his other arm. They continued down the street without a backward glance at the cousins.

"Well!" Judith exclaimed under her breath. "No introductions? What was that about?"

"Not my sweater," Renie griped.

"How old would you guess?"

"My sweater? I got it last year at——"

"No," Judith interrupted. "Klara."

Renie grew serious. "Forties, maybe? Hard to tell. She could be a bit younger or ten years older. Smooth skin except around the eyes and mouth. Hair may or may not be natural, though the texture is good and the color suits her. I figure she's stayed out of the sun, which is smart."

Judith didn't speak until they were across the street, headed for the police station. "So if Franz hasn't seen his father in several years, where's Klara been all this time?"

Renie shot Judith an irritated glance. "In prison? A convent? Outer space? How would I know and why do you care?"

Judith heaved an impatient sigh. "If I'm supposed to solve Herr Wessler's murder, I have to get background on the people involved. His son is a good place to start."

Renie grinned. "I think you've got a crush on Franz."

"That's dumb!" Judith cried, almost stumbling onto the curb at the corner by police headquarters. "He seems interesting. And he just happens to be the prime suspect in a homicide case."

"Gee, your kind of guy," Renie murmured, looking amused.

"Shut up," Judith snapped, almost hitting her cousin with the station door. "Focus on the case. You're supposed to be a sleuth, so act like one instead of making smart-assed commentary." She marched up to the desk, where a pudgy older woman was complaining to a weary-looking policeman whose gray eyes seemed focused on the far wall.

"Look, Mrs. Crump, your neighbors can't adjust their lives to Mr. Crump's schedule," he asserted. "There's no antinoise law for two in the afternoon. Can't your husband use earplugs?"

"Roscoe shouldn't have to do that," Mrs. Crump declared, wagging a finger. "He says they bother him, they tickle the hair in his ears. Now see here, Orville, we've lived in this town forever, long before all these newcomers moved here. We have longstanding rights!"

"Yes," Orville said in his beleaguered voice, "and you've been standing here long enough and often enough to tell me about it. You know we can't do anything about your neighbors."

"Hey," Renie said, barging past Judith to get next to Mrs. Crump, "your neighbors are going to file a complaint about Roscoe. His snoring all day is driving them nuts."

Mrs. Crump swerved to stare at Renie. "Who are you?"

"The name is Jones," Renie said somberly. "R. Jones."

Mrs. Crump looked puzzled. "You *are* Jones? That's it?"

"That's enough," Renie retorted. "And I know what your husband really does at night."

"Well!" Mrs. Crump put a hand to her big bosom. "I should hope not! His work is classified."

"That," Renie said with a world-weary sigh, "is how I know."

"I never . . . hrmpph!" The other woman turned around so fast that she almost ran into Judith. "'Scuse me," she mumbled, making her exit.

Officer Orville seemed bemused. "You two aren't by any chance the . . . um . . . er . . . women who . . . ah . . ."

"You betcha," Renie said. "Where's Fat Matt?"

Orville's leathery face darkened. "He's about to go to lunch."

"Lunch?" Renie repeated. "He just got back from coffee."

Orville nodded. "But it's way past noon and he's late for lunch."

Renie turned to Judith. "No wonder he's Fat Matt. He'll be known as Dumbo Duomo for his elephantine size before he solves this murder case. We need to see him *now*. As my husband would say, *boppin'*!" She clapped her hands for emphasis.

"Okay, okay," Orville said. "I'll buzz him. Hey," he said, his finger on the button, "how did you know Roscoe Crump works for security? You just got here."

Renie shrugged. "I know all things. It's what I do, it's who I am. Oof!" She winced as Judith stepped on her foot.

"Okay," Orville said, gesturing at a door to their left, "go ahead. He's in there. Can I ask what the *R* stands for?"

"Sure," Renie said, limping slightly as she led the way for Judith. "It stands for Results, which is what I get as FASTO."

The chief opened the door before Renie could grasp the knob. "There you are," he said. "I thought you got lost."

"No," Renie said, "we were attacked by a couple of Saint Bernards, but we fought them off. We're city girls, and used to violence. You ought to see Mrs. Flynn's cat. Or her mother." She shuddered. "Gruesome."

"Sounds god-awful," Duomo said, poker-faced. "Have a seat.

Don't mind Ernie. He nodded off about five minutes ago. He's one of those narcocalypso fellas. Or whatever they call 'em. Goes to sleep while he's walking down the street. Not much good on foot patrol, so I try to keep him on highway duty."

Sure enough, the deputy was asleep with his feet propped up on a filing cabinet. "Isn't his driving a problem?" Judith inquired.

Duomo shook his head. "Nah. He just puts on the cruise control. Okay. What've you got so far?"

Renie made a face. "Other than being attacked by dogs?"

The chief held up a hand. "Button up. I want the real FATSO."

Judith frowned. "Do you mind? 'Mrs. Flynn' or 'Judith' is just fine. We've only been on the case about an hour. What do you expect?"

Duomo shrugged. "It's a small town. Have you quizzed *anybody*?"

"Yes," Judith replied, "we have. Who's Klara and how is she connected to Franz and Dietrich Wessler?"

The chief leaned back and grinned. "Klara is Franz's ex. They split nine, ten years ago. She moved here to be the old man's housekeeper. Think the only room she keeps up is the bedroom. Why else hire Olga Crump as a cleaning woman?"

"Crump?" Judith echoed. "Is she married to Roscoe?"

"Ah. So you've met her, too?"

"She was complaining about neighbors . . ."

Duomo made an impatient gesture. "Yeah, she likes to do that. The Kotters are good people. Otto Kotter plays trombone in the oompah band. He has to practice and it keeps Roscoe awake. Not our fault."

Judith tried to ignore Ernie's snoring. "What exactly does Roscoe do on his security job?"

"Depends." He picked up a pencil and tapped it on his desk. "Usually he sort of wanders around to make sure nobody's where they shouldn't be. But with Oktoberfest, he checks for illegal immigrants."

"Uh . . ." Judith wasn't sure what Duomo meant. "What kind?"

The chief shrugged. "Anybody who isn't German." He nodded at Judith. "You're part German. Saw it when I did a background check."

"Yes, on my mother's side. She's a Hoffman."

He pointed at Renie. "You're not, but since you're with FATSO . . . I mean, Mrs. Flynn, you're okay."

"What," Judith inquired, still puzzled, "about the exhibitors? They aren't all of German descent."

"They have to pay a fee to set up their booths," Duomo replied. "That makes them honorary Germans."

"What's the point?" Judith persisted. "Oktoberfest and all your other activities are aimed at bringing in tourists. It doesn't make any sense. What do you do if a couple of French-Canadians show up?"

"We fine 'em. Five bucks—and give 'em a ten-buck restaurant coupon. Most folks think it's funny. Makes our budget look good."

Judith didn't dare look at Renie, knowing that they were both wondering if this wasn't the strangest of some very strange law enforcement personnel they'd ever met. Unless Duomo was kidding.

Judith changed the subject. "Let's see the witness list."

Duomo grunted while leaning far enough out of his chair to punch Ernie's arm. "Wake up, Major. Viet Cong got us surrounded."

Ernie Schwartz jerked himself into consciousness. "Huh? Wha . . . where? Oh." He rubbed his eyes. "What's up?"

"Mrs. Flynn wants our witness list from Wolfgang's last night."

The other officer yawned widely. "You're sitting on it, Chief."

Duomo looked surprised. "I am?" He raised his portly body and felt under his rear end. "Oh—that's where it went. Have we got more copies?"

Ernie nodded and stood up. "Orville has some out front. I'll get one for our sleuth."

The chief nodded once. "Good man," he said after his subordinate left. "Specially when he's awake. Got any more questions?"

"How about leads?" Judith inquired.

"Leads?" He wrinkled his nose. "You mean in the Wessler case?"

"It's a little late for the Lindbergh kidnapping," Renie noted.

"You," the chief said, shaking his finger at Renie, "keep quiet. You're the beard, remember?"

"Fine," Renie growled. "Then you're the gut."

Duomo shrugged. "Why not?" He drummed his pudgy fingers on the desk. "Okay, leads. Nope, can't think of any. Except for the knife."

"The knife?" Judith repeated. "What about it?"

"Fingerprints," he replied. "Lots of them. Smudged."

Judith reined in her patience. "Were *any* of them identifiable?"

"Nope."

"DNA?" Judith inquired.

"Not yet."

Judith persisted. "Any idea where the knife came from?"

"Nope. Unless it was off the food table by the roast beef."

"Hey," Renie said, "I never saw any roast beef! Where was it?"

"Never mind, coz," Judith said under her breath. "It was at the far end of the table." She raised her voice. "Who was carving the beef?"

"Anybody who wanted some," Duomo replied. "It was self-serve. Fact is, there were a half dozen of those knives by the meat platter."

"But one was missing?" Judith asked.

The chief shrugged. "Guess so. On the other hand, you know how folks like to pocket the cutlery. Don't know why. Doesn't everybody have knives at home? I do."

Before Judith could say anything further, Ernie returned. "Want these?" he asked, proffering a sheaf of printed pages to Judith.

"Yes, thanks." She perused the top sheet. At least fifty names were listed. "How many witnesses did you interview?"

"Ninety," Duomo replied, "maybe closer to a hundred, not including the hired help. You impressed?"

"Yes," Judith admitted. "It must've taken several hours."

"Damned near five," the chief said grumpily. "There was just Ernie here and me. I've only got a half-dozen full-time officers, but I'll be damned if I'll call in the sheriff or the state troopers. They always criticize how we operate. Who needs that? And they don't speak German."

"Do you?" Judith asked.

"No, but the major does." He looked at Ernie, who was nodding off. "So does Crump, our security guy. You want to keep that copy?"

"Yes," Judith said. "I need time to go through all these names."

"You do that." Duomo stood up. "Way past my lunchtime. Hey, Major, hop to it. Those little guys in their black pj's are lurking behind the jungle vines."

Judith and Renie got up. "Thanks. Enjoy your lunch."

"Will do," the chief said. "Don't be a stranger."

The cousins made their exit. Orville was on the phone and didn't look up as they passed by.

"Stranger is right," Judith said after they were outside. "Major Schwartz reminds me of Uncle Vince—always dozing off, even in the middle of Thanksgiving dinner."

Renie nodded. "Two years ago, he got his face stuck in the root vegetable dish. Orange doesn't become Uncle Vince."

"True. But how does this bunch keep law and order?"

"They must," Renie pointed out. "How often do you read about serious crime around here?"

"Well . . . not often. Unless they keep a lid on it. Little Bavaria is kind of isolated up here in the mountains." Judith paused at the corner. "Uh-oh. I hear music. The parade must be starting. How do we avoid it?"

"Go down a couple of blocks to where they were assembling and do an end run?" Renie suggested.

A dozen preschoolers, holding on to a thick red rope, were being herded by two young women toward the main street. Judith nodded at a group of laughing adults who were making their way toward the parade route. "We'll have to," she said with a sigh.

Before they could start walking in the opposite direction, a squad car pulled up next to the curb a few feet away. Judith put a hand on Renie's arm. "Hold it. There's somebody in the backseat. Let's see if an arrest has been made."

"Are you joking? If they busted someone, it's probably a shop-lifter pocketing cheap made-in-Myanmar German souvenirs."

They recognized Officer Hernandez when he got out of the driver's side. Apparently, he didn't notice them, but opened the rear door. Judith couldn't see who was getting out until after Hernandez moved away from her line of sight.

When he did, she gasped. The officer was escorting a hand-cuffed perp into headquarters. Renie let out a little squeal as cop and captive marched to the entrance.

"Good grief!" she cried. "Isn't that Eleanor Denkel?"

# Chapter Seven

**W**hat's that all about?" Judith said, trying to keep her voice down as more parade goers trickled past them and detoured vehicles used the side street for access. "Has Eleanor been arrested for being obnoxious?"

Renie cupped her ear. "I can't hear you. The band's too loud."

The only place to escape traffic and parade noise was in the alley next to police headquarters. Judith grabbed Renie's arm, steering her in that direction. Reaching relative quiet next to an unoccupied police van, the cousins caught their breath.

"Why is Eleanor busted?" Judith asked, still not raising her voice.

"Good question," Renie said with a smirk. "You tell me, FASTO. Maybe she's a hooker?"

"Hardly." Judith made a face. "Handcuffs, too. You don't suppose . . . ?" She let the question dangle.

Renie's brown eyes widened. "She dunnit? Her own grandfather?"

Judith shrugged. "Family ties are sometimes severed with a knife."

"Yes," Renie mused, "that can cut off a relationship. If we wait for Duomo to get back from lunch, it'll be time for his afternoon break."

"You're right," Judith agreed. "I don't know who else is on duty besides Orville, but he can't abandon his post." She grimaced. "Why does the concept of Ellie in a cell make me want to smile?"

"Because she treats you like compost?"

"There is that," Judith allowed, gazing up at the mountain that had become completely visible. "The B&B association is like high school—full of cliques. Not my style."

"You have to have certain things in common to be in a clique," Renie remarked. "How many other innkeepers find corpses?"

Judith glowered at her cousin. "Don't rub it in. Maybe we should watch the parade."

Renie turned mulish. "You know I'm not fond of parades."

"Have you ever watched an Oktoberfest parade?"

"No, and don't try to break my record for abstinence."

Judith shook her head and started walking down the alley before she realized her cousin wasn't behind her. "Why are you leaning against that van?" she demanded. "Isn't it the paddy wagon?"

"Probably," Renie called back. "I figure that they'll have to use it to haul away rioters and drunks from the parade. Then I won't have to walk back to Hanover Haus."

"Oh, for . . ." Judith was distracted by the screeching of tires. She glanced back to the street, where a squad car had just pulled up. "Hey—the chief's back!" she shouted to her cousin.

"He ate and ran? Not likely." Renie shook her head, but hurried to join Judith, who was already on her way to accost Fat Matt and Major Schwartz before they entered the building.

"Whoa!" the chief cried. "You hear about the break we got in the Wessler case?"

"Break?" Judith said. "You've only been gone ten minutes."

Duomo waved an impatient hand as he paused at the entrance. "Okay, so it's a confession. That's as good as a break. You going or coming?" Before Judith could reply, he looked beyond her to where Ernie was apparently asleep on his feet by the squad car. "Major!" the chief barked. "Land mine! Move it!"

"Huh?" The officer snapped to attention before jumping at least three feet across the sidewalk. "Damn! Sneaky commie bastards!"

"Better than an alarm clock," Duomo muttered, opening the door and allowing the cousins to enter first. He paused at the front desk, scrutinizing Orville. "Seeing how we got this case wrapped up," the chief said, "why don't you take that squad car outside and nip over to have Suzie put some lunch together for me? She knows what I like."

"But," Orville protested, "the parade's going down Main Street. I'd have to drive out of town to get to the pancake house."

"Hell, Orville, just turn on the siren and bust right on through. Hop to it, I'm starved."

"Yes, sir," Orville said with his usual careworn manner. Putting on his regulation hat, he came around from behind the counter to make his exit. "Pickles?" he asked, halfway out the door.

"Sure, the little sweet ones," Duomo replied.

"Got it." Orville departed.

"Now," the chief said to the cousins, "how do we work this? Probably not a good idea to let you in on the Denkel woman's interview. Why don't you two take over the front here while I listen in on whatever Hernandez is doing in the other room? Where'd Ernie go?" He looked around and shrugged. "Oh, well. Doesn't matter. It's all yours," he added with a wave of his hand before ambling off to the interrogation room.

"This is insane," Judith declared. "I'm beginning to wonder if this whole thing is some sort of hoax."

"You mean . . ." Renie's puzzled look suddenly disappeared. "Ingrid has decided to get even with you by staging a murder?"

"Exactly." Judith reluctantly moved around to the other side of the counter. "We'll play along for now. It could be fun."

"Am I still FATSO?" Renie asked, joining her cousin.

"Please—*FASTO*. Sure. We can play this game, too. If the chief and the other cops are in on it, they could blow your cover. On the other hand, we could've lied to them as well as to the B&B people."

Renie grimaced. "I think I'm confused. Am I still married to Bill?"

Judith looked exasperated. "Of course. Unless you prefer Joe."

"No!" Renie cried. "I mean, I like Joe and all that, but . . ."

"Skip it." She glanced toward the interrogation room on her left. "I wonder what they're doing in there. Laughing at us?"

"Probably." Renie sat down by the phone console. "I'm bored."

"You're nuts." Judith pulled a chair up to the computer. "This is a rare opportunity. We can access police files."

"Such as?"

"Let's see if the Stafford homicide is real."

Renie was leaning her cheek on her hand. "Real what?"

"As in it actually happened." Judith scowled at the screen. "I need a password. I thought this thing would be up and running."

Renie gazed glumly at her cousin. "Try 'Gestapo,'" she muttered.

"Not funny."

"Then try the local newspaper," Renie said impatiently. "You won't need a password to get online."

"I'm not sure what it's called," Judith admitted. "It'd be a weekly?"

Renie yawned. "Probably."

Judith typed in "Little Bavaria newspaper." The front page of the *Blatt* came up. "It *is* a weekly. It came out Wednesday. I'll put in Bob Stafford's name and see what . . . ah!" She stared at the headlines:

## LOCAL RESTAURATEUR'S BODY FOUND; M.E. CITES FOUL PLAY; CHIEF INVESTIGATES STAFFORD MURDER; DUOMO BAFFLED IN HOMICIDE CASE

"Sounds right," Renie murmured.

Judith shrugged. "At least we know that Bob Stafford really was murdered. This couldn't have been faked."

"I wonder," Renie mused, "if the city TV and print media covered the alleged killing of Dietrich Wessler."

As in most B&Bs, including Hillside Manor, there were no TV sets in the guest rooms. "We could pick up a daily paper," Judith suggested. "But if this is a hoax, they'd never release it publicly. Even if it was a genuine homicide, it might not make the news back home. Thank goodness," she added, relieved that Joe would be kept in ignorance.

"A regional two-, three-graph item," Renie remarked. "No other media coverage unless one of the TV stations is doing an Oktoberfest feature. I've seen no signs of that."

Judith smiled wryly. "If Mavis Lean-Brodie shows up," she said, referring to her longtime adversary and sometimes ally from KINE-TV, "I'll know Herr Wessler really did get killed."

"Mavis," Renie said with the same inflection she might have used for "plague" or "CEO."

The interrogation room's door opened. Chief Duomo stumbled out, mopping his forehead. "Tough cookie," he murmured, closing the door behind him. "Heart of granite. Never seen the like in my . . . twenty-five? Twenty-eight? Thirty . . . what the hell, I've been on this job too long."

"Eleanor confessed?" Judith asked.

"Oh, did she!" He stuffed his wrinkled handkerchief into his back pocket. "Well. That wraps it up. Thanks for your help. Now, if we could move on to that Stafford murder . . . after lunch, I mean. Where's Orville? How long does it take him to get my damned food?"

Judith had stood up. "Are you going to let her post bail?"

"Oh, sure," the chief said. "She can't miss Oktoberfest. See ya." He ambled into his office and shut the door.

"Now what?" Renie said.

"Hang on," Judith said. "I'd like to see how that stuck-up Ellie plays this hand. Will she post bail? It's Friday. I can't imagine there's a bail bondsman anywhere around here after noon on a weekend."

"Gee," Renie said, "I thought they'd be hanging out on street corners like hookers during a big beer blast like this."

Judith disagreed. "People don't get out of control. College kids don't count—they don't need an excuse to guzzle. Oktoberfest's more than beer drinking; it's Bavarian customs, history, and culture."

"Good," Renie murmured. "I don't want to get run down by a drunken tuba player."

"You won't." Judith paced the area behind the counter. "Where's Ellie? Where's Hernandez? Ernie's probably asleep somewhere. Lord, what a crew!"

"Hernandez is kind of cute," Renie remarked. "He seemed normal—by comparison. Whatever happened to Orville?"

"Who knows?" Judith's usual inexhaustible patience had snapped. She marched over to the door leading to the room Duomo had exited and knocked three times. There was no response. Frustrated, she turned the knob. The door opened, revealing an empty room. "What on earth?"

Renie joined her cousin. "There has to be another way to get out. I cleverly deduce that it was via that large open window that probably leads into the alley."

"Damn!" Judith exclaimed. "I didn't notice any window last night. I was too concerned about our own interrogation." She walked across the room and looked out. "It's a two-foot drop. Even I could do that."

"Why don't we? I'm bored again."

"Stop that!" Judith picked up a file folder from the table and scanned the papers inside. "Hey—this is Ellie's signed confession. It sounds almost enough like her to be the real thing."

"How about the short version?" Renie said, lounging against the doorframe. "Tweet will do."

Judith reread the statement twice before responding. "The motive is so predictable. Couldn't they be imaginative if they're writing fiction?"

"Skip the critique. Cut to the headline."

"Ellie stabbed her grandfather because he was going to change his will and leave everything to Klara."

"Oh. You're right. That is *so* not original. Let's go."

Judith hesitated. "The parade may be over. The route's short."

Renie turned around. "Hi, Orville. Hey, want to let me have a couple of those fries?"

"You want to get me fired?" Orville muttered before moving on.

"Jerk," Renie muttered as Judith joined her in the outer office.

"You're right," she said. "This game is dumb. I have to be at the town hall at four to attend the function with the Oktoberfest organizers."

"What am I supposed to do while you're there?"

Judith headed out the door. "Amuse yourself. You're creative."

"I have to be inspired," Renie said as the cousins paused before crossing the street. "I could check out some of the shops. Bill likes German stuff. Maybe I can find a nice bust of Goebbels."

They'd reached the main street, where the traffic flow was now normal. "Hey," Judith said, "isn't that Franz Wessler hurrying our way?"

"Gee," Renie said, "I'll bet he realized he's madly in love with you and wants to sweep you off your feet."

"Shut up, coz," Judith murmured as a worried-looking Franz approached them.

"Good afternoon," Franz said without his usual aplomb. "I dare not linger. I must see the police." He sketched a bow and hurried away.

Renie shot Judith a curious glance. "About Ellie?"

"Grab him. You can run, but I can't. Go!"

Her cousin looked reluctant, but she rushed away, calling after Franz. He stopped at the curb, obviously flummoxed. Renie took his arm, hauling him back to where Judith was ready and waiting to go straight to the point. "Is this about Ellie's confession?" she demanded.

Franz turned pale. "How do you know?"

"We were at the police station when she was brought in," Judith replied. "I have to level with you. I know Ellie didn't kill your father. This whole situation is absurd and you know it."

Tears welled up in Franz's eyes. "Yes, yes. I am aware of that." He swallowed hard, lowering his head before he stared straight into Judith's eyes. "That's why I'm going to the police. My niece didn't kill *Vater*. I did." He rushed across the street, heedless of oncoming traffic.

**J**udith watched Franz disappear into the side street. "Damn! Did Franz learn to act in L.A.? Those tears seemed real."

"I didn't get a good look," Renie admitted. "His back was to me."

"Now *I'm* confused. Can anybody give us a straight answer?"

Renie thought for a moment. "How about Inbred Heffalump?"

"She's not here," Judith said. "But," she went on, more slowly, "my guess is that she's the one who put this thing together—if, in fact, it is a payback hoax because of the bodies I've found."

Renie gazed at the people who were milling about on the sidewalks. Many of them were wearing Bavarian garb and obviously enjoying themselves. "That'd be too mean of her," she declared. "You're here at her behest and she pulls a stunt like this? Why doesn't she get her butt over here with the rest of the B&B gang?"

"She's an administrator," Judith explained. "There are only a couple of dozen B&B owners in town. Ingrid made all the arrangements, but her presence isn't necessary."

"So what do we do now?" Renie gazed at the town hall's clock tower. "It's one-fifty. We've got almost two hours to kill. So to speak."

Judith stepped aside for two 'tweenaged girls in dirndls running down the street and giggling their pigtailed heads off. A brass ensemble playing a merry tune could be heard in the distance. The sun was out, pale gold against a blue sky. What should have been a pleasant day now tasted sour.

"Let's go to the booth," Judith said after a pause. "I don't know who's on duty, but there may be some innkeepers I haven't met. We can gauge their attitudes about this whole mess."

"That sounds like so much fun, I'd almost rather shave my head with a potato peeler." But Renie fell into step with her cousin.

Judith spotted Connie Beaulieu at once, but the plump older man with her in the booth was a stranger. A dozen people, including children, were perusing brochures and chatting with the innkeepers.

"Want me to break this up?" Renie asked quietly.

"No! They're potential guests."

"Not if you wait for those tots to grow up. You don't allow children."

"But parents need getaways."

Renie sighed. "So do I. Hey—we missed lunch."

"I think there's food available a couple of booths down," Judith said, recalling the exhibitors' layout from her travel package. "Go eat something before you get surly . . . er."

"I'll do that." Renie stalked away.

At least five minutes passed before Connie and the other innkeeper were free. Judith had amused herself by gazing at the passing parade that included two teenagers wearing antlers, several adults loaded down with shopping bags, a young man on crutches, and a redheaded woman mounted on a handsome gray hunter that looked like a show horse.

"Judith!" Connie exclaimed. "Come meet Eldridge Hoover! He's from the other side of the mountains, so he's staying with the eastern contingent at the Bavarian Inn. I just love him to pieces!"

Eldridge put out a pudgy hand and chuckled. "Call me 'Ridge,' " he said, "given that I'm sure not rich. Ho-ho-ho."

"Hi, Ridge," Judith said, shaking the man's soft hand. "How's everything going?"

Eldridge's jovial expression changed. "To hell in a handcart. I'm glad I missed the cocktail party last night. Terrible tragedy. That poor old man—he lives to a great age and then somebody stabs him like a chunk of beef!" He shook his balding gray head and hooked his thumbs into his blue suspenders. "Why would anybody do such a thing?"

Connie leaned toward Judith. "I heard the most incredible rumor. Ellie is supposed to have confessed! That's ridiculous. I was with her when it happened. How does such gossip get started?"

Judith was wide-eyed. "You were with her? Really?"

"Of course," Connie said indignantly. "We didn't take part in the dancing. I don't know those steps. She and I were about to get something to eat when it happened." She shuddered, blond curls glinting in the autumn sunlight. "Were you there?"

"Yes," Judith admitted, "but we left right away. Too gruesome."

"But," Connie said, puzzled, "I thought your cousin was . . . you know." She winked.

"Serena prefers distancing herself from the immediate crime," Judith explained. "The ensuing chaos clouds her . . . brain."

Connie nodded. "I understand. She must be very deep."

Out of the corner of her eye, Judith saw Renie approaching with a white-and-brown paper bag. She was stuffing a large clump of dark chocolate in her mouth. "Yes," Judith remarked, "she likes to savor things. I'll leave you in peace. I see more visitors approaching."

"Oh, yes," Connie said. "See you at four."

Eldridge was beaming again. "Nice to meet you, Judith. How about being my date for the beer tasting later on?"

"Uh . . ." Judith was already backpedaling away from the booth. "I have to see what my cousin's schedule is. She's been sleuthing, you see. Very conscientious, very thorough."

"Oh?" Eldridge was befuddled. Maybe he hadn't heard of the infamous FASTO. "See you there, then," he said, sounding disappointed.

Judith managed to get in front of Renie before Connie and Eldridge could notice the melted chocolate that almost covered her cousin's chin. "You're a wreck," she muttered. "Didn't the candy booth have a napkin?"

"No," Renie said, after swallowing the chocolate she'd managed to get inside her mouth and not on her person. "Why?"

"Skip it." Judith gazed at their surroundings. "Let's take a break from murder, real or otherwise, and browse some of the shops."

"Okay." Renie pointed to a clothing store. "Bill's always wanted a cape. Maybe I can get him one of those Tyrolean-style things like the one I bought when we visited Innsbruck years ago."

Judith was dubious. "Bavaria meets the Tyrol?"

"Hey, most people can't tell one part of the Holy Roman Empire from another."

"Clean yourself up. You don't want to get chocolate on the merchandise."

"No problem," Renie said, popping another chocolate cluster into her mouth. "That's the last one. Ha ha." She used the empty bag to wipe off her face. And her neck. And both hands. "I'm good. Let's go."

The shop was nestled between a cobbler and an antiques store. Judith refrained from chastising her cousin for her piggery. The worst part was that Renie could eat so much and never gain an ounce. *Metabolism,* Judith thought—*some pigs got it, some pigs don't.*

The clothing shop was fairly small and very busy. While Renie browsed outerwear, Judith looked at sweaters. Christmas wasn't that far away. Maybe she could find something for Joe or Mike and his family. A forest-green lamb's-wool pullover caught her attention. It would suit Joe, but was available only in small and medium sizes. A navy-blue mohair crewneck suited Mike, but for all Judith knew, he might be sent to Florida on his next assignment. Frustrated, she moved on to the children's section. Before she could get past the lederhosen, someone tapped her arm.

"Judith?" said George Beaulieu. "Have you seen my wife?"

"Why, yes," she replied. "I talked to her just a few minutes ago at the B&B booth."

"She's not there now," he said, looking worried. "She was supposed to come off duty at two. We were going to have a late lunch."

"Who's in the booth now?" Judith inquired.

"Ah . . ." George tweaked his handlebar mustache. "Two innkeepers from the eastern group. They thought she'd headed this way."

Judith shrugged. "She's not here. But there are several other stores in this building, including up on the second floor. Maybe she went to the bookshop. It's right above us. Did you happen to see Mr. Hoover? He was with her in the booth."

"He's not there now," George said, his high forehead creased with concern. "I met him when I walked Connie to the exhibit. This whole situation makes me anxious. What does your cousin think about it?"

Looking for Renie, she spotted her cousin at the cash register. "She's still in the early interrogation stages. You've heard about Ellie?"

George nodded. "It's a mistake. Eleanor couldn't possibly have killed her grandfather. She must be taking the blame for someone else. That's the trouble with Ellie. Connie says the woman is so noble." He grimaced. "I must be on my way. If you see my wife, please tell her I'm worried." He paused, staring into Judith's eyes. "I still think you must be part Gypsy. Don't be offended."

Before Judith could comment, George hurried from the shop. Judith joined Renie at the counter. "What did you buy?"

"A snap-brim corduroy cap," Renie replied. "No capes that wouldn't make Bill look like a bat." She waited to get her receipt from the young woman at the register. "Who was that guy with the revolting mustache?" she asked as they started out of the store.

"Connie's husband. He lost her somehow."

"I don't blame him," Renie said, pausing on the walkway. "Let's go up to the bookstore. Bill gave me a list of World War Two books he thought they might have here."

Judith glanced at the stairs leading to the second story. "Why not? Joe likes those books, too, though he's not as avid about history as Bill."

The cousins climbed up to the balcony that jutted out from the front of the Bavarian chalet. They passed a crafts shop and a photography studio before arriving at Sadie's Stories.

The store was small, but one wall was so tall that a ladder was positioned by it. A half-dozen customers were browsing the fiction section. To Judith's dismay, the family of four from the train was among them. Thurmond was wrestling with a stuffed bear by the children's section. Ormond was chewing on the edges of a kiddie board book. His parents seemed absorbed in legal thrillers.

Renie nudged Judith. "Is it too late for me to get a restraining order for those little twits?"

"Ask their parents," Judith whispered. "They're the ones checking out the lawyer books."

"Just don't let them near me. Here's the history section," Renie said, pointing to a shelf behind her cousin.

"You know more about the subject than I do," Judith said. "Recommend something."

Renie, however, was studying Bill's list, printed in his small neat writing. *The Gestapo: Hitler's Horror,* she murmured. *The SS and Racial Cleansing. Himmler Does Hamburg.*

Judith looked over Renie's shoulder. "That can't be a real title."

"It's not, but all of these sound so gruesome," Renie said. "Whatever happened to *Fun with Adolf and Eva?*"

"They didn't end up having much of that," Judith pointed out.

"Serves them right. Oh, here's one Bill has marked with an asterisk—*Kommandant Killer: Hitler's Avenging Angel.*"

Judith winced. "That sounds even worse."

"It's all bad," Renie declared. "I was old enough by the end of the war to read newspapers and magazines. I was horrified." She perused the shelves. "I don't see Bill's priority title. Maybe I should ask Sadie."

Noting the auburn-haired girl behind the counter, Judith smiled. "I'll bet she's not Sadie. It's such an old-fashioned name."

The cousins waited for the clerk to ring up a young man who was buying a hiking trail book. After he left, Renie leaned on the counter. "I'll bet you a ten percent discount you're not Sadie."

"Bet's off," the clerk replied, giggling. "Sadie's been dead for thirty years. I'm her granddaughter, Jessica. Call me Jessi—with an *i.*"

Renie showed Jessi the list Bill had made out. "My husband

especially wants the Kommandant book. I don't know why—he already runs our house like a stalag. But I can't find this one on the shelf."

"Let me check," Jessi said, going to the computer. "We can probably order it from . . ." She frowned. "Weird. It's been deleted."

"Out of print?" Renie asked.

"No," Jessi replied, still frowning at the screen. "It's a recent release. That's really odd. We had some computer problems a couple of days ago, but a techie customer fixed it. What else is on your list?"

"Here," Renie said, pushing the slip of paper across the counter. "Take your pick. My husband starred only the one you can't get."

"We have the first two," the clerk said. "I'll get them for you." Jessi started around to the other side of the counter but paused, her fair, fresh-scrubbed face lighting up. "Barry! I thought you had to work."

The cousins recognized the younger bartender from Wolfgang's Gast Haus. "Barry fits him better than Fritz," Renie whispered.

Barry was focused on Jessi. "I don't have to work until later," he said, before noticing the cousins. "Hey—weren't you at the cocktail party last night when Wessler got killed?"

The parents of the little boys turned away from their legal thrillers to stare at the newcomer.

"We escaped right after the carnage," Renie said. "Where were you? The bar wasn't being tended the last time we sought refills."

"Both of us Fritzes had to see what happened when the music stopped," Barry said. "Then we served brandy for the people in shock."

Jessi touched his arm. "I'm glad I wasn't there. It sounded grim."

"It was," Barry said solemnly, "though I never got a good look."

A loud crash startled Judith, who turned to see the floor covered with chunks of plaster of Paris. Thurmond was screaming his head off.

"Thomas Mann!" Jessi cried. "The kid busted his bust!"

"Thurmy!" the mother shouted, racing to her son. "Did the nasty head fall on you? My poor little man!"

"What about Herr Mann?" Jessi said under her breath. "Kids!"

Thurmond kept yelling. His father smiled fondly. "He's okay, Gina. A good thing that statue wasn't marble." He turned to Jessi. "You should keep stuff like that out of children's reach. It's dangerous."

"It's hollow," Jessi snapped. "He shouldn't have climbed the ladder. And your other little guy is ripping up *The Cat in the Hat*."

The mother turned around sharply. "He doesn't like Dr. Seuss. Ormy is very fussy about what he eats. I mean, what he *reads*." She glared again at Jessi. "Maybe the plaster thing didn't harm Thurmy, but what about that bottle? If it broke, it could've cut him."

Judith and Jessi both hurried to see what Thurmond's mother was talking about. Sure enough, there was a small bottle lying among the pieces that had once been Thomas Mann's bust.

"Hunh," Jessi said, puzzled. "There's no label. It looks empty."

Barry joined her after the miffed mother had picked up the blubbering Thurmond. "Hey," he said, "maybe it's something used by whoever made the bust. A glaze or paint?"

"No idea," Jessi responded, bending down to pick up the item.

Renie was leaning over Jessi's shoulder. "I'm a graphic designer, so I've seen bottles like that, but I wonder why there's no label."

Judith took a closer look. "A medicine or a small liquor bottle? An exotic cooking ingredient?" She turned to Renie. "You're right—why is there no label or any other identification on it?"

Jessi turned around. "If the kid hadn't broken Mann's head, we'd never have seen it." She looked from Judith to the parents. "Hey, I don't want any trouble. It's okay. But you should keep an eye on your children. The bigger one could've fallen off that ladder and hurt himself."

"Aw," the father said, "little boys like to explore."

"Yes," the mother chimed in, taking Thurmond in her arms and jiggling him in an effort to quiet him. "If you had children, you'd understand that they must be allowed to experiment and test their limits. Furthermore, we didn't find anything of interest in your shop. Don't you have any *good* books?"

Renie looked belligerent. "Maybe Ormond would enjoy eating a cookbook. Check the parenting section. You might learn something."

"That does it!" the mother cried. "We're out of here!" She headed for the door. The father scooped up Ormond and was right behind her.

"No, you don't!" Renie yelled, rushing after the quartet and grabbing the father by his sleeve. "Citizen's arrest! Shoplifting!" She pulled a paperback legal thriller from the father's coat pocket. "Call the cops! Let's pat down the others—especially the kids."

"No!" Jessi shouted. "Let them go! I don't want a fuss!"

Renie shrugged. "Your call. Beat it, you crooks."

The not-so-happy family bolted out of the shop. Renie handed the paperback to Jessi. "Maybe you should have this checked for prints and run them through the ASIS database."

"Why bother?" Jessi said wearily, shelving the book. "Hey, Barry, want to help me clean up the mess the little brat made?"

It was Judith's turn to step in. "I hate to harp, but maybe you'd better not touch the bottle. If I were you, I'd turn it over to the police."

Barry stared at Judith. "You're serious?"

Judith hedged. "There's something about that bottle that bothers me. Maybe I'm overreacting, but I'd like to know how it got there."

Jessi seemed mystified. "Are you spooked because of what happened to Mr. Wessler?"

Judith didn't bother to lie, fib, or pretend. "Yes. Who wouldn't be?"

# Chapter Eight

**B**arry looked startled. "Did you know the old guy?"

"No," Judith replied. "But as witnesses, the police questioned us."

"Me, too," Barry said. "They told me he was stabbed."

Judith nodded. "I realize that. I'm not suggesting any connection between the bottle and Mr. Wessler." She turned to Jessi. "You'd toss it, right? So you won't care if my cousin and I take it with us."

Jessi eyed her with suspicion. "Why?"

Judith was forced to use subterfuge. She put a hand on Renie's arm. "Mrs. Jones is a private investigator who's following up on an illegal drug-labeling case. She's working with law enforcement officials all over the state, including Chief Duomo."

Jessi was incredulous. "Jones? Is that her real name? Prove it."

Renie reached into her handbag. "Here's ID for my purchase."

Jessi scrutinized Renie's driver's license. "You're a PI? My God! How come you've got chocolate on your elbow?"

"I do?" Renie looked at her arm. "Oh. Guess I missed that. I was interrogating people at the candy store. I really go deep on the job."

Two elderly ladies entered the shop. Jessi put on her customer-friendly face. "How may I help you?" she asked.

"Quilts," the plumper of the women said. "Do you have . . ."

Judith brushed past Jessi. "We'll clean up," she whispered.

"Better start with the detective," Barry said. "I'll get a broom and a dustpan."

"And a plastic bag," Judith murmured. Seeing Barry's puzzled look, she clarified her request. "Not for Mrs. Jones—for the bottle."

Barry disappeared through a door by the counter. Renie was using a Kleenex to wipe the chocolate off her elbow. "Glad I didn't wear a long-sleeved sweater," she remarked.

Judith was already gathering the plaster shards together while not touching the bottle. "It must've been put inside the bust through the hole in the bottom," she said, lowering her voice. "There might be prints on these pieces, too."

"You got a theory?" Renie asked.

Judith shook her head. "Only a question. Why would anyone put an unlabeled bottle in a bust of Thomas Mann?"

"Somebody who didn't think he should have won a Nobel Prize?"

Barry reappeared with the broom and a plastic grocery store bag. "No dustpan," he said.

"No problem," Judith said, standing up straight. "I'm going to sweep everything into the bag without touching it."

"Wow." Barry also kept his voice down, glancing at Jessi, who was handing crafts books to her new customers. "You're serious."

"Crime is serious," Judith said.

Barry posed a question to Renie. "Is she your assistant?"

Renie nodded. "She's not too bright, but she can do the dirty work. And she notices things, like that bottle. I operate on a higher intellectual plane. Thus, I let her do the grunt work. Like sweeping."

"Wow," he repeated, oblivious to the harsh look Judith gave Renie.

"Tell me," Judith said, securing the plastic bag with a rubber band. "I mean, tell *us* what you know about Bob Stafford's murder."

Barry was startled. "I don't know much more than anybody else. I arrived in town a few days after it happened. The cops seem baffled. I've been studying in Heidelberg, where I'm working on my doctorate in seventeenth-century history. My focus is the Thirty Years' War."

"Too long," Renie said. "Not as bad as the Hundred Years' War, but still . . ." She waved a hand in disgust. "Didn't those armies get *tired*?"

"Hey," Barry said, "if you don't mind . . . I mean, I only know the bare facts about the murder. Why don't you talk to the police?"

"We will," Judith said, then deferred to Renie. "Won't we?"

"Huh? Oh, sure. I've got it on my list of . . . STIFF. That stands for . . . 'Suspects To Interrogate For Future.' "

"Of course you would." Barry seemed uncertain. "I'd better do . . . something." He grabbed the broom and left through the side door.

"You're an idiot," Judith said between gritted teeth. "Aren't you paying attention?"

"I was," Renie replied, looking chagrined. "Then I saw that coffee-table book on Givenchy. It distracted me. You know I've always loved his fashion designs. What an eye for understated elegance!"

"Let's get out of here," Judith said, grabbing Renie's arm. "Did you pay for your books?"

"I never had a chance," Renie said, allowing herself to be propelled toward the door. "Jessi was interrupted by the kid busting the bust. I hope she hangs on to the books for Bill."

Judith sighed as they went out onto the balcony. "That's okay. We'll come back later."

"Small towns," Renie muttered, starting down the stairs. "At least the witness pool is smaller than in the city. Unless, of course, all the suspects are staying at your B&B."

"Not funny," Judith shot back. "I'll admit, I still don't know what to think about Herr Wessler. The entire population, visitors included, is taking his death seriously. But that doesn't explain why two people have already confessed to murdering him."

"Maybe they both stabbed him," Renie suggested.

"You're reaching." Judith paused, seeing two dozen uniformed Camp Fire Girls heading down the main street toward the exhibits. "Oh," she went on, "I forgot there's a Camp Fire booth near ours. It's ten after three. I wonder if Connie's husband ever found her."

"I thought you were going to take that bottle and those plaster chunks to the cops."

Judith nodded. "Let's do it."

The cousins had to wait for a horse-drawn carriage to pass by. The now-familiar blue-and-white-checkered Bavarian flags fluttered from the carriage's roof. The bearded lederhosen-clad driver waved. Judith and Renie waved back.

"The local version of a taxi?" Renie wondered aloud. "Why didn't we hail it? I'm tired of walking. You must be pooped."

"I am," Judith admitted, "but we have to play the game. If it is a game. Frankly, I have doubts."

"So you said. I'm beginning to feel the same way. For one thing, I can't see Inbred Heffalump going to all this trouble to bug you."

"True. It'd involve too much coordination, cooperation, and imagination—and Ingrid doesn't have much of the third commodity." Judith didn't speak again until they were on the other side of the street. "If Eleanor was released after confessing to a homicide Connie insists she couldn't have committed, where is Ellie?" She didn't wait for Renie to answer. "And what's with Franz Wessler? Did he also confess? Either this is the most inept bunch of cops I've ever come across or . . . ." She shook her head. "I just don't know."

"Baffled, huh?" Renie said cheerfully. "It's about time."

They'd almost reached the corner across from the police station when a squad car pulled out. "Hey," Judith called, seeing Duomo behind the wheel. Frantically, she waved her hand.

The vehicle almost slammed into the curb. "Got something for me?" the chief asked, sticking his head out of the window.

"Yes," Judith replied. "Should we come back later?"

"Heck, no," Duomo said. "Hop in. We're going to the beer tasting."

"But . . ." Judith began—and stopped. "Sure, why not?"

The cousins got into the backseat. Ernie was up front with the chief. "Gosh," Renie said, "now I feel like a perp."

Judith ignored the remark, but had a question for the chief. "Isn't the beer tasting this evening?"

"Yeah," Duomo said, heading for the main street. "But the city budget's tight. We're the health inspectors, too, so we have to sample the brews." He glanced at Ernie. "Helluva job, huh, Major?"

Ernie grunted his assent.

They were headed down the main street, approaching the exhibitor booths. "We found a bottle in a bust," Judith said, leaning forward to make sure Duomo could hear her.

"Whose bust?" the chief asked. "Did somebody get busted?" He turned back to his subordinate. "Did I miss a collar around here?"

Ernie shrugged.

"It was at the bookstore," Judith finally said.

"The bookstore?" The chief sounded puzzled. "Hell, I haven't been in that place for years. Don't have time to read books. Same thing with Ernie here. Says they put him to sleep. Ha ha."

Judith was practically gnashing her teeth. "I'll explain when we stop. Where *is* the beer tasting?"

"Just beyond the pancake house," the chief informed her. "It's a little park that goes halfway down the bank to the river. Real nice."

Judith glimpsed the B&B booth, which looked busy. Moments later, they pulled into the small parking area. All of the spots were taken. Duomo stopped the squad car at an angle, blocking a half-dozen cars from making an exit.

"Damn," he grumbled, "they were supposed to reserve a VIP slot for me. Didn't Orville put in my request?"

"Guess not," Ernie said—and yawned.

"What the hey," the chief muttered before turning around. "You want to show me whatever you've got there, Mrs. Flynn?"

"I can't pass it through the screen between us," Judith said.

Duomo sighed. "Okay, let's do it." Huffing and puffing, he got out of the car and opened the door for the cousins.

After Renie give her a boost, Judith placed the plastic bag on the hood. "We went to Sadie's Stories," she explained. "A little boy knocked over a bust of Thomas Mann. It broke and—"

"Who?" the chief asked.

"Thomas . . . never mind." Judith opened the bag so Duomo could look inside. "That bottle was in or by the hollow bust. It has no label, so I'm curious why anybody would ditch an empty bottle."

"Yeah, it could be one of those little shots they sell on planes and trains," the chief said, studying the bag's contents.

"I don't think so," Judith said. "This looks more like a medicine bottle. It's the wrong shape for the kind sold to travelers. Besides, the brand name is usually on the cap's top and there's nothing on this one."

Duomo chortled. "That calls for a cap joke, but I can't think of one. Can't even think of one about a derby."

"Skip the jokes," Judith retorted. "Shall I hang on to this or could Ernie take it back to the station?"

The chief mulled over the query. "Well . . . I guess." He glanced into the car. "The major dozed off. Only guy I know who sleeps it off *before* he drinks." He leaned inside to shake Ernie's arm. "Firefight! Move on out!"

The cousins backed away while Ernie received his instructions. He got behind the wheel and was about to drive off when Judith yelled at the chief to take the plastic bag off the hood.

"Right, right," Duomo said wearily. "I hate these high-end investigations. Suspects and witnesses and . . ." He handed the bag to Ernie and started for the beer-tasting tent.

"Wait!" Judith called.

"Now what?" Duomo asked, exasperated.

Judith's patience was strained, but she remained civil. "You want our help solving this so-called case. Why did Franz Wessler go to headquarters earlier today?"

"Oh, that," Duomo said, shaking his head. "He tried to tell me he'd killed his father. That's bull. He's covering for somebody."

"Eleanor Denkel?" Judith said.

"No. She's got some ax to grind, always does. Besides, she has an alibi. A pal of hers showed up a little while ago to say they'd been together when Wessler got stabbed. Friends alibi friends, and that's a fact, but I kind of believed this . . . what was her name?" He scratched his bald head. "Bowlegs? Boohoo?"

"Connie Beaulieu," Judith said. "Yes, I heard the same thing. Who do you think Franz is protecting?"

Duomo shrugged. "His ex-wife, Klara? That doesn't make much sense, since she seemed kind of keen on the old guy. Still, it could be a lovers' quarrel. Never could figure out what was going on with that bunch. I mean, old Wessler was getting up there. That is, I wouldn't think he could get it . . . never mind. I better test those beers."

"That," Judith said after Duomo disappeared inside the tent, "is one sorry excuse for a law officer."

"Maybe the small-town hick is an act to fool criminals," Renie said.

"Then he's got it down pat," Judith declared. "*I* believe it. Though . . ." She eyed her cousin curiously. "This situation is different from most cases we've run into. In small towns, we've usually dealt with county law enforcement. If Duomo doesn't have the money or the personnel, why doesn't he call in the sheriff or even the state?"

"Bad PR," Renie said. "*Der Alte* is whacked just as the Oktoberfest event kicks off? This town's built on tourism. Otherwise, it would've died when it ceased being a timber and railroad town. The population's around a thousand hardy mountain souls. Yes, they've got winter sports, but there are other towns nearby. If any of them had two homicides in as many months, they'd set some sort of per capita record."

"I keep forgetting that you're involved in PR with your graphic-design business. However," Judith went on, going back to the main street, "years ago, you told me that murder was good for *my* business."

"That's different," Renie said. "You're in the city. People expect murders. And I don't see that it's hurt your bottom line."

"That's difficult to judge." Judith paused as they approached the busy exhibitors' area. In the past few minutes, clouds had rolled in from the north and the air had turned cooler. She wondered if the change would dampen the visitors' spirits. Murder hadn't seemed to faze them. "Most of my guests don't know I'm FASTO," she went on. "As long as Ingrid doesn't blackball me or pull my license, I should be okay."

"Sure, until your next guest checks out permanently."

"Shut up!" Judith cried, walking faster. "Let's switch subjects. What will you do while I'm at the town hall organizers' meeting?"

"Take notes," Renie replied. "I'm still the sleuth, aren't I?"

"I suppose you are," Judith conceded. "I don't imagine anybody will ask for your bona fides."

"I don't have any," Renie said, "unless you count my HMO ID and my Nordquist card. Think I maxed that out last August. It's fifteen to four," she went on, looking up at the clock tower. "Maybe I'll buy a warmer sweater. I saw one I liked where I bought Bill's cap."

"Why not just go back to the inn and get one of your own?"

Renie shrugged. "It's more fun to buy something new."

"How are you going to pay for it?"

"Huh? Oh—I've still got my debit card. If Bill hasn't gone to the bakery to buy his special treats, I should have a couple of grand left in that account. Those napoleons and Italian slippers tend to add up."

Judith shook her head, marveling anew at how the Joneses could keep up with their spending—let alone keep up with anyone else named Jones. The cousins parted company a block and a half from the town hall. The two-story building was located on the block between the bandstand and the police headquarters.

After crossing the street, Judith gazed up at the numerous flags flying from what she assumed was a replica of an original Bayern village town hall. She already recognized the blue-and-white-checkered state flag of Bavaria, but there were several variations. Cities, towns, municipalities, she thought, or counties—if there were counties in Germany. The trip that she and Renie had taken before their respective marriages hadn't included much information about the nuts and bolts of the country's government. The cousins had been too enthralled sailing up the Rhine River, attending High Mass at the Cologne Cathedral, exploring Heidelberg's ancient castle above the River Neckar, and marveling at how efficiently Munich had been rebuilt despite extensive Allied bombing. But the flags intrigued her, particularly a playful depiction of a comical boar tromping through the forest against a black-and-white background.

"Quite the display, eh?" said a voice behind Judith.

"Oh!" She turned to see Delmar Denkel looking obsequious. "Yes, I was wondering if the flags represented cities within the state of Bavaria. Do you know anything about German government divisions?"

"Well . . ." Delmar cleared his throat. "Dachau is in Bavaria."

"It is?" Judith said in surprise. "I didn't realize that."

"So is Bertesgarten, Hitler's mountain retreat."

"Those sites weren't on our itinerary forty years ago."

"They wouldn't be, would they?" Delmar said quietly.

"People visit those places now," Judith said, feeling a stiff wind from off the mountains. "It's a lesson in how wrong a country can go under a charismatic but evil leader."

"Yes," Delmar agreed, looking around as if he expected to see an SS officer eavesdropping on them. "A reminder to future generations."

"You've visited Germany?" she asked.

Delmar nodded.

"Recently?"

"This spring. Eleanor and I were there for two weeks." The words seemed wrung out of him, as if they were a confession.

"Ah . . . how *is* Eleanor?"

"She's resting today." He gestured helplessly. "You understand."

Judith wasn't sure she did. But she tried to look sympathetic. "Are you going inside to meet the Oktoberfest organizers? I mean, if Ellie isn't up to it . . ." She let the rest of the sentence dangle.

"I don't know," Delmar replied, pulling up the collar of his suede jacket around his scrawny neck. "I really don't. I'll walk a bit now."

He went on his way. Judith stood still, wondering what to make of the conversation—and of Delmar Denkel. A handful of other people were heading for the town hall. Judith decided to join them, but took one last look at the flags that were now snapping in the chilly autumn wind.

She shivered, not sure if it was from the sudden change in the weather—or something more sinister from out of the past.

The town hall was aptly named. The pine-paneled walls in the open area led to offices on two sides, a single staircase, and an elevator. Directly in front of Judith was the hall itself, also covered in mellow pine. A balcony went around three sides. She calculated that the large room must take up more than three-fourths of the building.

At least fifty people were already gathered, sipping wine and beer from casks mounted on a trestle table where the bald Fritz II held sway. Judith didn't see any of the B&B contingent. In fact, the only person she did recognize besides the bartender from Wolfgang's Gast Haus was Suzie Stafford, who was chatting amiably with an older couple wearing Bavarian garb.

Feeling ill at ease, she approached the trestle table. Being neither a wine nor a beer drinker, she motioned to Fritz II. "What would you suggest?" she asked diffidently.

"A nice Liebfraumilch?" he suggested with the hint of an accent.

"Um . . . sure." While Fritz II poured the white wine into a large sturdy goblet, she looked up at the assortment of mounted animal heads, including a tiger. "Where was that poor cat shot? In a Bavarian zoo?"

Fritz shook his head. "No. In India, by Herr Wessler on one of his hunting trips." He moved a thick finger around the room. "All these animals are his trophies. He was a great hunter."

"I didn't know that," Judith said. "I also don't know the actual organizer of the Oktoberfest."

"Herman Stromeyer," he said, handing her the goblet. "But he's got the flu, so I'm filling in for him this evening. I'm the mayor."

Judith stared and almost sloshed wine on the blue-and-white-checkered tablecloth. "You are? Why are you tending bar?"

He shrugged his broad shoulders. "I like doing it during Oktoberfest. I enjoy meeting people."

"Is your name really Fritz?" she asked.

"Yes. Fritz Gruber. I was born in Bremen. I came here twenty years ago with my American bride. She's from Omaha."

"But you ended up here," Judith remarked before taking her first sip of wine.

Fritz nodded. "Herr Wessler was a distant relation. He urged us to move to Little Bavaria. He thought Omaha was too flat. He was right. It's best to live where one can look at mountains."

Judith nodded. "I've grown up with them." She savored the wine. "This is quite good."

"You have no palate?"

"I don't," she admitted. "My first husband owned a restaurant and I tended bar there sometimes. I got used to the hard stuff." *Not to mention,* she thought, *the hard times keeping the place afloat.*

"Ah. A shame. Wine is better for you."

"Yes," Judith allowed, "you may be right. I should offer condolences about Herr Wessler. He was what—a cousin?"

Fritz grimaced. "Yes, though I never knew him in the old country. But our kinsmen kept in touch."

"Speaking of family, here's my cousin Serena," Judith said, spotting Renie in a red cable-knit sweater. "She's also ignorant of wine."

"Hi, coz, hi, Fritz," Renie said, waving her hand at one of the casks. "Pour me a blistering dark brew, thick as malt, brown as a bear's butt."

Judith took a backward step. "You sound belligerent."

"I am," Renie replied, eyeing Fritz warily. "Don't shortchange me," she warned him, before turning back to her cousin. "I had to fight off some beefy broad for this sweater. As if she could fit into it, even if it is a large. I left her flat on her ass somewhere in dirndls."

"Coz!" Judith cried. "You didn't!"

"Yes, I did. I had my eye on this sweater. You think I'd let some big mama get her paws on it?" Renie twirled around. "How do I look?"

"Like the Red Menace," Judith said. "Take it easy. This is Fritz Gruber. He's the mayor."

Renie regarded Fritz with a dubious eye. "The hell you are. I'm not even sure you're Fritz."

"Ah, but I am," he replied, looking amused. "Do you want your beer in a bucket?"

"Why not? Or I could just lie on the floor and you could open the tap." But Renie held up a hand. "A stein will do. Are you really a Fritz?"

"I am indeed. Are you otherwise enjoying yourself?"

"Oh, yes," Renie said. "It's started to rain. That always cheers me."

Fritz handed Renie her stein. "How jolly do you get with snow?"

"I resort to weaponry." She glared at Judith, who'd glared at her first. "Let's stop annoying Fritz. He's got other customers lined up." She flashed a smile at the bartender and moved away from the trestle table.

"It's a good thing I don't recognize most of this crowd," Judith grumbled. "You not only embarrassed me, but I never got a chance to ask Fritz about his version of Wessler's demise."

"Crikey," Renie said indifferently. "You'll get another crack at him. What on earth are you drinking?"

"Liebfraumilch," Judith said, still annoyed. "Doesn't Bill sometimes like to have a glass of . . . oh, no! Here comes Connie."

"Has she confessed to the murder yet?"

"Maybe," Judith replied. "I wonder what happened to Delmar?"

"Who?"

"Eleanor's husband. I saw him just before I came—" Judith broke off, forcing a smile as Connie approached. "Hi, how are you? I missed seeing you after your stint at the booth."

Connie looked puzzled. "Why were you looking for me?"

"I wasn't," Judith blurted. "George was doing the looking."

"George," Connie said truculently, "fusses too much." She glanced over her shoulder. "Speaking of which, I heard from Ingrid Heffelman today. She told me not to believe a word you told us. It's a wonder she let you join the rest of us for our exhibit. She also related a horrifying story about how you were almost killed last winter in your B&B."

Judith forced a laugh. "That's Ingrid's way of protecting my cousin." She darted a glance at Renie. "Remember that poor man who fell out of his wheelchair and knocked me down?"

Renie nodded. "It's a good thing Arlene came back with that tomato paste, so she could help you get up. How come Arlene uses so much tomato paste? She must make a lot of casseroles."

"She does," Judith said. "She got into the habit while raising five kids. And Carl loves a casserole."

"So does Bill." Renie wrinkled her pug nose. "I wish I did. You got any really good casserole recipes, Connie?"

The other woman was looking perplexed. "George doesn't care for noodles. Here he comes. He'll take forever to choose a wine. His dream is to have his own vineyard." Connie moved off to join her husband.

"Twerp," Renie remarked, after taking a swig of beer.

Judith made a face. "How did Ingrid hear about my near-death experience last January? The media was shut down by the police."

Renie shrugged. "All it takes is one person with a big mouth. Okay, so what now? Collar Suzie about the late and allegedly lamented Bob? Maybe if she gets loaded, she'll reveal something."

"Not a bad idea," Judith agreed. "She, too, is heading for the bar."

"She cleans up pretty good," Renie remarked.

Judith discreetly studied Suzie Stafford as she waited her turn at the trestle table. Her tall, rangy figure was dressed in a black satin blouse and slacks, accented by a double strand of pearls. The dark hair she'd tucked into a net at work now fell gracefully onto her shoulders. "Mourning? Or prowling?" Judith murmured.

"Hey," Renie said, also lowering her voice, "even you weren't looking for another husband two months after Dan died."

"I never was. I just happened to find Joe again two years later."

Renie smiled wryly. "Reunited over a corpse. How romantic."

Judith shot Renie a sharp look. "How's your beer, big mouth?"

"Not bad," Renie replied, "considering it's beer."

"You're drinking it like you love it."

Renie frowned at the half-empty stein. "Huh. So I am. Huh."

"Behave," Judith whispered. "Here comes Suzie."

"Good. I can sleuth," Renie said.

"What are you two doing here?" Suzie asked, holding a glass of red wine in both hands. "I thought you were just passing through."

"We decided to stay for the Oktoberfest," Judith replied. "It takes my mind off my late husband."

"Yeah," Renie said, "he won't get here until seven. Ha ha."

Judith glared at her cousin. "That's not funny!"

"Good grief," Renie said. "Tell Suze the truth and get it over with."

Judith blanched, but knew Renie was right. "Look, Suzie, I *have* been widowed, but I've remarried. Chief Duomo told us about Bob's death and I'm very sorry for you. But he also asked for our help."

Suzie looked incredulous. "Fat Matt wants *your* help? Why?"

Judith touched Renie's arm. "My cousin Serena Jones is a private investigator. The chief is short-staffed. He asked her to consult not only on Wessler's death, but your husband's as well."

Suzie's incredulity seemed to increase as she stared at Renie. "You're a PI? You've got to be kidding!"

"Hey!" Renie cried. "Watch it! The spouse is the prime suspect."

"Back at you!" Suzie shouted. "You look about as much like a detective as I look like Ava Gardner!"

"You look more like Ava's gardener," Renie snarled. "Or maybe you look more like Ava *now,* since she's dead!"

"Coz!" Judith used her free hand to grab Renie's wrist. "Stop it! You two are creating a scene."

Renie and Suzie both looked around. At least a dozen people, including Connie and George Beaulieu, were gaping at the pair.

"Screw it," Renie muttered. She took another swig from her stein and stalked off toward the stuffed tiger.

Judith felt a hand on her arm. "Mrs. Flynn, are you okay?"

Feeling slightly dazed, Judith didn't recognize the young man at first. "Gabe! I'm fine. I think." She saw Suzie stomping in the opposite direction from where Renie had gone. The Beaulieus had melted into the crowd. "My cousin and Mrs. Stafford got into an argument, that's all."

"Why don't I get you a refill on your wine?" Gabe offered. "I think you spilled some of it when you grabbed your cousin."

"Oh!" Judith looked down at the serviceable carpet and saw a large stain. "Goodness, I didn't mean to make a mess. You're right—my glass is almost empty. I'll go with you."

Gabe glanced at his watch. "We'd better hurry. It's six-thirty. Mr. Gruber is giving his mayoral spiel in a few minutes. I don't know if he's tending bar solo or . . . he isn't. There's the other Fritz from Wolfgang's."

Judith had also spotted Barry. "Hi," she said as Gabe approached Fritz Gruber. "I thought you had to work at the Gast Haus tonight."

Barry shook his head. "I'm only filling in. Between this event and everybody waiting for the beer tasting, there's not much action at Wolfgang's. This is a short gig. Then I'll take Jessi to the beer garden." He lowered his voice. "How's Mom?"

Judith blanked. "Mom?"

"Oh—Suzie. Guess I didn't formally introduce myself at the bookstore. I'm Barry Stafford, Suzie and Bob's son."

# Chapter Nine

Judith was stunned. "I'd no idea. I'm sorry about your father."

"Me, too." Barry shrugged. "That's why I came back from Germany sooner than I expected. I couldn't leave Mom alone. She seems tough, but . . . she looked upset when she was talking to you and your cousin."

"Serena and your mother kind of got into it," Judith said reluctantly. "My cousin's feisty and your mom is obviously walking a thin line. Not that I blame her."

Barry nodded. "I noticed Mrs. Jones doesn't take prisoners when I was at the bookstore. Was she ever in Roller Derby?"

The idea of the uncoordinated Renie zooming around competitors on a fast rink made Judith laugh out loud. "Oh, no! She's not athletic."

"Ah . . ." Barry was looking beyond Judith. "I won't comment on that. Hi," he said to Renie. "You need a refill for that stein?"

"I sure do," Renie said, barging past Judith. "Fill 'er up. I just faced off with a tiger. I won. I have bigger teeth."

"Bigger mouth, too," Judith muttered, stepping aside to join Gabe.

"You make friends easily," he said, handing over the wineglass. "That's a must for an innkeeper. I have to force myself to be outgoing."

Judith shrugged. "I like people. I always have." Her gaze followed Fritz Gruber, who was putting on his blue Bavarian jacket. Moving from behind the trestle table, he paused to greet several guests before exiting the hall. "Where's he going?" she asked.

"Upstairs to the balcony," Renie said, holding her refilled stein. "They have a stage behind those movable panels in back of the bar setup, but Barry told me they didn't want to bother moving everything. Fritz will be mercifully brief. For a German."

"Watch it," Judith warned.

Renie frowned at Gabe. "You're German, too?"

Gabe laughed. "No, I'm English and Swiss."

A cowbell sounded over the crowd's chatter. Judith looked up to see Fritz Gruber on the balcony, smiling benignly at the gathering. *"Willkommen!"* he called. Virtually all of the guests applauded.

"Good," Renie said under her breath. "If the whole thing's in German, I can nod off."

But Fritz immediately switched to English. "We are delighted to have so many fine exhibitors at Oktoberfest. Each year we attract more visitors as well as merchants and organizations. We only have one main street, but it goes both ways . . ."

"Double yawn," Renie murmured. "Civic blah-blah. Same as corporate blah-blah. I'm bored. Maybe I'll go hit somebody."

"Don't embarrass us," Judith said through clenched teeth.

"Okay." Renie gestured at the entrance to the hall. "Here comes Fat Matt and Hernandez. Are they going to arrest me?"

Judith turned around to look. "Maybe. They're headed this way."

Fritz Gruber was winding down with a final German phrase that Judith translated as "Let's party!" but for all she knew, it could've been "Avoid catching a social disease!" Whatever it was, the crowd cheered and applauded. Taking a short bow, Fritz headed back to the staircase.

Gabe Hunter looked anxious. "What the . . ."

Judith turned her gaze away from the balcony and gave a start. Hernandez was holding a pair of handcuffs. "Gabriel Philip

Hunter, you're a person of interest in the murder of Dietrich Wessler. Will you come along quietly or do I need to cuff you?"

All eyes shifted away from the balcony. The gathering was stunned into silence. No one looked more shocked than Gabe Hunter.

"I . . . I don't know what . . . yes, of course . . . but . . ." he babbled.

Duomo nodded once. "Then let's hit it."

The chief walked on one side of Gabe, Hernandez on the other. Judith realized that Duomo hadn't seen her standing next to Gabe or, if he had, didn't care. Her perplexity concerning the local top cop was growing blurrier by the minute.

*Or maybe it's the wine,* she thought, noticing that her second glass was half empty.

"Hey," Renie said, "I could use a refill. How 'bout you?"

"You're cross-eyed," Judith said.

"Can't be," Renie said, rocking a bit on her heels. "Never been able to eyes my cross. I mean—"

"No more refills," Judith declared. "Not for both of us. I mean, *either* of us." She frowned. "Don't I?"

"Don't you what?"

"I don't know," Judith admitted. "Let's get out of here."

"Okay." Renie drained her stein. "Let's go to the beer tasting."

"We can't," Judith said. "I mean, we shouldn't." She winced. "Oh, what the hell . . . why not? We can walk it off."

"Good idea," Renie said, thrusting her empty mug at a startled silver-haired dowager. "*Wiedersehen,* Frau Chump."

A soft rain was falling when the cousins reached the street. Being natives, they hardly noticed. Judith suddenly realized she was still holding her wineglass. "Damn! I have to take this back."

"Just put it on top of that parked . . . wow—it's a mega Mercedes!"

Judith gazed at the sleek dark blue sedan. "Oh, why not?" She walked to the curb and placed the glass on the car's hood. Glancing at the windshield, she gasped before scurrying back to where

Renie was waiting. "Good grief! I just caught part of an X-rated show!"

"What kind of show? Live or taped?"

"Live, very much alive. It was just . . . bodies," Judith said, hurrying to the corner crosswalk. "Moving bodies."

"Moving's good," Renie said. "That means they aren't dead."

"I wonder who it is," Judith mused as they crossed the street and passed their own inn. "There's your boar, cavorting with those kids and some guy in a blue-and-white-checkered shirt."

Renie followed her cousin's gaze. "That's a sixteenth-century tabard with the Bavarian colors. If *I* were an actual sleuth and not a cross-eyed sot, I'd say that vanity license plate on the Mercedes is a . . . what do you real detecting types call those things? A clue?"

Judith stopped abruptly to stare at her cousin. "What was it?"

Renie spelled it out. "W-E-S-L-E-R."

Judith put a hand to her forehead. "As in 'Wessler'?"

"Yes. You know that with this state's vanity plates, you can't use more than six numbers or figures."

"Of course." She narrowed her eyes at Renie. "You're not drunk."

"Of course I'm not," Renie replied impatiently. "I just wanted to get out of there. I'll bet the next thing we would've had to endure was another oompah . . . oh, no!" she cried as the sounds of a brass band could be heard from farther down the street. "They're coming this way!"

"We're going the other way," Judith said. "Keep walking."

The cousins did just that, wincing slightly as the oompah band tromped past them a few yards away from the now-shuttered B&B booth.

"It's not that I don't like the music," Renie murmured as they approached the beer garden. "It's just kind of *loud*."

"What?" Judith said, the cheerful noise from the tented area in front of them seeming to resonate off the mountains.

Renie merely shook her head.

The beer-tasting event was jammed. Boisterous laughter filled the tent, though no one seemed to be openly intoxicated. Judith noticed that a table had been set up with food, including various *Bratwürste*.

"I'm hungry," she said in Renie's ear. "I'm getting something to eat. How about you?"

Renie eyed the offerings with distaste. "Sorry, coz. Bill likes bratwurst, but I don't. I'll just stand here and starve. As my mother would say, 'Don't worry about me.'"

"I won't," Judith said, making her way to the table. The selection was mouthwatering. When Judith and Dan McMonigle had lived in the otherwise bleak Thurlow neighborhood, one of the few stellar attractions—unless you counted the hookers near the airport—was a shop featuring German delicacies.

"What do you like best?" Eleanor Denkel inquired.

Judith hadn't noticed her fellow innkeeper behind the table. "Ellie! I thought you were at Hanover Haus."

"Or in a prison cell?" Eleanor retorted. "You must think I'm insane."

"Hardly," Judith replied, distracted by trying to choose between the Kulmbacher and the Würzburger brats. "I think you signed a false confession to divert the police. Duomo doesn't take you or Franz Wessler seriously. Nice try, though. I'll have a Würzburger with the works."

"You would," Ellie muttered. "If you're not FATSO, how do you know that?"

"I told you, my cousin is *FASTO*. And don't stint on the mustard."

Ellie glared at Judith. "Which kind?"

"The hot one."

"You would," Ellie repeated. "Does your cousin know who killed my grandfather?"

"She's working on it." Judith glanced over her shoulder, but couldn't see Renie anywhere in the crowd. "She's been interrogating suspects. You might not think so to look at her, but she's very smart."

"She hides it superbly," Ellie growled, slathering condiments on the brat. "I should ask Ingrid what she thinks about your claim not to be the innkeeper who can't keep her guests alive."

Judith shrugged. "Go ahead. It's very hard to disabuse Ingrid of an idea once she gets it in her head. I gave up years ago. It's not my fault if I happen to be with Serena every time she comes across a corpse." She paused. "I assume you know that a person of interest was taken from the town hall to headquarters just minutes ago."

Ellie almost dropped the meat fork. "No! Who?"

"Another innkeeper," Judith said casually. "You may know him. Gabe Hunter from the Kingfish Peninsula."

Ellie handed over the bratwurst and its lavish condiments. "I've met him," she said, puzzled, "but he hasn't been in the business very long. His parents were the former owners. That doesn't sound right. Has the chief lost his mind?"

Judith cradled the plate and leaned closer. "When's your grandfather's funeral?"

The other woman's face tensed. "Why? Do you plan to attend?"

"I assume you wouldn't hold it during Oktoberfest."

Ellie had regained her aplomb. "It's scheduled for Saint Hubert's feast day. I believe you're Catholic, so you realize the local church is named for him. In fact, *Grossvater* was a member of the Knights of Saint Hubert, awarded for his service in postwar Germany. Saint Hubert's feast day is November third. That's almost two weeks away. I trust you'll be gone by then," she added with apparent pleasure.

"Yes. Are you and Uncle Franz making the arrangements?"

Ellie's face tensed again. "No. Klara is in charge. She knows the priest who says the weekend Masses. Father Dash will be here Sunday."

Judith wasn't sure she'd heard correctly. "Father Dash?"

Eleanor nodded. "That's what Klara calls him. Excuse me, Judith. Other people are waiting to be served. Please move on."

*And just when it was getting interesting,* Judith thought, clutching her plate and searching among the beer tasters for Renie. The red sweater ought to have been easy to spot, but there was no sign of her cousin. Judith contented herself with standing near the tent opening and enjoying the bratwurst and its numerous accompaniments.

She had finished eating when she felt a tap on her shoulder. "Hi, coz," Renie said, entering the tent with a big bag of popcorn and a large Pepsi. "How's the brat?"

Judith recovered from her surprise. "You mean what I ate or Eleanor Denkel?"

Renie scowled. "Eleanor's here?"

"She's manning the *Bratwürste,*" Judith said. "Ellie admitted she didn't kill Herr Wessler. But it seems as if he's really dead."

"No kidding," Renie said, after slurping down some Pepsi. "Have they got him propped up here with the beer kegs?"

Judith shook her head. "They'll hold the funeral at Saint Hubert's Church. The way Ellie talked about it, I don't think she was lying. That means we really have to sleuth."

"I thought we already were," Renie said, before tossing a big handful of popcorn in her mouth.

"Well . . . I always hedge my bets." Judith couldn't quite quell her mixed emotions. "It has to be the most peculiar case I've ever come across. And I'm not just talking about the local cops. What on earth does Gabe Hunter have to do with Herr Wessler? I wonder what kind of background check Duomo ran on him."

Renie had stuffed more popcorn in her mouth. "Mebedint."

Judith had learned to translate her cousin's eat-and-speak long ago. "He must've checked out Gabe. The chief would need to make a connection in order to find a motive. As for witnesses, we know what a zoo that must've been like at the cocktail party."

Renie swallowed the popcorn. "We would? We left, remember?"

"Now I wish we'd stayed." Judith took her empty plate to a nearby bin. "Where did you get popcorn and Pepsi?"

"I remembered I didn't like beer that much," Renie explained. "Besides, you have to buy tickets to sample the various different kinds. I'll only drink beer if it's free."

"Good thinking," Judith said. "So where'd you get your snack?"

"They're showing old German movies on a screen in a tent down the street. I've seen plenty of Fritz Lang, so I stayed only for the food and pop part. Hey, you look gloomy. Want to go have some real dinner?"

"Huh?" Judith had only half heard her cousin. "Oh—dinner? No, I'm full. Ellie didn't cheat on the serving. Maybe we can have a late supper. Can you last that long?"

"Sure," Renie said. "I just wish they'd put more butter on the popcorn. I asked for extra, but got extra small." She frowned at Judith. "What's bothering you? Should I attack somebody as a diversion?"

"No," Judith replied, peeking outside to see if the rain was falling any harder. It wasn't—in fact, it looked like a mere drizzle. "Let's go to Wolfgang's. We need to ask some questions."

Renie smirked. "You have a theory."

"Well," Judith said as they made their exit, "not exactly. But I wonder if all this confessing and arresting isn't a stall. The organizers—including Fritz Gruber—wouldn't like a real homicide charge until after Oktoberfest is over, right? That'd make for bad publicity. I wonder if they've closed ranks."

"Isn't that dangerous?"

"Oh, come on, coz," Judith said, surprised to see how many people were on the street, cheerfully milling about and enjoying the damp, fresh autumn air. "You've worked with PR types for years. You know how they react to anything that's negative."

"Sure," Renie said, making way for a couple with a baby in what looked like the Rolls-Royce of strollers, "but it seldom involves murder."

"It can," Judith said, "as we both know."

Renie sighed. "Hey—you've walked too much, you've been standing too long. Let's stop at . . ." Her gaze swung left. "Wolf-gang's bar."

"That's where we're going."

"I know," Renie said, "but I had visions of you accosting the first person we met inside the door and interrogating everybody right down to that grumpy chef. We need to take a break."

Judith didn't argue. The crime-scene tape was gone from the entrance. A sudden calm met them in the lobby. During the past few hours, Judith had become so inured to the raucous sound of revelry that she suddenly realized her need for peace and quiet. Even the front desk was deserted. An arrow pointed to the dining room and bar in the opposite direction from where the cocktail party had been held the previous night.

Except for a couple who seemed absorbed in each other, the bar was empty. No one seemed to be serving drinks, though the occupied table had wineglasses that appeared to be at least half full.

"You have to ring for service," the male customer said. "There's a bell on the bar."

Renie rang the bell. Loudly. "Now what?" she said to Judith.

"We could serve ourselves," Judith murmured. "I have experi-ence."

"I don't have experience as one of your Meat & Mingle clien-tele," Renie responded. "Do I have to drool on the counter and cuss a lot?"

"Not funny," Judith retorted. "I've tried to squelch those mem-ories for over twenty years."

The harried Ruby appeared through a rear door. "You again," she said, her eyes showing a spark of amusement. "What'll it be this time?"

"You have two jobs?" Judith said in surprise.

"I'd have three, if I could find another one," Ruby snapped. "Burt blogs, but he doesn't earn. Well? You thirsty or what?"

"Scotch-rocks," Judith said. "Water back, house brand will do."

"Canadian," Renie said, "with ice, 7UP, and rocks. Make it Crown Royal and I'll pay for it."

Ruby shot Renie a disapproving look. "Lose the popcorn and the soda. We don't allow outside food in here."

"It's not outside," Renie said. "It's already here."

"You heard . . ." the waitress began.

Judith snatched the offending items away from her cousin and handed them over. "Ignore her. She's from the Meat & Mingle. If she gets rowdy, I'll toss her."

Ruby's eyes widened. "The Meat & Mingle? You mean that old dump in the Thurlow part of the city? I thought that place went broke right after my dad got arrested there."

"Ah . . ." Judith was speechless.

"Hey," Renie said, leaning on the bar, "did he get busted for stealing the owner's wife's purse?"

Ruby seemed almost as shaken as Judith. "Yeah, except it was her wallet. Another drunk ratted on him to an off-duty cop. How do you know that? It was twenty years ago, when I was still in high school."

"Ah," Renie said, "then the drinks are on you. Meet the victim, the former Mrs. McMonigle, now Mrs. Flynn, but always Judith."

"I'll be damned," Ruby murmured. "Do I need your ID as proof?"

Judith had found her voice. "Was your father fair-haired going bald, five ten, two hundred pounds with a wart over his right eye and a USN tattoo on the left forearm? Hung out with a guy called Big Bad Something-or-Other."

"Yep," Ruby said, shaking hands with Judith. "Jimmy Tooms. He croaked not long ago. His Harley went off the road after he came up here to borrow money. Mom had already dumped him."

"Jimmy," Judith said, weighing the name with all the pain and suffering that had gone along with the rest of the Meat & Mingle's tawdry clientele. "I don't recall—did he do time?"

"Twice," Jimmy's daughter said, pouring Scotch from a bottle Judith didn't recognize. "Not for pinching your wallet, though. What happened to Mr. McMonigle?"

"He blew up," Judith said. "What kind of Scotch is that?"

"You probably wouldn't know it," Ruby said. "It's from a new distillery in Scotland. Old Presentation, just released this year."

"So how did you end up here?" Judith asked.

"Long story," Ruby said, her gaze veering past the cousins. "Better check on refills before I head back to the dining room." She made an endrun around the bar, heading for her other customers.

"Darn," Judith said under her breath. "She's a source. Maybe we'll get lucky and most people will be at the Oktoberfest events. There's the concert and some other events tonight." She smiled wanly as Ruby returned to the bar. "If we need refills, do we ring the bell again?"

"Help yourselves," Ruby said. "You've got experience. Heck, you can wait on anybody who needs a drink. I've got dinner patrons."

"Maybe," Judith said after Ruby had briskly finished her tasks and exited the bar, "we should eat here. I wonder why Barry didn't have to work. He mentioned taking Jessi to the beer tasting, but I didn't see them there while I was waiting for you."

"Slow night with everything else going on," Renie noted. "As for Fritz Gruber, he apparently tends bar as a lark. I suppose he's involved in some of the other doings."

"Probably," Judith conceded, noting that two young women had sat down at a table near the door. "Am I really supposed to play bartender?"

"Why not? After twenty years, you don't want to lose your touch."

"I also don't want to fall down. This Scotch is really powerful."

"Want me to serve them?"

"Lord, no! Have you got something against Wolfgang's?"

"Other than a corpse last night?" Renie shrugged. "No, if I had that kind of reaction, I'd never come to your B&B."

Judith sighed. "Fine. I'll wait on the newcomers."

The strawberry blonde and her raven-haired chum ordered a

drink Judith had never heard of. "I'm sorry," she confessed. "I'm not familiar with a cocktail called Between the Sheets. What are the ingredients?"

Both young women giggled and jiggled. "Wow," the strawberry blonde said, "this is *really* small-town! I thought everybody knew what goes into Between the Sheets." They both giggled some more.

Judith finally got the basics out of the duo. "Ever heard of a Between the Sheets?" she whispered to Renie.

"Only when I lose my Big Red chewing gum at night and it gets stuck to the sheets—and Bill. Then I hear plenty."

Judith juggled brandy, rum, triple sec, and lemon juice in the hope that she was close to the correct amounts. "Why do I feel as if I'm past my pull date?" she muttered, adding a lemon twist to each drink. "When I started tending bar at the Meat & Mingle, I served anyone who wanted a mixed drink a martini because it was the only cocktail I knew how to make. They didn't care. I could've poured lighter fluid and they'd have been happy."

"I thought you did," Renie said. "To cut costs, I mean."

Judith ignored the comment and carried the drinks to the young women. "I hope I made them the way you wanted," she said.

The raven-haired giggler sampled hers. "Close enough. Is it true that some old dude got whacked here last night?"

"I'm afraid so," Judith said.

Miss Strawberry beamed with pleasure—or maybe it was excitement. "Can we go see where it happened?"

"I don't know," Judith said. "It may still be a crime scene."

The young women looked thrilled. "Tell us where the old guy got offed," Miss Raven begged. "Can we leave our drinks to check it out?"

"Sure, why not?" Judith said wearily. "It was in the ballroom."

"With the wrench or the lead pipe?" Miss Strawberry asked, green eyes sparkling.

"It's not a game," Judith declared. "It's a tragedy."

Both young women sobered. "We know that," Miss Straw-berry said, looking defensive. "We came here to party, not go all grim about some poor old geezer who got himself killed just because he was a Communist. Who cares about that stuff now? It's so last century."

Judith stared at the young woman. "Where did you hear that?"

"At the ski shop," Miss Raven said. "A really cute guy told us."

Miss Strawberry waved a hand in dismissal. "That guy was a snowboard geek. The girl who was hanging out with him said the old man was a Nazi chef."

Miss Raven made a face. "Here?"

"No, in Germany. You know, when they had that war over there."

"Which war? Did I see the movie?"

"Hey!" Ruby had come out from behind the bar. "I was kid-ding. You don't have to work. I'll take over. We've got a dining lull."

"No problem," Judith said, reluctantly moving away from the two young women. "I'm a bit lost with some of the newer cock-tails, though."

"Who isn't?" Ruby said. "It's all about the name, not the booze."

Renie, who'd watched Judith from her bar-stool perch, grinned at Ruby. "I managed to pour some Canadian without spilling it."

"Good for you." Ruby wiped down the bar anyway. "Those two on the prowl?" she asked under her breath, nodding at the young women.

"They want to see the murder site," Judith said. "Ghoulish."

"Oh, yeah," Ruby agreed. "I saw it. The murder, I mean."

Judith couldn't hide her surprise. "You mean the stabbing?"

"No, just after the crowd moved away from old Wessler. It wasn't too long after Burt and I talked to you. He'd gone to the can, so I wandered over to get some roast beef." She grimaced. "That's when the band stopped and it got so damned quiet. Then everybody moved—and I saw Wessler. Blood was all over the floor. How many times was that poor old coot stabbed?"

The cousins traded glances. "Once," Judith said. "Or so we heard."

Ruby shook her head. "Were you there?"

Judith grimaced. "Yes, but we fled. We were in a state of shock."

Ruby's face was grim. "Then you didn't see all the blood. It looked like a butcher shop. I bet they're still working on the stains in the floor."

"Did you see the body?" Judith quickly clarified the question. "I mean, right away?"

"Of course," Ruby said. "Everybody did. Wessler's son sort of took over, trying to calm people until the cops and the EMTs got there. But it was really gruesome. I had to go throw up."

Judith had drained her Scotch during Ruby's recital. "You didn't wait for the cops?" she asked, nudging her glass across the bar.

"Hell, no!" Ruby said, pouring out a generous amount of Scotch and adding more ice. "I was afraid I might pass out. I didn't come out of the can for at least ten minutes. I wasn't the only one either. Four or five other gals were sick, too. That ex-wife of Franz Wessler—Klara—was hysterical. Somebody finally slapped her silly. I came in here to calm my nerves. That's where I found Burt. He missed the whole thing. He thought I was crazy, but I asked what he thought all those sirens were for—it wasn't just another car going off the mountain pass."

"Were you questioned by the police?" Judith asked.

Ruby shook her head. "I kept a low profile." Her gaze followed the couple as they left the bar. "'Scuse me. I better make sure they didn't shortchange us on their tab."

Renie gulped down more Canadian. "How fried do I have to get before we can have dinner? Now I *am* hungry."

Lost in thought, Judith gave a start. "You're . . . what?"

"Hungry," Renie said, baring her teeth.

"Okay. Let's see if we can take our drinks into the dining room," she said as Ruby returned to the bar.

"Sure," Ruby said. "Open seating right now. Everybody's going to the concert. I hope Klara pulled herself together. She's going to sing."

Judith registered surprise. "She's a singer?"

Ruby nodded, topping off Judith's drink. "Opera. I'm heavy metal. Uh-oh. Here come the dudes. Maybe the Giggle Sisters can get lucky."

"What's your dinner suggestion?" Judith asked.

"Venison steak," Ruby said, heading for two young men who had sat down near the girls. "I'll remind Chef Bruno to hold the antlers."

The cousins found their way to the dining room. Only a half-dozen tables were occupied. The walls were decorated with sketches of Mozart, Beethoven, Handel, and some other composers Judith didn't recognize. Renie, however, rattled off their names. "Wagner, Schubert, Richard Strauss, Papa Haydn, Bach, Brahms, and some guy named Dortmunder."

"Dortmunder?" Judith said, sitting down in a booth for two.

"Something like that," Renie said. "It's a composer whose work I don't like. Too modern."

"I'll take your word for it. What did you think of Ruby's blood-bath description?"

"Hey, we're going to be eating," Renie said, giving Judith a dirty look. "Can we lighten up?"

"What about those girls saying that someone at the ski shop told them Wessler was killed because he was a Communist—or a Nazi chef?"

"Politics," Renie muttered. "Almost as distasteful as murder. Those twerps wouldn't know a commie or a Nazi from an oven mitt."

"I wondered," Judith said. "Well?"

Renie picked up a menu. "A socialist, a republican, an autocrat—who knows? He could be a royalist and Mad Ludwig's his ancestor. I can imagine the rumors flying around this town. You know how things get twisted, especially in a . . . hey, they've got nefle!"

"They do?" Judith's dark eyes lit up. "Do you suppose it's like Grandma Hoffman used to make?"

"I never ate hers," Renie said, referring to Judith's maternal grandmother. "But Grandma Grover made it, too. Let's hope it's not really spaetzle. That's like eating surgical tubing."

"Here comes Ruby," Judith said. "She'll know."

"Hand-cut," the waitress replied. "Bruno—the chef—is fussy."

As Ruby went off to put in their orders, the cousins briefly waxed lyrical over serious German cooking, recalling the weeks they'd spent in Germany. Just as they were growing almost misty-eyed, Ruby reappeared with their red-cabbage-and-beet salads.

"By the way," she said, lowering her voice, "I think sex won out over homicide. The Giggle Sisters left with the two dudes. That other couple took off, too. I'm freed up in here until somebody rings that damned bell. Maybe I can have an early night for a change."

"She's had a hard life," Judith mused after the waitress had departed. "I wonder how she ended up here."

"She ran out of gas?"

"Figuratively, maybe." Judith paused. "How 'bout that weapon?"

"Forget it," Renie said, looking bored. "If the chief thought it came from the buffet, it probably did. I'm not convinced there was that much blood on the floor. Some people pass out from a paper cut. I think Ruby likes dramatizing. She's not bad at it. Look at you—you're the best liar I've ever met. Bill says you've raised lying to an art form."

Judith almost dropped a beet slice off of her fork. "That's not so! I never lie! I occasionally tell a small fib when it's necessary."

"Bingo," Renie said under her breath. "You did it again. But you didn't fool me this time. Oh, Bill and I both admit we've swallowed most of your outrageous lies. We're gullible. But at least we're on guard."

Judith crumpled her napkin and threw it on the table. "I should leave you here to talk to yourself!"

"You won't," Renie said complacently. "I give you one word—*nefle*."

"Well . . ." Judith retrieved her napkin and put it back in her lap. "I haven't had real nefle in years. Mother used to make it now and then."

"That I believe," Renie said.

"Okay," Judith said, her equilibrium restored. "Let's look at what we really know."

Renie was wide-eyed. "We know something?"

"Yes," Judith declared with a touch of impatience. "Please. Let's stay reasonable for a few minutes. It was your idea for me to unburden myself. You were right—I was feeling frustrated—and tired."

"Go ahead. Tell me what we know. I'm all ears."

"Dietrich Wessler is dead. It's not a hoax. Maybe he was murdered. In fact, let's assume he was."

Renie nodded as she polished off her salad.

"Bob Stafford was murdered."

"Two corpses. Got it."

"Several people somehow involved with Herr Wessler are concerned about someone close to them who may be the murderer of . . . well, at least of Wessler. For now, we'll separate the two deaths."

"Good idea."

"The cops really are baffled."

"Of course."

"No one is trying to make a fool of me."

"Uh-huh. Say, we didn't get any bread."

"We don't need it. There are far too many connections between various people, which makes me wonder if—"

"We always get bread with salad," Renie said. "You ate a big sandwich. You don't need bread. I do."

"You ate popcorn. Shut up and let me—"

Judith was interrupted when Ruby arrived with their entrées.

"Here's the venison," she said, placing their plates on the table. "Medium rare. That's how Bruno does it."

"It all looks great," Judith said. "Nice green beans, too."

"How about some bread?" Renie said.

"We're out," Ruby replied. "The baker got too busy to make enough for us even on a slow night. He had to do all the other stuff for the various events. Sorry." She tensed. "Damn. There goes the bell from the bar." She took off.

"Where were we?" Judith said.

"Wondering what happened to the bread," Renie replied.

"No, we weren't," Judith insisted. "We were talking about false confessions. Which brings us to poor Gabe Hunter being hauled off for questioning. How on earth is he connected to this case? He hasn't been in the B&B business very long. I'd never heard of him until now."

Renie had swallowed her first taste of venison and appeared to be having an out-of-body experience. "Mmmm . . . ohhh . . . my!"

"Good grief," Judith said crossly, "you sound like Meg Ryan in *When Harry Met Sally*. It's a good thing nobody's watching us."

"You try it," Renie said. "It really is orgasmic."

Judith ate a mouthful and conceded the point. "You're right. It's very . . . good. But I'm not about to pass out from ecstasy."

"That's because you already ate a bratwurst," Renie said. "So why don't you call Inbred Heffalump and get the lowdown on Gabe?"

"Because I don't want her to find out what's happened," Judith replied. "She'll blame me for Wessler getting killed. I wonder if she already knows. I wouldn't put it past Connie or Ellie to tell her."

"You're paranoid," Renie said. "They're all too busy confessing."

Judith was about to grudgingly agree when she saw Franz Wessler enter the dining room. "Franz just came in."

Renie turned around. "Hi, Franz," she called out. "Over here."

Looking startled, Franz came to their booth. "Have you seen Klara?" he asked.

Judith shook her head. "Not since earlier today, when she was with those dogs. Was she supposed to be here?"

"Well . . ." Franz made a face. "She left her music here last night. Originally, she was going to sing a number of welcome to the guests, but . . ." He spread his hands in a helpless gesture. "She *thought* she left the music here in all the . . . chaos that ensued. It's an original piece she wrote just for this occasion, so she's never performed it in public before."

"What is it?" Renie asked with feigned innocence. "Some of that rockin' lied stuff about love in a cow pasture?"

"Not precisely," Franz replied through tight lips. "It's rather more . . . *Volk*-like, with apropos warmth and charm."

"Darn," Renie said. "I was so hoping it'd be all idyllic romance." She turned serious eyes on Franz. "I thought you might be in a more tender mood tonight. Death can do that to you. *Liebestod* and all that."

Franz's lean face darkened. "I've no idea what you're talking about. Excuse me, I must find Klara." He turned on his heel and hurried away.

"*I* don't know what you're talking about," Judith said angrily. "Are you nuts? Furthermore, you don't speak German. What's up with that?"

Renie uttered an impatient sigh. "Your sighting of something erotic—or at least romantic—going on in the fancy Mercedes. I don't speak German, but I know something about Wagnerian opera. The Liebestod is a famous aria that Isolde sings about loving somebody to death. Or dying for love. Maybe it's loving to die." Renie wrinkled her nose. "I didn't put that very well—but you get the idea. I tend to nod off before she gets done singing the blasted thing. It's Wagner, it's German, it's *long*. No wonder she goes to sleep permanently. She's worn out."

"Oh." Judith's anger faded. "Your remark did seem to hit home with Franz. Now I wish I'd taken a closer look into that car."

"Just as well you didn't," Renie said, after devouring more venison. "You might have fainted. You only like bodies when they're dead."

"Coz . . ." But Judith's mind was following a different path from mere reproach. "I suppose it could've been Franz and Klara reuniting in their mutual sorrow. Comforting each other over their loss."

"Gack," Renie said. "How do you like the nefle?"

"It's really good." But Judith wasn't focused on food. "I wonder if Franz and Klara had children together."

"Ask. You usually do."

"I really haven't had a chance to talk to Franz," Judith said. "In fact, he might have opened up if you hadn't annoyed him just now."

Renie made a dismissive gesture. "No room for him in this booth. Besides, he was trying to find Klara and her charming little lied."

"Maybe," Judith said after a pause, "we should talk to the cops."

"Why?" Renie asked. "They're dumber than we are."

"We should find out if Gabe Hunter is still being held."

"Why?"

"Because," Judith persisted, "he's a fellow innkeeper. I would think Eleanor, being in charge of the booths, might come to his rescue, but can you see her doing that?"

Renie polished off the last of her venison. "Let me think. Ellie confessed to the murder, recanted, and now wants to exonerate Gabe. Of course. That makes perfect sense."

"That's what I mean," Judith said, trying not to grind her teeth. "It doesn't. In fact, even if Ellie hadn't done all those things, she doesn't strike me as a humanitarian."

"But what about the strudel?"

"What strudel?"

"Didn't you see they had strudel listed as their dessert of the day on that chalkboard when we came in?"

"Why not? It's Little Bavaria. No, I didn't notice it."

"Hunh. And you call yourself observant."

"What kind?"

"Peach or pear."

Judith sighed. "I'm going to gain ten pounds on this trip. You don't have to worry about your weight. You have that weird metabolism that burns up every calorie. And your damned hair doesn't turn gray. You're not only annoying, but weird."

"Freak of nature," Renie said complacently. "Stop fussing. You'll walk off any weight you gain. Besides, you're so tall it never shows."

"I can still feel it."

"Eleanor isn't."

"Isn't what?"

"Refocus. A humanitarian. In fact, she must be a lousy innkeeper. She lacks warmth, which you ooze. And it's real."

Judith pondered Renie's statement. "True, but not all innkeepers are outgoing. Some people get involved in running a B&B for other reasons—like Gabe Hunter. He took over the business from his parents when they retired. I have no idea how Ellie got involved with innkeeping. She's what? Maybe early forties? Sometimes when the empty nest syndrome strikes, the parents don't want to move out of their big house, so they turn it into a B&B. I know of some people who've done that. Maybe that's what happened to Ellie."

"Something happened to Ellie," Renie murmured. "She's a pill."

Judith looked up to see Ruby approaching. "Dinner was excellent," she told the waitress. "We should order dessert before coz here pitches some kind of fit. I'll go with the peach strudel."

"Make mine pear," Renie said.

"They're both good," Ruby assured them. "Bruno's pastry chef does a mean strudel. Good thing he makes his own dough so we don't have to rely on the baker."

"Say," Judith said, as if off the top of her head, "how did you end up here in Little Bavaria? It's a long way from the Meat & Mingle."

Ruby sneered. "I could say the same for you. And it's a long story." She swiftly collected their plates and dashed away.

"Not a happy story," Judith remarked.

"You already mentioned something to that effect," Renie said. "Is there a reason for asking her or just your usual interest in humanity?"

"Well . . ." Judith fiddled with her wedding ring. "Maybe it's because her father was the jerk who stole my wallet. Sometimes kids came to the restaurant—they couldn't come in the bar—to haul their parents home, especially the dads. So many of them spent their paychecks on booze. I wonder if Ruby was one of those kids."

"Why do you care?"

"I don't know." Judith folded her hands in her lap before succumbing to a childish urge to bite her fingernails. "Is my brain going? I feel like everything that's happened here is hopping around like mosquitoes in my head and never alighting long enough to make sense."

"You could put an ad for your brain in the local lost-and-found or whatever. That's what Oscar does when he mislays his orange pillow."

Judith glared at Renie. "Don't talk about Oscar. *Your* brain left the premises years ago."

"Okay. Did you hear what Clarence did the other night when I went down to the basement to tuck him in?"

"Lose the bunny, too. I mean, don't lose him, but refrain from discussing his cutesy antics."

"You're jealous because Sweetums is such a wretched beast. Clarence is sweet in every way."

"Oh? Even the bunny poop he leaves on your basement floor?"

"I clean it up every night. It's good for the garden. Clarence likes to go outside to nibble chickweed and clover. Bill or I always—"

"Stop!" Judith held up a hand, but her dismayed expression changed when a young man in a chef's jacket arrived with their strudel.

"Who's the pear?" he inquired.

"That's me," Renie said. "Where's Ruby?"

"She went home," the young man replied. "Slow night." He slid their bill onto the table and ambled away.

Judith frowned. "That's odd."

"Why? Ruby said something about maybe leaving early."

"But before she served us?"

Renie made a face. "We aren't royalty."

Judith didn't argue. Her watch informed her it was going on nine. "Maybe they close the dining room early during Oktoberfest."

"We're missing the concert," Renie said. "Don't you want to hear Klara sing? Or will she sing a different kind of song to the cops?"

Judith slowly shook her head. "Who knows? All I understand now is that Bruno's pastry chef has talent."

"So he does," Renie said, lapping up slices of pears with cinnamon-and-sugar-covered crumbs.

"In fact," Judith said after a few moments of silence, "I think we should give our compliments to the chef."

Renie winced. "Why do I think it's Chef Bruno's turn to be grilled?"

"Because," Judith said, studying the bill, "that's what I plan to do. You owe me forty bucks."

"With tip?"

Judith nodded. "I included our bar bill, too."

"Fair enough," Renie conceded, getting out her wallet. "Why are you grilling the chef?"

"Because," Judith replied, "chefs count knives. I'd like to hear if one of his ended up in Herr Wessler's back."

# Chapter Ten

As might be expected Chef Bruno didn't look pleased to see the cousins invade his domain. "We're closed," he announced gruffly.

"Exactly," Judith said with a big smile. "My late husband and I owned a restaurant. That's why I feel guilty about interrupting your work. I wanted to thank you on behalf of us innkeepers who are here for Oktoberfest. You run an amazing kitchen."

"Well . . ." The chef glanced at his helpers, who had stopped scurrying around the kitchen to stare at the newcomers. Bruno himself suddenly stared at them, too. "Didn't you two come in here last night?"

"Yes," Judith admitted, deciding that honesty was the best policy. "We'd just witnessed the discovery of Mr. Wessler's body. We were horrified and fled the scene. It must've been chaos here after that."

Bruno used a towel to wipe off some perspiration from his high forehead. "That's for damned sure. Never seen anything like it." He glared at a young man with a blond goatee. "Almost lost my pastry chef."

Judith smiled sympathetically. "Oh, no! His strudel was amazing. But," she went on quickly, resorting to a semifib, "I heard you lost a knife. I've always wondered why people feel free to take souvenirs."

Bruno scowled. "You mean a buffet knife?"

"Yes. Some of the people who were here last night mentioned that one or two had gone missing. That's just plain thievery."

"Hunh." Bruno's gaze took in his half-dozen staff members. "How many did we get back? I didn't count them."

A dark-skinned young man glanced at what might have been a cutlery drawer. "We've got six of the ones we put out for the beef. I used two tonight." He looked at his coworkers. "Anybody else got one?"

The pastry chef nodded. "It's right here. I took one to cut up the pears and peaches."

"That it?" Bruno inquired, wiping perspiration from his bald head.

"You have one," a curly-haired redheaded man said. "It's under the edge of that platter."

The chef peered at the counter. "So I do. That makes ten. All accounted for." He turned back to Judith. "Why are you asking?"

"Ah . . ." Judith grimaced. "I heard that several were missing. I mean, stolen. Or borrowed. Or something."

"You heard wrong," Bruno said. "Now, if you don't mind, we've got work to do." He picked up the knife he'd been using and ran his finger down the flat side of the blade. "Glad you liked dinner. G'night."

Judith decided they had no choice but to leave. "Damn," she said when they'd gone out through the lobby, standing in a slight drizzle by the exhibitors' booths. "Bruno reminds me of somebody—maybe it's one of the chefs we had when Dan didn't feel like cooking. Or working." She sighed. "Let's go back to the inn. I *am* tired and I hurt. I should call Joe to see how things are at home. Tomorrow is another day."

"Okay, Scarlett," Renie agreed. "It's early for me, but I don't mind."

"Say," Judith said, walking slowly along the still-busy main street, "how come your mother hasn't called you about six times?"

"I told her I'd be out of range in the mountains."

Judith automatically glanced up, though cloud cover and darkness obscured the nearby peaks. "That might almost be true."

"It would, in the Himalayas—that's where I told her we were going."

"You did not," Judith said.

"Well . . . not exactly. But I think she believed me. About the mountains and the interference, I mean."

"Are you going to call Bill?"

Renie shook her head. "You know he hates to talk on the phone. If he even bothered to answer, he'd probably hang up on me."

The cousins sidestepped some costumed teenagers dancing what looked like a cross between hip-hop and a polka. Judith and Renie could hear music as they drew nearer to the bandstand.

"I wonder if Franz found Klara's piece," Judith murmured.

Renie sniffed. "If he didn't and she wrote it, she can probably fake it. Why not? Everything else around here seems fake."

"You think so? I like it. It seems authentic."

"I mean the Wessler murder," Renie said and grinned at her cousin. "My God, don't tell me you've forgotten about that!"

"No," Judith replied wearily. "But I'd like to. At least for now."

Entering Hanover Haus, they found the lobby deserted. "Guess everybody's at the events," Renie remarked, starting up the stairs.

"You can't blame them," Judith said. "That's where all the action is. We're probably the only guests not in attendance."

Inside their room, Judith collapsed on the bed while Renie headed for the bathroom, saying she was getting ready for bed—if not for sleep.

"I'll read for a while," she said, closing the door behind her.

Judith waited a couple minutes to unwind before getting out her cell to call Joe. He answered on the second ring.

"It's about time," he said. "I thought you forgot about me."

"Never that," Judith assured him. "We've been busy. At least I have. How's everything at home?"

"Fine."

"Including Mother?"

"She moved out."

"Joe—"

"How do you think she is? With Carl and Arlene dancing attendance on her, she's in fine fettle." He chuckled. "That means I can ignore her—and vice versa. We both like it that way."

Judith propped herself up on a couple of pillows. "So everything's going okay with the B&B guests?"

"Uh . . . well, sure. Why wouldn't it be? The Rankerses are old hands at running this place."

"I know," Judith said, "but every so often the unexpected happens." She paused, waiting for any sign of knowledge from Joe about the murder in Little Bavaria. "I thought there might be some Oktoberfest TV coverage from the local stations, but I haven't seen any reporters or video cams. Maybe they're waiting for Saturday's big doings."

"Could be," Joe said. "You want to get interviewed?"

"Heavens, no!" Judith exclaimed. "I want . . . anonymity."

"Good thinking," Joe said, "given your track record."

"Now don't start in—" She broke off. "I assume Ingrid Heffelman hasn't asked you out on a date in my absence."

"Ah . . . no."

"You sound uncertain," Judith said, suddenly suspicious.

"Not about a date," Joe replied, after clearing his throat. "She did stop by yesterday morning."

"What?" Judith cried. "You mean at the B&B?"

"Where else? Ingrid told me an inspection is a regular thing every couple of years. It's a city regulation."

"There *is* a city regulation," Judith said, trying to keep the anger out of her voice, "as you well know, but the city sends its own inspectors, not somebody from the state B&B association. What's wrong with you? You were a city employee for almost forty years!"

"Well . . ." Joe cleared his throat again. "That's why I believed her. I was spending the morning going over some of those reports from the city hall investigation. Ingrid told me that because this thing has been going on since the first of the year—along with budget cuts—consultants have been hired to do some of the legwork. It made sense. The city's done that in other areas. She pointed out it was a good time to do it while some innkeepers were out of town. Sort of spring it on them when they'd have no chance to fix things up while she was inspecting other parts of the premises. You can't blame her for doing her job."

"Ordinarily it's not her job," Judith huffed. "It sounds as if the two of you had quite a chat."

"The least I could do was offer her a cup of coffee," Joe said, sounding defensive.

"And the most you could do?"

"Hey!" Joe shouted. "That was it. I left her to do whatever she had to do. Arlene came back inside about then. I went to my office."

Judith wondered how Arlene had handled Ingrid. With a left hook, she hoped. "Where was Carl?"

"He'd gone to the grocery store," Joe said, sounding more like himself. "You were low on eggs. Or bread. Maybe it was milk."

"Never mind. How long did Ingrid stay?"

"I don't know," Joe replied. "She was gone when I came down to get some lunch. Ingrid said you'd get her report in a few days."

"I'll bet it'll be a doozy," Judith muttered. "Okay, sorry I got snappish. You know how Ingrid riles me."

"Forget it," Joe said. "She seemed nice, never criticized anything about you, not even your deadly track record."

"Joe! Don't!"

"I'm kidding. But I mean it—it was a very pleasant visit."

"Right." Judith sighed. "So no other problems?"

"Nothing except a jealous wife. It's kind of flattering."

"Men!" But Judith smiled. "I'm broad-minded. It's just that Ingrid showing up on Hillside Manor's doorstep is galling."

"At least she left alive."

"That's not funny!" But Judith was still smiling a few minutes later when she hung up just as Renie emerged from the bathroom.

"You look happy. Have you cracked the case?" she asked.

Judith explained about the phone call with Joe. Renie was amused. "You should call Arlene. I'll bet she didn't take kindly to an intrusion on her temporary turf, especially the pushy Inbred Heffalump."

"I will call Arlene," Judith said, "but not until tomorrow. She and Carl go to bed early. It's after ten. They probably went home and left Joe to lock up."

"Everything else okay at the B&B?" Renie asked.

Judith nodded. "I didn't ask Joe if he'd heard from Mike, but if he had, he would've told me. Mike probably hasn't been notified yet about his new posting."

"No point in worrying about that," Renie said, lying down on her own side of the bed. "Our kids are all so far away that Bill and I are lucky to see them two or three times a year. Thank goodness for e-mail and cell phones. Of course Bill never answers their calls when I'm not home. Good thing he doesn't. They often want money. Mom's a soft touch. Oh, heck, so's Bill. How," she asked, snuggling under the covers, "are Carl and Arlene getting along with the B&B?"

Judith made a face. "Fine, I think."

"Why are you looking so grim?"

"Oh, it's stupid, really," Judith said with some reluctance. "Ingrid Heffelman showed up to inspect Hillside Manor."

Renie burst out laughing. "She did? Why? Or was she really inspecting Joe?"

"That's what *I* wonder. Ingrid's never done that before. In fact, nobody from the state board has ever conducted an inspection. It's all done through the city."

Renie had put on her reading glasses. She peered at Judith with a wry expression. "And her excuse for showing up on your doorstep was?"

Judith waved an impatient hand. "Oh, the city hall investigation and all the departments being shorthanded and budget cuts and——"

Renie interrupted. "How did she know Joe would be home?"

"Maybe she called first and talked to Arlene."

"Arlene wouldn't have been aware that Ingrid didn't do such things as inspect B&Bs," Renie pointed out. "Makes sense. So where were the Rankerses while Ingrid was trying to seduce Joe?"

"Stop! They only had coffee together." Judith paused. "It was later in the morning. Arlene and Carl were checking out the guests."

"While Ingrid was checking out Joe. *I* suspect that maybe what you suspect could be right. But Ingrid's attempts at seduction wouldn't faze Joe. I've never seen the woman, but I always assumed my nickname of Inbred Heffalump wasn't far off the mark."

Judith considered her cousin's comment. "To be fair, Ingrid's not *un*attractive. She's a big woman, a little overweight, but tall and imposing. In fact, well, she's kind of like . . . me."

Renie sighed. "Oh, dear. Just Joe's type. Sorry about that."

"*You're* sorry?" Judith retorted. "How do you think I feel?"

"Oh, coz, don't be stupid! Joe would never cheat on you. He waited too long to finally hook up with you. You know that."

Judith frowned. "Men are . . . men."

Renie had opened her book. "Don't be a jackass. We are, after all, kind of old. There *are* limits."

"That's part of the problem," Judith said. "If Ingrid is really chasing him, Joe can't run as fast as he used to."

Renie ignored the remark. Judith pouted a bit. And then realized she was too old to pout. Instead, she turned off her lamp and went to sleep. In her dreams, an elephant was chasing a lion with a red-gold mane through Hillside Manor's backyard. The elephant suddenly stopped in front of the toolshed. Sweetums leaped off of the birdbath and growled at the elephant. Gertrude appeared by the statue of Saint Francis, singing, "You can have him, I don't want him, he's too dumb for me." The elephant ran off and disappeared in the Rankerses' giant hedge, apparently devoured by the mass of glossy laurel leaves. Judith wasn't surprised that she woke up smiling.

**J**udith didn't have to be at the B&B booth until ten. She had awakened shortly before eight, but decided not to call Arlene until after nine-thirty. Her stand-in would still be busy with the guests' breakfast. Maybe she shouldn't call at all.

Renie was again sleeping in, which was just as well as far as Judith was concerned. An early-rising Renie was not a pleasant Renie. Judith showered, dressed, combed her hair, and put on her makeup before heading down to breakfast. She arrived just after eight-thirty. The rest of the B&B contingent was already in place, looking, as Gertrude would say, "like the pigs ate their little brother."

Judith's polite "good morning" was greeted with a mixture of mumbles and blank stares. She selected a croissant, green melon balls, a couple of very thin ham slices, and pale coffee. Gabe Hunter's place was vacant, but Judith decided to sit in her previous spot by the Beaulieus.

"The Gypsy," George murmured, picking at a bran muffin. "What do you see with those eyes this morning?"

"Food," Judith said pleasantly. "Did you go to the concert?"

"Yes." George put a muffin crumb on his tongue and rolled it around in his mouth. "Quite enjoyable," he said, after swallowing the morsel. "Too many marches, though. I don't care for military music, especially the German variety." He shuddered slightly. "All I can think of are panzer divisions mowing down everything in sight."

Connie leaned around her husband. "Pay no attention to George. He's seen too many war movies."

George sat up very straight. His handlebar mustache seemed to bristle. "Nonsense! I was there. I lived through the war."

"You were a baby when it ended," Connie said. "You never saw a German soldier in that village in the Dordogne. Carmaux wasn't exactly a strategic spot, darling."

George glowered at his wife. "The Germans could've overrun us at any moment. You never knew what would happen. It was *war*."

Connie giggled. "Oh, George, you must have your drama!"

"Nonsense!" George huffed. "Even infants can sense danger."

Ellie, who was across from the Beaulieus, sneered. "You must've outgrown it, George. Why didn't you sense danger night before last?"

"As I recall," George said with a haughty look for Ellie, "I was in the men's lavatory at the time of your grandfather's demise."

Connie put a hand on her husband's arm. "If George had been with me, maybe I wouldn't have reacted so violently and gotten sick. Besides, Ellie, I still don't understand why you went to the police to tell them you killed your own grandfather."

"Because," Ellie replied with a toss of her head, "I blamed myself for asking him to speak to the cocktail-party attendees. I had to coax, which I should never have done, as he was elderly and yet so accommodating. I believe that's what caused him to have his heart attack and die. I'm still overcome with guilt." To make her point she dabbed at her dry eyes with her napkin.

"Heart attack?" Judith said. "He was stabbed."

Ellie's jaw jutted. "He happened to fall on a knife someone dropped. So careless. Some people can't hold their liquor."

"Or their knife," Judith shot back. "But that's not what the police say happened."

"Oh, for heaven's sake!" Ellie exclaimed. "In a small town like this, you don't expect to find clever policemen. Chief Duomo told me there'd be an autopsy. I'll call on them later today to hear the results."

Delmar Denkel was nodding vigorously. "Little Bavaria is a world unto itself. In great measure, I might add, to Ellie's grandfather. He resurrected this town from the dead."

"Too bad he couldn't have done the same for himself," Judith said, with a severe look at the Denkels. "I haven't heard anyone question the fact that your grandfather was murdered. Will there be an inquest?"

Ellie glared at Judith. "The autopsy report will have to be concluded first. Gossip here runs like so many mice in a cheese cave.

Naturally, the initial reaction was that poor *Grossvater* was stabbed to death, but that's erroneous."

Judith wasn't cowed by Ellie's steely gaze. "What about Gabe Hunter? Where is he, if not being held by the police?"

"I've no idea," Ellie declared. "Maybe he slept in." She pushed her plate away and stood up. "Come, Delmar, I'm finished here."

With Delmar trailing her like a small mutt, Ellie departed.

George was still toying with his muffin. "Could we change the subject? Dead people spoil my appetite."

The Beaulieus had spoiled Judith's. It was exactly nine o'clock. She wasn't due at the B&B booth for another hour. Her partner for the two-hour stint was a woman she knew only slightly, Evelyn Choo. The Choos owned Pearl House near the city's hospital district. Excusing herself, Judith got up and left. She took a deep breath and headed for the police station.

Gray clouds hung over the mountains, but the rain had stopped. Judith didn't bother putting up her jacket's hood even though the air was damp. The bright autumnal leaves clinging to the cottonwood and alder trees at the lower elevations seemed to beg for sunshine.

From the outside, headquarters looked quiet. Inside, however, was another matter. Duomo was berating Orville for some alleged mistake while Officer Hernandez was consoling a sobbing woman who was lamenting the loss of something—her purse, her cat—or maybe her mind.

Fat Matt stopped cussing out Orville long enough to acknowledge Judith with a curt nod. Apparently, his subordinate had mislaid a statement—and the chief's morning doughnuts. Just when Judith decided she might as well return to Hanover Haus, the woman stopped crying and Duomo finished tongue-lashing Orville.

"You got anything?" the chief asked Judith.

"Questions," Judith said briskly, gesturing at Duomo's office.

"Sure, come on," he said affably, and led the way. Just before reaching the door, he called over his shoulder to the distraught woman. "Don't worry. Nobody will keep the Red Baron for long. He's too quick."

The chief closed the door behind Judith and grunted as he sat down. "Damned nuisance. Why can't people keep track of stuff?"

Judith sat down in one of the other chairs after removing what looked like a white bakery bag from the chair and setting it on Duomo's desk. "I assume this is yours," she said.

"Ah!" he said with a heartfelt sigh. "*There's* my morning starter. Why'd Orville put it where I couldn't see it?"

Judith ignored the rhetorical remark. "The Red Baron is who?"

"It's not a who, it's a ferret," the chief replied, opening the bag. "Want a cruller? Got some chocolate-covered ones."

"No thanks," she said. "I won't take up much of your time, but I'm wondering if you're taking up mine." She noted the puzzled look on Duomo's face as he bit off a large chunk of cruller. "First, what happened with Gabe Hunter last night after you brought him in here?"

"Oh." The chief chewed hurriedly. "Alibi was fuzzy. Claimed he wasn't at the cocktail party when Wessler went down. Witnesses saw him just before it happened. Kept insisting he'd arrived just after the fact. The major couldn't remember seeing Hunter. Maybe he'd dozed off. Got it squared away, so I let him go." He paused to eat more cruller.

"I spoke with Chef Bruno last night. He accounted for all his knives," Judith said. "What do you think of that?"

"I think Bruno counted the wrong knives," Duomo replied, wiping some chocolate off his chin. "Sounds like him. My brother's an idiot."

Judith stared at the chief. "Bruno's your brother?"

"Yeah. My other brother's the baker. Frankie, real name Francis, but he'd slug you if you called him that. He's almost as dumb as Bruno. Makes good doughnuts, though." He polished off the cruller.

It was no wonder the chef looked familiar. There was a definite resemblance—especially the round bald head. In a small town,

Judith figured at least half the population must be related to one another.

"Let's get back on track," she urged. "One other thing really bothers me. This morning at breakfast with some of the other innkeepers, including Eleanor Denkel, Mr. Wessler's granddaughter, there was talk that he wasn't murdered, but had a heart attack and fell on a knife. Eleanor also said there's an autopsy. Is that true?"

Duomo put down a glazed cruller he'd taken out of the bakery bag. "Yeah, sure, autopsies are good. The local doc who's in charge of our hospital is the coroner, but he's backed up with all these screwy tourists getting themselves banged up and falling down and whatever else they do when they get crazy at Oktoberfest. Hell, they had a deer come into the ER yesterday morning. Nothing wrong with the deer, just curious, I guess. Anyways, Doc Frolander will get to it later today, maybe. But pay no attention to what people say. Gossip's a big hobby around here."

"Eleanor Denkel isn't local," Judith pointed out. "She may have family in Little Bavaria, but she's not part of your regular grapevine."

"It's contagious," Duomo stated. "Ten minutes inside this town and everybody's cackling like a bunch of damned hens."

"So it's definitely homicide?"

"Unless Doc Frolander says different." He bit into the cruller.

"What happened to the bottle that was found at the bookstore?"

"It's . . . somewhere. The lab, I guess. You don't know how long that bottle's been at the bookstore. Hell, whoever made that busted gizmo might've had lacquer in it. Or would that be a glaze?"

"It could be either one," Judith said irritably and stood up. "I'll check back with you later on the autopsy."

The chief waved a hand for her to wait while he finished another bite of cruller. "Hold it. You haven't given me anything. What've you been doing? Larking around town drinking beer and rubbernecking?"

Judith leaned both hands on the desk and looked Duomo straight in the eye. "I have never come up against a case as confused and frustrating as this one. I can't get straight answers, witnesses have wildly different reactions to the same things, people make false confessions, and I still haven't been able to sort out who's related to who. For all I know, you're Herr Wessler's illegitimate son."

The chief dropped the cruller. "Whoa! How did you know that?"

# Chapter Eleven

Judith was speechless—but only for a moment. Regaining her composure, she forced a sly smile. "I'm FASTO, remember?"

Chief Duomo still looked shaken. In fact, his eyes had misted over. "Francesca Duomo was my mother. She came from Italy—from Pescia, a Tuscan hill town. She fell in love with Wessler." He paused to dab at his eyes with a stubby finger.

"He must've had great charisma," Judith said, though she thought of several other attributes the deceased might also have possessed.

Duomo nodded. "My mama married an American alpine skier. He died young. That's why they lived here. I never knew him. Neither did my younger brothers."

"Ah . . ." Judith was momentarily nonplussed. "Wessler was also Bruno and Frankie's father?"

The chief nodded again. "'Course." He narrowed his small eyes at Judith. "You think my mama played around?"

"Oh, no," Judith said hastily. "I didn't realize the birth order of you and your brothers. Is she . . . ah . . . still alive?"

Duomo shook his head. "Passed back in '92. One of those damned aneurysms. Bingo!" He clapped his hands once. "She was gone. Just turned sixty the week before."

"Herr Wessler must've loved her very much."

"He loved everybody very much," the chief said. "Think I got about three, four dozen half brothers and half sisters between here and Germany. Real friendly kind of guy." He smiled wistfully before stuffing the rest of the glazed cruller in his mouth.

Judith was rarely at a loss when eliciting personal information from virtual strangers, but she was having a problem phrasing tactful queries about Matt's father and the gaggle of illegitimate Wessler offspring. "So," she finally said, "you're related to Franz Wessler and Eleanor Denkel."

Swallowing first, Duomo tapped his fingers on the desk as if he were running a calculator. "Right, right," he finally said. "Franz is a half brother, Eleanor's a . . . half niece? Hard to keep track. We're all spread out." He rubbed his paunch. "More ways than one. Get it?"

"Yes." Judith smiled obligingly. "Do you have any other half siblings here in Little Bavaria?"

Fat Matt frowned. "No, don't think so. Used to, but they all moved away. Let's see . . . there was Hans and Leah and Stan and . . . damn, can't recall that one half sister's name. She left when she was still in her teens. Nice-looking gal, but kind of standoffish. Never got to know her. Think she was about ten years younger than me. Oh, there was a boy, but his ma took him back east when he was just a little kid. She hated German food." Duomo scowled. "You writing my life story?"

"Hardly," Judith said. "If Wessler was murdered, his heirs would be possible suspects. As you know, money is always a good motive."

The chief shrugged. "I s'pose. But he gave most of his away, either to the lady friends or the town. Hell, I don't even know if he had a will." He scowled again. "Are you saying *I'm* a suspect?"

"You would be—but you weren't at the scene," Judith pointed out. "Unless, of course, you conspired with someone else."

"That's a bunch of crap," he declared, digging into the bakery bag. "Plain? What's wrong with Orville? He knows I don't like crullers without frosting. Oh, well."

"You asked for my help and that's what I'm giving you," Judith said. "If you're trying to remove suspicion from yourself, prove it."

The chief finished chewing. "I wouldn't go to all that trouble to kill anybody, let alone *Vater* Wessler. I'd just frame him for some crime, shoot him, and claim he was trying to escape."

Judith tended to believe Fat Matt was innocent, but didn't say so. Instead, she stood up. "I have to be going. If you want to help me help you, figure out if any of your other half siblings might be involved. Ellie already confessed, if only because she felt guilty about begging Wessler to take on the B&B exhibit and host the cocktail party."

"Hunh. That one's new to me. She did natter on about him asking her to do it. Felt he couldn't live forever and didn't want to get senile and decrepit. Thought it'd be kind of spectacular for the town. You know—going out in style. I guess."

"You bought that tale?"

"'Course not. It's like she was trying out different motives to see which one I liked best. That's why I let her go. Or maybe she was trying to make me look like a fool. It'd be like Ellie. She's not my favorite relative. Too high-and-mighty. Couldn't wait to get out of town. She headed for the big city the day after she graduated from high school."

"I won't argue the point about her arrogance," Judith said, "but that's not the version I read in her statement."

Duomo scowled. "You snooping around here when I'm gone?"

"Of course. How else can I find out anything? Now I've got two different versions of why Ellie claimed to have offed her grandfather. Three, if I count her signed confession about the will."

"Multiple choice," the chief muttered. "They're all bull."

"That I believe," Judith snapped, slinging her handbag over her shoulder. "I'll check in later about the autopsy."

"The . . . oh, sure. Hey—on your way out, tell Orville he's an idiot. It'll save me a trip."

Judith barely managed to refrain from rolling her eyes. But she didn't bother to say good-bye.

Evelyn Choo was waiting for Judith in the parking lot at Hanover Haus. They shook hands as Evelyn explained that she always went for an early walk before starting breakfast for her guests.

"It's the only way I can wake myself up to start the day," she said. "But since I don't have to make breakfast, I decided to take my walk after I ate. I'm staying at the Valhalla Inn on the edge of town by the river."

"It's good to change your routine," Judith remarked as they started down the almost deserted main street.

Evelyn nodded absently. "I suppose. I expected it to be so quaint and peaceful here after city life. I never came close to a homicide until last night. Ironic, isn't it?"

"Yes," Judith agreed, hoping Evelyn had never heard any FASTO tales. "Where were you when it happened?" she inquired, involuntarily looking up at Sadie's Stories with its "Closed" sign.

"I wasn't in the ballroom," Evelyn replied, turning up the collar of her suede jacket as a sudden breeze blew down from the mountains. "My husband had called to see if I'd arrived safely, but I couldn't hear him over the din of the band, so I went into the lobby. We chatted for a few moments—and then the party got so quiet. I assumed someone was speaking to the guests, but before I could ring off, I heard sirens. I didn't think much of it—the highway is treacherous. Then the sirens stopped and suddenly all those emergency people rushed inside. I didn't know what had happened until I went back to the ballroom." She shook her head. "So sad. So . . . strange."

"Strange?" Judith echoed.

"Theatrical, like a stage play or a film. Didn't you think so, too?"

"I did," Judith said slowly, "though almost subconsciously."

Evelyn put her hood up over her short black hair. "Maybe I reacted that way because it seemed so incredible. A small town, holding a big festival, everyone having a good time." She paused as they neared the exhibition area. "Oh, Eleanor's already at the booth. I heard she's the victim's granddaughter."

"She is," Judith replied, trying to put on a pleasant face as they approached the prickly Mrs. Denkel. "Are we all set?" she asked, hoping to sound cordial.

"No," Ellie replied crossly. "The two innkeepers from the Lake Shegogan B&B didn't clean up properly last night. I'm reorganizing the brochures and displays. Really, some people are very slapdash. I'd hate to see what their inns look like. How do they stay in business?"

Judith couldn't detect any serious disarray except for some maps that apparently had blown off the counter. "Vandals and Huns, maybe?"

Ellie glared at Judith. "You and your little jokes. I'll let you and Evelyn finish cleaning up."

"Sure," Judith said. "It's quiet this morning. Everyone must be recovering from last night's events."

"Perhaps," Ellie allowed through pursed lips. "You're five minutes early. If you were being paid, you'd probably demand overtime."

Evelyn arched her perfect black eyebrows at Ellie. "You have your own little jokes, Eleanor. You seem tired. Maybe you need a nap."

Ellie didn't bother to respond. She picked up her clutch purse and all but ran from the booth.

"Why," Evelyn said, joining Judith, who'd reached the counter first, "does she have to be unpleasant? Most innkeepers are personable."

"Maybe Ellie's grieving for her grandfather."

"Well . . . perhaps. But I have to wonder if she and Mr. Wessler were close. She doesn't seem to know the town all that well."

"She was raised here," Judith pointed out.

Evelyn looked surprised. "Really?"

Judith nodded. "She moved away after high school, which was

probably before Little Bavaria was turned into a tourist attraction. That might account for her lack of knowledge. I understand
all the buildings along the main street were completely renovated
in the Bavarian style."

"That would indicate Eleanor doesn't visit very often."

"Yes," Judith said, "it may explain her unfamiliarity with all
the changes. Tell me, how do you get along with Ingrid Heffelman?"

Evelyn laughed, but waited for the clock tower to chime ten.
"Ingrid and I sorted out our differences about running a B&B.
She's not unreasonable, just a bit hidebound. Do you have prob-
lems with her?"

Judith omitted the body count, assuming Evelyn didn't know
of her reputation. "Maybe it's a personality clash," she hedged.
"I spoke to my husband last night. He told me Ingrid had come
to inspect Hillside Manor. With the city's budget crisis, they're
farming out certain jobs."

Evelyn shrugged. "That makes sense. She does run the state
association. I don't think Pearl House is due for inspection until
next year. Maybe the city will be in better financial shape by then."

"I hope so," Judith said, noticing that the main street had
grown busier in the last few minutes. In fact, two dark-skinned
couples were headed their way. The men wore casual clothes, but
the women were dressed in elegant saris. Judith and Evelyn put
on their friendliest smiles and went to work.

The next hour and a half was busy. Some sixty people stopped
to chat and study the brochures, photographs, and maps. At least
half were Americans, and over a dozen were Canadians. There
were also visitors from Costa Rica, Argentina, Thailand, and
the United Kingdom. The first two couples had turned out to be
from Bangalore, India.

Judith was saying good-bye to a woman from Sarasota, Florida, when she spotted Renie approaching with Barry Stafford.

"You're awake," Judith said to her cousin.

"Sort of," Renie replied. "I ran into Barry outside of the bookshop. We're heading for the pancake place. I haven't eaten breakfast and he's ready for lunch. Want to meet us there?"

"Sure," Judith said. She turned to introduce Evelyn, but her fellow innkeeper was still talking to a young couple who looked sufficiently dewy-eyed to be newlyweds. "Save me a place."

Renie said she would. The cuddling couple had moved on. A lull followed as pedestrians stopped to watch a juggler on the sidewalk.

"Who was that?" Evelyn inquired.

"My cousin Serena," Judith replied.

"I assumed you might be related," Evelyn said. "You don't look alike, but your mannerisms and the way you speak indicate a resemblance. I meant the young man. He seems familiar."

"Oh," Judith said, "that's because he tended bar at the cocktail party at Wolfgang's night before last."

Their conversation was interrupted by two middle-aged couples, chattering cheerfully in German. The respite was over. For the next half hour the booth was busy. Judith was glad to see Eldridge Hoover and even Connie Beaulieu show up for their stint. Gathering up her purse and the notebook in which she'd jotted down potential B&B guests, she asked if Evelyn wanted to join her for lunch at the Pancake Schloss. The other woman declined with polite, even sincere, regret. She was meeting an old friend who owned an inn on Chavez Island.

"Jeanne Clayton Barber?" Judith asked in surprise.

Evelyn smiled. "You know her?"

"Yes, from way back. In fact, I B&B-sat for her a few years ago after her husband died."

Evelyn's face fell. "No! Were you there when a man got killed?"

Judith flinched. "Unfortunately, yes. But somehow I managed to survive that tragic episode."

Evelyn shook her head. "It must've been terrifying. Weren't you traumatized? How could you stand the stress?"

"Ah . . . well, you know how it is—you just keep going."

"I don't know if I could do that. I mean, to be involved in something as sordid as murder. Do you still have nightmares about it?"

Judith was trying to remember exactly who had gotten killed and why. All she could recall at the moment was thinking that Renie had hit the victim over the head with her dinner plate. At first, Judith had thought her cousin had killed him for trying to swipe her meal. "Time heals all wounds," she murmured. "I'd better meet my first susp—I mean, first *cousin*. She's the impatient type. Tell Jeanne hello for me."

Evelyn, looking faintly dazed, promised to convey her fellow innkeeper's greetings.

By the time Judith reached the restaurant, it was almost full. At first, she didn't see Renie or Barry, but her cousin stood up and waved from a booth near where they had sat the previous day.

"Suze and I declared a truce," Renie announced when Judith sat down next to her. "Barry told her I was an orphan who had to work in a New England shoe factory as a child and she felt sorry for me."

Barry laughed. "Mom's sort of hotheaded sometimes, too. She kind of likes it when somebody mixes it up with her. She can't insult rude customers, so she saves her hostility for private gatherings."

Judith glanced at Renie. "My cousin's less discriminating."

"Hey, watch it," Renie said. "Suze always lets Barry eat on the house. His guests, too. Don't criticize me or she might renege."

"One of my few perks," Barry noted. "Mom figures she fed me and my buddies for the first eighteen years before I started college. She decided she might as well go on doing it while I'm in town."

"Very generous of her," Judith said, seeing that Renie had already demolished most of her Swedish pancakes, eggs, and ham. "You two hooked up this morning at Sadie's Stories?"

Renie had stuffed her mouth with more ham, so Barry answered first. "I was just coming out of the shop. Jessi and I overdid it last night at the beer tasting." He gave Judith a rueful look,

Suzie suddenly appeared at the booth. "What'll it be?"

"Oh!" Judith exclaimed. "I haven't looked at the menu."

"Try the Reuben," Barry suggested. "Serena told me you like them. Mom serves a killer version." He pointed to the remnants on his plate. "That's what I had."

"Why not?" Judith said, smiling at Suzie. "And some lemonade?"

"Got it." Suzie wheeled away with a squeak of rubber-soled shoes.

Renie had polished off her Swedish pancakes. "Dessert?" Barry asked her. "Mom gets her pies from Frankie the baker."

Renie shook her head. "Not after breakfast. Somehow it seems so wrong. Go ahead, you had lunch and it's free. Never refuse a mom."

Once again, the mom under discussion materialized as if from nowhere. She set down a large Reuben and a generous side of German potato salad in front of Judith before looking at her son. "I saved some rhubarb pie for you—à la mode?"

"Sounds good," Barry said, grinning. "Thanks, Mom."

She turned to Renie. "And you, Weenie?"

Renie's eyes narrowed. "I'm full. But thanks for asking, Floozie."

Suzie laughed. "I like you. You're spunky." She wheeled off again.

Barry leaned closer to the cousins. "Maybe I shouldn't bring this up," he said, looking serious, "but I've been doing some research."

"About what?" Judith asked. "Your studies?"

"Not exactly. It's more about what's going on here." Barry's gaze shifted to Renie. "That book your husband wanted—*Kommandant Killer: Hitler's Avenging Angel.* The fact that Jessi discovered it had been deleted made me curious. Even if a book's out of print, there's often a link to used booksellers. The more I thought about it, the more intrigued I got. I'm not focusing on the Nazi era for my thesis, but I have to know as much as I can about

German history to understand what came before and after the Thirty Years' War. Germany's only been a nation for a little over a hundred years."

"Bismarck," Renie said. "There was a girl in my high school history class who insisted his name was Otto von Bisquick. I tried to correct her after class, but I gave up. She thought he shouldn't be called the Iron Chancellor because he was only half-baked."

"Coz," Judith said with a withering glance, "there are times when your knowledge of history is best kept under wraps. Let Barry continue."

"Phooey on you," Renie muttered. "Spoilsport. History's fun."

To Judith's dismay, Barry was smiling. "She's right. If you focus on historical figures, it's just a lot of old gossip. Sure, politics and ideology and all the rest are important, but you have to understand that individuals put all those things into motion in the first place."

"Don't encourage my cousin," Judith warned as Suzie wordlessly delivered her son's pie à la mode before hurrying off again. "Go ahead, tell us about the Kommandant book."

Barry paused after tasting his pie. "Mmm. Good. The local baker turns out some really good stuff."

"Did you know he's the chief of police's brother?" Judith asked.

Barry frowned. "If I did, I forgot."

"Hey!" Renie cried, slapping at Judith's arm. "I didn't know that."

Judith couldn't resist looking smug. "Fat Matt's other brother is Bruno, the chef at Wolfgang's. They're all Herr Wessler's sons."

Renie punched Judith's upper arm. "Get out of here! You made that up!"

Barry, however, merely nodded. "That's true. Which kind of leads into what I was going to say about the book."

It was Judith's turn to look incredulous. "It does?"

"It sounds strange," he admitted, putting down his fork, "and bear in mind I read that book three, four years ago in the original German. It wasn't what you'd think from the title."

Renie frowned. "That book isn't about a concentration camp or a battle? Bill must be slipping."

"Kommandant's a military title," Barry said, pausing to make sure no one else could hear him. "You've probably read books or seen movies about Hitler clones. Fiction, of course, but there were rumors all over Germany and elsewhere that the phenomenon was real. The book in question was about a German officer who was no fan of the Führer, but loyal to his fatherland. Thus, after the war, he wanted to avenge himself on Hitler by populating the world with good people." Barry stopped again, either for effect or to take up his fork and eat more pie.

Renie wrinkled her nose. "You mean this is a feel-good read? My husband's a psychologist. He can only bond with nut jobs." She swiveled around to glare at her cousin. "Don't you dare say it!"

Judith's dark eyes widened in feigned innocence. "Say what?"

Renie didn't respond.

"So," Judith said to Barry, "to cut to the chase, Herr Wessler was this Kommandant?"

Barry shook his head. "The guy's name was Gerbald Wulff." Barry spelled it out for the cousins. "He was a Prussian, from Konitz. But it does make me wonder."

Judith wondered, too. "Have you mentioned this to your mother?"

"No," Barry replied. "I didn't think too much about the title at first because I remembered the book in German. It was only this morning that I began to get curious. Jessi agreed it was all very strange."

"Very," Judith murmured. "But it could be a coincidence."

Barry waited to swallow some of his ice cream. "How so? That the book is unavailable? That Herr Wessler seems to have fathered a large chunk of Little Bavaria's population? That he's been murdered?"

"All of those things," Judith said. She turned to Renie. "Do you know why Bill was so anxious to get that particular book?"

Renie frowned. "No. I just assumed it was the usual nasty Nazi horror story. Being a shrink, Bill likes to study the better side of Germans during the war. He's fascinated by people like Maximilian Kolbe and Dietrich Bonhoeffer, especially their spiritual aura."

Barry nodded. "This book would fall into that category. Gerbald Wulff was a religious man. Lutheran, in fact."

"Wessler's Catholic," Judith said. "The idea of any connection between him and Wulff is probably far-fetched. The book's non-availability is curious, but may mean nothing. Can Jessi call one of the big chains to see if they can order it? If not, that'd eliminate any notion about it being tied into what's going on here in Little Bavaria."

"Good idea," Barry said. "I'll ask her." He finished his pie and sighed. "We'd better vacate this booth for the paying customers." He glanced at Judith's plate and looked embarrassed. "You're not finished."

"No problem," Judith assured him. "This Reuben is huge. I'll save the other half for later. The rest of the potato salad, too."

Renie sighed. "Coz likes to do that. It's her way of dieting. It'll take her the rest of the weekend to finish it."

Five minutes later, they were out on the busy main street. The clouds had begun to lift and the wind had died down. Maybe, Judith thought, the sun would shine after all.

Barry was gazing down the street at the clock tower. "It's still the noon hour," he said. "I won't bother Jessi now. That's always her busiest time. Heck, it's always busy with Oktoberfest."

"Don't," Renie said, getting out her cell. "Coz thinks I'm an idiot, but I can phone a bookstore. I'll move away from the street noise."

Judith was juggling her purse and the box that Suzie had provided for the leftovers when she spotted Klara Wessler coming down the street with the two dogs. "Oh, no! They'll go for my sandwich!"

Barry laughed. "I'll make sure they don't. Hi, Klara. Are you singing again tonight?"

"Yes," she said, straining at the leashes. "If I don't collapse from walking these beasts." She nodded vaguely at Judith. "I wish Franz would take them to California. I know so little about animals. They miss Dietrich and cannot understand why he isn't at home."

Barry reached down to pat each of the dogs. "Can't you find someone here who would take them?"

Klara shook her head. "No. And Mrs. Crump—the cleaning person—complains all the time about them now. She wouldn't dare when Dietrich was alive." Tears glinted in her eyes. "It is all so sad."

Barry shifted from one foot to the other. "I haven't yet decided when to head back to Europe. Maybe I'll stay on for the funeral."

Klara nodded. "That would be very kind. It will be . . . difficult."

The dogs had pulled Klara closer to Judith. They were definitely on the scent of her Reuben. She backed away—into a lamppost. The impact was slight, but she dropped the container. The dogs pounced.

"Oh!" Klara cried, tugging at the leashes. "Stop! No, no!"

Her commands proved fruitless. The dogs gobbled the sandwich and most of the potato salad before Barry could grab the miscreants by their collars and pull them away.

Klara stared helplessly at Judith. "I'm so sorry. Really," she said, relinquishing the leashes to Barry. "Have we met? You look familiar."

Renie had returned from making her call. "Yeah," she snarled. "The last time your furry friends tried to ruin my cashmere sweater."

Klara clapped her hands to cheeks that had turned pale from Renie's onslaught. "I . . . feel . . . ill," she gasped.

Barry intervened again. "Klara, I'll walk you and the dogs home."

"Oh . . . please! Thank you!" She fastened on to Barry's free arm.

"Later," Barry called as they headed toward the corner.

Judith was seething. "I don't know if I'm madder at you or Klara."

"Maybe it's a dead heat," Renie said calmly, picking up the residue from her cousin's leftovers and taking them to a garbage bin by the lamppost. "I wish I liked dogs better. I prefer bunnies. Clarence is so adorable with his lop ears and twitchy whiskers. When I dress him in his sparkly tutu . . ." She stopped, staring at Judith. "Now what?"

Her anger evaporating, Judith squared her broad shoulders. "You said it—*dead*. Come on, coz, we're going to the cemetery."

# Chapter Twelve

**W**here *is* the cemetery?" Renie asked, looking around as if she could discover tombstones and monuments somewhere between the *Fachwerk* of the Bavarian half-timbered buildings. Instead, the only sign of the dead were some Halloween goblins in the window of a crafts shop across the street.

"We'll ask Suzie," Judith said, heading back to the restaurant.

Suzie was still hustling. "The cemetery?" she said, barely pausing as she juggled plates of food. "You have to drive. First turnoff by the high school, quarter of a mile north. Got a car?"

"No," Judith replied.

"Take mine," Suzie said. "Green Ford Escort, parked out back. Keys are in my purse on the desk in the office. I'm not going anywhere."

Before Judith could ask where the office was located, Suzie was out of earshot with her lunch orders.

"It can't be hard to find," Renie said. "Maybe near the kitchen?"

Judith had already moved in that direction. "There's a door. My God, Suzie's a trusting soul."

Renie shrugged as they circumvented tables where customers chatted between mouthfuls of Suzie's servings. "Small-town people are more trusting. Except when they get killed, of course."

"She doesn't even know us," Judith countered, opening the door to what proved to be a small, cluttered office.

"We probably got a good word from Barry," Renie said. "You intend to search her wallet for clues to Bob Stafford's murder?"

Judith found the key ring on top of the other items in the no-nonsense black handbag. "Even I wouldn't be that crass."

"Yes, you would," Renie retorted, "but if we're in a rush, I don't know why. The people in the cemetery aren't going anywhere."

Suzie paid no attention when the cousins came out of the office. She was taking an order from Eleanor and Delmar Denkel, who both wore persnickety expressions. Suzie remained stoic, even as Ellie shook her head and Delmar peered at the menu as if looking for typos.

"What a pair of pills," Renie muttered after the cousins were outside and walking around to the back of the restaurant. "Even Inbred Heffalump can't be that big a pain in the butt."

"That depends upon your point of view," Judith said, "not to mention the size of Ingrid's butt. Ample does not begin to describe it."

"Wow—you really don't like her, do you?"

Judith had spotted the Ford Escort parked on the grass outside of the building. She couldn't help but pause to take in the view. The river's white riffles glinted in the autumn sun. On the opposite bank, with their orange leaves and black bark, the poplar trees seemed dressed for Halloween. Her eyes lifted to the great swath of evergreens, a third stand of timber, judging from their size. Farther up she saw the bare mountain ridge where new snow had not yet fallen. Despite the busy main street not more than fifty yards away, the only sound she heard was the whistle of a freight train as it passed through the north side of town.

"Gorgeous setting," she murmured at last. "Darn. I forgot to ask Barry or Suzie about that marker along the trail. They must know what or who it stands for. It's on their property."

"HRH? Gee, you're losing your grip. You must be tired. Slow down. You're pushing it."

They reached the Ford Escort. "Oh!" Judith exclaimed after the cousins were in the car. "I forgot to ask where the high school is located."

"I saw a sign from the shuttle," Renie said. "It's at the east end of town. Take a right out of the parking lot."

Judith had to wait for both vehicles and pedestrians to get out of the way. On this Saturday of Oktoberfest, Little Bavaria seemed as busy as a big city. At last she made the turn, though the going was slow.

"Hey," she said, keeping her foot on the brake, "what did you hear from the bookstore about the *Kommandant* availability?"

Renie shook her head. "I called the shop on Heraldsgate Hill, but they were busy during the lunch hour. I'll ring back later."

"Maybe it's just a glitch," Judith said, picking up a bit of speed. "It doesn't sound as if Wessler and the Kommandant are one and the same."

Renie agreed.

They'd reached the high school. On a Saturday afternoon, the playing field had been turned into a staging area for the Oktoberfest performers. Judith glimpsed horse-drawn carts, musicians with brass instruments, a woman untangling puppet strings, and two medieval court jesters practicing their swings at each other with giant bratwursts. She also spotted Barry and Klara walking the Saint Bernards up the hill. "Wessler's house must be around here," Judith remarked. "I wonder if it looks like a sixteenth-century *Schloss*."

"Probably," Renie said.

But just ahead of them on their right, the cousins saw a large brick-and-glass contemporary home perched on a hill. Only the mailbox by the road was built in the shape of a Bavarian half-timbered house. The name on it was Dietrich Wessler.

Renie laughed. "I suppose Herr Wessler had that house built before the town went Bavarian."

"I'm afraid so," Judith said, following the road that now was flanked more by forest than by civilization. She all but stopped at the train tracks to make sure they were clear. "Kind of disappointing. I expected something grander for the town *Vater.*"

"Circa the 1950s or even later. Not bad for that period, though."

"Not ostentatious either," Judith said, noting that they were now in the forest. "I wonder how far this is from . . . ah! There's the cemetery. The ground levels out here. It's a lovely woodland setting."

"Too bad the people buried here can't enjoy it," Renie remarked as Judith pulled onto the gravel road. "That view part in their advertising probably doesn't mean much to the folks who aren't coming back."

"Don't be a ghoul."

"Hey—I don't even know why we're here."

"Because," Judith said, opening the driver's door, "I want to see if Wessler's wife is buried here. He certainly had a lot of girlfriends."

"You couldn't just ask?" Renie said, before getting out of the car.

Judith waited to respond until they were both standing on the gravel road. "I get tired of asking questions sometimes," she admitted. "Besides, cemeteries are interesting." She paused, looking around at the large clearing, but not seeing any older tombstones or monuments. "Odd—this place looks like it hasn't been around very long. I wonder if it dates from when the town went Bavarian. Maybe they buried their dead in the next big town to the east. There's nothing much on the other side of the pass for at least thirty miles."

The clear mountain air was tinged with the scent of damp earth and evergreen trees. Judith took a deep breath before stopping at the first grave. "Mueller—husband and wife. He died in 1992. She lasted only two more years without him."

Renie scowled. "Hey, I can read."

"Sorry." Judith kept moving, but stopped when she saw signs of a new grave up ahead on a gentle slope. "Let's see if that's for Wessler."

"Wow! That might be a clue!"

"I should've left you back at the Pancake Schloss with the Denkels." Judith quickened her step, but the uneven gravel threw her off balance. "Oof!" she gasped, fearful of dislocating her artificial hip.

Renie was accustomed to such minor threats and reflexively grabbed her cousin's arm. "Now aren't you glad I came along?"

Judith's expression was sheepish. "Yes—unless you pushed me."

"Right. I just love those trips with you to the ER."

Judith stopped abruptly. "Look—here's Bob Stafford's grave."

Renie stared at the simple but handsome marker. "Gosh. He'd just turned fifty-three. Poor guy."

Judith nodded. "I sure haven't gotten anywhere with his homicide. Maybe it was some bum off the trains that go through here."

Renie gave her cousin a quirky look. "That'd be too simple. Senseless random killings aren't your style. You need motives, histories, relationships, all the things that your vaunted logic can deal with."

"Coz," Judith said forlornly, "I don't know zip about Bob Stafford except the basics. I haven't had a chance to discuss him with Barry."

"You will," Renie said as they moved on.

The cousins solemnly approached the newly turned earth at the foot of the slope. Maybe it was inspired by the praying angels on each side of a marble marker. Maybe it was the thought of Dietrich Wessler, who would be lowered into the open grave in a matter of days. Maybe it was the blank space left for the *Grossvater* beside the name of Julia Monika Wessler, b. July 11, 1917; d. December 24, 1953.

"You do the math," Renie murmured.

Judith calculated quickly. "She was only thirty-six when she died on Christmas Eve. I wonder what happened to her."

Renie had turned away to look down at a smaller marker. "Maybe this is part of the explanation."

"Oh, my." Judith read the inscription aloud in a melancholy

tone. "Anna Maria Wessler, b. June 3, 1953, d. Dec. 24, 1953. An accident involving mother and daughter? Or an illness?"

Renie grimaced. "Either way, it's awful."

"We should pray." Judith crossed herself, but didn't dare kneel. A faint breeze stirred the fir and hemlock trees, as if sighing for the departed souls.

"Over fifty years ago," Renie noted. "Someone must know what happened. How about Chief Duomo?"

Judith hesitated. "I figure him for about fifty, maybe a bit older."

"He'd still know," Renie pointed out. "Given Wessler's notoriety, a lot of people would even if they weren't around then."

"True." Judith gazed at an adjacent concrete slab set in the ground. "Josef Wessler, born August 12, 1947, died March 22, 1989. I wonder if that's Franz's brother. Look at this green marble stone below Dietrich Wessler's plot. Clotilde Elisabeth Wessler, also born in 1947 and died in 2003. I wonder if she was Josef's widow."

Renie came over to stand by Judith. "Looks to me as if Dietrich—assuming he was in charge of the burials—didn't like Joe as much as he liked Clotilde. Is your brain going in frantic circles?"

Judith made a face. "I can't help it. Franz doesn't seem too fond of his father. I wonder if after Josef died, Dietrich made a play for Clotilde?"

"Could we call her Tilly?" Renie asked in a plaintive voice. "Clotilde sounds kind of . . . formidable. Oh, I know there's a saint by that name, but still . . ." She zipped up her purple car coat as the wind grew stronger, causing the smaller evergreens to sway.

"You can call her anything you want. I'd like to know what Herr Wessler called her. Love muffin, maybe?"

"Which Herr Wessler? Josef or Dietrich?"

Judith pulled up her hood. "Good question."

They started back down the path, but were startled when an elderly woman suddenly popped up from behind a granite tombstone. "Excuse me," she said with a slight accent. "Could you help me with my vase? It's stuck in the ground."

"Let me," Renie said. "My cousin doesn't bend very well."

Judith followed Renie. The white marble bore the inscription Helmut Bauer, born 1922, died 1989. There was a vacant space for Astrid, presumably his widow and the old lady who had a bouquet of gold chrysanthemums at her feet. "My husband," she said simply.

It took Renie only a couple of tugs to loosen the vase. "I saw a faucet by the path," she said, standing up. "I'll fill this for you."

Mrs. Bauer looked at Judith through gold-rimmed glasses. "Your cousin is very kind."

"Yes, she can be. I mean, she is. Your husband was fairly young when he passed away."

The old lady nodded. "He died of grief."

For once, Judith was at a loss for words. "I'm so sorry."

Mrs. Bauer made a slashing motion with her gloved hand. "He had no reason to be ashamed! He was an innocent man, a good man."

Renie returned with the water-filled vase. "May I?" she said, gesturing at the mums.

"Oh, please," Mrs. Bauer said. "Thank you."

Judith finally found her voice. "Was he the victim of slander?"

"Yes, how did you know?" Her eyes narrowed with suspicion.

"I didn't. But if someone is innocent, then it indicates that lies have been told. In a small town, people gossip. That's often tragic."

Mrs. Bauer looked away. "So it was. Evil walks in disguise."

Renie had finished arranging the flowers. "Your husband was German?" She saw Mrs. Bauer nod. "But you're . . . ?"

"Swedish," the old lady said. "How did you know?"

"Your accent," Renie said. "And Astrid is more Scandinavian."

"Kind and clever," Mrs. Bauer murmured. "Thank you again."

Renie darted Judith a smug glance. "Can we give you a ride?"

"No," Mrs. Bauer said with a little smile. "I must say my prayers. I live not far away. I need to walk to keep my joints from growing stiff."

"Very wise," Renie said. "Take care."

The old lady offered more thanks before the cousins returned to the path and got into the car. "I wonder," Judith said, "if the town hall's open on Saturday."

"Dubious. Try reviving your lock-picking skills from when you used them to learn what financial crises Dan was hiding from you."

Judith shook her head. "How did I survive those years?"

"You had extraordinary patience or you'd have bumped off Dan long before he blew up—as you so indelicately put his demise."

"It beats explaining his diabetic condition." Judith slowed as they passed the Wessler house. "Klara has a gentleman caller at the door."

Renie looked out her window. "Franz. Why not? He *is* her ex."

"True. I doubt Suzie would mind if we drove to the town hall. I'm not used to walking on pavement this much. It wears me down."

Renie checked her watch. "It's only one-thirty. As Suzie said, she's not going anywhere. We, however, are."

"Good point."

As they approached the high school, traffic once again came to a virtual halt. A crowd had formed on both sides of the playing field. Lanes had been outlined in chalk, apparently for some kind of race. Judith didn't dare take her eyes off of the pickup ahead of her lest she rear-end the vehicle. "What is it? A beer-barrel race?"

Renie laughed. "It's a dozen dachshunds, wearing Bavarian hats and waiting to run a fifty-yard dash."

Judith laughed, too. "I don't remember that event, but there are so many on the list. We missed the keg-tapping for the festival opening."

"Isn't that where some local bigwig shouts *'O'zapft is'*? Or however you say 'let's get wasted' in German?"

"Probably," Judith said, inching forward.

"And there they go!" Renie shouted.

The pickup gained some speed. Judith had to move on to keep from getting Suzie's car hit by the SUV behind her. "I hope the dogs know when to stop or they might become Wiener schnitzel."

Turning onto the main street, Judith and the cars in front of her were forced to come to a dead halt. At least forty or more young people were dancing, singing, and forming conga lines. The unruly crowd appeared to be headed for the beer garden.

"I think they've already had enough for this early in the day," Judith said, looking dismayed. "College kids, I suspect."

"I thought the beer garden was open only in the evening," Renie said as a couple of young men waved to her on the passenger-side window. In retaliation, she made an obscene gesture. Laughing good-naturedly, the pair returned the favor and moved on. "Jack-asses," Renie muttered. "They'll regret it when they're puking up their innards."

"I'll regret it if we don't get out of this mob. Where's crowd control? Is Fat Matt sitting on his rear end having a midafternoon snack?"

"Drive up on the sidewalk and turn the corner. All the pedestrians seem to be in the street."

Judith was aghast. "I can't do that! I'll get arrested."

"By who? I don't see any cops. For all we know, they're dancing with the college kids. Gun it."

"Oh, for . . ." But Judith didn't have much choice as a roaring group of young sots began jumping on the cars in front of them. "Hang on!"

She turned the wheel with all her might, barely missing the pickup that was still in front her. It was just in time. A couple of girls and a trio of boys climbed onto the back of the truck, shrieking with glee. With a jolt, the Ford Escort mounted the curb to reach the sidewalk. Seeing no one in front of her in the thirty-odd feet ahead, Judith hit the gas, slowing only at the corner. Taking a right, she gently let the car slip onto the street where stragglers from the raucous crowd were catching their breath. Looking surprised, they scurried to get out of the way.

"That," Judith declared, easing off the gas, "is the nuttiest driving I've done since Mike missed the school bus and I had to pick him up before the Thurlow neighborhood hookers started pestering him."

"Gee, he was twelve," Renie said. "You were a really overprotective mom. Hey, I think I left my nerves back in the street."

"This was your idea," Judith reminded her.

"I've had worse ones, but I can't remember when. Going this way we'll end up in back of the town hall by the police station."

"I'd rather not get arrested for breaking and entering."

"Are you kidding? If the cops aren't out controlling that riot on the main drag, they're probably asleep under a pile of pastry."

"The action is behind us. It's almost deserted here."

"Everybody's having fun. I'm not sure I am."

"You'd prefer joining The Young and The Loutish?" Judith inquired, noticing only one squad car parked by headquarters.

"No!" Renie exclaimed. "I'm not sure I was ever *that* young."

Judith pulled up at the rear of the town hall. "Should we check the front to see if they might be open?"

"Doesn't that ruin your fun? On the other hand, we might get crushed by the mob that may have spread to that part of town."

Judith considered their options. "You're right. Besides, we probably can't park on the main street. Let's try the easy way."

The cousins got out of the car, making a quick surveillance of the side street, which appeared relatively deserted. The only living creatures they could see were a pair of crows teetering on a nearby power line.

"Locked," Judith announced as she tried the brass knob. "Okay, let's see if I can remember how to do this." She rummaged in her purse and found a paper clip, which she twisted into a single long wire. "You bend better than I do," she said to Renie. "Listen for a click. But keep one eye on the street."

"If I do that, I'll be wall-eyed."

"Shut up. Just do it."

Judith poked, twisted, jiggled, and turned. The only thing she heard besides the faint roar of the crowd and a couple of brass horns from the other street was Renie yawning. "Cut it out," Judith snapped.

"Here," said a male voice right behind her. "You need a key?"

Judith almost dropped the makeshift wire. "Major Schwartz! I didn't hear you yawn. I mean, I thought it was . . ."

The sleepy-eyed policeman nudged her aside and inserted a key. "The chief thought you might need help. We're headed out to bust some drunken kids. Can't they learn in college how to hold their liquor? Why pay tuition just to study?" He pushed the door open. "I assume you're sleuthing. Good luck." He sauntered off to the patrol car.

"Well!" Judith exclaimed under her breath. "That was lucky! Didn't you see him coming?"

"Sure," Renie replied as they entered a small hall that led to another door. "But you told me to be quiet. Anyway, I thought Ernie was sleepwalking. Look, there goes the boar."

Judith saw the man—or woman—in the boar suit chasing some laughing children down the side street in the next block. She suddenly shivered. "That thing creeps me out."

"Why? He's just another boring boar."

Judith forced a smile. "I know. But for some reason I had this sudden thought—about the Dead walking. Stupid, huh?"

Renie shrugged, but didn't comment.

# Chapter Thirteen

The cousins found themselves in the main hall, where the previous night's festivities had been held. They went out through the front, where a list of the town's departments was carved into a wooden cedar slab on the wall. Public records were in room three across the lobby.

The pine-paneled room wasn't much bigger than Judith's dining room. "I keep forgetting how small this town is," she said. "I suppose we should start with deaths."

"Why don't you do deaths while I do births?" Renie suggested.

"Good plan." Judith found the filing cabinet containing deaths right next to births.

"They can computerize this," Renie said, opening the top drawer.

"Maybe it's part of the old-world atmosphere," Judith said, trying to figure out if she should go by date or name. The filing system didn't seem to be in any particular order. "How are you doing with births?"

"Okay," Renie replied, "except for the three I birthed always being broke. Why?"

"I mean these records," Judith said, trying not to sound impatient.

"Oh. They're in chronological order so far. The most recent

one was born September nineteenth, a boy. That must be Suzie's waitress's kid. Remember—she's short a couple of servers."

"Right," Judith murmured. "But, to quote your dad, these files look like a bear with a crosscut saw went through them. There doesn't seem to be any order or sequence."

Renie leaned against the open drawer of her filing cabinet. "You're theorizing that somebody's gone through these files in a hurry or they want to stymie a snoop like you?"

"Yes, it might be one or the other, or both." Judith tapped the top of the cabinet with her nails. "Why? And when?"

"Rhetorical or serious question?"

"The latter. Wessler's certificate isn't here because the cause of death hasn't been officially determined. Even if Doc Frolander has finished the autopsy report, it won't be filed until Monday. I'm starting with his wife and child." Judith sighed. "The top-drawer records seem random by date and initials of last names."

"Maybe I should help you with dead people," Renie said. "I don't see how births matter so much in terms of satisfying your curiosity."

"Okay. Let's each pull out a drawer and sit down at the desk. There are two chairs, so we might as well be comfortable."

Fifteen minutes later, the cousins hadn't found anything remotely pertinent to the Wessler family—or to anyone else whose name they recognized. Renie, in fact, had found several nondeath certificates in the drawer she was perusing.

"I've seen at least a half-dozen divorces and twice that many marriage licenses," she said in exasperation. "Can't these people file things in their proper places?"

"Maybe the town clerk is another one of Herr Wessler's kids."

Renie paused, one arm draped over the filing cabinet on the desk. "It's sick," she declared. "All of this Wessler offspring stuff could lead to inbreeding like some of those Appalachian enclaves where everybody is related to everybody else and they all turn out weird."

Judith considered her cousin's words. "Well . . . not at this point. It's no secret when it comes to the locals acknowledging Herr Wessler's paternity. From what Chief Duomo told me, there are probably only a few of his illegitimate kids still around here. Now that he's dead, I assume there aren't any more on the way. Most of the people Fat Matt talked about are middle-aged."

"Given Wessler's vigor and good health," Renie said, flipping through more files, "I'm surprised there aren't dozens. Speaking of youth, small-town people marry young. I've just come across two certificates for teenagers. Guess there wasn't much to do before they went Bavarian."

"That's generally true of small towns, or at least it used to be," Judith agreed. "You're right, their system is really . . . hey," she said, turning to Renie, "what year was that? The teenage marriages, I mean?"

"Years," Renie corrected after going back to look at the marriage documents. "One was in 1980 and the other was"—she grinned— "in 1985. Groom's name was Albert Edward Plebuck and the bride's name was Eleanor Jean Wessler. How did I miss that the first time? I must've been too caught up in their ages."

Judith was smiling. "Well, well. Ellie's secret past. Whatever happened to Plebuck?"

"Should we search for a divorce?"

"Fat Matt told me she moved away right after high school. He didn't say she got married first. Maybe they eloped and left town."

Renie shook her head in mock dismay. "I don't know what the first husband looked like, but if Delmar Denkel is an improvement, then I marvel that Plebuck was ever allowed to cross the county line. Do the Denkels have children? I mean the kind that they don't have to hide in a root cellar because they're really terrifying?"

"I don't really know Ellie. Which is good—until now."

"You're considering another motive for murder by Ellie?"

"No, nothing like that. Do you see a phone book anywhere?"

Renie gazed around, came up empty, and started opening drawers in the desk. "Here's one. It's tiny. What am I searching for? Plebuck?"

"Right. He must've had parents."

"One would hope so . . ." Renie scanned the listings. "No Plebucks."

"Maybe they're in the cemetery," Judith said, tapping a pencil on the desk in an effort to ward off chewing her fingernails. "It probably doesn't mean anything. Let's keep looking for those death certificates." A sudden thought occurred to her. "If Ellie's maiden name is Wessler, where's the third brother? She's in her forties. Franz is younger than Josef, who apparently had no children. I don't get it. Even if Josef had kids who moved away, who is that third brother? We haven't come across any offspring of his."

Renie shrugged. "Then the unknown brother is Ellie's father."

"We'll ask Duomo," Judith said.

The cousins worked in silence until they heard the clock tower chime two. Judith finally found something of interest. "Ah! Bob Stafford's death certificate!"

"I didn't know we were looking for Bob," Renie said.

"It's sort of a bonus." Judith frowned. "Nothing we didn't already know. Blow to the head by person or persons unknown. Death placed between two P.M. and four P.M. on Friday, August nineteenth, 2005."

"That's it?" Renie asked.

Judith didn't answer right away. "Just attached notes from Doc Frolander's autopsy. Frankie Duomo was going fishing when he found the body around seven P.M. Frankie's the baker in the family. Initial reaction was that Bob had drowned . . . autopsy proved otherwise. Keep searching."

Renie heaved a sigh. "If I must. The divorce file is thin. I don't see anybody interesting. Mostly default decrees. 'De fault' of which spouse?"

Judith ignored the comment. Another five minutes passed before she hit pay dirt. "Here's Josef Wessler's death certificate."

She frowned. "He died from complications of a fall off the balcony of Hanover Haus, of which he was the owner. That's our inn."

"Our in to what?"

"The B&B where we're . . . you know damned well what I mean."

Renie shrugged. "Sure, but so what? The Wessler family's a big deal around here. Why shouldn't Dietrich's son own a local hostelry?"

"He wasn't very old when he died."

"You think he was pushed? Of course you'd think that."

"Okay, so I let my imagination run away with me," Judith conceded. "Still, I'm going to take another look at that balcony."

"I could push you and see what happens."

Judith shot Renie a dark glance. "Just keep searching."

Only a couple of minutes passed before Judith found Julia and Anna Wessler's death certificates. "Oh, no! They both drowned!"

Renie stared. "On Christmas Eve day? That's awful!"

Judith nodded absently as she read what few details were in the document. "The river might've flooded, if a sudden warming spell melted the mountain snow-pack. But why would a mother take her baby to the river in that kind of a situation? Some kind of weird flash flood?"

"We rarely have those around here," Renie said. "That's usually triggered by a dam bursting or someone using dynamite improperly."

Judith nodded. "Which makes this sound suspicious. I wonder who runs the local newspaper?"

Renie's shoulders sagged. "Gee—just when I thought *this* was tedious. What about the other Mrs. Wessler? Do we need to find her death certificate or assume she died of natural causes, like a runaway roller coaster or trampled by a herd of giant tortoises?"

"As long as we've gone this far, we might as well check Clotilde," Judith said. "And yes, I'll humor you. I think Clotilde is a classy name."

"You would," Renie mumbled, flipping through more documents. "Didn't you want to name Mike 'Balthasar'?"

"I did not," Judith replied indignantly. "It was 'Melchior.'"

"I knew it was one of the Three Wise Men. Why not 'Casper'? And if they were so wise, how come they didn't have better names? You know—like 'Tom,' 'Dick,' and 'Harry' or 'Groucho,' 'Harpo,' and 'Zeppo'?"

"I wish you'd been named 'Harpo,'" Judith said. "Then I wouldn't have to listen to you jabber."

Renie scowled. "I'm trying to liven things up."

"You aren't. Ta-da!" Judith cried, holding up a sheet of paper. "Perseverance. I found Clotilde."

Renie made a lethargic "yippee" motion with one finger. "I'm thrilled," she murmured. "Who done her in?"

Judith scanned the certificate. "Ovarian cancer. She died at home, not in the hospital. Home was . . . Hanover Haus. She must have taken over running it after Josef died."

"Family quarters downstairs? They'd have room since the lobby's small. Do you know where the bridal suite is?"

Judith shook her head. "Judging from the layout, it may be on the main floor, too. Maybe it was originally part of where Josef and Clotilde lived. Franz would know, of course."

"Ah! Guess who I found? Henry Rupert Hellman, suicide, born 1919, died 1979." Renie waited for Judith's reaction.

"The marker by the river," she said in wonder. "So is he buried there instead of in the cemetery because he killed himself?"

"Maybe, maybe not," Renie said. "Henry's suicide probably wouldn't have prevented him from being buried there, though I don't recall when the Church stopped banning people who offed themselves."

"I don't either," Judith murmured. "But why bury him by the river? Unless he did it by drowning."

"That wouldn't be as easy as you'd think," Renie said. "If the river's high enough, you get swept off your feet. Then you'd flop around and bump into rocks and fallen branches and make a big mess. It'd be way too much of a bother. Wet, too. You might catch cold."

Judith's shoulders slumped. "Your logic is so weird."

"My logic may not be as logical as yours, but it works for me." Renie began straightening the files in the drawer she'd been searching. "If the guy shot himself at home, they couldn't put him in the armoire. Can we get a snack or do we have to visit the weekly *Blatt?*"

"The newspaper can't be far from here," Judith said, tidying up her own portion of documents. "I'm kind of hungry, too, but at least we can find out where the paper is located while we still have Suzie's car."

"Too bad those dogs ate your leftovers," Renie said, shoving her drawer back into the filing cabinet. "Here, I'll put yours back, too."

"Thanks." Judith stood up, moving this way and that to work out the kinks in her neck, shoulders, and back. "I have to admit those other drowning deaths bother me."

"For once, I don't blame you," Renie said, putting on her jacket.

"That's why I'd like to see the back issues." Judith paused to make sure they'd left everything in good order. "It's so tragic."

Renie opened the first door and led the way to the outside entrance. "I wonder if they had a newspaper before the town became Little Bavaria, USA."

"I never thought of that," Judith said as they stepped onto the sidewalk. "They must have had . . . hey, where's the car?"

"You mean the one you parked in the no-parking zone?

*"What?"*

"Didn't you see the sign?"

Judith was flabbergasted. "I see it *now.* Why didn't you tell me?"

"I didn't realize you were blind," Renie said. "I thought you figured the cops would let you get away with it. I guess Schwartz didn't realize the Ford Escort was driven by you."

"Ohhh . . ." Judith stared across the street at the police station. "Somebody must be on duty." She paused, trying to hear if any noise was coming from the main street. "It's quiet around here. Let's see if Fat Matt is back from arresting a few dozen unruly beer-crazed kids."

"Where would he put them?" Renie asked as they crossed the street. "He can't have very many cells."

"I don't care if he put them in a bus and drove them across the county line. What do we tell Suzie if we can't get the car back?"

"You could tell her the truth," Renie said. "I know it's not your style, but just for once . . ." She shrugged as they entered the station.

To Judith's surprise, a redheaded young woman in uniform was behind the reception counter. "Yes?" she said in a brisk tone.

"You're . . ." Judith stopped. The officer wasn't wearing a nametag.

"I'm on loan," the officer responded. "The local police force is shorthanded during Oktoberfest. Shegogan County asked me to fill in. Double overtime. Why not?" She shrugged. "Call me Kitt, with two *t*'s."

"Okay," Judith said. "Here's the problem, Kitt. Our car has been towed from behind the town hall. That is, it's not *our* car, but we—"

"Right," Kitt interrupted. "I had it towed. You were in a no-parking zone. What did you expect? Or did you steal the car?"

"No," Judith said indignantly. "A friend let us borrow it. The car belongs to Suzie Stafford, who owns the Pancake Schloss."

Kitt's gray eyes were as chilly as snow clouds. "So? If you want it back, pay two hundred bucks cash and get it out of impound. I don't like pancakes."

"Two hundred cash?" Judith exclaimed. "I don't have that much on me." She turned to Renie. "Do you?"

"No," Renie said. "I wouldn't give ten cents to somebody who didn't like pancakes." She glared at Kitt. "What's wrong with you? People who don't like pancakes aren't normal."

"Watch it," Kitt said calmly. "You want to spend the night in a cell? This Fat Matt guy doesn't serve pancakes for breakfast."

Renie looked thoughtful. "What does he serve? I had pancakes this morning. I might enjoy a change."

"That," Kitt said coldly, "can be arranged."

"How about French toast or a nice omelet or——"

"Coz!" Judith exclaimed. "Shut up! We'll go to a cash machine."

Renie made a face. "You can't get an omelet from a cash machine."

Judith grabbed Renie, hauling her to the door. "We'll be back," she called to Kitt.

The officer didn't bother to look at the cousins. "Whatev'."

"One of these days," Judith said when they got outside, "you're going to get us into serious trouble."

"I'm not the one who parked in a no-parking zone."

"You should have told me!"

"Hey——you talk about serious trouble? How about all the times we've almost gotten ourselves killed because you were trying to finger who whacked whoever."

"Of course not," Judith shot back, feeling the stiff wind sting her cheeks. "But I've never asked a cop for an omelet."

"What about Joe's Special special? He used to be a cop."

"That's different. He likes to cook sometimes." Judith noticed that the main street was fairly busy, but there were no drunken revelers in sight. There were no signs of the police either. "Where *is* a bank?"

"How do *I* know?" Renie snapped. "I'm not the one who parked . . . oh, here come Connie and George Beaulieu. Ask them."

Judith waved at the couple, who were crossing from the other side of the street. The Beaulieus didn't seem pleased to see the cousins, but stopped on the corner.

"The bank?" George echoed in response to Judith's query. "I don't think it's open on Saturdays."

"Oh, Judith," Connie said, making a feeble effort to look concerned, "have you run out of money already?"

"No. I need cash," Judith said, in less than her usual kindly tone.

"Cash, eh?" George stroked his handlebar mustache. "That sounds odd. Everyone here seems to take credit or debit cards. Or have you exceeded your limits? Budget, that's the secret. I always tell Connie before we leave the house that we must first make a strict budget and keep to it. Very prudent approach."

Connie squeezed George's arm. "My husband is so practical. But of course he has to be, since he's a government agent."

"He is?" Judith asked in surprise. "What branch of government?"

"Now, Judith," Connie said, "you should know better than to ask that question. Let's just say his work is . . . covert."

George nodded. "Yes, deep cover, underground, you might say."

"How interesting," Judith remarked without enthusiasm. "Does that mean you might know where the bank is?"

The Beaulieus looked at each other questioningly. Finally George spoke. "I think it's a block or so west of the town hall on the same side of the street."

"Yes," Connie agreed. "George is right. Of course. It's next to the newspaper office. I had to go in there—the newspaper office, I mean—day before yesterday because they'd listed the wrong time for my innkeeping seminar this afternoon at four-thirty."

"You're giving a seminar?" Judith said in surprise. "I didn't know anyone from the state association was doing that."

Connie laughed. "It was Ingrid Heffelman's idea. She felt it would be excellent publicity to have someone like me tell not only prospective hostelry owners but guests what our business is all about. So sweet of her to choose little old me!"

"Yes," Judith murmured. *Ingrid* and *sweet* were two words she never expected to hear in the same sentence. "Good luck with that."

The Beaulieus had crossed to the other side of the main street. The cousins continued past the town hall just as the tower clock struck three. They reached the offices of the *Little Bavaria Blatt* first, but saw that it was closed.

"Drat," Judith said. "I'd hoped it'd be open. You think they'd be covering the Oktoberfest events."

"They probably are," Renie said, circumventing a trio of older people who had stopped to chat. "But if they publish midweek, they don't need to keep the office open. I assume they're probably taking photos and covering some of the bigger events. Hopefully, not Connie's seminar."

Judith sighed. "Sucking up to Ingrid. That galls me. You certainly were quiet when I talked to the Beaulieus."

"I was pretending they didn't exist."

"Good thinking. Here's the bank and there's the ATM. Damn. Forking out two hundred bucks wasn't in my budget. Even if I had one."

"We'll split it. I really should've mentioned the sign."

"You don't have to do that."

"No, but I will. I have my kindly moments. Quick, take advantage of this one. They never last long." ·

Judith smiled. "Thanks, coz. Let's hope this machine works."

Luckily, their transactions went off without a hitch. Five minutes later they were back at police headquarters, where Chief Duomo was engaged in a shouting match with Officer Kitt.

"You don't tow Suze's car! This is Little Bavaria, not some big, ritzy place like Lake Shegogan! Do you want to cut off my waffles?"

"How am I supposed to know who owns what car in this stinking little burg?" Kitt yelled back. "A no-parking zone means what it says where I come from! What kind of operation are you running here?"

"*My* kind," Duomo bellowed. "You don't know Jack about how law enforcement works in a small . . ." The chief suddenly noticed the cousins. "Hey there, FATSO, what's up?"

Judith winced, but decided she wanted Duomo as her ally. "Your extra help says I owe two hundred bucks for parking Suzie's car by the town-hall rear entrance."

"That's bull," Fat Matt declared, glowering at Kitt. "Hell, I could pay that fine out of petty cash for you or Suze." He turned back to the still-irate redhead. "Check the lockbox in that drawer and give the lady a couple of hundreds just for harassing her. She passed Go. Get it?"

"You get it," Kitt snarled. "It's your petty cash and I don't do charity when I'm on the job."

"Then do your job and go arrest somebody I don't like," the chief said. "Go on, hit the streets."

Kitt grabbed her jacket and hat, hurtled around the counter, and shot one last malevolent look at the cousins. "I should get triple overtime for this gig!"

"To be fair," Judith said, after Kitt made her exit, "I should've seen the sign. Were you serious about giving me the two hundred dollars?"

Duomo shrugged. "Guess not. I think there's only about thirty in petty cash. My idiot brother wants to start charging me for his pastries. Hey, what's family for?"

"Let's call it even," Judith said. "We still have our hunskies. What happened to the rioting young drunks?"

Duomo leaned against the counter. "We told 'em to take off. Where would I put a mob like that? Maybe they're walking out of town. They're too drunk to drive. Hell, they're too drunk to walk. If they try to flee justice, Orville and Ernie are waiting for them at each end of town. Maybe we could make some money off of that bunch. Anybody hungry?"

Renie raised her hand.

Duomo nodded. "I'll call that redhead and have her get something. Patrol's a waste of time during Oktoberfest. How 'bout some brats?"

Renie shook her head. "I don't like them. A burger and fries sound good, though."

"Sure," Duomo agreed. "I'll give the redhead a few minutes to cool off. Kind of a good-looker, though. Too bad she's so ornery."

"While we're waiting," Judith said, tired of propping herself up against the counter, "could we talk about some things my cousin and I found in the town records?"

Fat Matt shrugged. "Why not? Couldn't take you too long. The old town hall burned down years ago. Glad I wasn't the chief back then. They never did figure out who set the fire."

Judith stared at Duomo. "You mean it was arson?"

"So it seemed. Just as well it got torched. Wessler would've built a new one anyway to fit his plan for Little Bavaria. Follow me. Hernandez should show up any minute."

The chief's office smelled of cigars and Limburger cheese. Judith and Renie both made sure they weren't going to sit on any leftovers before seating themselves across from Duomo.

"We went to the cemetery this afternoon," Judith began. "We found the Wesslers' graves."

The chief yawned. "So? They haven't moved for quite a while."

Judith got to the point. "How did Wessler's wife and child drown?"

Fat Matt looked unmoved. "They fell in the river. Julia couldn't swim. Neither could the baby."

"Why," she persisted, "were they by the river on Christmas Eve?"

"How would I know? I wasn't born yet." Fat Matt took in Judith's irked expression and sighed. "It was during the day, not night."

"It seems odd," Judith persisted, "especially if the river was high."

"I don't know what the river was like," the chief said impatiently. "The story was she'd gone to get greens for decorations, slipped on a wet rock or something, and fell in. If she was carrying the kid, she probably couldn't let go to grab anything. It was a freaky thing. Nobody ever said anything different. Real sad, but those things happen."

Judith considered the explanation, which was credible, if not necessarily true. "How were they found?"

"Hell, I don't know." Duomo was opening drawers, maybe searching for something to eat. "I suppose Wessler went looking for them when they didn't show up. All I know is that it wasn't long after that he started having kids with other women. Guess he was making up for lost time or some damned thing."

"Why," Judith asked, leaning closer, "do you never call him 'Dad' or 'Papa' or whatever most people call their fathers?"

The chief shrugged. "Too confusing. With so many of us, a

half-dozen kids yelling for 'Dad' would've been kind of weird. Anybody could've called him that when I stop to think about it. Face it, Wessler was the town's father figure in more ways than one."

Judith nodded. "How did your father get along with his sons?"

"You mean the legit ones?" Duomo leaned back in his chair and gazed at the ceiling. "Oh . . . not sure I recall. I was a teenager back then. Not much interested in grown-up stuff. Didn't have much to do with my Wessler cousins—Joe and Tilde's kids."

"Tilde!" Renie exclaimed. "That's not too bad."

The chief stared at her. "Too bad for what?"

"A name," Renie said. "Clotilde bothers me."

"She never bothered me," Fat Matt said. "I didn't see much of her. Kept herself to herself, as they say. Fussy woman. Franz was kind of snooty. No wonder Klara dumped him. Not that she isn't a little strange. All that singing stuff. Why can't she just yodel and get it over with? The tunes she sings last about half an hour. Or maybe it just seems like it."

"Lieder," Renie remarked.

"Leader of what?" the chief said. "She's never had a Girl Scout troop or a bunch of Camp Fire Girls. Too snooty, like Franz."

"I meant . . ." Renie stopped. "Skip it."

"You mentioned cousins," Judith said, trying to get back on track. "Does Franz have other siblings besides Josef?"

"You mean legit ones?" Duomo saw Judith nod. "Nope, just the baby sister who drowned."

She changed the subject. "Has the autopsy been concluded?"

A knock sounded on the door. "What?" Duomo barked.

Hernandez entered, nodding vaguely at the cousins. "Doc Frolander sent this over," he said, handing the chief a manila envelope.

"About time," Fat Matt grumbled. "Where's that redhead?"

Hernandez frowned. "She took off in her own squad car."

"You mean," the chief said, his face reddening, "she left town?"

"No," Hernandez replied. "She had to break up a dogfight.

Those dachshunds mixed it up with Wessler's Saint Bernards. Franz was walking them. Dolph ate a couple of the dachshunds' hats."

"Oh." Duomo sat back in his chair. "Guess the redhead's sticking around. You might as well take over the front desk until she gets back."

Hernandez departed. The chief set the manila envelope aside. "Damn. Now I can't send out for a snack."

"Hey," Judith said, practically reaching out to grab the autopsy report, "are you going to read that thing or not?"

Fat Matt looked startled. "Huh? Oh. Yeah, guess I'd better."

Judith watched Duomo scan the report. It seemed to take him forever, though there were only three pages.

"I'll be damned," the chief finally said. "Wessler wasn't stabbed to death after all. Doc says he was poisoned. How 'bout that?"

# Chapter Fourteen

Judith didn't know what to think. "How was he poisoned? What did he eat or drink? Was he injected? Did he take medication?"

The chief held up a hand. "Slow down. All these big scientific words . . ." He ran a stubby finger under a couple of lines in the report. "Aconite—that's a short word, but it sounds like flooring. Or an altar boy? Wessler wanted all his sons to learn how to serve at church. I thought it meant I had to be a waiter. So did Bruno. Fact is, when he found it wasn't like that, he decided to become a chef. Maybe that's why Frankie wanted to be a baker. Never thought about that till now."

Judith felt one of her headaches coming on. "Please. An 'acolyte' is someone who serves at Mass. Serves the priest, that is. I mean, *helps* the priest celebrate Mass. 'Aconite' must be something else, but offhand, I don't know what it is. Doesn't Doc Frolander explain it somewhere?"

Duomo scowled at the last page of the report. "Yeah, it's called monkshood in plain English. Hell, that sounds like more church stuff."

The cousins exchanged dismayed glances. "Monkshood is also known as wolfsbane," Judith said. "It grows around here."

"I'll be darned," Duomo said. "Don't think we've ever had a poisoning case before."

"Why did somebody stab Wessler?" Judith asked, still reeling from the latest news. "He must've already been a goner."

Duomo grimaced. "I left out something. You'll get mad at me."

Judith narrowed her eyes at the chief. "What?"

"Well . . ." He cleared his throat. Twice. "The stabbing part. I mean, he wasn't really stabbed. It was one of those joke knives, the kind that kids have for Halloween. Otto Kotter, the trombone guy, did it. He likes a good gag. Orville didn't know Otto was in on the setup and tried to stop him from fleeing the scene."

Judith vaguely recalled Renie mentioning something about a cop and a trombone player. "But what about all the blood?"

"Hey," Fat Matt said, now on the defensive, "if you'd stayed around instead of flying off like a wild goose in winter, you'd have been able to see that a real knife wound like that wouldn't have spilled so much blood. It was another one of those Halloween gag deals—fake stuff. It might've fooled the witnesses, but you'd have caught on right away."

Judith held her head. Renie leaned forward, resting an arm on the desk. "That was a cheat on poor coz," she declared angrily. "Why didn't you tell her the truth from the get-go?"

"You don't have to get all cranky about it," Duomo huffed. "Truth is, I needed your cousin's help in the Stafford case. The Wessler thing was a throw-in because you were there. If you'd stayed put, she'd have figured it out on the spot."

Judith had collected her wits, though her temper was still frayed. "You thought Wessler was playing a joke?"

Duomo sighed. "At first. But he was dead, so I figured it was a pretty bad joke. Backfired, or something, probably had a heart attack in all the hoopla and excitement. Face it, he was my old man, so I let Doc Frolander do an autopsy. Imagine my surprise when all those morons like Ellie started confessing. That made me kind of suspicious."

"No kidding," Renie muttered.

"Hey," Duomo said, wagging a finger, "the old guy was in darned good shape for his age. Frankly, I was surprised he'd keel over like that."

Judith was shaking her head. "You must be disappointed in me. I haven't gotten to first base with Bob Stafford's homicide. You forced me to get sidetracked with this Wessler thing."

"Yeah, right," Duomo agreed. "Poor strategy on my part. Though now it turns out for the best. You've already done your homework on Wessler. Let's see if we can't get two for the price of one."

"You're *paying* me?" Judith asked.

"Not exactly," Fat Matt hedged. "Suze will probably give you a free dinner. Maybe a lunch, too."

"Gosh," Renie said, all brown-eyed innocence, "you're the cop. Can't you figure it all out so we can go home Monday?"

"Don't be a smart-ass," the chief said. "You've got FATSO here to sleuth. If I wasn't baffled before, I sure am now."

"It's *FASTO*," Judith all but shrieked, digging into her purse to find some Excedrin. "Where can I get a glass of water?"

"Uh . . . go ask Hernandez," the chief replied.

Renie jumped up. "I'll do it." She practically ran out the door.

Judith set her elbows on the desk. "May I see the report? Surely the doctor has more toxicology details. And yes, I've seen autopsy reports before. My husband's a retired police detective. On occasion, he'd let me see the results of a poisoning death after he'd closed a case."

"Think we should call him?"

"No! I mean, he's very busy. In fact, he's doing an internal investigation of our city's police department."

The chief grimaced. "Guess calling him is a bad idea. I wouldn't want him investigating *us*."

"You sure wouldn't," Judith murmured, taking the report from Fat Matt. "May I assume that Doc Frolander is competent?"

"You mean as a doctor?" Duomo didn't wait for an answer. "I guess so. He went to John's Hoppin' med school."

"You mean Johns Hopkins University in Baltimore?"

Duomo rubbed his bald head. "Yeah, that sounds right."

"He must be brilliant," Judith said as Renie returned with a paper cup of water. "That's one of the best med schools in the country."

"It is?" The chief seemed unimpressed.

Judith popped the Excedrin into her mouth and swallowed most of the water. "Thanks, coz. I'm studying the autopsy report."

"I can see that," Renie said, sitting down. "Anything of interest?"

Judith didn't answer right away. "I'm trying to find out how quickly monkshood or wolfsbane works. Wessler seemed in fine fettle before he died." She paused, studying the details. "It works fairly fast. The only sign of it is asphyxia, which, of course, could be caused by so many other things. At least that answers one question."

The chief looked surprised. "It does? What's the question?"

Judith managed to hide her impatience. "Whoever poisoned Wessler hoped to conceal the fact. Maybe the killer thought a small-town medical examiner wouldn't have the means to figure it out."

Renie poked her cousin's arm. "Back up. Are you considering that Bob's murder could tie in to any of this? I'm asking because I'd like to know if Mother Wessler and child drowned where Bob's body was found."

Judith stared at Renie. "Why?"

"How many people in one small town drown? The Wessler house is close to where Bob's body was found, right? I know the incidents are separated by many years. But wouldn't that be the same area where Mrs. Wessler would go looking for Christmas greens?"

Judith shook her head. "There were no evergreens near that side of the river. Why would she go there at all?"

"Having worked on graphic designs for Wirehoser Timber," Renie began, "there may've been trees along that river at one time. They were cut or swept away by a flood. The usual undergrowth has taken over part of the path. The river could've even changed channels. So it's plausible that years ago Mrs. Wessler was gathering Christmas greens. But why did Bob Stafford go there in the first place?"

Duomo shot Judith a sharp glance. "You sure she's not FATSO after all?"

Judith felt stupid. "I was so busy admiring the view that I didn't notice. But my cousin's right—which makes me wonder if Bob was killed by the river or somewhere else."

The chief scowled. "And somebody hauled him down there? He was a fairly big guy. Not fat or anything, but at least average. You met Barry, his son?" He saw the cousins nod. "About the same height, only with another twenty pounds or so."

Judith exchanged quick looks with Renie. "Are you suggesting something symbolic about the third body being found by the river?"

Renie didn't answer right away. "Sorry. My stomach's growling so loud that I can barely hear you. It could be connected, symbolic or otherwise." Her expression grew self-deprecating. "Maybe I'm nuts."

"Probably," Duomo said, turning back to Judith. "I thought we were staying on track with Wessler and what really killed him."

"I can see a possible connection with the place where Mrs. Wessler and Bob were found dead, but not with what happened to your father," Judith admitted. "We don't know where he was poisoned since he'd just arrived at Wolfgang's. The stomach contents don't tell us much. Wessler hadn't eaten for at least an hour, but he'd drunk some wine before arriving at the cocktail party. It doesn't state where he did that."

The chief shrugged. "Don't know where he'd been before he showed up and croaked. Home, maybe. He wasn't a big drinker, so maybe he'd gone to some other shindig before—" Duomo's phone rang. He stared at it as if he could make it stop. Finally, after five rings, he reluctantly picked up the receiver. "What now? I'm in conference."

Judith watched Fat Matt's expression change from annoyance to exasperation. "Okay, okay—hell, can't you dumbbells control a riot?" He slammed down the receiver, grunted as he stood up, and grabbed his cap. "Those damned kids are tearing up the beer garden. It isn't even open yet. I thought they left town. Maybe I'll shoot a bunch of 'em. We got more room in the hospital than in the jail. Keep sleuthing. Gotta go."

Duomo went. "Great," Judith grumbled. "Every so often he seems almost like a policeman. And then he goes all Keystone Kop on us."

Renie leaned her head on her fist. "Do you really think he's as stupid as he seems?"

Judith considered the question. "No, but I don't think he's any genius either. Maybe it's an act to fool perps. I hope he kept that bottle from the Thomas Mann bust. I wonder if it contained poison. I also like your idea about the river site."

"I could get more ideas if I ate something," Renie said.

"Let's try one of the food stalls," Judith suggested, checking her watch. "It's not quite four."

"No bratwursts," Renie said.

"Fine," Judith said. "How about Frankie's bakery?"

"Duomo's brother's place? Sure, why not? Where is it?"

Judith had gotten up and moved to the door. "Let's find out."

Kitt had returned to desk duty. Judith asked if she knew the bakery's location. She didn't know and didn't much care. "I don't live here, remember?" she said, refocusing on the paperwork in front of her.

The cousins left. At the corner, Judith suddenly remembered seeing a bakery across the street from Sadie's Stories. "Hey—isn't it time for you to check back with the Heraldsgate Hill Bookshop?"

"You're right," Renie said. "I'll do it now before we're caught in another riot." Getting out her cell, she dialed the number from memory.

Judith turned to look toward the main street where a half-dozen children were bouncing along in a pony cart driven by an older man who was apparently telling them stories that made them giggle. Another man was playing the accordion on the far corner while his audience sang along and clapped their hands. Judith smiled, admiring the pleasure that people of all ages seemed to derive from the Oktoberfest celebration. For a few moments she forgot about her headache and the tragedies that had triggered her frustration.

"Helene can order the book," Renie said, breaking her cousin's reverie. "Bill should've gone to the neighborhood bookstore in the first place. I told her to get it and she thought it would be in by next Wednesday. Obviously, it's only unavailable in Little Bavaria."

"There's a reason," Judith said as they crossed the street, "but I can't think why. From what Barry told us, it doesn't have anything to do with Wessler. I wonder what he did to get that Saint Hubert's award? I bet Father Dash knows. It's too bad he won't be here until tomorrow."

"What about Klara or Franz? They must have a complete biography of Wessler," Renie said, turning the corner onto the main street. "Even if they don't know details, they have to put something together for the funeral eulogy."

"You're right," Judith agreed. "Let's get a snack at the bakery and pay a call on whoever may be in at the Wessler house." She stopped suddenly, startling Renie.

"What's wrong?"

"The car!" Judith exclaimed. "We forgot to collect it. We'll need it to get to the Wessler house. I'm not walking that far. Then we can take it back to Suzie before she thinks we stole it."

"Bayern Bäckerei first," Renie said, pointing to a sign between a dry cleaners and a hat emporium. "I can translate that."

The bakery was crowded, and customers had to take a number. Renie found the dispenser near the door. "Thirty-three." She looked up at a digital counter on the wall. "We've got ten people ahead of us. Can you see how many clerks are waiting on customers? I'm too short."

"Three," Judith replied. "Two women and a guy who looks like Fat Matt except he's not as fat and not completely bald."

"That's not too long a wait," Renie said. "But we can't see what's in the bakery cases until some of those other people leave."

Unfortunately, one of the customers moving away from the counter was Eleanor Denkel. "Judith," she said in a cheerless voice. "I didn't think you liked sweets. No wonder you don't like to be called FATSO."

"It's *FASTO*," Judith said grimly, "and it's not me, it's my cousin, remember? Does she look fat to you?"

Ellie eyed Renie with disdain. "No, but those teeth of hers could devour an entire shelf in a hurry."

Renie folded her arms across her bosom. "I'll step outside with you, Ellie, and we'll discuss that further, okay?"

Ellie looked shocked. "How dare you!"

Renie shrugged, moving just enough to block the door. "It's not a dare, it's a challenge. Well? Or do you need a second, such as that wizened little critter you call a husband?"

Ellie's face turned a color akin to puce. "I should call the police! You're threatening me."

"Go ahead," Renie said, her eyes flashing. "Ask for Kitt. I'd love to see her hustle your butt off to jail. In fact, I'll go with you." She looked at Judith. "You know what I like. I'll get the car while I'm watching Ellie get busted for interfering with an officer of the law."

Ellie's eyes widened. "You've been deputized?"

"The term is 'special consultant to the chief of police.' Well? What are you waiting for?" Renie backed into the door, pushing it open. "Move. Put your mojo where your mouth is."

"Oh, for . . ." Ellie turned in every direction. "Excuse me, I forgot something." She brushed past Judith, went back toward the counter, and tried to wedge herself between four other customers, who were crowded together at the end of the counter.

Renie grinned and moved away from the door to let two patrons make their exit. "I called her bluff."

"Coz, someday you'll go too far. But this time wasn't one of them. I kind of enjoyed it."

"Look," Renie said, "Ellie's sneaking out the back way. Ha ha."

Judith smiled ironically. "So she can be intimidated. I wonder—"

Renie interrupted. "Two more just left. I mean it, you buy me something wonderful while I get the car and then pick you up. Bye." She followed the departing customers out of the door.

Judith finally got up to the display case. Some of the trays were already empty; others held only a few items. She scanned the length of the baked goods, dismissing muffins, crullers, and any cookies with nuts from her wish list. Renie's allergies were no joke. She spotted some cinnamon twists in the end tray. Her cousin liked those. Judith's taste buds were tempted by a lone custard-filled Danish, but one of the buxom blondes behind the counter scooped it up and handed it to a bearded man next to her.

"Hungry?" a voice behind her inquired.

"Franz!" Judith turned around. "What happened to the dogs?"

"Oh!" He chuckled. "They were just frisking with the dachshunds. No harm done. Those hats didn't suit them. They were the orange ones and the green looked so much better. But of course it was easier to keep track of the racers with different-colored hats."

"We only saw them start the race," Judith said as two more customers, including the bearded man, left the shop. Franz Wessler moved up beside her. "Serena and I were coming back from the cemetery. We saw some of your family's graves."

Franz frowned. "Do you always have cemeteries on your itinerary?"

"As a matter of fact, we do," Judith said, telling only a small fib. "We found some fascinating ones when we were in Scotland last year."

"Yes," Franz said slowly, "I can see how that would be of interest, especially if you know the area's history."

"That's the point. It's one of the ways you learn the history. For example, we found your mother's and your sister's graves."

"Yes, of course." Franz's face grew melancholy. "Very sad."

Another customer left. Judith realized she was only one number away from being called. Glancing at Franz's ticket, she saw that he was thirty-two, just ahead of her. "My father died young," she said. "Do you remember much about your mother and sister's tragedy?"

"No," Franz said, avoiding Judith's gaze. "It happened when I was too young to understand. In fact, my father was so grief-stricken that he sent my brother, Josef, and me back to Germany to live with relatives for a time. This town was very small then. We had no high school, no doctor, no dentist, and of course no hospital. There was only a run-down motel. None of those facilities and services were available until the 1980s when my father began his campaign to create Little Bavaria as a tourist attraction. Josef returned before I did, but I stayed in Germany until I was in my midteens. I virtually had to learn English all over again. Our German relatives treated us well, but I felt as if I were divided between two worlds, the new and the old."

"Your father must've recovered from his loss," Judith said. "Is that why he became involved in creating Little Bavaria?"

"Not quite, though he . . ."

Frankie Duomo called number thirty-two. Franz turned, glanced at the baker, and pressed his ticket into Judith's hand. "Go ahead, you've waited a long time. You look tired. I'll take your number instead."

"But . . ." Judith began, puzzled.

Franz smiled, though his eyes were hard. "Please."

"Okay." She handed over her own ticket and passed Franz's across the counter. "Hi," she said to Frankie. "I'd like two cinnamon twists and one of your chocolate chip cookies."

"That's it?" Frankie asked, his gaze flickering in Franz's direction as he moved farther away to the other end of the display case.

"Ah . . . I'll take a lemon Danish, too, please."

Frankie complied wordlessly. He bagged the items and rang them up. Before he could give Judith the total, one of the buxom blondes called number thirty-three. "That comes to six dollars and fifty-four cents," Frankie said.

Judith gave him a ten. While waiting for change, she saw the blonde chatting amiably with Franz. A moment later, she was outside where the Ford Escort had pulled up in the store's small parking lot.

"I didn't run over anybody," Renie announced. "What did you get?"

"Here," Judith said, first removing the cookie. "It's all yours."

"Yum! I love twists. Too bad Bill's not here—lemon Danish is one of his favorites." She bit into a twist. "Goddedatwisfirs. Den-wllgo." She swallowed and stared at her cousin. "You look weird. What's wrong?"

"I don't know. But pull out."

"Weird" didn't quite describe Judith's feeling. It felt more like apprehension. Or maybe even fear.

# Chapter Fifteen

**R**enie bit off more twist, but complied with her cousin's request to keep moving. A moment later, they were headed east on the main street, driving slowly as pedestrians, pony carts, strolling musicians, and a medieval jester impeded their path.

"Are we calling on the Wessler manse?" Renie asked.

"I don't know," Judith repeated.

Renie frowned. "What did you do in the bakery? Take stupid pills?"

Judith shook her head. "No. But Franz Wessler was there and he seems to have an aversion to Frankie Duomo. He made me switch numbers with him so Frankie couldn't wait on him."

"Maybe Franz wanted to check out the buxom blondes," Renie said as they came to a full stop when a trio of acrobats tumbled across the street. "I assume Klara's not putting out."

"Who knows?" Judith said. "I wonder if we should call on Klara. Do you think we'd scare her? She seems like the nervous type."

"I'd be nervous, too, if I had to drag those big Saint Bernards around," Renie said after she'd polished off the first twist. "Are we going to the concert tonight or do you have an official function I don't know about?"

"Ohh . . ." Judith rummaged in her purse. "I forgot. There's a small cocktail party for the innkeeping contingent at the Valhalla Inn. My gosh! I *am* losing it! What happened to Gabe Hunter after Duomo let him go?"

"Gee," Renie said as they crept past the exhibit booths, "why don't you ask him? He's on duty with some woman I don't recognize."

"Can you pull in somewhere?" Judith asked, twisting around to see Gabe and his companion in the booth. "Oh! That's Jeanne Barber. You know—the woman I filled in for when we were on Chavez Island?"

Renie groaned. "Another one of our misadventures with a corpse. She does look familiar, but her hair's a different color. It's been at least ten years." She turned the steering wheel, aiming at a spot on the sidewalk that was conveniently devoid of pedestrians. "Hang on—this could be b-b-bumpy."

Judith gasped as the Ford Escort climbed the curb. "We're lucky if we don't wreck Suzie's car before we get it back to her."

Gabe, Jeanne, and the half-dozen visitors at the booth stared in surprise. Judith turned to Renie before getting out. "Drive around someplace while I talk to them, okay?"

"Hey," Renie said, "with all these meandering people, I may only get half a block away. Just go so I can get off the sidewalk."

Judith went. Before she reached the B&B booth, Jeanne Clayton Barber let out a shriek of recognition. Signaling to her old high school chum to ignore her and continue talking to two young women, Judith discreetly stepped off to one side. A couple of minutes passed before Jeanne suddenly came out of the booth and embraced her.

"It's been ages!" Jeanne cried. "You've hardly changed one bit since I saw you at that B&B meeting five years ago."

"It was eight," Judith said, but smiled and wished she could say the same for Jeanne. The dyed auburn hair didn't suit her pale complexion and her angular frame looked downright scrawny. But the gray eyes still had a sparkle and the wrinkles indicated she had laughed more than she'd frowned. "I heard you were here,"

Judith said after Jeanne stepped back. "I worked the booth earlier with Evelyn Choo."

Jeanne nodded. "Yes, I've known Evelyn for years. She and I served on a couple of committees together." She grimaced. "You know how Ingrid Heffelman loves to coerce us onto committees."

"Fortunately," Judith said, "I've been spared most of that. Just lucky, I guess." In fact, she knew that Ingrid preferred keeping her least favorite innkeeper a deep, dark secret. Or so Judith had always figured.

"We must get together," Jeanne said, glancing at the booth, where Gabe Hunter was still involved with a quartet of people wearing Bavarian garb. "I assume you're attending the party for us tonight at the Valhalla Inn. Our host is Herman Stromeyer, the Oktoberfest chairman. The inn is such a cozy place at the west end of town—perched out on the riverbank, it's a veritable aerie. You can imagine you're on the Rhine. I can practically hear the Lorelei calling."

"I not only haven't met Mr. Stromeyer, I haven't been that far down the main street," Judith said.

"Nor have I. He was supposed to address us at the cocktail party, but he never got the chance because of the tragedy. Evelyn Choo told me he came down with flu later that evening. Or maybe he was overcome by what happened to Mr. Wessler." She shuddered as the clock tower struck four. "My goodness! The time flies so. I can't believe Gabe and I are finished already." She lowered her voice. "That poor young man! Can you imagine being hauled off by the police for no reason? How embarrassing!"

Judith saw Gabe nodding and smiling at the Bavarian-clad foursome. "Who's relieving you?"

"Oh," Jeanne said, "Ellie and her husband are filling in because so many of us want to attend Connie's seminar. Are you coming?"

Judith's expression was noncommittal. "I thought that whatever Connie is doing was aimed at travelers, not innkeepers."

"It's both," Jeanne said. "So many people signed up for it that the venue has been changed to a larger room."

Judith saw Eleanor and Delmar Denkel approaching from the other direction. "I'll have to see about that. My cousin Serena is with me. You remember her from our stay on Chavez Island?"

Jeanne looked faintly startled. "Yes. Yes. She's . . . memorable."

"She is that," Judith conceded. "Here comes Gabe. I'll see you at the cocktail party, Jeanne."

"What?" Glancing over her shoulder at the Denkels, Jeanne suddenly seemed distracted. "Oh, yes, the party. Excuse me, I should speak to Ellie and make sure we left everything in order."

Jeanne and Gabe nodded and smiled as they crossed paths. The young man approached Judith in a diffident manner.

"You must think I'm some kind of screwup," he said, adjusting the hood on his ski parka.

"You mean the mix-up with Chief Duomo?" Judith laughed. "Did he have you going in circles?"

"You know that guy?" Gabe asked. "He's kind of strange."

"He's certainly different from most law enforcement officers I've . . . known," she said. "My husband is a retired police detective."

"He's different from just about anybody I've ever met," Gabe said. "The weird thing was that it was like he was trying to get information out of me about other people. But he went about it in such an oddball way that I didn't know what was really on his mind. Even after that other officer—the guy with the sleepy eyes—admitted he remembered I'd gotten to the party at Wolfgang's just as the old guy was killed, the chief still kept asking me a ton of questions."

"By then, he may've considered you a witness, not a suspect."

"I don't know. If so, why did I have to spend the night at the jail?"

Judith didn't answer right away. It suddenly occurred to her that maybe Duomo had done that for Gabe's protection. "Did he focus on any certain individuals when he asked you about the other people?"

The sound of a bass drum, a flugelhorn, and a brass saxhorn kept Gabe from answering immediately. The trio appeared from in back of the booths and continued down the street.

"Wow," Gabe said under his breath. "I think they're advertising tonight's band concert. They sure like their music around here." He paused and blinked twice. "What did you ask . . . oh, if Duomo focused on anybody in particular. He kept pretty much to the B&B group, mostly focused on on Ellie Denkel, but I really don't know her. That'd be natural, since she's the one in charge of us."

"She's from here," Judith said. "But she already confessed."

Gabe shook his head. "Falsely, right? Why? Is she shielding somebody? Delmar's a Realtor. He's not involved with running B&Bs."

"Delmar sells real estate?" Ellie's pint-size mate didn't strike Judith as a typical high-pressure salesman.

Gabe shrugged. "I guess. I heard her say he was involved in residential and commercial properties."

"Oh." Judith scanned the street for the Ford Escort, but only saw a dozen stalled vehicles in either direction waiting for a group of Girl Scouts to cross. "I'm glad you weren't further detained."

"Me, too. I better go." Gabe checked his watch. "I'm attending Connie's seminar. Being new in the business, I need some tips."

"Good luck," Judith murmured. Gabe hurried off down the street, avoiding the Girl Scouts, who had reached the sidewalk.

Finally, she saw the Ford Escort. To her horror, there was a deer on the hood. Judith waited anxiously for Renie to pull over to the curb. It was only then that she realized the deer was a large stuffed animal whose glassy eyes nevertheless seemed to stare at her in reproach.

"Hey," Renie called, leaning out the window, "could you haul that thing inside? I feel like an idiot."

"You *are* an idiot," Judith said, wrestling with the deer. It wasn't very heavy, but the legs and antlers made it difficult to remove from the hood. "And now *I* feel like an idiot," she declared, stuffing the deer in the backseat. "Everybody's looking at me like I'm some kind of poacher. Dare I ask how that happened?"

"Sure," Renie said. "I was trying to turn around by the U.S. National Forest booth down the street and I hit the deer they had standing outside. Guess it got caught in the headlights."

"The headlights aren't on," Judith said.

"Did I say they were? The headlights are still *there*."

"No wonder Bill complains about your driving."

"You know I haven't got any depth perception. It's not my fault, it's genetic. Just stop griping and tell me where we're going."

"Oh . . . we should call on Klara. Let me think of a viable excuse."

"We could give her the deer as a hostess gift," Renie said, waiting for a Boy Scout troop to cross the street.

"That would really make her nervous," Judith said as they reached the high school turn. The dachshund racecourse had been replaced by a replica of Mad Ludwig's castle with a courtyard that served as a stage for a puppet show. Judith assumed it was probably a fairy tale enactment.

As often happened with the cousins, Renie read Judith's mind. "I bet it's Grimm, but not too grim for the kiddies."

"I hope so. There's too much grim stuff around here already."

There was little traffic on the side street. Renie pulled into the curving driveway. "Lots of steps to get to the porch. Can you manage?"

"I'll have to," Judith said. "You can't carry me."

Judith was relieved to see there was a handrail. The cousins climbed the curving stone stairway to face an oak door with a brass knocker. Renie lifted it, discovering a buzzer underneath. She banged only once. A half-dozen musical notes resounded inside the house.

"What is that?" Judith asked.

Renie frowned. "Maybe the overture from Wagner's *Meistersinger*?"

Judith shrugged. "You know more about opera than I do."

There was no immediate response. Renie was about to bang the knocker again when Olga Crump opened the door. The housekeeper peered suspiciously at the visitors. "Do I know you?" she asked.

"Yes, you do," Renie said, edging her way inside. "We're here to tell you Roscoe is off the hook for snoring all day. The Kotters conceded that he has a right to nod off anytime he wants. It's in the Constitution under 'Freedom of Sleep.' Where's Mrs. Wessler?"

Olga, looking confused, pressed her hands against her big bosom. "Is she expecting you?"

"Expecting us to do what?" Renie asked. "Of course. Tell her that Mrs. Flynn and I have come to explain why we're here."

Still looking puzzled, Olga stomped off down the long hallway. Judith gazed into the living room with its big stone fireplace and comfortable furniture. The only sign of the Wessler ancestral heritage was a plaque on one wall with what looked like a family crest.

Renie tugged at Judith's arm. "Sit. Klara can't throw us out if we look as if we're settled in."

"We can't be *that* impolite," Judith protested.

"Why not? Do you think Klara would faint?"

"Maybe," Judith said, hearing voices close by. "Here they come."

"They?"

"Klara and Mrs. Crump," Judith whispered before turning around. "Hello, Mrs. Wessler. How kind of you to let us inquire about your dogs. Are they recovered from their fracas with the dachshunds?"

"Oh!" Klara said, her glacial-blue eyes round with surprise. "Yes, it was a frisky romp. How did you know?"

"We ran into Franz earlier," Judith said. "My cousin also wanted to offer you her apologies for taking Siegfried and Dolph to task." She nudged Renie with her elbow.

"I'm terrified of dogs," Renie said, trying to look abject. "My cousin will explain why. I can't really talk about it." She put a hand to her forehead and turned away.

"Please sit," Klara said, ushering them into the living room. "No worries. The dogs are outside." She paused as the cousins sat down on a big forest-green divan. "Is there something Mrs. Crump could fetch you before she feeds Siegfried and Dolph? A glass of wine, perhaps?"

"No, thank you," Judith said. "I'm attending a cocktail party this evening." She smiled disarmingly. "I don't want to impair my faculties."

Klara waved a hand in dismissal of Mrs. Crump. "Very prudent," she said, carefully arranging the pleats of her rust-colored skirt before sitting down in a brown gold-studded club chair. "I appreciate your kindness in offering an apology, Mrs. . . . . ?"

"Jones," Renie said with a facile smile. "Serena Jones."

For some reason, Klara laughed, a fittingly musical sound. "You," she said, after reining in her merriment and looking at Judith, "are . . . ?"

"Judith Flynn. I'm part of the innkeeping group."

"Oh, yes. I believe Franz mentioned that." A slight frown creased her high forehead. "Where *is* Franz? He's been gone for quite some time."

"We saw him at the bakery," Judith said. "That was probably twenty minutes ago."

"Oh." Klara bit her lower lip. "Maybe he's catching up with old friends, though after living away from here, he's lost track of so many."

"He must know Frankie the baker," Judith said innocently.

Klara's face tightened. "Franz distances himself from his father's other offspring. He finds them . . . an embarrassment." Her expression grew melancholy as she changed the subject. "I've lived here only a few years. Los Angeles was a fine place for my career, but after Franz and I separated, I needed a more tranquil setting to revive my spirit. Little Bavaria seemed like Eden— until now." Her eyes glistened with tears.

"You must've been very fond of your father-in-law," Judith said.

"Oh, yes." Klara sniffed and dabbed at her eyes with a finger. "He was such a sympathetic, understanding man. You might not think he would be so kind to his son's former wife, but that was not so. He invited me to live here. Dietrich was the epitome of compassion."

"So we hear," Judith said. "Everyone seems to have loved him."

Klara nodded. "He truly had not an enemy in the world. That is what is so terrible." She stopped, looking forlorn.

Judith nodded. "I can't imagine why anyone would wish him harm. I heard he was made a member of the Knights of Saint Hubert. It's a very prestigious award. How did he earn such an honor?"

Klara tugged at a perfect pink earlobe. "For his work with refugees. So many displaced persons, not only Germans, of course, but from other countries. Many had fled the Baltics to Germany to escape the Russian Communists. They lived like hunted animals during the war. Some of the Germans resented them. Dietrich saw to it they were treated kindly and not persecuted because they were foreign."

"That sounds like a very noble endeavor," Judith said. "I didn't realize that Germany was considered a safe haven for people from Lithuania, Latvia, and Estonia."

Klara nodded. "My parents were Latvian. It was so difficult for them, during the war, and even afterward. You'd be shocked how even some good German people behaved. Understandable, but inhumane."

"Mr. Wessler's honors seem well deserved," Judith said. "I can't help but wonder if whoever . . . stabbed him was deranged."

Klara's eyes widened in shock. "Deranged? Oh, no! Surely not!"

"Well . . ." Judith raised her hands in a helpless gesture. "Who else but a crazy person would want to harm Mr. Wessler?"

"I know of no one so crazy," Klara said in a tremulous voice. "I think perhaps it was a bizarre accident. I was never in the ballroom, so I only know what I heard later. I had to rest my voice that night."

Judith glanced at Renie, an unspoken signal for her cousin to speak up. "An accident? It wasn't a sword dance. Do you mean Mr. Wessler slipped and fell on a knife?"

Klara's oval face exhibited perplexity. "A freakish thing. Franz described it as so much movement and loud music that it was a blur, like a bad dream that doesn't come into focus."

"True," Judith agreed, realizing Duomo hadn't had time to make the autopsy report public. "Serena and I were there, and Franz is right about the circumstances. We were never sure if Mr. Wessler was dancing or simply caught up in the midst of those who were."

Klara smiled faintly. "Dietrich was a fine dancer. He may have joined in. Franz couldn't tell. He was at the bar when it happened."

Judith thought back to the last time she'd seen Franz at the party, but couldn't remember. "I assume," she finally said, "Mr. Wessler was in good spirits when he left for the event at Wolfgang's that evening."

"Oh, yes." Klara smiled more brightly. "He was very happy. He was always especially joyous during Oktoberfest. We'd had guests in that evening. Dietrich was ever so jolly."

Judith smiled back. "He must have been a connoisseur of German wines. He seemed to appreciate the good things of life."

Klara nodded. "He did. Wine, music, food." She lowered her head for moment. *You left out women,* Judith thought.

Klara, however, continued quickly. "He had plans for a vineyard about seventy miles from here. He'd already made an offer on some property. I'd like Franz to carry out his father's plan. It would be a living memorial to Dietrich."

Renie leaned closer. "I'd think the revival of this town would be his memorial. It's certainly alive—and lively."

"That is so," Klara agreed, "but the town is not authentic. The vineyard would grow grapes from vines in Franconia, the part of Bavaria known for its excellent wines. The Maindreieck district is famous for growing Silvaner and Müller-Thurgau grapes. Dietrich wished to experiment with the Silvaner, though he also planned to cultivate the more common grapes—Riesling, Bacchus, Domina . . ." She paused. "You are familiar with Franconian wines?"

"Only Deux Franc Charles," Renie said. "We're not into enology."

Klara seemed mystified. "Deux Franc . . . ? I don't understand."

Judith wanted to kick her cousin, but merely shook her head. "Serena is teasing you. We're both ignorant when it comes to wine."

Klara nodded. "Sometimes I miss conversational nuances. What I mean is that Dietrich's plans were temporarily suspended when his partner died."

"His partner?" Judith said.

"Yes. It was just a short time ago," Klara explained. "Very sad, too. My father-in-law had gone into the vineyard business with the owner of the Pancake Schloss, Bob Stafford. He also met a tragic end. I wonder if the vineyard is cursed before it's planted?"

# Chapter Sixteen

Judith also wondered if Dietrich Wessler and Bob Stafford were cursed. She didn't say so out loud, but instead commiserated about the two unfortunate deaths.

"It's terribly sad for the whole community," Judith said. "From what we've heard, Bob was also a fine man. A hard worker, too."

"Yes." Klara's gaze roamed to the family crest that was on the opposite wall. "So is his widow, Mrs. Stafford. But I don't know if she was as enthusiastic about the vineyard project. She is very involved with her pancakes." Only a touch of sarcasm was hinted at in her tone.

"Hunh," Renie said. "So who gets the loot? Mr. Wessler's, I mean."

"The . . ." Klara's blue eyes widened. "Forgive me, I don't know that word unless you mean the lute Dietrich kept in the music room."

"That lute, too," Renie replied. "I mean, who inherits everything?"

"Oh." Klara stared at her bronze ballet flats. "I have no idea. Perhaps Franz knows." She brightened. "Or Mrs. Stafford. Bob— her late husband—handled all of Dietrich's affairs. He was a lawyer before he became involved with pancakes."

"That so," Judith remarked softly. "I'd forgotten that Bob practiced law before he and Suzie moved here."

The grandfather clock by Klara's chair struck five. "Oh, my!" she exclaimed, getting to her feet. "I must rest. I'm singing at the concert this evening. You will be there?"

Judith opened her mouth to hedge, but Renie spoke first. "What's on your program?"

"A potpourri," Klara replied. "Some of what you might call 'popular' songs as well as German and Viennese selections."

"Sure," Renie said, also standing up. "We'll be there at least for part of it. My cousin has some other duties. Break a leg—or should I say strain a vocal cord?"

Klara blanched. "Whatever do you mean?"

"It's showbiz talk," Renie said, hoisting her purse over her shoulder. "Don't take it to heart, okay?"

Klara looked uncertain as she walked the cousins to the door. "You must forgive me. My nerves are frayed to the bone."

"Of course," Judith said softly. "We'll see you this evening."

Nodding dumbly, Klara opened the door slowly, but quickly shut it behind her departing guests.

"That was a bust," Renie declared.

"What do you mean?" Judith asked, gazing in every direction at her surroundings, which included a fallow garden, a bird feeder, and a pond.

"You didn't get a chance to ask Klara about the guests who were at the predeath party."

"No," Judith said, "but that was interesting about the vineyard."

"You figure some rival winery or vineyard put Bob and Wessler out of business?" Renie asked as she started down the steps. "Hey—are you coming or not?" she yelled, seeing Judith still on the porch.

"Pipe down," Judith said, motioning with her hand. "I'm taking this short flight of stairs that must lead to the back of the house."

Renie sighed wearily. "Fine," she said, scurrying onto the porch. "You *have* noticed," she continued after they'd descended the steps, "it's gotten colder now that the sun's setting. I should've brought my furs."

"You don't have any furs," Judith said, admiring the tidy, graceful landscaping that flanked both sides of the walk.

"I do if you count Oscar and Clarence," Renie said as they reached a tall wooden fence and gate. She jiggled the handle. "It's locked."

Judith elbowed Renie aside. "Yoo-hoo!" she called. "Mrs. Crump!"

The Saint Bernards barked in response. "See what you've done?" Renie hissed. "Those beasts may get loose and attack . . ."

The gate swung open, almost hitting the cousins. "Yes?" the housekeeper said. "What's wrong?"

Judith's expression was apologetic. "I left my gloves in the living room. Is there any chance you could let us in the back way?"

Mrs. Crump frowned. "Oh," she finally said, "follow me."

The dogs were in their kennel, but barked again when they saw the visitors. The fenced portion of the backyard featured a patio, now stripped bare of summer furnishings. A few doggie toys were scattered on the lawn. Judith noticed a big hole dug next to the house, apparently by the Saint Bernards. The cousins went up a short flight of steps that led directly into the kitchen. Stainless-steel appliances and sleek contemporary furnishings lent a twenty-first-century aura. The only item that didn't match was a big, old-fashioned, black cast-iron stove.

The housekeeper apparently noticed Judith's interest. "Wessler brought that from Germany. He said it cooked better than newer stoves. That was his opinion. I like the modern ones just fine."

"Yes," Judith said, "so do I, but if Mr. Wessler entertained a lot, two stoves might have been better than one. I understand he had a party here the night of the tragedy. Did you have to cook for the guests?"

Mrs. Crump shook her head. "Cold appetizers, that's what the young Mrs. Wessler wanted to serve." She wrinkled her blunt nose. "Fancy cheese and funny little crackers. She insisted it went well with the wine. She ought to know—she drinks enough of it. Not that I should criticize. She's an 'artiste' and they're all kind of queer."

Judith's expression was sympathetic. "Do you cook and clean?"

"Sometimes." Mrs. Crump brushed off some almost invisible dust from the vintage stove. "But usually just for guests."

"Did you have a big crowd the other night?" Judith inquired.

"Mostly big shots from the Oktoberfest." She scowled at Judith and Renie. "Who are you? Cops?"

"No," Judith replied with a little laugh. "My husband is a retired policeman and he wanted me to drop by to say hello to Chief Duomo. They've known each other for years."

Mrs. Crump snorted. "That dunderhead. How he ever got be a police chief is beyond me. Must've been who he knows, not what he knows. Roscoe thinks he's on the take."

Judith feigned surprise. "Really? Did you mention that your husband works undercover? Is that how he knows?"

"Roscoe knows plenty," Mrs. Crump said. "But he doesn't tell tales. Can't. He'd lose his job."

"Of course," Judith said, trying to think of some way to get the housekeeper back on track. "Was Chief Duomo at the party here?"

Mrs. Crump shook her head. "It was only for the Oktoberfest folks. Herman Stromeyer, a couple of German visitors from the old country, and some of the people in charge of the exhibit booths."

"Oh," Judith said. "Were the Denkels here from our B&B group?"

"Could be," the housekeeper said. "Are you an innkeeper?"

Judith nodded. "Yes. You must have had a houseful."

"Not really," Mrs. Crump replied, casting her eyes to see what Renie was doing. "About a dozen, I guess. Is she one of yours?"

"She's my cousin," Judith said. "Sometimes she helps me."

"Why is she looking in the fridge?"

"Ah—she's buying a new one," Judith said. "Right, coz?"

"Hunh?" Renie shut the refrigerator door. "Oh, right. Our old one is sort of . . . old."

Mrs. Crump scowled. "That one cost a bundle. Wessler

should've put more money into new pipes. The sink got plugged just before the party. The local plumber was closed and his backup charged the world. He knew we were in a bind. But money's no object in this place." She shook her head before looking at Judith. "You better find your gloves."

"I will," Judith said. "Is it okay if we leave through the front door?"

"Just be quiet about it," Mrs. Crump said. "I have to be heading home. It's time to wake up Roscoe."

Judith and Renie followed the long hall out of the kitchen to the living room. "You didn't have any gloves with you," Renie said when they were standing in front of the fireplace.

"I know that," Judith said. "But if it gets much colder, I'll wish I did." She walked over to study the family crest. "Nice. Just the name Wessler and something in German that I can't read. Can you?"

Renie studied what was probably a family motto. "No. *Liebe Winter Nicht.* Something to do with love and winter, maybe."

"Hunh." Judith looked into the adjoining dining room, but saw nothing of interest. "Drat. This visit hasn't been all that helpful."

"You expected items marked 'clue'?"

"I was expecting something," Judith replied, going outside and grasping the handrail. "I suppose we should return Suzie's car."

"That means we'll have to walk back to our inn," Renie said over her shoulder. "Why can't we see if Barry can collect it for us?"

"We don't know where Barry is," Judith replied, reaching the level ground. "He may be tending bar. Besides, that'd be an imposition. Suzie probably wonders where we've been all afternoon."

"She probably hasn't had time to notice the car's still gone."

"We should return it now anyway," Judith said, pausing at the Ford Escort's passenger door. "Maybe you should drop that deer off by the Forest Service booth first."

"Oh." Renie peered into the backseat. "Damn. It's still there. I hoped it had run away."

There seemed to be a late-afternoon, early-evening lull in the Oktoberfest action. It took less than two minutes to reach the exhibitors' area. Renie had some difficulty dislodging the stuffed deer from the car, but declined Judith's offer of help.

"If I can wrestle our tall and stalwart children to a buffet, I can handle this," she asserted. "Stay put."

Gazing at the Forest Service booth, Judith wondered if Mike had heard anything about his next assignment. Deciding to check in with Joe, she got out her cell and tapped in her home phone number.

"Hey," Joe said, "I thought you ran off with some Bavarian stud."

"Not my type," Judith said, smiling at the sound of his voice. "We've been busy." She paused, watching Renie dump the stuffed deer in front of a forest ranger. "It's a fascinating town." She paused again, seeing the tall, uniformed man point first at the deer and then at Renie.

"Staying out of trouble, I assume?" Joe said.

"Oh," Judith responded, wincing as Renie stood with fists on hips and feet planted apart, "of course." Apparently, either the city media hadn't carried the story about Wessler's murder or else Joe hadn't been keeping close track of the news. "How's everything at home?"

"Fine," Joe replied. "Your dreaded mother's helping Arlene make the guests' appetizers."

"She is? She's never so much as offered to do that for me," Judith said while Renie and the ranger went toe-to-toe in a shouting match. "Where's Carl?"

"He and I raked leaves in both our yards this afternoon," Joe said. "He's home, taking a nap. I think I'll do the same before dinner. Arlene's making lasagna."

"Nice," Judith remarked, cringing as Renie backed up and swung her purse at the ranger. Luckily, she missed. "No further harassment from Ingrid Heffelman?"

"Uh—no."

Renie was stomping back to the car. The ranger stood his ground but Judith could hear him yelling what sounded like very unpleasant words. Judith, however, tried to focus on her husband. "You seem uncertain about Ingrid."

"Oh, it's nothing," Joe said, his voice strained. "She dropped by this noon to give me a copy of her inspection. I mean, give *you* a copy."

She flinched as Renie bolted into the driver's seat and slammed the car door. "Did she stay long?" Judith asked Joe.

"No, she was in a hurry. What's going on? Who's cussing?"

"Renie," Judith said as her cousin revved the engine, hit the gas—and almost sideswiped the ranger who had followed her to the curb. "I'd better hang up now. Oh—have you heard from Mike?"

"Not yet," Joe said.

"I wish . . ." She dropped the phone as Renie roared off down the street toward the Pancake Schloss. "Damnit! What did you do now?"

"That stupid ranger accused me of kidnapping his ugly stuffed deer! Like I'd want a stuffed animal sitting around the house? I've already got Bill. I mean, Oscar. Well, Oscar isn't really—"

"Oscar isn't real and would you please shut up? I can't bend down to pick up my cell. I don't think I disconnected Joe."

"It disconnects itself," Renie said, veering around a slow-moving truck. "At least that's what one of my kids told me."

"Be careful! We almost ran into that oncoming SUV."

"Almost doesn't count," Renie muttered, careening into the parking lot. "I told Ranger Ruggiero I'd report him to . . . somebody."

"Ruggiero?" Judith gasped. "Are you kidding?"

Renie slowed down as she headed to the rear of the pancake house. "No. So what?"

"He's the guy who's in charge of Mike's transfer. You didn't mention my name, did you?"

"No. Why would I?" Renie pulled into the place where Suzie had parked the car earlier in the day. "What if I had? Mike goes by McMonigle, not Flynn."

"I've got to talk to him," Judith said. "Did he see me in the car?"

"How do I know? He probably didn't. He was too busy harassing me about the stupid deer."

"Can you reach my cell?" Judith asked, undoing her seat belt.

"You're going to call Ranger Rude?"

"No, of course not, but I need—"

"You need a lot of things," Renie griped, leaning over to grab the cell. "You're lucky I don't dislocate my other shoulder." She handed over the slim black phone. "You need a little sympathy for *me*."

"Coz . . . skip it. You give Suzie the car keys while I walk back to the Forest Service booth. We have to go in that direction anyway. When you see me talking to Ruggiero, pretend you don't know me and keep going."

"Hey—I'll walk on the other side of the street," Renie said, getting out of the car. "You want me to ask Suzie about the vineyard?"

"You probably can't. It's the dinner hour. The lot's almost full."

The cousins parted company. Judith took her time traversing the block and a half to the exhibit area. She was shivering by the time she reached the Forest Service booth. Not only had it gotten colder, but she could smell snow in the air.

The stuffed deer was leaning against the side of the booth. Apparently Renie must have broken one of its legs. Ruggiero was easy to spot, being the tallest of the three rangers on duty. She approached him just as he finished talking to a couple of men in hunting gear.

"Hi," she said, forcing her warmest smile. "I don't think we've met, but I know you." She extended her hand.

Ruggiero peered at her with shrewd gray eyes. "How is that?" he inquired, shaking hands with a firm but brief grip.

"I'm Mike McMonigle's mother," Judith said. "I've been here in

Little Bavaria with the innkeeping group since Thursday, so I've been out of touch with Mike." She decided not to use subterfuge. "Do you know where his next posting is?"

"Yes."

Judith felt her heart start to beat a bit faster. "Where is it?"

"I can't say. It's not official."

"But . . ." Judith was flummoxed by the ranger's stern expression. "How soon will we—will he know?"

"He knows now," Ruggiero replied. "But he can't tell anyone until it's official. That's how it works with the U.S. government."

She started to say something, realized it would be futile, and clamped her mouth shut. Ruggiero started to turn away, but Judith couldn't let him get off the hook so easily. "Why isn't the U.S. government doing something about the murders around here?"

The ranger swung around to face her. "What are you talking about? That old geezer who got knifed in the bar brawl the other night?"

*So that was how the murder's being played,* Judith thought. "Yes." She gulped. "I was there. It was awful."

"Look," Ruggiero said as if he were talking to a third grader, "this Oktoberfest thing is basically an excuse for tourists to get drunk and go nuts. So far it hasn't been too bad. The people here have a pretty good grip on how to run this kind of show. But you wouldn't believe what I've heard from other parts of the country where they hold these shindigs. Talk about the Italians and the French getting sloshed at their celebrations—the Germans do a damned good job of it, too. If I were you, I'd keep clear of these people. They can be dangerous."

"I suppose so," Judith said meekly. She shivered again, and this time it wasn't only from the cold night air.


**J**udith and Renie didn't meet up until the last few yards before reaching the entrance to Hanover Haus. "I thought you'd been busted by that ranger as my accomplice," Renie said, panting a bit.

"I practically ran the last two blocks to make sure you were okay."

"I am," Judith said, "sort of. Let's talk after we get to the room."

While changing clothes, Judith related her frustrating—and disturbing—encounter with Ranger Ruggiero. "The most interesting part was how Wessler's murder is being played to the public. I suppose that's why Joe doesn't seem to know anything about it."

"Be relieved," Renie advised, taking an orange cowl-neck sweater out of her suitcase. "So Ingrid showed up again? Is she stalking Joe?"

"I'm beginning to wonder. Is she just trying to annoy me or is she really hot for him?"

"Never having met her, I can't tell you much," Renie said, slipping the sweater over her head. "I spoke briefly to Suzie about the vineyard. She had Barry waiting tables before tending bar at tonight's party."

Judith was applying makeup in front of the bureau's oval mirror. "What did she say?"

Renie had almost finished putting her mascara on. "Suze said the plan was on hold. I got the impression she'd like to leave it that way."

"Did she seem annoyed by the inquiry?"

"Why would I annoy her?" Renie scowled at Judith. The mascara wand slipped and fell on the floor. "Damn! See what you made me do?" She snatched up the wand and stared in the mirror. "Now I look like Raccoon Renie. I'll have to start over."

"Sorry. I only meant the question itself, not you. I mean, the two of you did get into it the other night . . ."

Renie had gone into the bathroom to remove the errant mascara marks. "Suze and I are as one," she called out, having left the door open. "The only problem was she got distracted when Franz Wessler came in."

"Franz?" Judith's hand bobbed, sending her lipstick into her left nostril. "Now you've done it!" She got up and joined Renie in the bathroom. "Hurry up. We're going to be late."

"Ha ha. You look funny."

"Mop yourself up so . . ." Judith froze. "What's that?" she breathed.

Renie stepped away from the sink. "What's what?"

"Shhh. It sounded like someone out on the balcony."

"So?"

"I saw a shadow outside, as if someone was looking into our room."

"Watching us turn ourselves into clowns? Aren't there better things to do during Oktoberfest?"

Judith held up a hand, signaling for Renie to be quiet. "Listen." But the only sound they heard was a hunting horn off in the distance.

Renie stalked out of the bathroom, marched to the window, and shouted, "If you got the money, honey, we got the time!"

"Coz!" Judith hissed, coming out of the bathroom. "Stop that!"

Renie ignored the advice, opening the balcony door and looking out. "Nothing to see here, as the cops would say, but it's snowing."

Judith finished wiping off the lipstick smear before joining her cousin. "Fresh footprints, but no tread on the soles. That's odd."

Renie shrugged. "It just started snowing. Was someone listening the whole time before the snow started?"

Judith took one last look before closing the door. "Maybe. Fairly big footprints. That's kind of scary. At least I didn't imagine it."

"No," Renie agreed. "Man or woman?"

"I can't tell. The prints will be obliterated in a few minutes. I'd guess whoever it was must be fairly tall. The eavesdropper must not be staying here. A guest could listen at the other door. Unless it was a ruse to make us think that."

"Maybe it was your run-of-the-mill window peeper," Renie said. "Every community has at least one of those."

"You don't believe that," Judith said, making another attempt at putting on her lipstick, but discovering her hand was unsteady.

"Okay, we can't dwell on it. How distracted was Suze by Franz's arrival?"

Renie waited to answer until she'd finished reapplying her mascara. "I wouldn't call it 'agog,' but she seemed definitely interested in his arrival. Usually, she's unflappable on the job."

"Hmm. I wonder if she was in the car the other night with Franz. I don't recall seeing her after you two parted company at the town hall."

"You think Suze and Franz *really* got together? Not a bad idea. I mean, for them."

"Suze certainly had gone to some trouble to look like . . . maybe not Ava Gardner-esque, but not like Pancake Suzie either."

"Could be a strategic move," Renie said, pulling on her glossy brown leather boots. "Something to do with the vineyard?"

"Maybe." Judith sat down on the bed. "Can you help me with my boots? I'm too tired to bend that far."

"Sure," Renie said. "What would you do without me?"

Judith smiled. "Well . . . I can never accuse you of being dull."

"Thanks." Renie put on the first of Judith's low-heeled snow boots. "I never think of not being dull." She tugged on Judith's other boot. "It's a lot better than thinking of being dead."

"Right," Judith agreed, standing up. "Why do I have the feeling that's what we have to worry about?"

# Chapter Seventeen

The snow fell in feathery flakes, indicating that the temperature wasn't far below freezing. The wind had subsided, apparently coming off the mountains and blowing east. Judith envisioned a white world of orchards and farms in that part of the state.

"Winter wheat," she said aloud, walking along the next block past more shops and cafés.

"What?" Renie asked. "Are you obsessed with crops now?"

"I need a reminder that most people's lives are ordinary, ordained by the seasons. How many other people do you know who are afraid that someone may be lurking around the corner waiting to kill them?"

"Plenty, if I count the shoppers at Falstaff's Grocery when I drive into the parking lot."

Judith shot Renie an irked glance. "You know what I mean."

"Just enjoy the snow." Renie gestured at a group of young people who were trying to make snowballs in the middle of the street. "Look, they're probably so gassed they don't know the snow is too wet for weaponry. They'll have to wait a while to pelt each other."

Judith shrugged. "They're having fun. How far is this place?"

"How would I know? It can't be too far. We're past the bandstand and that other inn. The town virtually ends in another block or two."

They trudged on for another half a block before seeing a sign and an arrow pointing toward the river. "There it is. The Valhalla Inn," Judith said. "I can see the roof. There better be stairs."

There were zigzagging stone steps already almost clear of snow from the arrival of earlier guests. Judith held on to the handrail and took her time. From what she could tell through the thick snow that was now falling, the inn looked older and more rustic than the rest of the town's architecture. It was built into the side of the hill above the river, its bottom two floors made of sandstone. Rough-hewn logs covered the second- and third-floor facades. The steep pitch of the roof indicated it had been constructed to withstand heavy snows when there had been even harder winters in the first half of the twentieth century.

"I bet this was the original ski lodge," Judith said, pausing at the pine door to listen to the river ripple in the mountain valley. "It reminds me of our family cabin."

"Yeah?" Renie retorted. "So where's the outhouse?"

"Forget it." Judith opened the door. The river's flow was drowned out by the sound of cheerful voices, hearty laughter, and a lively accordion. "We *are* late," she murmured. "Stay out of trouble, okay?"

Renie made a face, but didn't say anything. She was too busy trying to unzip her black hooded ski parka.

Eldridge Hoover and Jeanne Barber both rushed over to greet Judith. "We were afraid you weren't coming!" Jeanne cried, gripping her in a rib-crushing hug. "Everybody's here."

Managing to unlock herself from Jeanne's embrace, Judith scanned the crowd in the rustic room. She spotted the Denkels, the Beaulieus, Gabe Hunter, and several others from the B&B contingent. Barry Stafford was tending bar while Jessi kept him company. Evelyn Choo was talking to a slim, trim, silver-haired man Judith hadn't yet met.

"Connie must've finished her workshop," Judith said.

"Yes," Jeanne said. "I learned all sorts of new tricks from her."

"I didn't know Connie was turning tricks," Renie said, sidling up to her cousin.

Jeanne looked puzzled; Eldridge let out a little snort that sounded like a stifled laugh.

Judith changed the subject. "Is that Mr. Stromeyer with Evelyn?"

Jeanne nodded. "He seems very nice, but he came down with flu a couple of days ago. That's why we haven't seen much of him. Mr. Stromeyer is much older than he looks. Isn't he distinguished?"

Judith studied the chairman's erect figure. "Ex-military?"

"Yes," Jeanne said. "Despite the German name, he was born in this country. He fought for our side."

"So did Eisenhower," Renie remarked.

"I should meet him," Judith said. She abandoned Renie to the two other innkeepers, but paused at the bar to ask Barry for a Scotch-rocks.

"You got it," Barry said with a wry smile. "You can't get drunk if you're not drinking,"

Jessi, who was sipping some sort of bubbly wine, shook her head. "Don't encourage any more mayhem around here, Barry. This town is starting to make me nervous." She nodded in Stromeyer's direction. "He's such a wonderful old guy, but he looks pale. Maybe he should've stayed home tonight after putting in so much work for the festival."

"Could you introduce me?" Judith asked. "I'd like to thank him for everything he's done."

"Sure," Jessi said. "Follow me."

To Judith's dismay, Ellie and Delmar Denkel had just approached Stromeyer. "Judith," Ellie said, lifting her glass in a vague salute. "You must meet Herman Stromeyer. Delmar and I feel like he's a dear friend."

Judith thought Herman looked older up close. He offered her the hand that wasn't holding an empty wineglass. "How do you do, Mrs. . . . ?"

"McMonigle," Ellie put in hastily.

"Flynn," Judith said firmly.

Ellie snickered. "I forgot you finally married that cop."

Jessi volunteered to get Herman a refill, but he demurred. "I don't want to upset my stomach after the flu. Just sparkling cider, my dear."

Jessi took his empty glass. "Sure, Gramps. Be right back."

Judith didn't hide her surprise. "Jessi is your granddaughter?"

Herman offered her an engaging smile. "She is indeed. My Sadie passed away a long time ago. She's my youngest daughter's little girl."

"Goodness," Judith said, "I'm used to the city. I forget how everyone in small towns seems connected to everybody else."

Ellie nudged Judith. "You're drinking Scotch? How could you with all these amazing German wines?"

"I have no palate," Judith admitted.

"Pity," Delmar said, tapping his glass. "I've studied up on the differences between regional wines. This Silvania is top-notch, straight from the old country."

"*Silvaner,* darling," Ellie said, putting a hand on her husband's back. "Oh, I realize you're making one of your little jokes."

Herman looked slightly pained, but attempted a smile. "It's not easy keeping track of wines and their regions. I'm no expert, like Dietrich Wessler, but, as they say, I know what I like." His expression brightened as Jessi reappeared with the sparkling cider. Renie wasn't far behind.

"Jerk," she said into Judith's ear. "I had to listen to Jeanne Barber blah-blah about the wonders of island living. Evelyn abandoned me."

Ignoring the comment, Judith introduced Renie to Herman. "Not another innkeeper, eh?" he said in a jovial tone.

"I'm a cousin-keeper," Renie said meekly. "I don't get out much."

"That's not a bad thing," Ellie murmured.

Judith held her breath as her cousin's eyes sparked. "Watch it, Mrs. Dingle," Renie said softly. "One thing I'm keeping is my temper."

Ellie whirled around so fast that she bumped Herman's arm, spilling some of the cider on the parquet floor. "You're rude!" she cried. "What did you do with your manners?"

Renie assumed an innocent air. "I gave them to you for your birthday. You never thanked me."

Judith realized that several heads had turned in their direction. Jessi was motioning to Barry, who had come out from behind the bar. Ellie swerved toward Judith, who accidentally stepped on Barry's foot, causing him to bump into Herman and slosh cider on the hardwood floor.

"Don't move," Barry said. "I'll wipe this up and get Herman a refill."

"Sorry," Judith whispered to Barry, handing him her glass. "Could you top this for me?"

"Sure." He hurried back to the bar.

"Excuse me," Ellie said, her head held high. "Come, Delmar, we must get out of the disaster area. We, too, need refills." She flounced off with her husband taking up the rear in his docile pet Chihuahua role.

"Chicken," Renie said, after taking a swig of her bourbon. "The old hen's twice my size and still is scared of me. It must be the big teeth."

"And the big mouth," Judith said under her breath. Glancing at Herman, she saw that his smile was ironic.

"Ellie's soured with age," he murmured. "She was always difficult. Spoiled, I think, by her mother to make up for her father's alcoholism."

Judith felt her eyes widen. "Her father drank?"

"I'm afraid so," Herman said, frowning. "Being Dietrich Wessler's elder son was a burden for Josef. The younger one, Franz, had it easier and later moved away. Josef's death was untimely in the sense that he was drunk when he fell off the balcony at Hanover Haus. He died immediately of his injuries." He smiled in his ironic manner. "Ellie's mother was more relieved than grief-stricken. Tilde was known around town as the Merry Widow."

"I didn't know Ellie very well until now," Judith said, still feeling confused about the Wessler family tree. "We've had no chance to talk about backgrounds. Was Dietrich a harsh father or merely demanding?"

"He wasn't cruel," Herman replied after a pause, "but let's say he held great expectations, particularly for Josef as his firstborn."

Barry had returned to wipe up the floor. "Refills on the way with Jessi," he said. "I had to give the Denkels another hit on their drinks first. Mrs. Denkel doesn't like to be kept waiting."

"She never has," Herman said softly.

Barry finished his task and rushed away.

"Sad, really," Judith said. "Ellie's upbringing, I mean. Speaking of tragedies, something just occurred to me. If the cemetery is relatively new, why are Mr. Wessler's wife and baby buried there? They died over fifty years ago."

Herman's mouth twisted. "The cemetery was created on land owned by Dietrich. Frau Wessler and her child were buried there in the forest. It was a logical place to put those who passed on later."

"That makes sense," Judith said. "How did they drown?"

Herman's shrewd blue eyes regarded her with something akin to amusement. "Are you writing a history of our little town?"

"I am," Renie said, raising her hand. "I'm a graphic designer. I thought I'd tell the story in 'toons."

"Why not?" Herman responded. "It's had its comic opera aspects."

He paused to accept the glass Jessi offered him. "Thanks, Jess. Mrs. Jones tells me she plans to write a book about us. Or draw one." He raised his glass and took a deep sip.

"Really?" Jessi said, turning to Renie. "Are you an artist?"

"Sort of," Renie replied. "I do graphics."

Judith couldn't resist putting another question to Herman.

"My cousin and I happened to see the marker for a Henry Rupert Hellman. I understand he was a suicide, but why is his marker there?"

Herman looked askance. "That's a story in itself, but nobody knows how much is true and how much is rumor. He'd come here from Germany around 1950. I've only been in Little Bavaria since 1982. Hank, as he was called, had a wife and a son, but they kept to themselves. Mrs. Hellman was in poor health and died young. Some people—not all our residents back then were as broad-minded as they are now—thought he felt awkward being Jewish. He couldn't openly practice his religion because there was no temple or synagogue." Herman shook his head. "Then one day he hanged himself from a lamppost near the town hall. Very sad."

"What about his family?" Judith asked.

"The son had moved away. I never knew them."

"No, not if you didn't come here . . ." Judith stopped as Herman grasped his throat, dropped the glass, and reached out to Judith. Unable to support his weight, she stumbled backward into Jessi, who let out a little scream before trying to help with the stricken man.

"Gramps!" Jessi cried. "What's wrong?"

He didn't respond. Somehow, the three women eased him onto the floor. It wasn't easy, given his size and the broken glass. Barry was running toward them. So were several other guests, including the Beaulieus and Evelyn Choo, who were coming from the bar behind Barry.

Evelyn had her cell out. "I'll call 911," she said, a ship of calm in a sea of shock. She stepped out of the way while Judith frantically tried to loosen Herman's tie and unbutton his white shirt. The old man was turning purple, still fighting for breath. Barry was trying to keep more gawkers from crowding around them.

"Please!" he shouted. "Step back. Make way for the EMTs."

Hands shaking, Judith tried to remember what to do from her Red Cross classes. But Herman had passed out. Or . . . she didn't want to think about the alternative. Putting a hand on his chest, she realized he was still breathing, if in a shallow, labored manner. Her own head felt strange. The headache must be coming back . . . it had been a long time since she'd taken the Excedrin . . . hours and hours and . . .

The last thing she heard was Ellie saying in her strident voice, "Now see what you've done, Judith. You've killed Herman Stromeyer."

**J**udith came to in a room that was so bright it almost blinded her. She blinked several times before realizing that she was looking up into the lights of a hospital corridor.

"It's okay," Renie said. "You passed out. You're exhausted."

"Where's Herman?" Judith asked, making a vain effort to sit up.

"They're working on him," Renie said, gesturing down the hall.

Judith felt a sense of relief wash over her. "Was it a stroke?"

"I don't know. The medics arrived just after you fainted. They only had room for Herman, so Duomo put you in the paddy wagon. I rode along with you."

"What?" Judith tried to lift her head, but couldn't quite manage it. "How long was I out?"

"Seven, eight minutes. The hospital's just past the high school. It took less than five minutes for the EMTs to do their thing."

"Good grief." Judith flung an arm over her eyes. "That light is killing me. Have you got some Excedrin?"

"Yes," Renie replied. "I also brought your purse. Have you got something in it that's stronger than the Excedrin we both carry because we're old and enfeebled? I think I'll take a couple just for the hell of it."

"Hand me my purse and get some water," Judith said. "Have you seen a doctor?"

"No, I don't have to." Renie gave the purse to Judith. "I feel fine."

"I mean, have you talked . . . skip it." Judith didn't know

whether to laugh or hit Renie. She did neither, saving her energy to find her pills.

After her cousin went off to find some water, Judith located her pills and studied her surroundings. The hallway was lined with doors leading to what might have been exam rooms. She couldn't see any personnel, so assumed the staff was working elsewhere.

Renie returned with a paper cup of water. "Doc Frolander and an intern are the only ones on duty. Doc is tending to Herman. I overheard the term 'gastric lavage,' so they're pumping his stomach."

Judith groaned. "That indicates they think he was poisoned."

Renie nodded. "I wondered. Think it was the wine or the cider?"

"I don't know," Judith said, after swallowing the pills. "Duomo noted that Wessler may not have died immediately after consuming whatever killed him. Did you see food at the party tonight?"

Renie shook her head. "If I had, I'd have eaten it. I'm hungry."

"Who else came here with Herman?"

"Jessi," Renie said, peeking around the nearby corner that led to another hallway. "In fact, here she comes now with Fat Matt and a thin nurse. I thought I heard voices."

The police chief took one look at Judith and chuckled wryly. "Don't tell me you got poisoned, too."

That hadn't occurred to Judith. "I don't think so. I'm just really tired. I'm not used to walking so much on pavement."

"Tell me about it," Duomo said. "Sure glad I don't do a beat anymore. 'Flatfoot' is right. Hey, the nurse wants to check you out."

The chief, Renie, and Jessi moved away. The nurse began taking Judith's vitals. She spoke only when she'd finished. "Stomach pains?"

"No. Just light-headed when I collapsed."

"No other complaints?"

"No."

"Your pulse is fine, no fever, but your blood pressure is elevated."

"It does that sometimes," Judith replied.

"Do you take medication for it?"

"Yes."

"Very well. I recommend that you stay here for at least half an hour. If you want to see a doctor, you may have to wait longer. We just got word of a bad accident up at the summit."

"I don't think I need to bother anyone else," Judith said. "Thanks."

The nurse moved swiftly around the corner and disappeared. Judith tried to sit up, but required a hand from Renie. Jessi looked pale and her eyes were red-rimmed.

"How," she asked of no one in particular, "could Gramps get poisoned? *Why* would that happen to him?"

"Could be food poisoning," the chief said. "Did he eat before the shindig?"

"I don't know," Jessi said. "I worked until closing the shop. I'd brought my good clothes with me to save time so I'd be ready when Barry came to get me. He had to help set up the bar at a quarter to seven."

"Right," Duomo said absently. "I should've stopped in. I've missed a lot of this year's functions. Damned job. Have to tend to business to impress the tourists. Oh, well. See you all later." He started toward what Judith thought must be the exit.

"Hey," she called in a feeble voice, "don't you want to question us?"

"Huh?" Fat Matt turned around. "Not now. You're sick. I'll catch you tomorrow." He disappeared around the corner.

Judith grappled with the thin blanket that covered her. Jessi was nowhere in sight. Apparently, she had gone off to check on her grandfather. "I can't lie here like a lump," Judith said. "How do we get back to Hanover Haus? I sure can't walk."

"You could crawl," Renie suggested.

Judith didn't bother to comment. She started to sit up, but

found the effort too draining. "I'm really worn out," she said in frustration.

"Maybe I can steal an ambulance," Renie said.

"Forget it. They're peeling people off the road up at the summit."

Renie scanned the hallway. "There must be something I can steal. Be right back." She went off and out of sight.

Judith finally managed to raise her head enough to take the Excedrin. A moment later, Barry came around the corner.

"How are you doing?" he asked. "I followed Jessi here in Mom's car. No word yet on her granddad."

"How old is he?" Judith asked.

"Eighty-eight," Barry replied. "He's a good guy. Jessi's folks retired to Arizona last year. Her dad likes to golf."

"Nice," Judith murmured, before taking in what Barry had said previously. "You have your car here?"

"Yes." Barry smiled. "You want a ride back to your inn?"

"You should stay with Jessi, but . . ." She stopped, hearing a rattling noise nearby. A moment later, Renie showed up, pushing a hospital bed.

"Hey, coz," she called, "get Barry to hoist you onto this. I can wheel you back to Hanover Haus."

Barry burst out laughing. Judith shook her head. "We have transport. Barry has a car."

Renie evinced surprise. "A car? What a novel idea!"

Five minutes later, Judith was in the passenger seat of the Ford Escort. "It's Mom's car," he explained. "She didn't need it tonight."

"I thought it looked familiar," Renie said from the backseat. "We got it impounded this afternoon. Good thing I got rid of the deer."

"The deer?" Barry asked from behind the wheel. "What deer?"

Renie explained about the stuffed buck. Judith told Barry why the car had gotten impounded.

"Mom didn't tell me you'd borrowed the Escort," he said as they drove down the busy main street. Vehicle and foot traffic had already turned the snow to slush. "Guess she was too excited about her date."

"Your mother has a date?" Judith said. "How nice."

Barry nodded. "Some people might think it's too soon after Dad died, but Mom needs somebody to lean on. I can't stick around here forever. She seems independent and tough, but underneath . . . well, it's kind of a facade. Besides, this guy is really one cool dude."

"Dare I ask who?"

"Sure," Barry said, pulling up to the entrance of Hanover Haus. "He's a bigwig forest ranger, name of Rick Ruggiero."

Judith and Renie didn't let on they knew Ruggiero. Given Renie's fractious encounter and Judith's rejected pleas about Mike, their history with the ranger didn't add anything positive to their own résumés. Nor was there much opportunity to discuss Suzie's date. Judith could walk through the small lobby, though she had to lean on Barry to steady her. The woman behind the desk glared at the trio and mouthed the word *drunk*. Renie mouthed a couple of unprintable words in return and moved on to help Judith take the stairs one at a time.

Inside their room, Judith thanked Barry profusely. Before he left, she begged him to let her know what had happened with Herman Stromeyer. Barry promised he would and departed.

"So Suzie's not hot for Franz," Judith murmured, lying on the bed. "Just as well. Ruggiero's the strong, no-nonsense type. He must be stationed here. I wish I knew where Mike was going."

"You'll find out," Renie said, checking her watch. "It's not yet nine. You don't intend to send me off to that concert to sleuth, do you?"

"I hadn't thought about it," Judith said. "But now that you mention it, the bandstand's only a little over a block away."

Renie tipped her head to one side and looked pitiable. "Coz . . ."

"Klara said it would be popular music. You wouldn't mind that, would you? I mean, it's not that long, drawn-out stuff you hate."

Renie groaned. "It's snowing, it's cold, it's dark, it's . . ." She picked up the parka she'd tossed on a chair. "Okay, but you owe me."

"I already do," Judith said with a wan smile. "You were a trouper at the hospital. Just don't mix it up with anybody, okay?"

"I never make promises I can't keep," Renie said, putting on the parka. "Maybe I can find some food. See you."

Judith's headache was beginning to ease. She considered sitting up so she could read one of the two paperbacks she'd brought with her, but felt more like taking a nap. Turning off the bedside lamp, she closed her eyes. Moments later, she was sound asleep.

A knock at the door woke her up. Judith fumbled for the light switch. Her watch informed her it was nine-forty. By the time she struggled out of bed, the knock sounded again, louder and more insistent. "Who is it?" Judith asked, wishing the door had a peephole.

"George Beaulieu," said the muffled voice. "Please let me in."

Judith hesitated, but decided if she needed help, she could stay near the balcony and yell down at the festival patrons who were probably all over the main street.

"What's wrong?" she asked, seeing George's stricken expression. His overcoat and watch cap were dusted with melting snowflakes.

"I must talk to someone," he said in an anxious voice. "I chose you, with your Gypsy eyes. May I sit?"

Judith gestured at one of the two simple armchairs. "What's upset you so?" she inquired, sitting in the other chair and relieved that she hadn't bothered to get undressed.

"It's Connie," George said, nervously smoothing his handlebar mustache. "She's leaving me."

"No! Why would she do that?"

George sniffled. "She's in love with another man."

Judith took a deep breath. "How long has this been going on?"

"Ever since we went to Disneyland," George said, taking a handkerchief out of his pants pocket.

Judith refrained from asking if Connie had fallen in love with Pluto. Or Goofy. "What did Disneyland have to do with it?"

George paused to blow his nose. "We went there a year ago last summer. I had to attend a training seminar in Anaheim. We'd taken our children to Disneyland years ago, but as long as we were staying close by, we decided it might be enjoyable to go by ourselves. One of the rides we went on was Splash Mountain—the one featuring Brer Rabbit."

Judith nodded while George caught his breath. "My first husband and I took our son on that ride when we visited Disneyland." It wasn't exactly true. Dan McMonigle's girth couldn't fit into the craft that plied Splash Mountain's waterway. For a moment or two Judith was lost in reverie, and missed a beat in George's account.

". . . Connie met Franz, who was filming a folktale documentary. At first, I thought she was infatuated with the Possum, not the man."

Judith waited for George to continue, but he was blowing his nose again. "You say 'infatuated.' Do you mean that or something more serious? Did Franz reciprocate?"

"Unfortunately, I caught a cold," George said with a mournful expression. "Franz was staying at the same hotel. He and Connie had dinner together one night. She returned very late, insisting they merely talked, mostly about his films. I was fool enough to believe her."

"And?" Judith urged.

"I believe that since then"—he grimaced—"they've *texted*."

"Oh," Judith said. "Oh, that's . . . too bad."

"And now they're . . . together." George blew his nose again.

"You mean . . . ?"

"When I asked if you knew where Connie had gone the other day, I'm sure she was with Franz. Last night they left the concert arm in arm. I suspect the worst."

"Why didn't you leave with Connie before she could go with Franz?"

"I was overcome by Klara's singing. I was among those giving her a standing ovation. She has such a lovely voice." George leaned forward in the chair. His face—or what Judith could see of it with the sadly drooping handlebar mustache—was full of appeal to her better nature. "Those Gypsy eyes. Please convey your wisdom to me. I'm in agony."

"I'm no wiser than most people," Judith said firmly. "You should discuss this with Connie. Or have you already done that?"

"Not tonight," George replied. "How could I? Connie and Franz are at tonight's musical event. I couldn't bear to be around them. Of course I broached the subject when we were in Disneyland, but I was ill, and not able to adequately articulate my concerns. She merely laughed and said they had only talked. But I know they've been in touch. This comes at an awful time—we're about to celebrate our silver wedding anniversary."

"All the more reason to talk this out," Judith said.

George stared at his bony hands. "Connie would only deny any wrongdoing."

Judith hesitated, feeling helpless in the wake of George's reluctance. "I recall you and Connie talking about your job being undercover. That indicates you might have resources to investigate what's actually going on between Connie and Franz. It may sound extreme, but are you willing to try a backdoor approach?"

George scowled. "How? By checking our sewer line? I already did that today for Mr. Stromeyer, but he needs a plumber."

"Huh?"

He let out a big sigh. "I'm a sewer inspector for the city. Connie likes to make me sound mysterious. I'm not. I considered my task at Stromeyer's as a goodwill gesture. No charge."

"Very kind. I still think you two ought to talk. It's the best advice I can offer. It seems to me that your suspicions are a bit flimsy."

"Flimsy?" George snorted and retrieved his handkerchief. "I saw one of those texts. They were making plans to rendezvous at an expensive hotel in Vegas. She wanted to know which one Franz would choose. We've never been to Vegas, but he has. Isn't that solid evidence?"

*Of what?* Judith wanted to say, but retained her sympathetic manner. "Your wife runs a B&B. She may've been inquiring on behalf of a guest. George, I think you're overreacting."

He blew his nose and retreated into his glum state. "I disagree."

The door burst open and Renie practically fell into the room. "Wow, I had a great time! They played some of my favorite . . . oops! Hi, George," she said, seeing him where he'd been hidden by the open door. "Were you at the concert? Klara has a spectacular voice."

He looked dazed. "Not tonight. I'm unwell."

Renie nodded. "You look it." She turned to Judith. "How are you feeling? Did you take a nap?"

"Yes, I did. Any news?"

Renie glanced at George. "Jessi says the other patient is better."

"Good," Judith said, getting out of the chair slowly, but surely. She turned to George, who looked blank. "I hope you'll take my advice."

"What? Oh, yes, thank you. I'll try," he responded, "though I'm pessimistic." With apparent reluctance, he, too, stood up. "Thank you for hearing me out." He nodded absently at Renie and left.

"Well?" Renie said. "Did he confess to killing Herr Wessler, too?"

Judith sank back into the chair. "No. He thinks Connie is carrying on with Franz Wessler. I think George is nuts."

Renie grinned. "I saw Connie with Franz—an odd couple."

"I agree," Judith said, "but I think George is making a mountain out of a molehill." She quickly described his suspicions. "It's likely those text messages between Franz and Connie were to find a Vegas hotel as a surprise anniversary present for George."

Renie, who had taken George's place in the vacant chair, shrugged. "Could be. Connie didn't look like an enamored wayward wife when she left with Franz. In fact, I thought she looked scared."

"You mean Connie went with Franz unwillingly?"

"No, not that," Renie said. "She seemed frightened or worried."

"Maybe I should talk to Connie," Judith murmured. "It's a shame I haven't warmed to her." She stared at Renie. "Why did Ellie choose Connie to give that seminar? It wasn't on the original event schedule. Maybe you should chat her up tomorrow. I wonder if the Beaulieus are Catholic. George was born in France. I'm on duty at the booth at eleven with Eldridge Hoover, right after Mass."

Renie didn't answer right away. "No. You've been in the hospital. I'll do your stint with Eldridge while you have a sit-down with Connie. But you're going to have to pry George loose."

Judith, however, protested. "You don't know how to run a B&B."

"What's to know? I just hand out some poorly designed brochures and bare my teeth in a pseudo smile."

Judith was too tired to argue. "We'll sort this out in the morning. Tell me more about Herman Stromeyer."

"Not much to tell," Renie said, getting up and starting to undress. "They pumped out his stomach and he's in some kind of condition. I forget what. Maybe upgraded from dire straits to so-so."

"Could they tell what he ingested?"

"Poison, I guess," Renie said, from underneath the sweater she was pulling over her head.

"You guess? Did Jessi say it was poison?"

Having discarded the sweater, Renie glared at her cousin. "Of course not. They have to run tests. You know that."

Judith leaned back in the chair. Her headache was better, but she was still bone tired. "You're right. I'm worn out. Do the booth, but don't mouth off to anyone. Eldridge will help you. You're used to dealing with people in your graphic design business. What could possibly go wrong?"

# Chapter Eighteen

**R**enie tried to discourage Judith from attending Mass the next morning, but failed. "I *can* go to church," she said. "Maybe I can talk to Father Dash about Mr. Wessler. But I'll come back here to rest."

Renie looked dubious, but didn't argue. She obviously wasn't quite awake at nine-thirty in the morning. They skipped breakfast. Judith wasn't very hungry and Renie figured she could get something somewhere somehow after Mass.

The church was a block and a half uphill, but only one block east of Hanover Haus. The snow apparently had stopped not long after it had started, with less than two inches on the ground. The streets and sidewalks had been cleared, but the cousins took their time. The plain white church with its steep roof did not have the elaborate onion-shaped dome that was typical of southern Germany, but it definitely had a European feel inside.

"Baroque simplified," Renie whispered, entering the wooden pew.

Judith agreed. The interior evoked the style of the seventeenth century, but was less lavish. The sanctuary featured colorful statuary of the Virgin Mary holding Jesus on her lap with Saint Joseph hovering behind them while cherubs watched under a deep blue sky.

The church had filled up by the time the priest and two teenage acolytes processed to the altar. Father Dash was of Asian descent, but his English was perfect. By the time he approached the pulpit to deliver his sermon, Renie nudged Judith.

"Check out the statue on my right. If that's Saint Hubert, how come he's dressed up as a hunter and eyeing that stag?"

Judith turned to look at the arched niche with its not-quite-life-size statuary. "I don't know," she whispered, "but that deer is better-looking than the one you were driving around in Suze's car."

The cousins kept quiet while Father Dash delivered an articulate if uninspiring sermon about the disciples trusting in Jesus, casting off their fear of drowning, and getting into the boat. Judith drifted, wondering how Mrs. Wessler and her baby had drowned, trying to picture Bob Stafford by the river before his assailant's attack, and if there was a connection between the two recent homicides. She was snapped back into the present when the lector read the petitions for the fourth Sunday of October. The next to the last was for the recovery of Herman Stromeyer; the final prayer was for Dietrich Wessler and all the souls of the departed.

Judith and Renie had exchanged relieved glances at the mention of Herman's survival. So had several other members of the congregation. The liturgy continued, with the last blessing and dismissal at precisely eleven o'clock. The church bells rang, echoed by the chiming of the nearby clock tower. There was no announcement about a postliturgy get-together. Instead, Father Dash informed his worshippers that Dietrich Wessler's Requiem Mass would be held at eleven on Thursday, November 3, the feast of Saint Hubert. "For those of you visiting Little Bavaria," he explained, "the deceased was a beloved patron and father figure to the town, respected by all for his untiring diligence in re-creating a moribund village as a vibrant center of Bavarian culture."

"Are you okay to walk back to the inn by yourself?" Renie asked as they moved outside with the rest of the parishioners and visitors.

Judith nodded. "I'd still like to speak to Father Dash, but he's surrounded by some of the locals." She nodded discreetly as they saw the priest standing in the midst of at least a dozen people.

"You could collapse again to get his attention," Renie said.

"No, I'll wait inside. I can catch him on his way to the sacristy."

Renie hesitated. "You're sure you want to do that?"

Judith insisted she did. "Go on, I'll be fine. Grab something to eat before you rip some tourists apart with your bare teeth."

Renie didn't need any further prodding. Judith went back inside the church. Only two elderly women remained, both saying the rosary. Judith guessed that the door to the left of the sanctuary led to the sacristy. She tried to visualize the building's exterior, but couldn't recall seeing any indication of a basement. If there was a rectory and a social hall, perhaps they weren't connected to the church.

One of the old ladies got out of the pew, moving to the nearby shrine of a nun. Judith recognized the parishioner as Astrid Bauer from the cemetery. When the old lady tried to light a votive candle, her hand shook so badly that she dropped the match and let out a little cry of dismay. Judith got out of the pew, but before she could take any action, the flame sputtered out.

"No harm done," Judith said softly. "Let me do it for you."

"Thank you! Oh! You were with that sweet, kind woman who helped me with my bouquet."

Judith smiled as she struck another match and lighted the wick. "There," she said. "Who is this saint? I don't recognize her."

"Saint Birgitta of Sweden," the woman replied, her wrinkled hands still trembling, though a faint smile touched her thin lips. "I gave this statue to the church in memory of my daughter. It was all I could do."

"That's a lovely memorial," Judith said.

Mrs. Bauer nodded, her gaze straying to the flickering candle. "My daughter was named for a saint who was never accepted by Rome. That nun is as lost to church history as my daughter is lost to me."

"I'm so sorry," Judith said. "Your daughter died young?"

Mrs. Bauer looked away. "No. She is dead to me, but not to God." Crossing herself, she bowed her head, apparently in prayer.

Judith had no choice but to move down the aisle, where she saw Father Dash enter the sanctuary. She smiled as she met him by the confessionals. "I know you must be busy," she said, "but may I speak to you for a moment? I have questions about Mr. Wessler's Requiem Mass."

If the priest was surprised by her request, he didn't show it. "Fine, tag along while I get out of my rig. I have to say another Mass at a mission church this evening, but I can spare a few minutes now."

Father Dash led the way. Judith had to hustle to keep up with him. She wondered if Dash was a nickname. It was one of the first questions she had for him when they entered the small room where the vestments and other Mass items were kept.

"I gather you're on the road a lot," she said.

"I am. Three, sometimes four different churches every weekend." He paused as he took off his chasuble. Judith figured him for midforties, medium height, sturdy build, and balding. "During the week I work in the chancery office. I'm a canon lawyer."

"You're an American," she said, and was embarrassed that it sounded like an accusation.

"I am now, but I was born in Indonesia." He grinned. "My last name's not Dash—it's Wirahadashikudumah." At least that's what Judith thought he said. "I came to this country when I was eight. You are . . . ?"

"Judith Flynn, part of the innkeeping group." She shook hands with the priest. "Have you served in Little Bavaria for a long time?"

Father Dash finished removing his vestments and carefully hung them on a padded hanger. "About five years." He tucked a plaid shirt into his denim jeans. "Cute town. Enthusiastic bunch of people. Terrific beer." He looked closely at Judith. "You *are* Catholic, aren't you?"

"Yes, a cradle Catholic," Judith said.

"I thought so. You didn't look shocked when I mentioned beer. What did you want to ask about the Wessler service?"

Judith decided to level with Father Dash. "I'm helping the police with their inquiries about Wessler's death—and Bob Stafford's, too."

"No!" The priest burst out laughing. "You're serious?"

"I'm afraid so."

"From what I've seen of the local police chief, God love him, he's not the brightest bulb in the law enforcement marquee. But then I don't really know him. With a name like Duomo, you'd think he'd come to Mass sometimes. I never met Stafford—not Catholic. Say, I haven't eaten yet. I had to fast before saying Mass. Any chance you're hungry?"

"Yes," Judith admitted as her stomach growled to prove it.

"Okay." Dash put on a black leather jacket. "We'd better avoid the Pancake Schloss if we're going to discuss the late owner. There's a crêpe place tucked away by the hardware store a block from here. Shall we?"

"Sounds good." Judith smiled gratefully. "I'm kind of worn out."

"You look a bit weary around the edges," Dash said, holding the door open for Judith. "Oktoberfest can be tiring. Just as well I don't stick around here for too long at a time. I'm used to a less raucous life."

The sun was trying to break through the clouds when they got outside. A band played in the distance. They turned a corner a block away from police headquarters, venturing down a side street Judith hadn't yet seen. Werner's Crêperie was between Hansel's Hardware and Gretchen's Kitchens. Father Dash must have been a regular, as the effusive white-haired woman who greeted him seated them immediately.

"Helga and Werner are Lutherans," the priest said, handing Judith a menu, "but she must have some French in her. She makes great crêpes. They also offer a couple of German pancake specialties, too."

"I didn't realize how hungry I was until now," Judith said. "I see they also have Swedish pancakes. That reminds me—do you know the woman who was praying by the statue of Saint Birgitta?"

"Mrs. Bauer?" He nodded. "She's Swedish, but converted years ago when she married . . . Helmut, I think. I never knew him. He died before I started coming here."

"She was praying for her daughter. It sounded . . . very sad."

Dash was studying the menu. "I guess so. From what little I've heard, the girl went off the rails. She wouldn't be a girl now, of course, probably middle-aged. Mrs. Bauer must be in her eighties. I think I'll have the crêpes with the boysenberry jam."

The many choices made Judith indecisive. "Oh, I guess I'll get the applesauce ones. They sound more German." She put the menu aside. "Mrs. Bauer referred to a saint who wasn't a saint. I mean, in reference to praying to Saint Birgitta. Do you know who she meant?"

Dash frowned. "Not offhand. You mean somebody who's alive?"

"No. Someone from the past. Apparently, Saint Birgitta is as close as she could come to the other person who was never canonized."

"I'd have to look it up," Dash said. "There's a Saint Brigid, but she's Irish and definitely was canonized."

"Yes, I know about her."

A very young-looking waiter came to take their orders. After he had gone off, Dash asked why Judith was helping the police with their homicide inquiries. She reluctantly told him about her reputation as FASTO. "Please don't mention it to anyone. I'm trying to keep a low profile while I'm here. I don't want to get kicked out of the B&B association. The woman who runs it thinks I'm a magnet for murder."

Their meal arrived. "Good service," Dash remarked. He eyed Judith curiously. "Why here? Why now?"

Judith swallowed a bite of crêpe. "What do you mean?"

"You say Duomo asked you to help. How'd he find you?"

"I assume he came across the FASTO site on the Internet. I never look at it. Maybe it's cross-referenced under B&Bs or innkeepers."

"Not word of mouth?"

Judith felt stupid. "I doubt it. He'd have mentioned it. Duomo seems desperate. He wasn't getting anywhere with the Stafford murder. Then Wessler got killed and last night Mr. Stromeyer was poisoned."

"Poisoned?" Dash almost dropped his fork. "I thought he had a heart attack. Are you sure?"

Judith explained how she had been a witness at the Valhalla Inn and then had ended up in the hospital, too. "I know it all sounds improbable, but I haven't yet heard the results of the tests on Mr. Stromeyer. I'm glad he's stable. Isn't that what you were told?"

Dash nodded again. "Yes, Doc Frolander's son is one of my altar boys. He asked me to pray for Stromeyer. I don't know Herman. He's Lutheran, but he's another big wheel around here. Not as much as Wessler was, though."

"Tell me about the Knights of Saint Hubert," Judith said, sprinkling more powdered sugar on her crêpe. "How is the honor earned?"

"Wessler got it for helping refugees after the war." Dash paused while the young waiter refilled their coffee cups. "He worked mainly with displaced persons. A few of them—along with several of the Germans—followed him to America. Wessler emigrated around 1950, but settled somewhere else first. The Midwest, if I remember right."

"Omaha, someone told me. Speaking of Saint Hubert, my cousin and I wondered about the statue of him as a hunter."

Dash chuckled. "It may be a myth. In fact, it may have been handed down from another saint who probably didn't even exist."

"The one Mrs. Bauer mentioned?"

"No, this one was a guy, known as Saint Eustace. He was supposed to be a general under Trajan and an unholy terror on the battlefield. But as the legend goes, he went hunting in his quieter moments and a stag with a crucifix in its antlers appeared to him.

He became a Christian and allegedly was martyred. Or maybe arrested by the local game warden for poaching. Anyway, somehow that tale became confused with Saint Hubert, who was a very holy eighth-century bishop of Ardennes. No martyr—he died in some sort of fishing accident. I suppose that may be how his life story got mixed up with the one about Eustace. The hunter association fits Wessler better, though."

"I saw some of his big-game trophies at the town hall."

"Not just that kind of hunter." Dash grew serious. "He's done some other hunting—of people. Nazis, to be precise. Or so I've heard."

"You mean in this country or in Germany?"

"I don't know specifics. Stromeyer knows the background. He served in Germany. Franz Wessler would know, too, of course."

Judith grew thoughtful, but gave a start when the waiter brought their bill. "Could Wessler's Nazi hunting be a motive for murder?"

"Don't quote me. Oh, go ahead, it's a story that's gone around town for a long time. Maybe it's a myth, like Eustace. But the stag apparition is a better-looking visual than some poor dude falling out of a boat. Especially given today's sermon. How bored were you?"

Judith couldn't help laughing. "I have to admit I was still tired from my spell last night."

Dash waved a hand. "Forget it. I'm better at writing legal briefs than I am at sermons. Not my strong suit."

"We're lucky at Our Lady, Star of the Sea," Judith said. "Father Hoyle is one of the few priests I've known who gives a good homily."

"I admire that," Dash said, reaching for his wallet. "Let me make up for the sermon by paying the—"

"No!" Judith protested. "I only put five dollars in the collection. It's the least I can do. Please?"

Dash hesitated—and shrugged. "Okay. If you're here on business, deduct it twice on your income tax—once for business, once for charity."

"Isn't that a sin?"

He shook his head. "Not unless you're using counterfeit money."

Judith and Dash parted company at the corner. He headed for the rectory, which, as Judith had guessed, was separate from the church. The priest was meeting at one o'clock with Klara and Franz Wessler to begin plans for the Requiem Mass. Feeling much better after a good meal and the priest's company, Judith decided not to go directly to Hanover Haus. Instead, she walked across the street, heading for the police station. Maybe Fat Matt had the analysis of Herman Stromeyer's stomach contents by now.

Judith felt she shouldn't have been surprised when Orville said the chief wasn't in. "The wreck on the pass was a real mess," he explained. "We got three in the hospital here and a couple of dead people headed for somebody else's morgue. The boss was so upset he kind of tied one on at the beer garden. He should be in around one. Or two. Or so."

"I suppose that's why he wasn't at church," Judith said pointedly. "Did you get the report on Mr. Stromeyer from the doctor yet?"

Orville nodded. "I put it on the chief's desk."

"Good," Judith said, and headed for Duomo's office.

"Hey," Orville said in a mild tone, "you can't go in there."

"Watch me." She opened the door. "See? I'm doing it now."

Judith heard Orville sigh as she closed the door behind her. The report was in plain sight in a manila envelope stamped with Frolander's name and the hospital's address. Before sitting down, she made sure that there was nothing in the chief's chair—like a bag of doughnuts.

The doctor's findings were what Judith expected. Traces of aconite—or wolfsbane—had been found. Herman had eaten a light supper before the cocktail party. The report contained nothing more of interest, other than mentioning that the amount he'd consumed wasn't fatal. She was getting up from Duomo's chair when Ernie Schwartz came into the office.

"Have you taken over for the chief?" he asked.

Judith noticed his droll expression. "I wanted to see the results from Herman Stromeyer's brush with death last night."

Ernie eased himself into one of the chairs on the other side of the desk. "You seem to have recovered from whatever happened to you. I thought maybe you were poisoned, too."

Judith shook her head. "I think it was exhaustion."

"You need more sleep." He yawned. "I could use a nap myself."

Leaning forward in the chair, Judith made sure she was making eye contact. "Ernie—tell me about Wessler's Nazi-hunting exploits."

The sleepy eyes sparked. "Why?"

"Isn't my curiosity natural? Aren't we looking for motive?"

Ernie's shoulders sagged. "I see your point. But that all happened in Germany." He sat up straighter. "There were rumors when I was a kid that somebody around here was suspect. Assumed name maybe, new identity, respectable, you know the drill for those guys who tried to start over. But whoever it was never got fingered by Wessler. He died several years ago. The rumors dried up."

"What was his name when he was in Little Bavaria?"

Ernie fingered his chin. "The wife's still around. Must be getting up there in years. Her husband's name was Helmut Bauer."

# Chapter Nineteen

**I**'ve met Mrs. Bauer," Judith said. "She told me her husband had died of shame because of malicious lies."

Ernie yawned. "Could be."

"Had Mr. Bauer actually done something despicable?"

The major gripped the table with both hands. "I'm Jewish, I know what those SOBs did to some of my relatives. You want gory details? I might not like the replay, but do you think I've forgotten?"

"Of course not," Judith said, realizing that not only were the major's eyes wide open, but they seemed to almost sizzle. "Nobody should ever forget it. Not only Jews, but Catholics, Lutherans, Gypsies, Communists, political dissidents, and so-called defective human beings."

Ernie leaned back in the chair. "True. As for Bauer, I'm not sure what the accusations were. Maybe he was at one of the camps."

Judith thought it might be wise to change the subject, lest Ernie work himself up into a frenzy—or nod off. Maybe, she thought, that's why he fell asleep so often. It might be his way of not envisioning the horror that was Hitler. "What happened to Bauer's daughter?"

"Hmm." Ernie frowned. "She was a year or two younger than I was. I can't remember her name . . . Isabel? Irene? Something like that. Tall, fair-haired, not the kind a guy would stare at, but not homely either. By the time I got back from 'Nam, I think she'd moved away. At least I don't remember much else about her except from high school."

"It must've been a small class," Judith said.

"True, but she was at least two years behind me." He smiled faintly. "You know—in high school the older kids don't pay much attention to the underclassmen."

"How did you end up here?"

"My folks spent the war in an English village. They'd gotten out in 1938. After the war, they thought about moving to Israel, but that wasn't happening yet, so they emigrated to the States. They had relatives in New York, but Pa and Ma were small-town people who hated cities. My father dreamed of owning a grocery store. A cousin of his worked for the Department of the Interior. He'd spent a lot of time around here when they were building dams on this side of the mountains. After the cousin retired to Lake Shegogan, he urged my folks to move here. They ran the local grocery store for thirty years."

Judith smiled. "I didn't mean to pry. I wondered how a Jewish family would feel about moving where there were so many Germans."

"Back then, there weren't as many," Ernie said. "That came later, after Wessler started beating the drums to turn the town around. When I was a kid, most people were logging and railroad workers." He looked at his watch. "The chief should be showing up soon. I'd better get some shut-eye before he comes in. Good luck with whatever it is you're doing."

After Ernie ambled away, Judith decided she'd better move on, too. She felt better, but guilt niggled at her. If she took her time, the two-block walk to the B&B exhibit shouldn't tire her out. Assuming, of course, that the booth was still standing. Judith didn't want to think about the havoc Renie might wreak if aggravation overcame her.

The sun had come out while she'd been in the chief's office.

It was a beautiful fall day, crisp and clear, with new snow on the mountains. The ground in the village, however, was all but bare. Judith figured the temperature must be in the high thirties. As she started down the main street, she glanced up at the clock tower. It was ten minutes past noon. On a whim, she decided to stop in at Sadie's Stories. Maybe Jessi would have fresh news about her grandfather's condition.

The streets were more crowded than ever, but the bookstore wasn't busy. Judith figured most visitors were in search of lunch or brunch during the noon hour. Jessi was behind the counter ringing up a half-dozen children's books for a family of five. Barry was helping a young couple choose a travel atlas. Only two other customers, both elderly women, were browsing the shelves.

"Hi," Jessi said after the family exited. "How are you feeling?"

"Much better," Judith replied. "How's your grandfather?"

"Improving." Jessi checked to make sure no one was listening. "The doctor said it was some kind of poison. I can't believe it!"

It suddenly occurred to Judith that she didn't know if the general public had yet learned the real cause of Dietrich Wessler's death. "Maybe someone made a mistake," Judith hedged, not wanting to alarm Jessi. "Did Doc Frolander go into details?"

"I didn't talk to him very long. He's worn out and was going to get some rest. I called my parents again, but told them not to come up here as long as Grandpa's better. They always spend Christmas here. Still, they're really upset."

"Of course," Judith said. "Do you have any books on saints?"

"You mean Catholic saints?" Jessi saw Judith nod. "Yes, I think we have two—one for children and one for adults. I'll show you."

She led Judith to the religion section. "It should be right here, but it's not. My fill-in, Mrs. Zook, must've sold it. Would the children's version be any help?"

"No," Judith said. "I'm looking for an obscure person." Seeing that the young couple had made their choice of an atlas, she let Jessi go to the register. Judith strolled over to the travel section, where Barry was straightening the shelves. "Have you got time to talk to me—and my cousin—about what happened to your dad?"

Barry adjusted a staff recommendation sign on the shelf featuring German tourist guides. "I don't know very much. As I told you, I wasn't here when it happened. You should talk to Mom, though she doesn't know anything more than the police do."

Judith nodded. "I'm on my way to meet Serena. Could we get together for coffee at the café downstairs in fifteen minutes?"

He glanced at Jessi, who was giving a smiling send-off to the couple with the atlas. "Sure. Maybe I can pick up some lunch there for Jessi and me. Hey, I'm glad you're feeling better."

"So am I," Judith said, returning to the counter. "Say, do you recall anyone who lingered around the Thomas Mann bust lately?"

"No," Jessi replied. "Only the brat who broke it. Why do you ask?"

"My cousin thinks the bottle might've contained poison," Judith said. "Chief Duomo is having it analyzed."

"I don't get it," Jessi said. "If somebody deliberately poisoned Grandpa, the bottle wouldn't have been there *before* it happened."

"A valid point," Judith said, "but Serena is so dogged about the tiniest detail of a crime she's working. She's got that kind of mind."

Jessi gaped at Judith. "She's investigating Wessler's death?"

"Gosh," Judith said, backpedaling to the door, "I thought you knew she's a supersleuth. See you later. Oops!" she exclaimed, bumping into a postcard display. "I'm meeting her now. She subbed for me at the B&B booth." *Or what's left of it,* Judith thought grimly, and wished that the book title she'd just glimpsed wasn't *The Last Train from Hiroshima*.


To her great relief, the booth was still intact. Several people were obscuring Judith's view of Renie and Eldridge Hoover. But as she got closer, she spotted her cousin bobbing up to hand over some brochures and what looked like a map. Amazingly, the would-be inn patrons seemed in a jocular mood.

"Hi, coz," Renie called. "Just took a reservation for Hillside Manor from these wonderful folks who live in Pocatello, Idaho. That makes sixteen so far. You're going to enjoy the Fawcetts," she added, gesturing at the middle-aged couple. "They're anything but a pair of drips! Right, guys? Meet your innkeeper."

The Fawcetts laughed like crazy.

"Hi," Judith said a bit uncertainly. "It's nice to meet you."

Eldridge leaned sideways to look at Judith. "We've had a swell time. Can't believe our stint is up already. Roonie here is a real funster!"

Renie held up her hands in a helpless gesture. "Hey, 'Dridge, being with you is like Christmas, Thanksgiving, and the Fourth of July rolled into one. Here come Phil and Jeanne. Much as I hate to say it, I'd better scoot." She grabbed her purse, blew Eldridge a kiss, and left the booth.

"If," Renie said, after they were out of earshot, "you ever ask me to do anything like that again, I swear I'll kill you."

"But you seemed to——"

"Of course I *seemed* to," Renie snarled. "I do this for a living. Be nice, I mean. I get paid big bucks for it. And then I go home and verbally abuse Bill, Oscar, and even Clarence. Oh, they ignore me, so I retreat to the kitchen and break something."

Momentarily distracted by the Bavarian boar who was driving a wagon full of laughing children, Judith didn't know what to say. "Did you really take sixteen reservations?"

"Of course. I charmed, wheedled, and entranced those suckers—just like a design presentation, only with comfort and cuisine instead of art and artifice. God, but I can be a phony! Sometimes I scare me."

"When?"

Renie glared at a dachshund wearing a purple hat before turning to shoot the same look at Judith. "When what?"

"When are the upcoming reservations?" Judith asked meekly.

"Four in November, two in December, and the rest in January—your slowest month. How do you like that for push and shove? Six of those people weren't even planning on coming to our fair city."

"Thank you. I mean it. But stop—we're going to Kreuger's Kuchen. It's right there below the bookshop."

"We are? You're going to feed me?"

"No. We're having coffee with Barry. You're the sleuth again."

Renie sighed. "Another hat for me to wear. Sheesh. Why not? It's a wonder you didn't have me assist at Mass or play the tuba in the marching band that's coming down the street and will probably take a detour so they can run us over."

The band kept marching. Judith and Renie kept walking—straight into the café. Barry wasn't there yet. Apparently customers seated themselves. Judith pointed to a table near the door. "That way Barry can see us," she said.

Renie practically fell into a chair. "I'm exhausted. Being nice wears me down. Why are we interrogating Barry? Is this the Stafford murder case? I like to know ahead of time what crime I'm solving."

"Yes." Judith noticed menus, but wasn't hungry. "I'm having a beverage. Go ahead, order something. I'll treat."

Renie looked indecisive. "I went to the bakery and bought a bunch of stuff. Frankie's kind of surly. Maybe that's another reason why Franz didn't want to deal with him yesterday."

"There's an undercurrent of tension with a lot of people around here," Judith said, relieved that her cousin seemed to be regaining her equilibrium. "Before Barry arrives, let me catch you up on some things I've learned since we parted company."

Judith quickly summed up her recent activities. The only interruption was by their server, a pert young woman who took the orders for Judith's mocha and Renie's root beer.

"You've got a book about saints at home, don't you?" Judith said when she had finished her recital.

"Three of them," Renie replied. "So? Bill won't answer the phone."

"Well . . . how else will we find out who the mystery nonsaint is?"

"Why do we care? It sounds like one of your dumber ideas. If this person was never canonized, she probably wouldn't be listed anyway."

"You told me a while ago that at least one of your books listed all sorts of nonexistent saints. Mrs. Bauer said this was a real person. If Mr. Bauer was suspected of being a bad Nazi, I'm interested."

Renie shrugged. "If we had a computer . . . Maybe they've got one we could use at Hanover Haus. Though I doubt the old bat who's usually at the front desk would let us use it."

"Jessi might," Judith suggested. "Or the cops."

"You're right, especially if Duomo is still hungover." Renie nodded toward the entrance. "Here comes Barry."

"Sorry," he apologized. "The store got busy all of a sudden. I have to get takeout for Jessi and me because she wants to see her grandfather this afternoon. I'm going to sub for her."

"Say," Judith said, "why don't you go with her? Serena and I can fill in. I'm a librarian. I worked for years at the Thurlow Public Library."

"No kidding?" Barry grinned. "Are you sure you want to do that?"

"Yes," Judith replied. "Serena did an amazing job at the B&B booth. She can sell books to people who don't know how to rea . . . oof!"

Barry looked alarmed as Judith winced in pain. "Are you okay?"

"Yes, yes, I'm fine," Judith said, trying to smile even as she retaliated for Renie's kick by stamping on her cousin's foot. "Just a little twit. I mean, *twinge*. Here's the waitress with our dinks. That is, *drinks*. Are you going to order now?"

"Ah, sure," Barry said. He took a quick look at the menu, ordered chicken-salad and ham-on-rye sandwiches with side salads to go. His immediate request was for a double tall latte. "Okay, I'm set, but I can't offer much about Dad's murder. It seemed like a random thing."

Judith licked her lips to get rid of any mocha residue. "Did you see the letters he received from the disgruntled client?"

"I did," Barry said. "Duomo thought they were mildly threatening, but the guy sounded more like a griper. I'm guessing it was a guy because the legal issue was how he got screwed over in a child custody dispute. He blamed my dad for mishandling the case."

Renie nodded. "Your garden-variety sorehead. But why wouldn't he sign the letters? How could he expect your father to know which case it was? He must've handled tons of custody battles over the years."

Barry didn't answer at once. "I never thought about that, but it's true. Growing up, I heard Dad talk about clients. Face it, the majority of Legal Aid clients are low income or uneducated. Maybe he just wanted to blow off steam, but stay anonymous. That doesn't make him a killer."

Renie agreed. "It'd take time and trouble to come here to murder somebody. When did your dad stop practicing law?"

"Ten years ago, except for some cases he took on as favors."

"Local clients?" Judith asked.

"Mostly." Barry passed a hand over his forehead. "I wasn't around all the time. Either I was in undergraduate school or studying for my advanced degrees. I recall only a couple of cases. One was a property dispute and the other was a messy divorce."

Judith started to speak, but waited until the waitress brought Barry's latte. "Are any of those litigants still in town?" she inquired.

Barry leaned back in the chair, looking up at the mosaic ceiling. "The property involved was where an old gas station used to stand. The original owner had died and left the land—and everything else including the gas storage drums—to his granddaughter. She'd moved away and didn't want it. Too much trouble to get rid of the contaminated soil. Then a cousin who'd worked at the station asked her to give him a quitclaim deed and he'd take care of it for her. She thought he was pulling a fast one, and refused." Barry laughed softly. "Mr. Wessler got into the act, trying to be a peacemaker. He liked to do that. He meant well, but it only caused more trouble. He was the heiress's paternal grandfather." His jaw dropped. "You know her—Eleanor Wessler Denkel."

Judith stared at Barry. "Let me get this straight. The maternal grandpa left her the property, right? Was the cousin a Wessler?"

"Well . . . yes," Barry said. "It was Frankie Duomo, one of Wessler's illegitimate kids. He wanted to open a bigger bakery there."

"Who won?" Renie asked.

"Dietrich Wessler," Barry said. "He paid off both Eleanor and Frankie, assumed the deed to the property, got it cleaned up, and that's where the beer garden is now. Franz Wessler pitched a fit. He came roaring up from L.A. to try to talk his father out of the deal. Franz wanted to open a small theater on the site. There's never been a movie house in this town. That's why they show the German movies in that tent down the street. To be honest, I thought Franz had the right idea."

Judith took her last sip of mocha before posing another question. "Did that cause a serious rift between Franz and his father?"

"Mom told me it caused more than that," Barry replied, smiling wryly. "I'd forgotten what happened until now. Franz didn't want to show only theatrical releases, but to preview his documentaries. And Klara wanted to use the theater as her private concert hall. That's why she moved up here—to con Franz's father into making the deal. The irony was that she blamed Franz for not getting her way. That's when she divorced him and moved in with Wessler."

Judith felt as if her head was spinning. "Did Klara think she could get Wessler to change his mind?"

Barry shrugged. "Who knows? She found a soft life with him. The old boy doted on her. I figure he left all his money to her."

"Hold it," Renie said. "Where did Klara get her divorce?"

Barry looked puzzled. "Where? You mean . . . ?"

"Was it here in Little Bavaria or in California?"

"I don't know," Barry said. "I don't think Dad or Mom told me."

Judith eyed her cousin. "What are you getting at, supersleuth?"

Renie made a face. "I'm not sure. But when we were going through those records at the town hall, I don't recall seeing anything about a Wessler divorce. In fact, there weren't that many divorces. I'm wondering if Klara and Franz aren't still married."

Barry shook his head. "Sorry. If Dad handled that one, I don't remember. Maybe Franz started the divorce proceedings in Los Angeles." He checked his watch. "Are you serious about filling in at the bookshop?"

Judith took in Renie's benign mood. "Yes. Serena still has to pick up those books for her husband."

"Right," Renie said. "Bill won't speak to me for at least ten minutes if I don't bring him those books. And Oscar will have a fit."

"Oscar?" Barry said with a puzzled expression.

Judith stood up, digging into her wallet. "Never mind. Oscar's a terrible grump. I'd tell him to get stuffed—except he already is. We'll have Jessi come down here so you can eat in peace before you visit her grandfather at the hospital."

Leaving a twenty-dollar bill on the table, she headed for the exit. Five minutes later, the cousins had taken over the bookstore. Renie had already agreed to check out the noncanonized saint on the shop's computer while Judith waited on customers. There were a half-dozen people browsing the shelves. Jessi had been effusive in her thanks, insisting that Renie take Bill's books without charge.

"I won't, of course," Renie said to Judith after Jessi had departed. "You can ring me up. Where should I start with the nonsaint?"

"Birgitta was Swedish," Judith said, keeping one eye on the customers. "Back then, all of Scandinavia was Sweden, right? See what you find by cross-referencing Birgitta with whatever might work."

"Got it," Renie said, scooting behind the counter. "Anglicized as Bridget, I suppose."

"Right," Judith said as a ponytailed girl approached with a Twilight book.

A half hour passed before Renie began to grow impatient. "I've tried every which way to go at this and come up empty," she said under her breath to Judith, who'd just finished ringing up a frail old lady who'd bought four volumes of erotica. "I've done all the Scandinavian saints through three centuries, famous Scandinavian women of the same period, every Ingamoder and Ingeborg and Inglenook or whatever along with Rikissa, Kristina, and Agda. Got any other ideas?"

"Maybe we shouldn't stick to Sweden or Scandinavia. Why don't you try putting in just medieval Catholic saints?"

"Oh, for . . ." Renie held her head. "Do you realize the hits I'll get? I'd have to expand it to more than a two-century time span for Scandinavian saints. I'm not sure why we're doing this in the first place."

"If I told you it's a hunch, would you hit me?"

"No." Renie took a deep breath. "Your hunches often work." She turned back to the computer.

Twenty minutes later, Judith heard Renie let out a little squeal. Trying not to rush the gray-haired man who couldn't remember whether he'd read the latest Michael Connelly paperback or the one before that or even if he'd ever read any of them, Judith finally suggested that maybe he should confer with his wife, who was perusing romance novels.

"What is it?" she finally whispered to Renie.

"I think I found her," Renie said softly. "Look."

Judith saw the name of the Swedish woman whose cause for canonization had been dropped during the Reformation. "Good Lord!" she exclaimed under her breath. "I don't believe it!"

The cousins exchanged startled glances.

"Maybe," Renie suggested, "it's a coincidence."

"Maybe," Judith said, her voice unsteady. "Let's hope so. I'd hate to think this might lead us to the killer."

The unofficial saint's name was Ingrid.

# Chapter Twenty

**B**ut," Renie said, lowering her voice, "it's only a coincidence."

"Maybe," Judith admitted. "There must be a ton of Ingrids in this part of the country. Lots of Scandinavians. They were a major influence in this whole area. What are you doing now?"

"Checking the usage of Ingrid as a first name," Renie murmured.

The couple who couldn't seem to make up their minds had settled on a cookbook. Judith rang them up while Renie kept searching.

"Just as I thought," Renie said after the customers left. "Ingrid Bergman popularized the name circa 1940. I can't get a hit on anyone before that except for the ersatz saint. Is Heffelman her maiden name?"

"I don't know. She's divorced. But what does Ingrid have to do with Little Bavaria? I've never heard her refer to the town until she organized the Oktoberfest exhibit. Nobody has mentioned a local connection with Ingrid. I assumed she'd grown up in the city. Is that a local phone book under the counter?"

"Yes." Renie picked up the directory and flipped to the *H* listings. "No Heffelmans." She turned the pages back to the *B*s. "One Bauer, initials A.L., the mother from the cemetery and the church. Coz, you've got Inbred Heffalump fever. She's not even here, yet you've been obsessing about her ever since we left home."

Judith made a face. "So I have. Face it, she's the only part of my job that drives me nuts. She's been on my case ever since the fortune teller was killed at Hillside Manor early on in my B&B career."

"So? You're still in business, aren't you?"

"Yes, but now she's showing up on my doorstep when she knows I'm not around. The few times she's met Joe, she's always been kind of flirty with him, which isn't Ingrid's usual style."

"Gee," Renie said, lowering her voice as two young men entered the shop, "with tough competition like Delmar Denkel and George Beaulieu, I don't see how Joe would stand a chance with Ingrid."

"Not funny." Judith asked the new customers if she could help. They asked if she knew where the snowboarding books were. She pointed to the winter sports section. They began to browse.

"You trust Joe," Renie said quietly. "Stop worrying."

"It's just another reason why Ingrid has been on my mind lately." Judith glanced at the young men who were absorbed in snowboarding books. "You're right. I should forget about her and refocus."

"Do that. You still think two people are involved?"

"If not, somebody's protecting someone. Ellie and Franz are both likely candidates because they're related. But it still points to a Wessler family member—including Klara. Unless you count all the bastards."

"For that," Renie said, "I need a football roster. The other sports don't have enough players."

The young men each brought a trade paperback to the register—*The Illustrated Guide to Snowboarding* and *100 Classic Backcountry Ski & Snowboard Routes in Washington*. "Is this your first snowboarding adventure?" Judith asked as she rang them up.

"First time," the shorter, stockier of the duo said. "We need more snow. Guess we miscalculated."

"Guess we're unlucky," the taller, lankier young man said. "We went hiking around here last summer and some jerk told us to get off his property. I thought anybody could walk along a river in this state. We weren't going to fish. Who would on a hot August afternoon?"

"Right," said his companion. "That guy acted like we were crooks."

The other young man laughed. "That's because his buddy was wasted. He couldn't even sit up."

"So what?" his friend said. "Like we haven't seen drunks before?"

Judith kept her voice matter-of-fact. "When was this in August?"

"Oh," the stocky young man said, looking at his lanky friend. "Third week? It was a Friday, I remember that."

"Was it near the Pancake Schloss?" Judith asked.

"We'd just finished a late lunch there," the stocky one said.

Renie poked Judith. "As a police deputy, don't you think you should ask them to report what they saw? I'll stay here." Seeing the young men's wary expressions, Renie pulled a twenty and a five out of her wallet. "The books are on me. We should all do our civic duty."

"She's right," Judith said, coming around from behind the counter and grabbing her jacket. "Police headquarters is only a little more than a block away. Shall we?"

The dumbfounded pair took the refund and the books. "I guess," the lanky one said, "but this is too weird."

On their way to the station, Judith explained that a crime might have been committed by the man who had told them to go away. She avoided any mention of murder for fear of scaring off the young men. At the entrance to the station, she paused.

"I'm Judith Flynn. I should know your names before we go inside."

"Tyler Whalen," the lanky one said.

"Jordan Smith," the stocky one replied. "Really. It *is* Smith."

Judith smiled. "I believe you. It's too obvious to be made up."

Hernandez was back on duty at the desk. "Chief's not here," he said, eyeing Judith and the young men with curiosity. "He took the redhead out for drinks. Ernie's taking a nap break in one of the cells."

"Then you're it," Judith said, giving the officer a meaningful look. "These gentlemen want to make a statement about what they saw by the river August nineteenth."

It took only a moment for Hernandez to realize what Judith meant. "Okay, but we'll have to do it out here. I can't leave my post until Ernie wakes up. Let's get you settled in behind the counter."

Tyler and Jordan sat down in folding chairs, but still looked uncertain. Judith, who had seated herself in a chair Hernandez had fetched her, tried not to eavesdrop, but couldn't avoid it. The young men were apparently trying to figure out what kind of crime had occurred other than being drunk in public. Jordan remarked that if getting blotto was breaking the local law, about half the town could have been busted the previous evening.

Finally, they set to work, writing out separate statements. The task took less than ten minutes. "Here," Tyler said, handing over their accounts to Hernandez. "This is the truth. It's all we can remember."

The basic facts meshed, but didn't go much beyond what Judith had already heard. After Hernandez had also read the statements, she asked if Tyler and Jordan could describe either the man who'd yelled at them or the one who seemed to be intoxicated.

"The jerk was fifty or so," Jordan said, looking at Tyler, who nodded. "He was balding, sandy hair, average build. Tan chinos, tank top, I think. No facial hair, just an average dude."

"How tall?" Hernandez inquired.

"I couldn't tell," Jordan replied. "He was sort of squatting, propping up the drunk. If I had to guess, close to six feet."

"What," Judith asked, "did the other man look like?"

Tyler grimaced. "We didn't see much of him. We'd just come

down to the bottom of the trail when the dink told us to go away. I suppose we were twenty, thirty feet away. Brown hair, about the same age, bigger build, plaid shirt, dark pants." He shrugged. "That's about it. His back was turned to us. We figured he was throwing up."

Judith gazed at Hernandez. "The jerk could be anybody," she said.

"Hey," Tyler said, "I'm a cartoonist. I could do a sketch of Jerk-off."

"That might be helpful," Hernandez said without inflection, "I'll get paper and pencils." He went over to a cabinet by the far wall.

Judith wished Renie had come with her. Another artist's eye might help interpret whatever Tyler was going to draw. Trying not to bother the young man, she drew her chair closer to Jordan. "Do you two come to Little Bavaria often?" she asked in a virtual whisper.

Jordan shook his head. "This is only the third time. We skied up at the summit last year. Tyler wants to try snowboarding to show off for his girlfriend. Why not? It sounds pretty cool to me, too."

"Cool and cold," Judith murmured, watching Tyler out of the corner of her eye. He seemed to be working quickly.

He was, in fact, finished. "There," he said with satisfaction. "Take a look. See if you recognize this creep."

Hernandez, who had been doing paperwork, joined Judith. She spoke first. "He doesn't look familiar. But I don't live here."

After another long moment, Hernandez shook his head. "Nobody I know either. Of course, I've only been in Little Bavaria for a few months. The chief might recognize him."

Tyler seemed disappointed. "Maybe I didn't really capture him."

Judith smiled encouragingly. "You've injected character into his face. He looks angry."

"He was," Tyler responded.

"Dude," Jordan said, "you nailed him. I'd know him anywhere. But I don't want to." He turned to Hernandez. "What crime did he commit?"

Judith waited for the officer to answer the question. Hernandez opted for discretion. "I can only say he's a suspect."

Judith didn't say anything at all.

The young men hadn't exhibited further curiosity. They left almost immediately, telling Judith to thank the woman with the big teeth for giving them the snowboarding books.

"I gather," she said to Hernandez, "you think those two caught whoever killed Bob Stafford in the act?"

"Maybe not actually killing him," he replied thoughtfully, "but setting Stafford up to look as if he'd drowned."

"Their arrival must have scared the wits out of whoever he is," Judith said, then realized it was a stupid thing to say. "No," she corrected herself, staring at the sketch again. "There's no fear in his expression. He probably thought that if they asked what was going on, he could say his friend had fallen and hit his head."

"A cool customer," Hernandez remarked as Duomo came through the door.

"Hell's bells," the chief said, "that redhead could drink me under the table. What's she got, a hollow leg?"

"Her legs look fine to me," Hernandez murmured. "Where is she?"

"On patrol someplace," Fat Matt growled. "Sober as a judge." He saw the sketch on the counter. "Who's doing cartoons around here?" Finally, he seemed to realize that Judith was present. "You draw that? Am I supposed to arrest some guy from the funny papers?"

Judith tried to measure the chief's state of inebriation, decided he didn't seem much different from when he was sober, and informed him that the man in the drawing was a suspect in the Stafford homicide. She let Hernandez handle the rest of the explanation.

"The hell you say." Duomo squinted at the sketch. "Never seen him before in my life. Just what we figured—one of those random deals. We could put out an APB, maybe. Probably only get a bunch of crazies. Poor Bob. What would I do without those pancakes?"

"You can make copies and post them around town," Judith said.

Duomo looked aghast. "During Oktoberfest? That guy's mug would scare visitors. We'll wait until after everybody's gone."

Judith didn't argue. "May I get a copy of it? My cousin and I are leaving early tomorrow on the Empire Builder."

Duomo waved a hand. "Go ahead. Think I'll join Ernie for a nap. I'm getting too old to drink on the job." He ambled out of sight.

Judith stared at Hernandez, who was already scanning the sketch. "Is your boss for real?"

The officer smiled faintly. "Define 'real.'"

"Never mind," Judith said.

Five minutes later, she returned to Sadie's Stories. Renie was selling six Agatha Christie mysteries to two middle-aged women. "I can't believe you've missed her," she was saying in a chipper voice. "She's the Queen of Plots. Every author since has stolen from her."

The women thanked her profusely and departed. Renie shook her head. "I swear Christie invented every conceivable plot imaginable. I wonder what she'd have done with DNA. What's up?"

"It's snowing," Judith said. "I took my time coming back."

"I wondered. Someone mentioned the snow. It must've blown in fast. Business has slowed down." She checked the time. "It's almost two. Barry and Jessi should be back soon. What's in that envelope?"

Judith explained about Tyler's artistic talent as she took the sketch out of the envelope. "What do you think?"

"Of his talent? Not bad. He's caught a real person. Alas, the guy looks like a bad apple. You think he killed Bob?"

"Let's see if Barry recognizes him," Judith said, but paused before putting the drawing back in the envelope. "Can you make a copy of this so he can show Suzie?"

"Sure," Renie said. "They've got the same kind of all-in-one printer that I have. It'll only take a few seconds."

She'd just finished removing the copy of the sketch when Mrs. Bauer walked into the shop. Judith smiled in surprise. "You're very brave to come out in the snow," she said.

The old woman peered at her for a moment until recognition struck. "You were at church this morning. I didn't know you lived here."

"I don't," Judith said. "My cousin and I are filling in for a friend while she has lunch. Do you know Jessi?"

"Yes," Mrs. Bauer said. "A very nice young woman. I'm used to the snow. Jessi is holding an embroidery book for me. It has a long title—something about making projects for the home."

Renie scanned the shelf where Jessi stashed preordered books. "Here you go," she said, setting *Colorful Stitchery* on the counter. "It looks like it just came out this month."

Mrs. Bauer nodded. "Yes. Jessi knew I'd enjoy it, though I wish my eyes were not beginning to fail."

"Here's Jessi now," Judith said, seeing her arrive with Barry.

Jessi greeted Mrs. Bauer while Judith picked up the sketch and showed it to Barry. "Do you know this person?"

Barry stared at the drawing before giving Judith a quizzical look. "No. Should I?"

"Probably not." She lowered her voice. "Are you leaving now?"

"I don't have to," Barry said. "The snow's really coming down."

Judith held on to the sketch in case Jessi might know the man. She didn't want to explain why she'd asked Barry, but it was Mrs. Bauer who craned her neck to stare at the alleged suspect's likeness.

"Oh, dear God," she murmured, turning pale even as she adjusted her glasses. "No, no!"

"What is it?" Judith asked in alarm.

Mrs. Bauer peered at the drawing again. "Perhaps I am mistaken. It's been so long . . . surely it can't be . . . but I could swear that is Jack, the man who ruined my daughter."

All eyes regarded the old lady with puzzlement. "Jack who?" Judith finally asked.

Taking an embroidered handkerchief from her purse, Mrs. Bauer removed her glasses and wiped her eyes. "Jack Hellman, the son of the horrible man who tried to destroy my husband's reputation. Those Hellmans are the most evil people on earth! Please tear up that picture. I think I'm going to faint."

Mrs. Bauer did just that. Luckily, Barry caught her before she hit the floor. "Smelling salts, anyone?" Renie said in a weary voice.

"No," Jessi said, "but I'll get some water." She scurried out through the door at the end of the counter.

Barry had gotten down on the floor, propping up Mrs. Bauer with his knee. She seemed to be coming around. "Hellman?" he said softly.

"I think," Judith said reluctantly, "his father committed suicide. Before your time, though."

Barry shook his head. "Why have you got a picture of his son?"

Before Judith could explain, Jessi appeared with a glass of water and a damp facecloth. Mrs. Bauer had opened her eyes, but looked dazed. "I am so sorry," she mumbled. "Very foolish of me."

"Not at all," Jessi said, holding the paper cup to the old lady's lips. "You had a bad shock."

"Yes," she said, after sipping from the cup. "I may be wrong, but the drawing looks like Jack's father at that same age. Fifty, perhaps?"

"Probably," Judith said.

Barry waited for Jessi to wipe off Mrs. Bauer's face before helping her to stand. "I'll walk you home," he said. "Maybe you should rest for a few minutes. Let me get the chair from behind the counter."

"I'll get it," Renie said. "Hey, coz, why don't you and Barry go into the back room and get a bag for Mrs. Bauer's book?"

"Don't you have some bags . . ." Judith stopped. "Oh, you

mean the heavier ones. Sure, come on, Barry," she said, after he'd settled Mrs. Bauer in the chair.

Jessi looked mystified, but didn't say anything. Renie stealthily slipped the original sketch to her cousin. A moment later, Judith and Barry were in the shop's back room. Giving her a bewildered look, he asked what was going on with the drawing. "I told you I don't recognize the guy. I think I've heard the name 'Hellman,' but that's about it."

"You've seen the marker on the trail from the Pancake Schloss, though. Didn't you ever ask what it was for?"

"Sure," Barry replied. "My parents told me it was for some old nut who'd offed himself a long time ago. It was kind of creepy, but I never thought much about it."

Judith explained about the snowboarders. As her tale unfolded, Barry's expression changed from curiosity to abject horror.

"You mean . . . these guys saw who killed my dad?"

Judith nodded. "It sounds like it. If so, then Jack Hellman—the suicide's son—may be the killer. I think we should go see Matt Duomo."

Barry balked. "No. We have to tell Mom first. I'll walk Mrs. Bauer home, then get Mom's car and collect you. Deal?"

Judith hesitated. "Renie should go along to stay with Mrs. Bauer."

"Why?" Barry sounded puzzled. "She should be okay if she rests."

Judith shook her head. "The police are shorthanded. Mrs. Bauer may be in danger. You, of all people, know there's a killer out there."

Renie didn't argue with Judith's suggestion. "Should I be armed?" she whispered, putting on her jacket.

"Just be careful," Judith said under her breath. "You're lethal with a pickle fork. But try getting Mrs. Bauer to talk about her daughter."

Twenty minutes later, Barry had braved the snow to get the Escort to collect Judith, Renie, and Mrs. Bauer. Jessi had two new customers, a cheerful mother and daughter from Osoyoos, British Columbia, who didn't resemble homicidal maniacs.

Mrs. Bauer lived in a small frame house two blocks north of the police station and one block west of St. Hubert's. Along the way she had revealed some interesting, if perhaps misleading, information.

"Heinrich Hellman claimed to be Jewish," she said from the backseat, where she was sitting with Renie. "But one evening I came to church to light a candle for my daughter. He was praying at Saint Hubert's shrine. It was quite dark inside, so he did not see me. I waited for him to finish, then I followed him outside. It was the first time I'd confronted him with the lies he'd told about my husband, Helmut. He denied everything, of course. The next day he committed suicide."

She'd concluded the recital just as Barry had pulled in front of her house. There was no chance for Judith to ask questions. She'd have to leave that up to Renie.

"I guess I've missed a lot of background about Little Bavaria's history," Barry said, heading for the police station. "Did Mrs. Bauer mean that Hellman wasn't Jewish or that he was nuts? And what would his son have to do with my dad? I never knew any Hellmans."

"Major Schwartz might know," Judith said. "He's Jewish."

"You mean Ernie, the Dozing Cop?"

"Ernie may doze, but he's smart. The only problem is that he might not remember much about the Hellmans. Good grief," she exclaimed, "it's snowing so hard that your windshield wipers can hardly keep up with the flakes! Won't the weather hamper the festival finale?"

Barry shrugged. "It's barely above freezing. That's why the flakes are so big. It's not unusual to have a big snow in October. Sometimes it doesn't happen again until December."

Judith realized she shouldn't have been surprised. Even on the more temperate western side of the mountains, the weather could be unpredictable. After Barry parked the car within a few yards of the station, he insisted that Judith wait for him to help her get out.

Hernandez had been replaced behind the counter by Ernie, who looked awake. "We were expecting you," he said. "What took so long?"

"It wasn't Barry who ID'd the sketch," Judith said. "It was Mrs. Bauer. Did you know the Hellmans?"

"You mean the guy who offed himself? Sure. It happened a few years before I joined the force. What's he got to do with anything?"

"Was he really Jewish?"

Ernie laughed, a first for him as far as Judith was concerned. "I guess so. We ethnic types don't always hang out together. He was old."

"What about his son?"

Ernie frowned. "Jack Hellman? Yeah, I went to high school with him. He was kind of a jerk. We weren't buddies, though I guess he was Jewish, too. No high school in Little Bavaria then. We had to bus over to Lake Shegogan. There were quite a few students in our class because it was the only high school for this whole area. Jack left town not long after graduation. I haven't seen him since."

Judith showed Ernie the sketch. "Well?"

Ernie rested an elbow on the counter and stared at the drawing. "Yeah, that could be him after thirty years." He looked at Barry. "You ever see him with your dad?"

"I've never seen him," Barry replied. "I never heard of the family."

"Your ma seen this?" Ernie asked.

"Yes," Barry said. "I showed it to her when I went to get her car. She didn't recognize him either. This is crazy."

"Speaking of crazy," Judith said, "where's the chief?"

"Hey," Ernie said, "you dissing our boss?"

"Ah . . . I meant this whole thing is crazy," Judith said. "Maybe he can enlighten us." But Duomo hadn't shown much interest in the sketch.

Ernie shrugged. "Go ahead. He's back in his office. But knock first. He might be busy."

Judith made no comment as she and Barry traipsed to the chief's door. To her surprise, Duomo was alert and studying what looked like a report. "It's about time," he said. "Got the busted bust and the bottle back from the lab. Hey, Barry, you working for FATSO these days?"

Barry looked askance at the chief's form of address. "Mrs. Jones is the sleuth. I'm Mrs. Flynn's chauffeur. It's snowing hard."

"Yeah," Duomo said. "I should patrol the highway, but it's too dangerous. What's up?" He winked at Judith. "I mean, with your sister."

"My *cousin,*" Judith said, wishing she didn't spend half her time with Fat Matt trying to keep from shaking him. "Take another look at this sketch. I think, I mean *we* think," she added for Barry's benefit, "we may have fingered Bob Stafford's killer."

"The hell you say." Duomo gazed at the drawing. "This guy does look kind of familiar. Is he one of my brothers?"

"Not that I know of," Judith said. "Keep looking and add thirty years to what you might remember about the man." Automatically, Judith did the same—and something elusive tugged at her memory.

The chief apparently took Judith seriously. "Then I think back to a twentysomething type." He stared some more. "Yeah, could be the Hellman brat. His old man was the one who did himself in. Jim? Joe? No, *Jack,* was trouble. But he's been gone for years." Duomo turned to Barry. "Did you ID him?"

"No," Barry said. "Mom and I didn't recognize him. We wondered if he'd been a client of Dad's when he worked for Legal Aid."

The chief scowled. "The jackass who wrote the letters to your pa?"

Barry nodded. "Maybe."

Duomo tapped a pencil on his desk. "So who ID'd him?"

"Mrs. Bauer," Judith said. "She also told us a strange story."

Fat Matt sighed. "Let's hear it."

Judith repeated the old lady's tale of her encounter with the senior Hellman in the church that had been followed a day later by the older man's suicide. "That's why my cousin is staying with Mrs. Bauer right now. After recognizing Jack, she could be in danger."

"How?" Duomo scoffed. "Bob was killed over two months ago. If Jack Hellman is still around, somebody would've seen him. Hell, *I* might have seen him. But I didn't. This isn't New York or L.A. There's no place you can hide for long in Little Bavaria."

The chief had a point. "Okay," Judith finally said, "maybe there's no threat to Mrs. Bauer, but shouldn't you try to track down Jack in connection with Bob's homicide?"

"Yeah, sure, I'll do that." Duomo looked at Barry. "Tell your ma I'm on the job. Good thing we got statements from those two snowshoe guys or whatever they are. Go ahead, beat it, kid. I'll give FATSO a ride back to . . . wherever she's going. Suze is probably worrying about you. By the way, if you see Jessi, tell her that Grandpa's doin' real good."

"Thanks," Barry said. "That's great news." He regarded Judith dubiously. "You sure you want to stick around here?"

She nodded. "Yes. I have to report back to my cousin."

To Judith's surprise, Barry hugged her. "Thanks. You've really taken a load off of Mom and me." He stepped back. "I mean, your cousin has . . ." He broke into a grin. "You know what I mean."

Barry hurried out of the office.

"Nice kid," Duomo remarked. "Want a cigar?"

"No thanks," Judith said. "My husband enjoys them sometimes."

"I'll smoke one for him." The chief took forever to get the cigar lighted. When he finally did, he eyed the ash with disgust. "Now why'd I do that? It's time for my snack. Oh, well." He picked up the lab report. "Zip," he said. "No usable prints, too many smudges. The bottle was clean. But Frolander's seen aconite come that way. A dose that size would kill most people, even a tough old cuss like Wessler."

"What about Herman Stromeyer?"

"Same stuff. Different bottle. If it was in a bottle. Comes in all forms. Heck, the plant grows everywhere in this state, specially forests. Bunch of names and varieties, too. Bet you got 'em in your backyard. Invasive, but kind of pretty."

Judith nodded. Every year she found wildflowers in her garden that had sprouted from windblown seeds. "You'll talk to Suzie?"

Duomo frowned at the cigar, which had gone out. "Think I'll have dinner there." He grimaced. "She usually quits around eight, eight-thirty, so that means I'll have to eat late. Darn."

"See if you can get a list of Bob's clients," Judith said.

"Huh? You think Jack Hellman was a client?"

"Why not? Maybe he lived in the city. It's a stretch, but he might be your letter writer."

"That's not the worst idea I've heard lately. But that still leaves us with a dead Wessler and a poisoned Stromeyer. Don't stop sleuthing."

"I don't have much time do it," Judith said. "I told you, my cousin and I are going home early tomorrow morning."

The chief shook his head. "You can't leave me in the lurch."

"I have to," Judith asserted. "I have a B&B to run."

Duomo chewed on the end of his unlighted cigar. "I could arrest you. Then you'd have to stay."

"Then I'd have to sue you," Judith said. "I hope I've accomplished what you originally wanted me to do, which was find out who killed Bob Stafford. You're on your own with Wessler. Good luck."

Judith walked out of Duomo's office, through the reception area, and left the building. She hadn't seen such a heavy snowfall in twenty-five years when she'd had to walk two miles home from the Meat & Mingle. As she opened the station door, the dim memory of someone or something came back to her—and disappeared into the snow that obliterated Little Bavaria.

# Chapter Twenty-one

The snow blurred Judith's vision, preventing her from seeing more than one step ahead of her. Worse yet, she had no transportation except for her own feet. At least there was no sharp wind stinging her face. It was the quiet that disturbed her. No laughter, no music, no vehicles—just silence. She squinted at her watch: 3:10.

Judith was about to eat humble pie and go back inside to ask if someone could give her a ride to Hanover Haus when she saw a dim figure moving toward her from across the street. A moment later, she realized it was Renie.

"Why," her cousin demanded, "are you standing out here?"

"I'm an idiot," Judith admitted. "I forgot I didn't have a car."

"Hang on to me. The snow's soft, but not slippery."

Judith grabbed Renie's arm. "Why aren't you guarding Astrid?"

"A neighbor came who looked as benign as Mrs. Bauer. I told them to lock the doors and not let anyone in. I couldn't stay there forever."

Judith wiped away the snowflakes that were gathering on her face. "No, you couldn't. I wonder if tonight's grand finale is canceled?"

"Could be, unless it stops snowing so hard."

They paused before crossing the main street. "Did you get Mrs. Bauer to talk about her daughter?"

"No," Renie replied as they crossed the deserted thoroughfare. "But she did go on about the senior Hellman. I'll tell you more when we get back to our room."

Upon arrival, Judith took off her jacket and flopped onto the bed. "I'm tired. Again. Amuse me with tales from the crypt."

"That's sort of what it was," Renie said, tugging off her boots. "I insisted Mrs. Bauer—let's call her Astrid since she and I are now best buds—drink something stronger than water. She had an unopened bottle of Absolut vodka and, better yet, pickled herring. Thus, we whiled away almost an hour while she revealed all about the Hellmans."

"Wow! Tell me more."

"I will, but let me take off your boots for you while I do it." Renie tossed her own pair aside. "Astrid has done her homework. In fact, she has a copy of that Kommandant book Bill wants." She paused, grunting as the first of Judith's boots required extra effort. "Astrid apparently got the only copy Sadie's Stories had before the title fell off the radar. What she read confirmed her suspicions about the senior Hellman. In fact, he's not Heinrich Hellman, but Engelbert Vogel, a Nazi collaborator. Every lie he told about Mr. Bauer apparently was true about *him*, including a new identity and a change in religion. Oops!" Renie cried as she almost toppled over yanking off the other boot. "His crimes included turning Jews and other so-called undesirables over to the SS and the Gestapo."

Judith propped herself up on the pillows. "What was the original connection between Bauer and Hellman aka Vogel?"

"Bauer was hiding some Jewish friends in a small town where Vogel was an official. He found out about the family of seven and they were sent to the camps. Bauer and Astrid—who'd come to Germany to work as an au pair just before the war—barely escaped Vogel's wrath."

"And the men didn't cross paths until they met again here?"

"Right. Bauer and Astrid fled to another town, where they got married and moved in with some people who had taken in displaced persons." Renie sat down on the other bed. "Hellman—I mean, Vogel—had grown a beard, dyed his hair, and married an American woman at some point. Maybe, Astrid thought, a WAC. She died not long after giving birth to their son, Jack. That was before the cemetery existed. Astrid doesn't know where she's buried."

Judith grew thoughtful. "So who planted Vogel by the river?"

Renie's eyes sparkled. "Herr Wessler. Who else? He was the one person who believed Bauer was innocent."

"My God! That's a motive for murder."

Renie grinned. "It sure is. Now where do we find Jack Hellman?"

"Good question." Judith stared up at the half-timbered ceiling. "A disguise?" She shook her head before Renie could respond. "If Jack Hellman killed Bob *and* Wessler, did he hang around here for two months? That doesn't seem likely. Maybe we *are* talking about two murderers. But what's the motive for either killing?"

Renie fingered her chin. "Can we cross Jack off as the griping letter writer?"

"I guess." Judith sounded uncertain. "Wait. I've got an idea." She delved into her purse and took out her phone. "Can you grab that folder on the little table? It's got my information in it. I need the number for Wolfgang's restaurant and bar."

Renie got up, grabbed the folder, and handed it to Judith. "Who are you calling?"

"Ruby, the barmaid and waitress." Judith punched in the number. "I hope she's at work."

Ruby wasn't on the job, but whoever answered obliged with a home number. A sullen female voice answered. "Ruby?" Judith said.

"Yeah. Who's this?"

"Your sub from the other night when you were pulling double duty. Judith McMonigle Flynn. Have you got a moment?"

Ruby uttered a short, bitter laugh. "Sure. Time on my hands, nobody in my arms. What can I do for you?"

"This sounds odd," Judith said. "When did your dad die?"

"You want to send flowers? It's a little late." Ruby paused. "It was August, a Friday. I'd have to look at a calendar."

"How about August nineteenth?"

"That sounds right," Ruby said, sounding surprised. "Why? Are you suing his estate for what he stole from your bar?" She laughed again. "He didn't have an estate. I told you he was broke."

"Do you know how the motorcycle accident happened?"

Ruby paused again. "Well . . . no, and I wish I did. It was on one of those sharp, narrow curves. He was with some sleaze-bag buddy who took off, according to a witness. A trucker saw it happen and said Dad ran over an embankment. He always rode like a bat out of hell."

"Who was the buddy?"

"Let me think. Oh—it was that guy who hung out with him at your place. Big Badger or Bad Bull or some damned thing."

"Do you recall his real name?"

"No. I only saw him once or twice. I didn't see him when Dad stopped in to put the squeeze on me."

"Would you recognize the sleazebag if you saw him?"

"It's been a while. Hey, what is this? You working for the cops?"

"Yes." Judith was no longer playing games. "I'm a police consultant on the Bob Stafford homicide."

"Holy crap! You think Dad killed Bob?"

"No. I've got a sketch of his pal. Are you going to work?"

"I'll try. It's only three blocks. I live near the railroad tracks. I'll be there around four. Are you coming to Wolfgang's?"

"Probably not, but I can fax you the drawing."

After hanging up, Judith noticed that Renie was giving her a curious look. "What? Do you think I'm nuts?"

"No," Renie said, "but we don't have a fax machine."

"I mean, the cops can do that," Judith replied, not wanting to admit her cousin was right. "But we're missing something."

"Such as Jack Hellman or whatever his name is?"

Judith nodded. "Who burned down the original town hall? Was it someone who wanted to destroy the records?" Suddenly she brightened. "It happened when Jack's father was still alive. He hanged himself from the lamppost at the site. Wessler buried him by the river where his wife and baby died. That's the connection."

"You're reaching."

"No. I think it means something very important—symbolic. Wessler could've planted Hellman—and let's keep calling him that to avoid confusion—in the forest or the local garbage dump. What if Hellman killed Mrs. Wessler and her child? And why would he do that? Did she know the truth about him from when they lived in Germany?"

"If Mrs. Wessler knew, then so did Mr. Wessler." Renie clapped a hand to her cheek. "Of course! Astrid Bauer told me Wessler knew Hellman was guilty of war crimes."

Judith started to nod in agreement, but suddenly stared at Renie. "What if Hellman's death wasn't a suicide?"

"You mean . . ." Renie bit her lower lip. "Damn. It makes sense."

"It also makes a motive for Jack killing Wessler. Maybe Bob, too. He was Wessler's attorney and possibly a confidant. If the old guy was as decent as everyone says, he'd have to clear his conscience. His priest may be long gone. Next on the full-disclosure ladder is a lawyer."

"You're doing just fine," Renie said. "But where *is* Jack Hellman? He can't be hiding in plain sight."

Judith leaned back on the pillow. "Something's tickling my brain—evil and how it . . . damn! I forget. Do you recall hearing that?"

Renie rested her head on her hand. "Gee . . . we've talked to so many people. But it does ring a bell. Let me think."

"Okay. Meanwhile, I'll call the cops and ask them to fax that sketch to Ruby at Wolfgang's. If she doesn't get to work, there's a chance someone else might recognize it and have some information about Jack."

"Dubious," Renie murmured, still apparently in deep thought.

Hernandez took the call. In his usual no-nonsense manner, he agreed to fax the sketch to the restaurant. "I wonder," Judith said after disconnecting, "if he feels out of place with the rest of the local cop crew."

"They should lose the cop cruiser and have a clown car," Renie said. "Of course there aren't enough cops on the force for ten or fifteen of them to come out of one tiny vehicle. Besides, their uniforms aren't as funny as . . ." Her jaw dropped as she gaped at Judith. "Mrs. Bauer, at the cemetery, with the flowers."

"We're playing Clue again?"

Renie shook her head. "No. She was talking about the Hellmans and how evil comes in disguise."

"It was probably a figure of speech," Judith said. "Though Oktoberfest is a good place for a disguise, clowns included."

For a few moments the cousins were lost in thought. A knock on the door made both of them jump. Renie stood up. "If it's a clown, call the cops." She cautiously opened the door. "Are you a clown?" she asked Eleanor Denkel.

"I beg your pardon?" Ellie huffed as she stalked into the room. "Really, you don't have any manners, do you?"

"Guess not," Renie said. "Have a seat."

Ellie, however, remained standing by the bed where Judith had sat up and was eyeing their visitor with curiosity.

"What now, Ellie?" she asked.

The other woman's usual bravado faded. "You must think I'm an idiot." She took a deep breath. "You know I didn't kill my grandfather."

"I never thought you did," Judith said.

"But you don't know why I confessed. Three times."

"I'm listening," Judith said, her expression sympathetic.

Ellie took a deep breath. "Ingrid Heffelman made me do it." She moved to the vacant chair and pulled it closer to the bed. "If I didn't, she was going to pull my B&B license."

Judith couldn't hide her dismay. "I don't get it."

Ellie sat down. "Nor do I. She called me as soon as she heard about what happened to . . . Dietrich. I thought . . ." She winced, her eyes darting in Renie's direction. "If your cousin is a sleuth or if you are, do you know why she'd ask such a thing?"

Judith hesitated about being candid. Ellie seemed sincere. "Okay, I *am* FASTO. Serena is my able assistant." She was glad Ellie couldn't see Renie roll her eyes. "But I truly don't know unless Ingrid has ties to Little Bavaria. Is that possible?"

Ellie shook her head. "Not to my knowledge."

"Was it her idea for us to take part in Oktoberfest?"

"It was her decision." Ellie paused. "But we've had a presence at other events—state fairs, festivals, conventions. Several B&B owners have suggested Oktoberfest and small-town celebrations."

"True," Judith said. "This is a first for me."

"I've done a few others in the city," Ellie said. "This was convenient for me with family here." She looked away. "For a while, at least."

"I *am* sorry about your loss," Judith said solemnly. "What kind of pressure did Ingrid put on Connie?"

Ellie's head jerked around to stare at Judith. "You knew? She told Connie to make sure I confessed. She bribed her with that workshop."

"I don't get it," Judith admitted. "Why did Ingrid do any of this?"

Ellie sighed. "You tell me. You're the sleuth."

Another knock on the door startled all three women. Renie, who had been sitting in an unusual state of quiet, jumped up to open the door. Franz Wessler rushed into the room.

"Eleanor!" he cried. "You're safe."

Ellie swung around in the chair. "Of course. I got back here before the snow started coming down so hard."

Franz looked chagrined. "I'm sorry. Delmar is frantic. He thought you were stranded at the exhibit area."

Judith gestured at Franz. "Why don't you take the chair my cousin just vacated, Franz. You look cold. And weary. Please."

"No, thank you," Franz said, still looking at his niece. "I must tell Delmar you're safe. He's outside."

Ellie looked annoyed. "How silly of him. Go to the balcony and let him know I'm fine. And tell him to come inside, for heaven's sake."

Franz froze. "You know I can't do that."

"Oh!" Ellie put a hand over her mouth, turned pale, and bowed her head. "I'm sorry," she mumbled, removing her hand. "I didn't think."

"Never mind," Franz said, awkwardly patting his niece's shoulder. "I must go. I'll tell Delmar to come in on my way out." He made a little bow to the cousins. "Forgive the intrusion."

Renie moved away from the door to allow Franz to make his exit.

"What," Judith said to Ellie, "was that all about?"

Ellie sniffed before raising her head. "You don't know?" she asked in a hoarse voice. "No," she went on quickly, "even FASTO wouldn't know what happened between Franz and Josef."

Judith waited for Ellie to continue, but it was Renie who spoke first after pulling the vacant chair by the bed. "My cousin knows Josef was pushed off the balcony," she said, stretching the truth. "She just isn't sure who did it. I assume it was his brother, Franz. That's why he won't go near there."

Ellie stared at Renie. "Are you sure you're not really FASTO?"

Renie grimaced. "The pretense seems to have turned into reality. I'm starting to think like a sleuth. Scary, huh?"

Judith smiled at her cousin. "Serena has always helped me with my investigations. Was Josef drunk and abusing your mother?"

Ellie's face tightened. "Yes. He was trying to throw her over the balcony. Franz arrived just in time to stop him. They fought . . ." She hung her head again, fists tightly clenched in her lap. "Josef fell over the edge and was killed instantly. Dietrich never quite recovered from that. It created enormous tension between father and son. And I think Franz felt guilty for his own father's death. He thought maybe I *had* killed him."

Judith nodded. "I understand. Even the most admired people are flawed and few families live in total harmony. It's the human condition."

Ellie seemed to relax a bit. "You really are a nice person."

"Most of the time," Judith said. "It's pointless to rehash all this now. I do have a question, though. When you were growing up here, did you know the Bauer family very well?"

Ellie seemed surprised. "Only from church. Mr. Bauer died years ago and their daughter moved away. I don't remember much about her. She was ten, twelve years older than I was. We were never in school together. I doubt I'd know her if I saw her. Why do you ask?"

"We met Mrs. Bauer," Judith said. "Her husband was the victim of malicious lies, but your grandfather knew better."

"Oh." Ellie was starting to pull herself together. "Yes, that was typical of him—righting wrongs. Except," she added ruefully, "not always lenient with his own kin."

"Not an uncommon trait," Judith said. "I've heard he had high hopes for his boys, especially your father, being the elder son."

Ellie stood up. "Very dynastic of him, but very hard on Josef. I must go. Delmar needs comforting." She stood up, offering her hand. "Thank you, Judith. I'm grateful to you." She turned to Renie. "And you . . . Serena." Ellie seemed to have a bit of trouble getting out the name.

"I'll be damned," Renie said, after closing the door behind their guest. "Ellie's human after all."

"Aren't we all," Judith murmured. "You can go out onto the balcony without pitching a fit. See how hard it's snowing."

Renie went around the bed to open the outer door. "Still snowing, but not as heavy. Colder, though. Did you plan to do some sleuthing?"

"No. It's too deep. Is there much activity out—" She was interrupted by her cell phone's ring.

The caller was Chief Duomo. "Just thought I'd tell you Mrs. Bauer's still alive and kicking."

"You saw her?" Judith asked.

"Nah, too risky. She called to report a bear in her yard. I told her not to worry, they wander around here fairly often, foraging for food."

"Was her neighbor still with her?"

"No, but a relative showed up. Some kind of family reunion, I guess. Bear or no bear, the old lady sounded kind of cheerful. Gotta forage for my own food. Need to beef up if I have dinner late. Ciao."

Judith hung up. "Mrs. Bauer is fine except for seeing a bear in . . . don't bears hibernate this time of year?"

Renie nodded. "Usually. I suppose bears could still be on the prowl." Her eyes widened. "The bear that wasn't there?"

"Exactly." Judith grabbed her cell. "I'm telling Duomo to get his fat butt over to Mrs. Bauer's ASAP. I think I know where the killer's been hiding. That's no bear, that's the boar."

**H**ernandez answered her call to headquarters. "Sorry," he said, "the chief went to his brother's bakery. I can't believe he's *walking*."

Judith didn't care if Duomo sank up to his eyeballs in the snow. "Is someone on patrol?"

"The major just left. He's chained up. If he can get through, he's probably close to your inn. Why? You need a lift?"

Judith hesitated. "Yes. We'll be waiting out in front."

"Got it." Hernandez rang off.

Judith burst into action. "We're going with Ernie to Mrs. Bauer's. As usual, Fat Matt's a washout. Or a snow-out."

"Relax. It *could* be a bear," Renie said, putting on her jacket while also stepping into her boots. "Need help?"

"I can get into them when I'm not so tired. The *off* part's harder."

Two minutes later, they were in the parking lot. The snow was still falling, but in much smaller flakes. A few headlights and some foot traffic could be seen on the main street. The clock tower chimed the quarter hour after four.

"Hiding in plain sight," she said in dismay. "Why didn't I think of that? The boar was outside of Wolfgang's right after Wessler was killed."

"Don't beat yourself up. We've seen lots of people in weird outfits."

"True. Here comes Ernie."

"What's up?" he asked as Judith joined him in the front seat and Renie moved in behind them.

Judith quickly explained her suspicions. The major's reaction was skeptical, but he made his way to Mrs. Bauer's house as fast as weather conditions would permit. Trying to stay calm, Judith noticed how quiet the town had become, as if the snow had trumped the usual raucous closing of the Oktoberfest celebration. Or maybe it was the pall of death that hung over the town along with the heavy dark clouds.

Renie broke the silence. "Why do I get stuck back here in the perp's seat? I'm innocent."

"Not of some things I could mention," Judith said through tight lips. She saw the outline of St. Hubert's loom through the snow. "How far away are we from Mrs. Bauer's?" she asked of Ernie.

"Block and a half," he said, turning left.

"Shouldn't you call for backup?" Judith asked.

"What backup?" Ernie said wryly.

"Well . . ." Judith began, "I assume you have everybody working."

"Sure," Ernie said, slowing down as he carefully turned into an unplowed driveway, "but they're all out rescuing drivers and pedestrians who didn't have sense enough to stay inside." He stopped the cruiser. "Now what? Look for the bear or the boar or whatever beast is loose?"

"I don't see a house," Judith said, peering at the windshield, which was beginning to accumulate a dusting of snowflakes. "Where is it?"

Ernie pointed straight ahead. "About twenty yards, but I can't drive closer. The snow's drifted in the driveway. I'll check on Mrs. Bauer. If I see a two-footed animal, I'll bust him."

Ernie got out of the car. Renie leaned forward. "So we just sit?"

"I can't risk a fall in this stuff. The wind's blowing from the south. From what I can see, it looks like one big drift out there. The major should be wearing snowshoes."

"It's not snowing as hard, though," Renie said, straining to look out the window. "I can't roll this down to see how cold it is because I'm the perp. Any chance you can turn on the heat? It's chilly in here."

"I can't see the controls on the dashboard," Judith said. "I wonder if I can find a light somewhere."

"Use my key chain flashlight," Renie said, rummaging in her purse. "Damn! My fingers are so stiff I can hardly move them."

"Why don't you get out and sit in the front seat?"

"Because the rear doors are locked from the outside. On the other hand, I can't give you the flashlight through the grille between the seats. Can you get out and open the door for me without falling into a heap?"

Judith groaned. "This is so . . ."

To her surprise, the passenger door seemed to open on its own. At first, Judith could only see dark, bristly fur. She gasped as the creature lowered its head. Pointed ears, a broad snout, and two sharp tusks almost touched her face.

"Fool," a husky voice growled. "Meddling is *your* profession. Now you're finally finished trying to ruin me!"

Renie screamed as the gloved hands reached out for Judith's

throat. "Vermin!" the creature cried, lurching into the car and falling on top of Judith. Forced backward, her shoulder hit the horn. The boar uttered a stream of obscenities while Renie kept yelling.

The horn continued blaring into the stiff wind and falling snow. Judith could barely breathe, let alone move. If only Ernie would hear the horn . . . her mind fled back to the previous January when she'd found herself in the same dire straits and would've died if Arlene Rankers hadn't intervened. But Arlene was over a hundred miles away at Hillside Manor, readying for the arrival of guests . . .

"Die, you demon, die!"

The menacing word didn't come from the boar. Judith heard a high-pitched voice cut through the air just as the creature suddenly went slack, but the horn kept blaring.

"What the hell . . . ?" she heard Renie gasp.

The snout was pressing against Judith's forehead and her breathing was hampered by the weight of the inert body sprawled on top of her. Suddenly she heard someone —Ernie Schwartz, she thought vaguely, though he sounded unlike himself as he yelled at somebody to stop doing something and put their hands on . . . the cruiser?

"Coz!" Renie cried from the backseat. "Can you breathe?"

Judith couldn't answer. But before she thought she'd smother, the pressure was released when the creature apparently was dragged out of the front seat.

"You okay, Mrs. Flynn?" Ernie asked.

Slowly opening her eyes, Judith let the officer grab her hands and pull her into a sitting position. "Uh . . . huh," she panted, relieved that the horn had stopped honking. "What . . . ?" She blinked several times. She couldn't see anything of the boar, but the outline of what appeared to be a woman in ski pants and a parka was visible next to the cruiser.

"Take it easy," Ernie said, still leaning into the passenger seat.

"Backup's coming. Just relax. Your attacker is out cold, thanks to . . ." He paused, turning around to look at whoever was standing by the cruiser. "You got a name, lady?"

"Yes," Judith heard the woman say. "I'm Ingrid Heffelman from the state B&B association."

The last place Judith expected to find herself that afternoon was in Hanover Haus's private quarters. Flames danced from crackling pine and cedar logs in the stone fireplace as she sipped a hot rum toddy and snuggled under a hand-knit blue-and-white-checkered coverlet.

"Good work," Chief Duomo said between mouthfuls of buttered popcorn. "You, too, Mrs. Flynn. But our own Ingrid saved the day."

"Shut up, Matt," Ingrid snapped. "You know I never let anyone find out I came from this stupid little burg. I was too ashamed after marrying that total loser, Jack Hellman. It only took me two months of emotional and physical abuse to figure out what he was really like."

"Aw, Ingrid," the chief said, "don't be so hard on Little Bavaria. It was your idea to have your bunch come over here in the first place."

Ingrid sighed. "It was Suzie and Bob. I knew them as neighbors in the city before they moved. I never told them I was born here. When Bob got killed where the other horror had happened, I had a feeling Jack was involved. Then he tried blackmailing me— and not for the first time. But I *knew* he'd been involved in Bob's murder. One of his other ex-wives had raised some kind of ruckus over child custody and Bob had been his attorney at Legal Aid. I sent an anonymous letter to Dietrich Wessler, telling him to watch out for Jack. I don't know what the old guy did about it, but obviously not enough. I called Herman Stromeyer after I got here. He and Wessler were tight." She glared at Duomo. "Well?"

The chief shrugged. "Never heard a peep out of either of 'em.

You don't know how Wessler and Stromeyer handled stuff. They did things their own way, working like a couple of secret agents."

Ingrid nodded impatiently. "And it cost them, or at least Wessler. Of course, I wasn't at the cocktail party when he died. I didn't get here in time. But at long last, I've reconciled with my mother."

"How?" Judith asked.

"I finally went to see her," Ingrid said with a lift of her chin. "She stubbornly thought I still loved Jack. I promised I'd get even with him for what he did to my father. She decided I wasn't a lost cause. Silly old bat."

"Takes all kinds," Duomo muttered. "How come you changed your name from Hellman to Heffelman?"

"Oh, that." Ingrid gave the chief a condescending look. "My second husband was named Feldman. He drowned in a tragic birdbath accident. Frankly, he wasn't much of an improvement. I didn't want to sully the Bauer name any further, so I combined the two husbands' names as a reminder to never marry again. I'm unlucky in love. Unlike some." She glowered at Judith. "Of course, you did flunk the first time around," she added, before turning to Renie. "How come you're not wearing that red sweater you wrestled me to the ground for?"

"I already wore it," Renie said smugly. "I looked amazing."

Judith's eyes widened. "You mean . . . ?"

Renie scowled at her cousin. "I told you my foe was a big mama. How did I know it was Inbred Heffalump? We'd never met."

"How dare you!" Ingrid cried. "I'm not *that* big!"

"True," Judith said. "You're built like me." *Only more so,* she thought. "Did you visit my B&B to make sure I was in Little Bavaria?"

Ingrid sneered. "Of course not. Well . . . maybe."

"You certainly put pressure on the B&B contingent," Judith said.

"Yes," Ingrid said, with a swift look at Duomo. "I had to stir the pot to keep everyone on their toes, you included. When I heard you insist you weren't FASTO, I thought you might back off just when *I* needed you."

"Ha!" said Renie.

Ernie Schwartz entered the cozy parlor and addressed Ingrid. "The perp will recover. Where'd you get that stiletto?"

"It's a letter opener," she said. "That is, it's an antique weapon, but not what my mother uses it for. She's not a violent person."

"Good," said Ernie, stretching out as much of his lanky frame as he could manage on a velvet-covered settee. "I could use a nap."

"So," Judith said, "what about the poison bottle at the bookshop?"

"I put it there, though not *in* the bust."

"But nobody knew then that Wessler was poisoned," Judith pointed out. "Nor could you guess the little kid would bust the bust."

Ingrid looked exasperated. "Poison? Hardly. It was an empty eyedrop refill. I set it on the shelf and forgot about it. It must've gotten stuck under the bust."

"I guess," Judith murmured, "I jumped to conclusions. Why didn't you go to the police and warn them about Jack?"

Ingrid's sharp blue eyes went first to Duomo, who was polishing off the popcorn, and then to Ernie, who was already snoring softly on the settee. "Judith—that is the stupidest question I've ever heard!"

Judith winced. "Yes, I suppose . . . I mean . . ." She didn't know where to look. "Okay, so how did Jack poison your grandfather and Herman?"

It was Ingrid's turn to be disconcerted. "I don't know. Don't tell me your mighty brain is also drained?"

Judith started to admit she was also at a loss, but Ingrid's words inspired her. "Yes," she said, "I do. He was the plumber."

"Plumber?" Duomo repeated. "What plumber?"

"The one who came to the Wessler house just before the cocktail party and probably to Stromeyer's after George Beaulieu checked the sewer line. Mrs. Crump told us the plumber wasn't from here—the local guy had already closed up shop. Serena and I saw a big hole by the back of the house off the kitchen. We thought it was dug by the dogs. I'll bet Jack screwed up the plumbing and then gained entry to both houses—and managed to put poison into whatever Wessler and Stromeyer drank before leaving their respective homes."

Ingrid leaned back in her chair. "Contrived, but it sounds like Jack. He was cunning."

Ernie's eyes had opened. "The plumber did it?"

Judith nodded. "Too bad there wasn't a butler."

Ingrid made a face. "Too bad I didn't stab Jack a long time ago."

Duomo nodded halfheartedly. "Really too bad. Caused us a lot of work. Oh, well."

"Cheer up," Renie said. "The wurst is over."

The train pulled out on time from Little Bavaria the next morning. The snow had stopped, but at least six inches remained on the ground.

"Beautiful," Renie murmured after settling into her window seat. "How do you feel?"

"Still worn out," Judith replied, fingering the manila envelope Chief Duomo had handed her just before the cousins had boarded the Empire Builder. "But relieved. At least Ingrid should stop bothering me now. It's almost worth everything we went through to get her off my back."

Renie was silent for a moment, apparently admiring the snow-blanketed trees as they climbed up to the summit. "Jack's motive for killing Bob and Wessler doesn't make much sense. He'd been gone from Little Bavaria for thirty years. Why did he care what happened here?"

"His whole life was a disaster," Judith replied. "Broken marriages, children lost to him, and according to Ingrid, a criminal record and jail time. I suppose he met Bob and suddenly saw him as a symbol of his own failure. Jack hated the town, hated Ingrid, hated Wessler for knowing the truth about his father Helmut—or

Hank, as he was called. We'll never know if Wessler killed Hank or if he committed suicide, but one look at that marker on the trail by the river must've unhinged Jack. He unleashed all his rage on Bob. And then Wessler had to go. Stromeyer, too, because he knew the truth about the elder Hellman."

"Jack better not cop an insanity plea," Renie said. "Hey, what's in that envelope?"

Judith undid the clasp and noticed a handwritten note attached to a glossy photograph. " 'FATSO,' " she read aloud—and winced. " 'Here's a pix Ernie took of the perp. Thought you might want a souvenir.' As if," she muttered before looking at the photo. "Oh, good Lord! It's Jimmy Tooms's pal from the Meat & Mingle! Big Bull or Bad Bear or . . . I called him Boorish Boar! He had a handlebar mustache back then, kind of like George Beaulieu's. It reminded me of tusks. No wonder I had a creepy feeling about that snowboarder's sketch."

Renie grinned. "Just another Meat & Mingle memory."

"A really bad one, though there were . . . ouch!" Judith cried as something struck the top of her head.

"Gotcha!" Thurmond cried in glee. "Like my big wubber wurst? Daddy bought it for me. It's a knockwurst, so I knocked you."

Judith stared at the two brothers in the aisle. "No, I don't like it. Please don't do that again."

Ormond held up a similar item. "I got a brat."

"You *are* a brat," Renie said. "So's your brother. Go away."

The little boys' parents appeared from the other direction. "Thurmie! Ormie!" the mother cried. "There you are! You shouldn't run off . . . oh! Stay away from those bad women! They might kidnap you!"

"Are you nuts?" Renie snapped. "I'd rather wrestle a couple of saber-toothed tigers!"

"With those teeth, you'd win," the father huffed before hustling his boys away.

"Neener-neener," Renie muttered, sinking down into her chair.

Judith couldn't help laughing. "*You* said the wurst was over."

Renie shrugged. "I was wrong." She paused and grinned at Judith. "No, I was right. At least until the next time you find a corpse."

Judith's smile fled. "Don't say that! I'm done, finished, kaput!"

Still looking amused, Renie just stared at Judith and said nothing. The train entered the long tunnel that descended from the summit and everything faded to black.